Worlds Apart

Worlds Apart

Nicola Thorne

G.K. Hall & Co. • Chivers Press
Thorndike, Maine USA   Bath, England

This Large Print edition is published by G.K. Hall & Co., USA
and by Chivers Press, England.

Published in 1997 in the U.S. by arrangement with
Peters, Fraser & Dunlop Writers' Agents.

Published in 1997 in the U.K. by arrangement with
HarperCollins Publishers Ltd.

U.S.   Softcover   0-7838-8233-5   (Paperback Collection Edition)
U.K.   Hardcover   0-7540-1036-8   (Windsor Large Print)
U.K.   Softcover   0-7540-2019-3   (Paragon Large Print)

The text of this Large Print edition is unabridged.
Other aspects of the book may vary from the original edition.

Set in 16 pt. Plantin by Al Chase.

Printed in the United States on permanent paper.

British Library Cataloguing in Publication Data available

Library of Congress Cataloging in Publication Data
Thorne, Nicola.
    Worlds apart / Nicola Thorne.
       p.   cm.
    ISBN 0-7838-8233-5 (lg. print : sc : alk paper)
    1. Large type books. I. Title.
    [PR6070.H689W65 1997]
    823′.914—dc21
                                                    97-15346

This book is for
my dear friend Jane Biran
who not only said it was high time
she had another of my novels
dedicated to her,
but suggested the theme.
So she deserves it.

CONTENTS

PART 1

A Full and Useful Life

CHAPTER 1

Anna got tired of the joke: 'Mrs Livingstone, I presume?' She would react to it with the sort of polite, world-weary smile that she reserved for difficult clients, arrogant barristers, or patronising magistrates.

'Mrs Livingstone, I presume?' echoed down the years.

Anna reached across the desk, shook her client by the hand, and offered her a seat. Outside the window, the traffic at the busy road intersection rushed by, almost drowning her opening words.

The woman on the other side was pale-faced, thin, swamped by a heavy coat several sizes too big. Her spindly legs were encased in black leggings, and she wore a heavy pair of Doc Martens boots. Her spiky hair, sticking out like petrified electric shock waves, was a hectic shade of purple. She had rings on every finger and one through her nose. She was perhaps about thirty. Her name was Joyce Egan.

'I bet people say that to you all the time?' She smiled a cheeky, challenging kind of smile, as though pleased with her own cleverness.

'You could say that.' Anna glanced down at her notes. 'Now, what can I do for you?'

She joined her hands on the top of the desk

and, for the umpteenth time that day, assumed the helpful air, the encouraging smile which she hoped would get her clients to like her, confide in her and, above all, trust her.

'It's like this,' Joyce began, crossing and uncrossing her legs. Suddenly she seemed more vulnerable than self-confident.

Her story was about a landlord who had attempted to cut off the water and electricity, dumped rubbish on the stairs outside the back door, shoved excreta through the letterbox, anything to get her to leave. But, of course, she had nowhere to go. The kids were ill all the time, and her partner didn't have a job. He was on invalidity benefit, having served with the army in the Falklands. He was not, however, the father of Joyce's children.

But, still, there was the question of obvious harassment. Anna scribbled a note.

She had heard this tale so many times before it would be easy to be cynical about it. In a way people got themselves into their own messes and relied on others to get them out. But if you took that attitude you would condemn two thirds, if not more, of the human race.

There was still a lot Anna could do. The landlord was clearly acting illegally. He could be taken to court, but it would take time. The best thing was to refer her to the housing authority, the social services, and let the full panoply of bureaucratic welfare, now grinding rustily along on a treadmill, take control.

She explained to Joyce, whom she liked, her rights in a clear, firm voice, emphasising each point with a nod of her head. Joyce, who had at one time seemed on the point of tears, cheered visibly, reached over and shook Anna's hand warmly, stuffing into her vast pockets the sheaf of papers she'd given her.

Anna saw her to the door, looked out into the corridor which was empty. The front door was locked and the staff had gone home.

'Sorry to have kept you.' Joyce turned with a grateful smile as Anna followed her to let her into the street.

'No trouble at all,' Anna assured her. 'Let me know what happens.'

She drew back the bolt, unlocked the door and stood on the steps as Joyce blended into the flotsam and jetsam of mixed nationalities, people of all ages, shapes, colours and sizes, from all walks of life who swirled along the pavement round the corner from the tube station.

It was about seven o'clock on a summer evening and the heat rose from the stale city street, blending with the fumes of petrol and the noise of traffic.

Anna was very tired. She had come straight to the Law Centre from her office in Wigmore Street, pausing only to drink a plastic beaker of tea thrust into her hand by one of the volunteers who followed her to the empty office with a sheaf of files to brief her about the cases she was to see.

Twice a week, sometimes three if they were

unusually busy, she helped out at the Law Centre set up by a bunch of lawyers, supporters of the Labour Party, who gave their services free. Usually they closed at about nine, but on this particular evening, due to staff shortages, they closed the door at seven. Anna had already telephoned her husband Peter to say she would be late, because she had at least another half-hour making notes on the files to be left ready for the staff when they arrived the following day.

Anna opened a window that gave on to a narrow, airless cobbled passage that bisected the warren of streets. Its size and location were redolent of its nineteenth century origins, maybe earlier. Halfway up the wall of the building opposite were a door and a derrick, indicating that it had once been a warehouse or a storage area for grain. Recently it had been turned into a trendy art gallery, part of the transformation of Camden Town into the radical chic of the late nineteen eighties. At weekends, people flocked to the street markets, the canalside cafés, fashionable bistros and Greek restaurants offering amazing value for money.

Anna returned to her desk and drew the top file towards her, brow puckered, as she momentarily attempted to recall the first of the many clients she had seen in her two hours at the centre. Approximately five an hour, possibly a little longer than the average patient was allowed in an NHS surgery.

The law was a kind of surgery too (in fact these

sessions were called surgeries): a catharsis, a laying open of wounds, broken bodies and minds.

Forty minutes later she made her final note about Joyce, whom she'd rather taken to, put the files neatly together with a scribbled note on top for Mandy who ran the centre and, taking the jacket of her lightweight suit from the back of the chair slipped it on, grabbed her bag and briefcase, made her way to the outside door, locked it carefully behind her, and slipped the key back through the letterbox.

Then she wove her way cautiously through the stationary traffic of Camden High Street and strolled up Parkway towards the park where she'd left her car.

Inside the house all was quiet, except for the distant murmur of the television.

A quarter to nine. Anna felt guilty as she swiftly deposited her bag and briefcase in the hall, and stole towards the lounge, the door of which was ajar.

Peter, slumped in front of the TV, was fast asleep, long legs stretched before him, hands resting on his chest, head back, mouth slightly open.

Anna went over to the TV and was about to switch it off.

'Leave it, darling. It's nearly time for the news.'

Straightening up she smiled. 'I thought you were asleep.'

'I nodded off. Late again, Anna.'

'Sorry, darling.' She crouched at his feet. 'It

13

was my night at the Law Centre.'

'Why don't you give it up?' His hand affection-ately ruffled her hair.

'Are you crazy?'

'Yes,' deep sigh, 'I suppose I am. And you're not eating enough.' He looked at her critically. 'I'm not the first person to notice you're too thin. Fiona said just the same thing yesterday when you dashed out before breakfast.'

'Well that's quite deliberate.' Anna placed her hands neatly on either side of her waist, breathed in deeply. 'I did actually feel I was putting on weight. All this sitting around.'

'Well, now it's the opposite. Haven't eaten tonight, I suppose?'

'I'll get a sandwich.' She looked at her watch. 'Are the children in?'

'Fiona's in her room. Guy had cricket practice.'

Once a week Guy went to the nets at Lords. This year Fiona had GCSEs.

The signal for the nine o'clock news came on, and Peter leaned forward.

'Turn it up, Anna.'

She waited to see the headlines and then, re-turning to the hall, took up her bag and jacket and went upstairs to her bedroom, passing Fiona's shut door on the way. She paused, mo-mentarily seemed to steel herself, and then tapped firmly on the door.

No sound.

She braced her shoulders, tapped again, then almost simultaneously turned the door handle.

14

The room was empty, desperately untidy with clothes scattered on the floor, a pile of books flung on the unmade bed, and papers thrown on the desk, upon which was a light, still turned on as though she'd left in a hurry.

Well, nothing unusual about that.

Anna knew better than to try and tidy Fiona's room. She would be accused of interfering if she did, so she left it as she'd found it, closed the door firmly on the mess, and made her way up the short flight of stairs to the large back bedroom she shared with Peter, which overlooked the garden.

Here at least was peace and tranquillity. She even seemed to breathe more easily.

She switched on the small TV to get the rest of the news as she changed from her work clothes into a track suit and slippers.

As the weather forecast came on she went downstairs again and into the kitchen, which was also untidy with dishes on the draining board and, something that always irritated her, the door of the fridge left half-open.

She closed it with an exasperated sigh and, as she turned, she saw Peter lounging in the doorway, hands in his trouser pockets.

'I meant to clear up before you got home.' He sounded apologetic. 'I know how it irritates you.'

'Why should you? Let they or, I suppose to be truthful as well as accurate, I should say "she" who made the mess clear it up.'

'Fiona is busy working.' A defensive note came

15

into his voice. 'She went straight up to her room.'

Anna got salami from the fridge and put two slices of bread into the toaster. 'Well, she isn't there now.'

'Fiona's not upstairs?'

'Nope.'

'She might have told me she was going out.'

Anna said nothing, plugged in the kettle to make a mug of instant coffee.

Watched by Peter, she put the salami between the slices of toast and placed mug and plate on a tray. 'Anything interesting on the news?'

Peter shrugged and followed her into the lounge, and as she munched and sipped her coffee he poured a whisky from a decanter on the table.

'I'm dreadfully worried about Fiona.' He sat opposite her, hands clutching his glass. 'Not only the lack of commitment to her work, but the company she keeps.'

Anna dreaded what was coming next. All her fault, as she had opposed sending the children to private schools and wanted them educated by the state in accordance with her socialist principles, even though they were not her children but Peter's by his first marriage.

'She could have met those sort of people anywhere. This is the Metropolis. A private education doesn't mean you only meet the right people. Not in London, not out of it either if we are to believe what we read in the papers and see on TV. Don't blame me.'

'I'm not blaming you, Anna, you know that. I'm just saying that if we knew then what we know now we might have acted differently.'

'I tell you I don't think it would have made any difference.'

'And Guy should be home from cricket practice.' Peter's tone was querulous as he looked at his watch. 'It's nearly ten. It finishes at eight, eight-thirty.'

Peter used to insist on picking Guy up, but now that he was nearly fifteen he resented being treated like a baby.

Guy and Fiona went to the large comprehensive school nearby, and although they had different sets of friends they led similar lifestyles, except that Guy had a deep love of all forms of sport, especially cricket, while Fiona's main object in life seemed to be to have a good time.

Another restless, maybe sleepless night, was in the offing. Anna yawned, suddenly aware that she was dead tired.

'You go to bed. I'll stay up,' Peter said.

'You've got to work too.'

'Yes, but they are my children . . .' He stopped, realising too late the gaffe.

Without a word Anna went into the kitchen, and with her usual speed and thoroughness put her dishes, along with those stacked on the draining board, into the dishwasher. It was such an easy thing to do as she kept on telling the children; Peter was also an offender. It just took a few seconds, and look at the difference it made.

She wiped down the draining board, the kitchen table and work surfaces, set the dishwasher, put out the lights and went upstairs without looking into the lounge from whence came the sound of the ten o'clock news.

She passed Fiona's room, resisting for the umpteenth time the urge to go in and tidy it, past Guy's where the condition would be the same: unwashed socks and pants in a corner, dirty towels, sports gear all over the place.

She shut the door of her bedroom, opened the window and leaned on the sill, for a moment breathing in the warm, fragrant stillness of the garden.

The house in Belsize Park was a large, three-storeyed building that Peter and his first wife, Nancy, had bought when they married. It was a comfortable family house, with a sizeable garden, close to Haverstock Hill, Swiss Cottage and to all the amenities.

Anna had felt no aversion to living in a dead woman's house, because by the time she and Peter married all trace of Nancy had evaporated.

Actually she loved the house; its lived-in feel, its homeliness. When the children were small, bikes, balls, cricket bats and tennis racquets piled inside. The carpets were now rather shabby, and the whole place could do not only with redecoration, but with refurnishing as well.

The garden backed on to another garden, the huge trees now in leaf, and except for the sound of distant traffic, the red glow of the lights of

London in the sky, one could almost have imagined oneself in the country. A gentle breeze fanned her face.

She closed the window, drew the curtains and began slowly to undress. Thoughtful. Somewhere out there were Guy and Fiona, and somewhere, perhaps, not very far away, staring through windows or prowling restlessly about were anxious parents like Peter and herself, wondering where their offspring were, what they were up to.

She was anxious about the children, but not as painfully anxious as Peter — maybe because the blood bond was lacking. Yet when they were small, she'd felt for them as though they were her own.

Eighteen months separated them: they were two and three when their mother died, four and five when she married Peter, knowing quite well what lay in store.

Anna had been twenty-three when she met Peter at the home of Claude Rigby, the then senior partner, who was giving a dinner party to celebrate the completion of her Articles, her emergence as a fully qualified solicitor. Peter, whose wife had just died, was a friend of the Rigby family.

She remembered how sorry she'd felt for him, how hard and successfully he had tried to conceal his grief. He was a tall, distinguished looking, attractive 'older' man, but she wouldn't have dreamt of taking it any further. She was studious, a little naive, still sexually immature and unsure of herself. Besides, in the circumstances, it had never crossed her mind.

Six months later they met again when Claude Rigby, who was something of a socialite, took a crowd of people to Henley for the Regatta, and again, Peter was among the guests. This time, there was no doubt that Peter and Anna were attracted to each other; there also was a meeting of minds. Gradually he introduced her into his life. She visited his home, met his children; they became lovers.

When she married him eighteen months later she knew exactly what she was doing. She loved Peter and she loved his children, even though children as such had never figured very high on her list of priorities. She was willing, temporarily, to abandon her career and devote herself to them; the archetypal female sacrificing her ambition for the sake of husband, home and children.

They were adorable children. It would have been hard not to like them; tiny looking, intensely vulnerable, badly in need of a mother's care.

Loving Peter as she did, she also loved his children, had no jealousy of the woman who had borne them, and had died prematurely and painfully of cancer of the spine.

Somehow you wanted to love the children all the more because of that. Give them everything; maybe too much. Maybe spoil them.

She had a bath, got into bed, and so had begun to read when she heard voices raised in the hall two floors below. The shrill whining voice of

Fiona protesting innocence, the harsh angry tones of Peter. The voices rose to a crescendo and then there was the sound of hurried footsteps bounding up the stairs, a door banging. Probably tears on the other side.

Anna knew better than to go and try and comfort her stepdaughter. Anyway, the door would be locked.

Silence again in the house. She became drowsy and was putting down her book when there was another commotion. Guy. Guy and Peter at it again, as they always were. But Guy could shout louder than Peter and his voice had almost broken. He was tall, well-built, mature for his age. If only he would stick to athletics and not worry his father so.

Everyone said they were normal children, that all teenagers were like that. It was not all that long ago that she'd been a teenager herself, but she was an only child with a single, working mother who had not had much time or patience for unruly offspring. Besides Anna seemed to have been born conscientious, ambitious and anxious to succeed. Clever at school, good at games, always occupied, with lots to do. Painfully aware that her gentle, self-effacing mother, lacking the educational opportunities Anna had had, had been abandoned by her husband and left to raise Anna on her own. They'd lived in a suburb of Leeds and there was no way you could compare it, even then, to life in the Metropolis, though in the years since she'd entered adulthood the suburb had developed adolescent problems and a drug culture of its own.

The voices downstairs sank to murmurs and then stopped, and Anna guessed they had gone into the kitchen. Unlike rows with Fiona, which ended in explosions and tears, with Guy they tended to simmer down. Guy, perpetually hungry, always went in search of food.

Anna left the light on on Peter's side of the bed, put out her own, and tried to compose herself for sleep. She was desperately tired, over-tired, and she had to be at the magistrates' court in the morning to try and prevent a teenager from being sent to a youth detention centre. A teenager from a bad home with lots of problems. Never the chances that Guy and Fiona had.

The door opened and Peter crept in. Anna remained with her eyes closed not wanting to talk; tried to make her breathing regular, controlled. Finally she rolled on her back, head propped on the pillows, and gazed across at him, taking in his dejection, his utter weariness.

'I'm so sorry,' she said, stretching out a hand.

'And I'm sorry.' He went over to the bed, unbuttoning his shirt, and flopped by her side. 'I'm sorry about what I said . . .'

'It's true.' She shrugged. 'They are your children.'

'But I know you love them, care for them, worry about them as much as I do.'

Anna wasn't sure about that, but knew how hurt Peter would be if she said so. She knew she didn't have quite the agony, the almost visceral feelings of pain that he, and other parents had. Somehow although she cared, cared deeply and always had, she was detached. She knew that whatever happened to Fiona or Guy affected Peter in a much more profound way than her.

But she had to be the one to remain balanced, to keep sane. No use the pair of them going to pieces every time the children offended or did something they shouldn't, which was almost every day.

She knew that if she felt as Peter felt, her career would be adversely affected, her life.

Despite Anna's eloquent pleading, the magistrates, in their wisdom, decided to send her client to a youth detention centre for two years. They felt it was in his best interests. Anna knew that Mrs Bridges, the chairman of the magistrates, was a caring, compassionate woman, and she and her fellow magistrates would have taken time to consider the matter and reach a conclusion that they believed was just and fair.

But was it? Anna got together her papers and went into the lobby to confer with her client's probation officer, before going down to see the young man about to be taken into custody.

He was only sixteen, and none of his family had been present. He was a pale, pimply, unprepossessing yet infinitely pathetic youth, who clearly no one loved. The sort of person disadvantaged from the start, who had absolutely no chance in life, none at all; who flourished in the seed-bed of petty crime, and whose life henceforth could be predicted with utmost certainty. His time at the youth detention centre almost certainly would lead to more serious crime, and at some stage in his life incarceration, maybe for years, in prison.

The social worker grinned at her sympathetically. 'You did your best, Mrs Livingstone. Maybe if his parents had been here, or someone to give him a hand . . . I think Mrs Bridges thought so too.'

'Maybe.' Anna didn't like to give up on a client.

She felt depressed and anxious, not only on behalf of the young man. She'd had a bad night and was awake well before the alarm. As usual she had taken Peter a cup of tea in bed, called the children, and left the house probably before anyone was fully awake.

She went down to the cells for a final word with her client, Joe. He looked more wan, more hopeless than he had in the dock, and she resisted the urge to put an arm round his shoulders and give him a comforting hug. How long ago was it, she wondered, since anyone had done that?

'Joe,' she said sitting opposite him, 'I'm very sorry you got done in. I know the magistrates thought it was in your best interest.'

'Sod the magistrate,' Joe mumbled, wiping his nose on the sleeve of his T-shirt.

'Well I suppose you think that. Now, Joe, I'd like to contact your mother and try and persuade her to come and visit you. Could you let me have her address?'

Joe remained sullen, silent, staring at the surface of the hard wooden table between them.

'Dunno,' he said.

'You don't know where she lives?'

'Somewhere in the norf'.'

'The north of England?' Anna shook her head helplessly. 'The north of England is a big place.'

'I don't want to see my ma.'

'Don't you really?' She looked searchingly into his eyes. They were shifty, evasive. 'I think everyone wants to see their mother,' she continued softly, 'truthfully.'

'You don't know my mother . . .'

'And father? Brothers or sisters, Joe?'

Apparently there was an elder sister whom he sometimes saw. Anna would get her secretary to try and find her, have another word with the probation officer. She looked at her watch and stood up.

'Joe . . . I am sorry.'

It seemed so inadequate to say 'take care' or 'good luck'. Hypocritical, too. Besides, there was this awful seemingly lack of interest in his fate on the part of Joe, as though he were swept along by a tide he had no means of controlling.

She went back to the lobby to seek out his probation officer but she had vanished. Too many clients on her mind to concentrate on Joe.

Joe, now swept up in the impersonal, majestic, inexorable processes of the law, was no longer the officer's problem.

Neither, strictly speaking, was he Anna's.

She had spent most of the morning in court waiting for the case to come up, and there was a heavy schedule of work back at the office. It was half past twelve, and she was reminded that she had had no breakfast. Nor had she had time for coffee. There was a pleasant snack bar up the road, and she would allow herself half an hour. If she hurried she would get a table before the place filled up.

Coffee and a toasted sandwich. She shook out the *Guardian*. Time to unwind. She became absorbed in the day's news.

'Mrs Livingstone, would you mind if I joined you?' She looked up to see Mrs Bridges, cup and plate balanced precariously in her hands, looking apologetically down at her. 'There doesn't seem to be any more room.'

'Of course.' Anna moved along the bench and put her newspaper aside.

'I expect I'm disturbing the only peaceful moment you're going to have all day?' Mrs Bridges' cultured tones sounded more apologetic than ever.

'That's perfectly alright.' Anna smiled.

'Actually I'm glad of a word with you,' Mrs Bridges put her cup and saucer and plate on the table, 'because I do know how you felt about that young man. But,' she sat down next to Anna and slipped her jacket round her shoulders, 'I really do think it was for the best you know. We were all in agreement.'

'I think it was a little severe for a first offence.'

'We had his best interests at heart. No parents. No support. Desperately sad, isn't it?'

Mrs Bridges — comfortable, well-off Mrs Bridges, whose husband was a distinguished ENT surgeon, doubtless with a lucrative private practice and whose children most likely went to private schools. They lived, probably, in a large house without mortgage, up the road in Hampstead. But who was Anna to judge? Comfortably off, a middle-class professional herself.

'Have you any children?' Mrs Bridges enquired, stirring brown sugar into her coffee.

'I've got two step-children, a boy and a girl.'

'Oh!' There was always the pause after she announced her relationship to the children. It was, she imagined, a bit like saying you were adopted and had never known your parents. Out of the ordinary. People didn't like to say 'why haven't you any of your own?' although, of course, they wanted to know. 'It's not quite the same then, is it?' Mrs Bridges stared at her brightly.

'What isn't the same?'

'Well I never know.' Mrs Bridges waved a hand in the air. 'I hope I'm not being tactless. I probably am.' She buried her face in her cup.

Anna said nothing, deciding to let her suffer.

'I've three children,' Mrs Bridges went on hurriedly. 'All flown the nest. One is a doctor like my husband, the girl is a nurse and my youngest son is still at university.'

'Mine are both still at school,' Anna said without volunteering where and, glancing at her watch, 'I really must fly. I have a conference at two.'

'Is it that late already?' Aghast, Mrs Bridges looked at her watch. 'And I said the court would resume . . .'

'No you've got plenty of time. I have to think of the traffic.'

'So nice to talk to you, Mrs Livingstone, and please don't think you failed that young man.' She sighed. 'Frankly I think he's a hopeless case.'

Anna sped down the hill fuming with indignation. It would be a very different kettle of fish if one of the Bridges' offspring had appeared in court. Not for the first time she thought about the injustice of middle class people sitting in judgment on those who, for lack of any precise or better description, would be considered their social and intellectual inferiors. Probably the same could be said about representing them too.

Yet somewhere in the middle, between the hapless Joe and the Bridges' children, were Fiona and Guy. Their mother had died; their professional father loved them, provided a good home for them and, eventually, a good surrogate mother.

And she had been a good mother. After she and Peter were married she gave up work for a time because his took him abroad a great deal. It was difficult getting to know someone else's children, growing to love them, wanting them to love you and trust you in return.

Halting outside the chemist at the bottom of the hill just before the magistrates' court, Anna, thinking of children, remembered something, ferreted frantically around in her bag, searched the side pockets, her wallet, and then heaved an exasperated sigh and muttered under her breath, 'Damn!'

If only one didn't have to have prescriptions repeated for the oral contraceptive pill, life would be so much more simple. Then she hurried on towards her destination, through the doors of the courthouse.

Peter and Anna remained deeply physically in love, even after ten years and the trials, fairly recent, of the children growing towards adolescence. They had their rows, disagreements and moments of discord; but they shared a deep physical passion for each other that enabled them regularly to make the best of the brief time between going to bed and falling asleep. Somehow, no matter how tired, Anna was excited by Peter, his proximity, his touch. Willingly she made love, often she initiated it.

But tonight as Peter reached for her, she turned her face towards him and shook her head.

'Darling?' His brow puckered as he began tenderly to stroke her hair.

'I've forgotten my prescription for the Pill. I was due to start taking it again today.'

'Bugger the Pill,' Peter said, a hand continuing to stroke her hair, while the other began gently to fondle her breast.

Their lips met. His hand moved from her breast to her waist, further down. The desire for him was uncontrollable. Besides they were married, a couple together.

'It makes it more exciting like this,' he murmured, slipping into her with the easy familiarity of the practised lover. She folded her legs around his, locking him into her, linking her hands around his back, binding him indivisibly to her.

The excitement was intense, urgent. They thrashed about the bed like combatants, and afterwards they lay breathless, revelling in the kind of primitive joy that, although it was familiar, was also somehow new.

They joined sticky hands and looked at each other exultantly.

Maybe, their eyes seemed to say, unprotected sex occasionally was a good idea in a long, safe, happy marriage.

CHAPTER 2

The cottage in Dorset was part of Peter's past. It belonged to Peter, Fiona and Guy and their memories of Nancy, Peter's first wife, who had died at the age of thirty. She had lived in the house in London too, but somehow there wasn't the same association with Nancy that the cottage, where she died, possessed.

Although born in South Africa, she had no roots there and had lived in Dorset before her marriage to Peter. She had money of her own, and eventually bought the cottage in the Blackmore Vale where she used to take the children in the holidays and paint.

Nancy seemed to have been a beautiful, carefree woman, and although Anna was not considered conventionally beautiful, she had a natural élan and gaiety of spirit that made many people, who had known both women, say that in some ways, they resembled each other.

Like Nancy, Anna had ash blonde hair, blue eyes, well defined features, a hint of stubbornness about the chin. But here the resemblance ended. Nancy was considered elfin, petite whereas Anna was tall. Anna was athletic and liked to walk and swim, while Nancy had cosseted herself and had preferred to stay indoors, except when she painted her pretty rural scenes.

Because it was so far from London, the Dorset cottage was used mainly for holidays. It was really too far to travel just for weekends. This was just as well, because Anna was often busy, and the children, now that they were older, much preferred life in London to that in the country.

They had protested vigorously this time at being dragged away from their favourite haunts, if only for a relatively short time, but Peter put his foot down. He had taken a week off, so had Anna, just to be with them. Besides, they both wanted to encourage Fiona to get down to some serious studying as her exams were not far away.

Although a local woman came in regularly to air the cottage and make sure everything was functioning — no burst pipes in the winter — when the family arrived it always felt cold, deserted, almost neglected.

The garden was overgrown and untended, and Peter liked to don green wellies and do some serious digging. Then he and Anna toured the local garden centres and arrived home with a variety of plants and shrubs. By the time they left, the place was just about looking lived-in, and they were all sorry to depart until the next break, when they had to start all over again.

Fiona had arrived in a rebellious mood, but even she seemed to mellow under the influence of the peace, the calm, the beauty and, above all this year, the good weather. The village lay just under Bulbarrow, that great escarpment rising above the Blackmore Vale, giving spectacular, panoramic views for many miles around.

In many ways Little Halton was a picture postcard village, with a manor, a turreted church, two prosperous, well-stocked farms and a row of thatched cottages, of which theirs was one. It was at the end of the row, consequently it had a larger garden than the others, and also three bedrooms. Nancy had made a studio in the garden, and this was left as a sort of shrine to her. She had never enjoyed or really attempted any commercial success, regarding herself as an amateur painter. But her pretty, delicate canvases of flowers and rural scenes were still stacked against the wall, and the painting she was working on when she died was as she'd left it, on its easel.

The door of the studio was hardly ever unlocked or the room itself visited; but it remained as a memorial to Nancy who lay buried in the local churchyard under an elderberry tree.

The family left London on Friday at midday and were in Little Halton by five. They stopped for lunch at the service station on the M3, and again in Shaftesbury for petrol.

Mrs Hanson, the farmer's wife, who looked after the cottage, had left bread, potatoes and milk. The rest they'd bought. The fridge had been cleaned and switched on. The place was also clean and there was a large vase of flowers on the deal table in the kitchen, but still there was that slight air of must, of neglect, the feeling that windows should be flung wide and doors left open.

Peter immediately became transformed from a man of business and corporate affairs to a bluff, jolly countryman. Within minutes of arriving he was in his wellies and inspecting the garden, while Guy disappeared to look up his mate, Martin Hanson. Fiona and Anna were left with the woman's role of unpacking and preparing the evening meal, something which, surprisingly, Fiona seemed to like, though the atmosphere these days was always one of an armed truce.

Or perhaps it was only Anna who was aware of the tension in the cottage as if, instead of leaving their problems behind, they brought them with them. Maybe it was the close, enforced proximity that would last the week of the half term, and sometimes Anna felt that it was as though the shade of Nancy, though long dead, somehow remained to hover around them.

Or the simple explanation may have been that Anna, who worked so hard and for whom there were not enough hours in the day in which to accomplish everything, felt ill at ease with time on her hands.

By Sunday they had all settled in and established a routine. The church bell rang in vain for them, because they never attended service. It was the kind of village where people kept to themselves. It was quite a distance from the nearest town, and houses had become so expensive that the local population had tended to move out.

Therefore it was full of people like the Livingstones, who had second homes and went to the country to get away from busy lives. Thus they felt disinclined to socialise.

Some people — admirals, army officers and diplomats — had retired there, and they also kept themselves to themselves. No, it was not a friendly village, and the Livingstones rather liked it that way.

Fiona seemed to have decided that she was here to work, and she remained in her room attached to her Walkman, though Anna could never understand how the young continued to study while listening to their favourite pop music.

Guy, always a sociable boy, spent most of his time with his crony Martin, the farmer's son, who was keen on cricket, and they took over a field in which they endlessly bowled and batted to each other.

After they had settled in, Anna went up to thank Mrs Hanson at the farm and to buy some eggs. She was met in the strange reserved way the family seemed to have not only for her but for all newcomers. The Hansons were true Dorset people, and it was very easy to believe here that you came from a foreign land. Ted Hanson was a bluff, taciturn countryman, who actually seemed to harbour a feeling of resentment against all strangers, perhaps because he could see how they were encroaching on his land. Two of the Hansons' three daughters worked in Blandford

Forum, seven miles away, and one was married and lived in Bournemouth.

Ted Hanson ran the farm virtually single-handed, which could explain much that he had to be angry about. He always seemed to Anna, who tried fruitlessly to communicate with him, an angry, overworked and resentful man.

'Mr Livingstone well?' Mrs Hanson enquired of Anna as she packed the eggs from her cool larder into cartons.

'He's fine. He's started on the garden.'

'And the children?' Mrs Hanson didn't look at Anna, but her tone of voice subtly changed.

'Oh, they're very well. Fiona has her GCSEs this summer, in a few weeks. She's working hard.' Anna tried to make her tone sound convincing.

'What does she want to do then?' Mrs Hanson finished packing the eggs and gave them to Anna who stacked them carefully in her basket.

'She's not sure. Is anyone these days?'

'Will she go back to school?'

'Oh, I suppose so.'

As they came out of the pantry and into the yard, they could see Guy and Martin practising their cricket in the far field.

'Sometimes I think Guy would like to be a farmer,' Anna said. 'He hasn't much inclination for intellectual work.'

'You don't have to be a fool to be a farmer,' Mrs Hanson said crisply, examining the notes in her hand with which Anna had paid for the eggs,

36

and for her care of the cottage.

'Oh I don't mean *that* at all.' Anna was acutely embarrassed. 'Please don't think . . .'

Mrs Hanson gave her a frosty smile. 'Not that I don't think Ted hasn't made a lot of mistakes, and this so-called "agricultural policy" doesn't help us at all. In fact,' she paused as if considering whether or not she should continue, 'we'd like to get rid of the farm, I don't mind telling you, Mrs Livingstone. It's hard work. Our girls aren't interested, and our boy doesn't show much aptitude for it.'

Anna followed her gaze.

'What does Martin want to do?'

'I wish I knew. Always dissatisfied is Martin. Children can be a problem, can't they, Mrs Livingstone? But then,' she gave her a slightly patronising smile, 'as you never had any of your own . . .'

'Believe me, I know all about the problems of children,' Anna said firmly. 'I've looked after Fiona and Guy for ten years, watched them grow up.'

'Yes, but it's not as if they're your *own,* is it?'

'I feel they're my own.'

Irritated, Anna put her purse into the pocket of her jeans and picked up the basket. 'Thanks ever so much for these eggs and, by the way, thanks for all you do at the cottage. We do appreciate it.'

'It will be about ten years since Mrs Livingstone died,' Mrs Hanson seemed determined to

37

pursue her point. 'The first Mrs Livingstone, I should say.'

'It's ten years since I married Peter,' Anna said politely. 'He was a widower for almost two years when I married him. So she must be dead twelve years.'

'Twelve.' Mrs Hanson sucked her lower lip. 'I wouldn't have thought it was as long as that. She was a lovely lady. Very clever. Always pleasant and smiling. Well thought of, but then in those days the village was more of a village, if you know what I mean.'

'More local people lived here?'

'Oh yes, and that cottage which she bought, so she could have some peace to paint, was the only one that belonged to a "foreigner", as we call them in Dorset. After that, house prices began to rise and the rot set in, though we all liked Nancy. Don't think we didn't.'

Nancy. So they did call her by her Christian name, a familiarity they never attempted with her, and yet she had been coming here year after year for ten years.

But she still felt a stranger.

'Bye for now, Mrs Hanson,' Anna raised her hand.

'How long will you be staying, Mrs Livingstone?'

'Just the week.'

'Sometimes Nancy stayed here all summer, with the children. But then of course you're so busy aren't you, being a professional woman?'

Anna smiled. 'I couldn't stay here all summer, even if I wanted to.'

'Don't suppose you could stand the quiet.'

'Don't suppose I could.'

Anna smiled again and turned, walking carefully along the muddy track that led from the farm to the road. Though the weather was good now, it had been very wet and the ground was still soft. She passed Guy and Martin in the field, but they were too busy to see her wave. Beneath her, the valley simmered in the sunshine, and fat lambs basked in the protective shadow cast by their mothers. It was calm, it was idyllic, it was peaceful, and yet inside, Anna did not feel at peace. She felt somehow that this was the calm before the storm; that eerie stillness that presages thunder.

There was also that nagging worry that had haunted her for two weeks: a most unusual occurrence as far as she was concerned. Meticulous in all things, it seemed that her mind governed her body, and she was also used to regular periods governed by the Pill, routine bleeding lasting a few days, usually beginning twenty-eight days to the dot at the end of her menstrual cycle. But, for the first time for many years, the expected hadn't happened, and then she had recalled those carefree nights, no not just one but several, when, having forgotten to renew her prescription for the Pill, she had missed it altogether.

The theory in her mind at the time was, she supposed, that it was so unlikely she would conceive after all these years anyway. Some doctors were of the opinion that a number of years on the Pill could make you sterile, at least temporarily, and she had been on it continuously for twelve years, and on and off before that as her sex life waxed and waned. She first had it prescribed as a first-year student. There was the fumbling and groping leading to uneasy sexual intercourse which made her visit the college doctor. There had been a period of abstinence, and then a more profound affair at twenty which broke off when the man in question, a graduate law student, returned to the States.

Yes, it was very silly. It was unlike her, too; careless. They made love so regularly that a few nights without wouldn't have been a great deprivation. And yet, it would. The more you had of a thing the more you wanted it, so that sex became like a drug, or alcohol, or food: one became addicted.

There had been that curiously uninhibited joy at making love without the Pill, illogical, but true. Peter had said it was like flirting with danger. Subconsciously, did he want her child? Subconsciously, too, did she?

When she got back to the cottage Peter was at work in the back garden, planting out some bedding plants they bought at a brief stop at a nursery on the way down.

He grinned at her, running his forearm across his forehead.

'Hard work, this gardening.'

'Better give it a break and have a beer.' Anna kicked off her wellies at the door before entering the kitchen. 'Eggs from Mrs Hanson. No pork.'

'Pity,' Peter grimaced. 'How are the Hansons?'

'As well as the Hansons ever are, I suppose.' Anna went into the cool larder and began unpacking the eggs from their cartons and placing them carefully in open trays. 'They don't give much away.'

'Country people are like that.'

'She did, however, seem fond of Nancy.'

'She mentioned Nancy?' Peter looked surprised, and getting a can of lager from the fridge, opened it and drank from it.

'She said Nancy was much loved in the village, and that I couldn't really know about the problems of children as I hadn't any of my own.'

'You soon put her right on that!' Peter smiled, and raised the can again to his lips.

'I said I regarded Fiona and Guy as my own.'

'Quite right.' Peter put an arm round her waist and pressed her to him. 'You've been a marvellous mother to them. Better, I think, than Nancy would have been.'

'Really?' Now it was Anna's turn to express surprise.

'Oh, yes. I mean Nancy loved the kids but she didn't take her maternal duties very seriously. She came here for weeks on end to paint.'

'But the children came with her.'

'The Hansons' eldest daughter looked after them.'

'She didn't tell me that.'

'Darling, Nancy has been dead for twelve years. Why are we bringing this up?'

'That's what I keep asking myself.'

'There is nothing to be jealous about . . .'

'And I'm not, I promise.' Anna looked reassuringly at him, closing the door of the larder. 'It's just that, for some reason, the fact that the children are not biologically mine seems to have come up a lot recently.'

'Has it?'

'Well you mentioned it a few days ago. Before that no one seems to have given it a second thought.'

'And I apologised.'

'I know. Then the chairman of the magistrates, Mrs Bridges, mentioned it.'

'In what context?'

'Oh, I can't really remember.' Anna's hand brushed her brow. 'But I'd had rather a sad case at court of a young boy whose parents neglected him, put into custody for some petty theft. Mrs Bridges and I met by chance at lunch afterwards, and we talked about the case. She asked if I had any children and I said two step-children, and she trotted out with the business of it not being the same as having your own. I told her it was.'

Peter sat in the cane chair beside the kitchen table and stretched his legs. 'It is.'

'But *is* it? Is it, Peter? Am I as worried about them as you are, at a basic, visceral level?'

42

'Well, I think you are. You seem worried enough.'

'But you said . . .'

'I was a fool, and I apologised for it afterwards.'

'I know you did; but I *don't* think I worry quite as much as you do. I mean I can see in you a kind of exasperation which I don't feel. I love them, I'm anxious for them, I'm annoyed by them, made happy or sad by them, but not I think to the same extent as you.'

'That's because of the sort of person you are.' Peter put his lager on the table, got up and, walking over to her, stood behind her, placing his arms round her waist, hugging her tightly. 'You're a sensible, level-headed, unemotional woman. You wouldn't be able to do the kind of job you do if you weren't.'

'You really think I'd be like this if I were their biological mother?'

'I do.'

'You're saying I can't feel intensely?'

'No, I'm not.' He nuzzled her face with his mouth. 'I wish we were here alone, don't you?'

Oh yes she did. If they were here alone things would be very different.

Whenever they were away together, apart from the children, she didn't feel the same anxiety, the same feeling of tension, or the guilt.

That afternoon they went down to the coast, to the beach at Studland. Though it was still too cool for a bathe, some intrepid souls took to the sea, including Guy, who had brought Martin Hanson with him. The Livingstones had a hut on Studland beach which had been in the family since Nancy had first bought the cottage some sixteen or seventeen years before. They'd been down here at Easter but it had been too cold and wet to do much with the hut. This time, they spent the afternoon cleaning it out, and Peter did a bit of banging and resolved to come and start painting if he could accomplish all he had to do in the garden.

'I could do with two weeks here or even a month,' he added, and looked as though he would enjoy it.

'Maybe you're really a countryman at heart?' Anna was brewing tea on a butane gas stove. Fiona lay on her tummy on the beach, her Walkman clamped over her ears, letting the sand run through her fingers. Her feet rose up and down in tune with the music.

'Do you know I believe I am. Let's retire.'

'Chance would be a fine thing. We couldn't afford it.'

'Besides, you wouldn't want to.' Fiona who, despite the drumming in her ears, missed nothing, rolled over on her back and, hands over her eyes, squinted at Anna. 'Would you?'

'I don't expect so. Besides,' she paused in the act of pouring tea into mugs, 'I would never have the time. By the way, I've been asked to stand for the Council.'

The lack of an immediate reaction from Peter

and Fiona was highlighted by the sounds of people playing on the shore, calling to one another, by the breaking of the waves, and the cries of gulls.

'What Council?' Peter, standing on a ladder, paused in the act of battening down the roof, and asked abruptly.

'Our local Council.'

'You're joking!' Hammer in hand, Peter jumped down on to the sand.

'I'm not.' With a tense expression, Anna continued her pouring. Fiona's gaze never wavered.

'Who asked you?'

'Jimmy Wharton of the League of Labour Lawyers, among others. Several people have asked me.'

'You're sure to get on as a leftie,' Fiona said.

'I thought you were a leftie yourself?' Anna glanced at her sideways.

'I am. I didn't mean it nastily.'

'Well, the way you said it, it sounded nasty.'

'I didn't mean to. It's just that you misinterpret everything I say.'

'I try not to, really, Fiona.'

'You're too critical of Anna,' Peter said sharply. 'She feels it just as much, as if . . .' he paused and glanced at Anna, 'as if she were your own mother.'

'*If* she *were* my own mother I mightn't be so critical of her.'

'Fiona!'

'Well I mightn't, might I? Anyway,' she turned

over again on her stomach and resumed pouring the sand through her fingers, 'we will never know as my own mother's dead.'

'But what makes you want to bring it up now?'

'Bring what up, Dad?'

'This.'

'I didn't bring it up.' She turned round and stared at him. 'You did.'

'Yes, you did, Peter.' Finishing pouring the tea and looking, but not feeling, very calm, Anna sat back on her haunches and began sipping the brew. 'I think it's come up more in the last few weeks than it has ever since I married you.'

'Has it?' Fiona looked interested.

'Yes it has, and I think for some reason you're suddenly feeling it too. It's because you resent the criticisms I have of you, thinking your own mother would behave differently.'

'Well she might.'

'And she might not.' Peter carefully put his hammer and nails inside the hut and joined them on the sand, taking the mug Anna held out to him.

'I think Anna has been more than a good mother to you; she has been a wonderful mother. When I married her she gave up her career for a while to look after you . . .'

'Big deal,' Fiona muttered. For a moment, Peter, normally a controlled man, looked as though he would hit her. The mug shook in his hand.

'Best stop this conversation,' Anna said

abruptly, jumping up. 'It's quite futile. I guess all parents and children have a time when their feelings for one another verge on hostility. All people I know seem to go through it. This really came on because I said I might be standing for the Council. Of course it won't be until next year so there's plenty of time to think about it, and if you all are dead against it, then I won't.'

'*I'm* not against it,' Fiona said robustly. 'I'm all for it.'

'Don't you think she has enough to do?' Peter took up his hammer again, and began slowly to mount the ladder to continue his repair of the roof. 'She has a busy practice; she does a lot of voluntary work. She goes to bed late and gets up early . . .'

'But she must *like* it, Dad, or she wouldn't do it.' Fiona looked gravely at her stepmother. 'You *do* like it, Anna, don't you?'

Anna collected the mugs and put them in a bowl. 'I don't know that "like" is exactly the right word. I mean a lot of it I do from a sense of duty. I feel there is a whole segment of our society that needs help, and if I can give it, I shall.'

'So you will seriously consider standing for the Council?' Peter looked down at her, hammer poised in his hand.

'Yes,' Anna swallowed, 'I shall.'

She took the bowl containing the mugs and went across the sand to the sea where she knelt and began rinsing them. Glancing behind her, she saw that Fiona was standing by the ladder in conversation with her father.

For the first time she felt a sense of exclusion, of apartness, of being a stranger from the family. Oddly enough, this was a new sensation. She had been so wanted by them, so needed, when she married Peter, that the alienation as she, and they, grew older, was insidious. Ten years was a long time, but it was not a lifetime, and Fiona had been conceived between Nancy and Peter, and carried in her womb. She gave birth to her, and for three very special, formative years lived with her.

When Anna married Peter the children seemed already to have taken to her and welcomed her into the family. And it was true that, out of love for him but also for them, she had abandoned her law practice and devoted herself to the two motherless children in her effort to bond with them. This step had, in fact, held back her career. It was the reason that, at the age of thirty-six she was, though a senior member of the firm, not yet a partner. She had given a lot for the children and she realised that a real mother might feel it was her duty, whereas a stepmother might feel she had no such obligation and expect, somehow, to be rewarded.

Anna hadn't even expected that.

She knew how Peter agonised over them since they'd been teenagers, and realised that she never experienced that special sort of agony felt by Peter. Worried, concerned, but not agonised. What was it that Anne Elliot's sister said to her in *Persuasion*? 'You, who have not a mother's feelings', when she asked her to look after her sick child. How perceptive of the author, the childless Jane!

When Anna got back to the hut, Peter was hammering away at the roof and Fiona had disappeared, maybe to get an ice cream at the kiosk, or to wander away into the dunes.

She looked up at Peter, but he avoided her eyes and, wondering what had passed between father and daughter, the feeling of isolation, or alienation on Anna's part, deepened.

All week, Fiona, who ostensibly had come to Dorset to study, scarcely touched her work. She seemed to prefer the company of Martin and Guy and a girl called Honey who lived in a cottage along the lane. Honey, hitherto an acquaintance, was rapidly becoming a bosom pal.

Peter worked hard in the garden, occasionally helped by Anna who had, however, brought a load of her own work, to try and catch up with a backlog.

'I wish Fiona were like you,' Peter said one day, looking into the bedroom where Anna had put a working table. 'I don't think she's done a stroke all week.'

Anna removed her spectacles and smiled at him.

'You've done all you can. She said so.'

'We've done all we can,' he corrected her gently.

Anna sat back in her chair and gazed out of the window at the gentle slopes of Bulbarrow. 'I feel at the moment I must take a back seat with Fiona, so as not to isolate her. She may yet need me.'

'How do you mean?'

'She's going through a difficult phase. It's obvious she feels very close to you and somehow resents me. She's prickly and brittle towards me.'

'I think you exaggerate.'

'No, it's true. I realise now that it has been getting like that for some time. We know she's not going to get good grades, don't we, Peter? She's going to have to resit and then there will be the question of what to do and where to go.'

'You think she'll have to leave the comp?'

'Yes, don't you? A crammer, I think, that is if she wants to go to university.'

'Which she says she doesn't.'

'I don't want her at the age of twenty-one wishing she'd got A levels. Some people do, you know. So when these results come out, that's when she'll need me, and you too.'

'What about the Council? That will take a lot of your time.' His tone was aggrieved and she knew that although he hadn't said as much he didn't, in fact, want her to stand.

'Well the Council's not until next year. *If* I do it. I have been asked before, you know, but I did consider the children. Now as they're older I'm getting older too.'

'We'll have you standing for Parliament next,'

Peter slumped despondently on the bed. 'Don't you ever think of *me* as well?'

Ten o'clock and neither Fiona nor Guy were back. Peter was in his pyjamas, and feeling angry.

'I really think this is too bad. Heavens, we need our sleep for God's sake!'

Yet again Anna opened the front door and, going to the garden gate, looked up and down the deserted lane. It was no use worrying. At least the children were together.

She saw a light in Honey's house, the girl who Fiona played with, though 'play' was not exactly the right term at their age. Fiona usually picked up the girl, so Anna knew next to nothing about her. She slipped back into the cottage for a jumper, and as she shrugged it on said to Peter: 'I think I'll just pop along to that cottage down the road and see if they know where Fiona and Guy are. If they don't know, I'll try the farm.'

'But it's dark. I'd better come with you.'

'Don't be fussy, darling. It's perfectly safe.' Anna opened the drawer in the sideboard and rooted inside. 'I'll take a torch.' She turned and looked at Peter, who seemed tired and unhappy.

'Peter, do go to bed. Don't worry.'

'They are extremely trying.'

'Well, they're on holiday.'

'Fiona was specifically told she must work. We've hardly seen Guy at all.'

Anna went over to him and gently tried to erase the creases in his brow with her thumb. Then she stood on tiptoe and kissed him. Anna was considered tall for a woman, but Peter was six foot three. 'Go to bed, darling. *Don't* worry.'

'I love you,' Peter said reaching for her hand and taking it to his lips.

Clutching the torch Anna walked swiftly down the garden path, through the gate and along the road towards the only house in the village with a light on. People tended to go to bed early in rural Dorset.

When she got there she sensed her instincts were right, and immediately felt relief surging through her. The curtains were drawn, but the sound of youthful voices came from within.

She stood outside the door for a moment feeling apprehensive. She could just imagine what sort of reception she'd get from Fiona; the accusation that she was being spied on. For a moment she thought of turning round and persuading Peter that, after all, it *was* his job. But on reflection she decided it was hers too; until recently she would never have thought otherwise. Firmly she tapped on the door and the voices suddenly fell silent. There was no reply but she could hear furious whispers break out at the other side.

She knocked again, more firmly, and after a few moments a light went on round the side of the house and a female voice called out: 'Who's there?'

Anna hurried in the direction of the voice. In the light over the back door she saw a rather pleasant looking, youngish woman, dressed like her in jeans and a T-shirt. The woman had a cigarette in her hand and flicked the ash on to the garden path.

'Can I help you?' she enquired.

'It's just that . . . I'm afraid we haven't met, but I think my daughter Fiona knows . . . is it *your* daughter? Honey?'

'Oh, you're Fiona's mother,' the woman said pleasantly enough, but without inviting her in. 'How do you do? I'm Sal.'

'I'm Anna.'

'Yes, Honey is my daughter.'

'Are they there?' Anna, feeling rather chilly, looked towards the house.

'Yes. They're watching telly. They'll be home in a minute.'

'Is Guy there too?'

'Yes, and the boy from the farm. Martin, is it? They're alright, Anna. No need to worry.'

Sal turned towards the door, as if that was the end of the matter, but for Anna it was not.

'I'm sorry, Sal,' she called as pleasantly as she could, 'but I want to take the children home. Their father's worried about them.'

'There's no need to worry. They're *perfectly* alright. Watching a video. As soon as it's finished I'll send them home.'

'They have to come now, I'm afraid.' Anna's voice tightened. 'With me. Right away. Now.'

'My goodness!' Sal said mockingly, tossing back her hair. 'We *are* a disciplinarian, aren't we?'

53

Anna didn't like the woman's tone, or, now, her manner.

'Sal, it's well after ten. Fiona is supposed to be working for her GCSEs. Her father is very tired and so, in fact, am I. It's late and we want them both home.'

'What is it, Mum?' a younger voice called from inside.

'It's Fiona and Guy's mum. They have to come home. Get them would you, pet?'

'But Mum . . .'

'I said get them.' The friendly tone now became a sharp command, and Sal stood looking at the door. Anna began to shiver. From inside the house she could hear raised voices and then shrieks of laughter. Honey's voice, this time fainter, sounded from inside.

'They say ten minutes, until the end of the video . . .'

'Now,' Anna said in a commanding voice and walked firmly towards the door. 'I'm sorry, Sal, but I don't like this at all.'

'They're not watching dirty videos, if that's what you think.' Sal's tone was now contemptuous. 'I wouldn't allow it.'

'But I think you allow them to smoke pot,' Anna said quietly. The sweet, sickly smell that wafted towards the door was unmistakable.

'And you don't, I suppose?'

'I certainly do not.'

'Well they *all* do, you know. You might not know it or like it, but they *do*.'

'*If* they do, they do it without the knowledge of me or their father.'

'More fool you.'

'You realise that it's illegal?' Anna knew she was sounding like a schoolmistress and thoroughly alienating Honey's mother.

'What? Going to report us to the cops, are you?'

'Of course not, but it *is* against the law.' Anna pushed past Sal and into the kitchen, which was untidy, the sink and draining board stacked with dishes. The smell now from the living room was overpowering, and she guessed that Sal was smoking too. She went to the door and peered in. Through a thick haze she could see several people, including her stepson and stepdaughter, lounging about, propped up on cushions on the floor or lying on the sofa, draped in the large comfortable chairs. The television in one corner of the living room was on, but no one appeared to be taking much notice of it, if any at all.

When they saw her, however, the atmosphere changed completely as lethargy turned to panic. Guy rolled off the sofa on to the floor, face downwards as if to disguise himself, and Fiona turned her back to the door.

'Fiona, Guy,' Anna called. 'Time to go home.'

No one moved. Martin rose rather sheepishly to his feet, but Honey and a girl Anna didn't recognise and another youth remained where they were, gazing at her with expressions of derision on their faces.

'We'll come in a minute, Anna,' Fiona mumbled at last.

'*Now*, Fiona. Please.'

'Fiona's not a child,' Honey said aggressively.

'As a matter of fact, she is.' Anna crossed the room, stirred Guy's body with her foot, and took Fiona by the arm and tried to jerk her up.

'*Please*, don't make an exhibition . . .'

'You already have,' Fiona said petulantly, trying to release her arm. She aimed a vicious kick at Anna's shins, but missed.

'I'll go and wait outside the back door, and I expect you to join me in five minutes. OK? Five minutes. No more.' Neither of them looked at her. 'If not, I shall go and get your father. You give me no other choice.'

She went back into the kitchen where Sal, lounging against the draining board, a fresh cigarette in her hand, had now been joined by Honey, who was whispering feverishly into her ear. It was not hard to guess what.

'I don't think smoking pot is any worse than whisky,' Sal said in a tone of defiance to Anna. 'In fact it's probably better for you.'

'I don't think any of them are particularly good for teenagers. Guy is only fourteen.'

'They grow up very fast these days.'

Anna sized up Honey, who could have been eighteen but was, she knew, nearer Fiona's age. She was a tall, slim, attractive girl with crinkly brown hair, a smiling unmade-up face. With the right expression she would probably be pretty, but now her face was disfigured by an ugly scowl.

'I just want Fiona and Guy *home*,' Anna said in the same quiet, patient voice. 'Their father's worried. So am I.' She looked at her watch. 'It's after ten, and we didn't know where they were.'

'I feel sorry for you,' Sal said nonchalantly. 'Seems you have a lot to learn about kids nowadays.'

Anna opened the back door and breathed in deeply, feeling like a diver coming up for air.

Shortly after she was joined by a subdued Guy and Fiona, who followed several paces behind her, dragging their feet all the way up the lane and back to the house.

CHAPTER 3

Anna's doctor was a personal friend, a woman a little older than her, whom she'd known since their university days when they'd lived in the same hall of residence. Anna, who was hardly ever ill, took her few complaints to Katie Ward, who practised as a gynaecologist, was married to a GP and had two children.

The two women were of similar temperament; brisk, practical, outward looking, with well-developed social consciences. Katie did a lot of lowly or unpaid voluntary work in mother and baby welfare clinics in the disadvantaged areas of London, far from the fashionable ambiance of Harley Street and its environs.

Katie gave Anna a yearly check-up, smear test, breast examination, heart, lungs and, after pronouncing her fit, as she usually did, they would go off to have lunch. Katie's consulting rooms were in Wimpole Street, a short distance from Anna's law office in Wigmore Street.

Apart from that, they socialised occasionally, attended the same dinner parties, had one another to dinner. Katie's husband, Donald, was younger than Peter, but the two men got on well. The Ward children were considerably younger than Guy and Fiona, so the socialising was confined to adults.

If Anna made an appointment to see Katie apart from the annual check-up it was never for something trivial so, as Anna loosened her coat and sat down, Katie took a seat opposite her preparing to listen attentively after they had exchanged the usual preliminaries: how were husbands, children, etc.?

Katie opened Anna's file and flipped through the few papers it contained. 'I last saw you six months ago for the usual. Everything was fine.' She gave a brief professional smile, joined her hands together and looked across at her friend. 'What's the problem?'

'Well,' Anna, betraying her nerves, fidgeted with her rings, 'I think I might be pregnant.'

'Oh?' Katie's expression registered mild surprise. She was a small, neat woman with short dark hair, warm brown eyes, rather delicately featured, fine bone structure, and always discreetly but expensively dressed. Every inch the professional. 'Is that good news or bad?' She stared at her notes again. 'I see that I'm still prescribing the Pill for you. Did you stop taking it?'

'Briefly.'

'Oh!' Katie leaned back and nodded.

'I'd run out but I realised I'd left my prescription at home. Well, that night . . . you know how it is.' Anna fidgeted nervously again, and Katie nodded understandingly. Oh, yes, how well she knew.

'I thought that after taking it for so long there'd

be no problem.' Anna's hands fluttered towards the desk in front of her as if seeking reassurance. 'I've said nothing to Peter.'

'Let's see,' Katie said jumping up. 'Put you out of your misery.'

'You can tell? *Now?*' Anna looked amazed.

'Not absolutely. But pretty sure, ninety-nine per cent.' Katie went over to a cupboard and began searching through the contents. 'No need to inject it into frogs and wait for ages.'

'*It?*' Anna looked puzzled and Katie turned towards her and smiled.

'Pop into the bathroom and give me a sample, there's a dear. You know the routine.'

Moments after the sample was delivered, Katie emerged from the examination room next to her consulting room smiling as she wiped her hands on a towel.

'False alarm.'

Anna felt she could have wept with relief.

'You're *sure?*'

'Pretty sure. Ninety-nine per cent.' Katie tossed the towel to one side and, resuming her seat at her desk, drew Anna's file towards her and scribbled a note. 'There is absolutely no trace of the dip stick changing colour, and if you missed two periods,' she looked up with a thoughtful expression and began to count on her fingers.

'Yes, two.' Anna found herself choking back the tears. 'Gosh, I was so worried.'

'Were you?' Katie sat back and regarded her

friend solemnly. 'As much as that? Why?'

'Well . . .'

Katie was surprised by the attitude of the normally articulate Anna. It was so unlike her, losing her cool like this. 'Did you never *seriously* consider having a family, Anna?'

'Yes, we considered it. Naturally. But that was years ago before I resumed work.'

'And not since?'

'No. Guy and Fiona seemed to need all the parenting I could give.'

'And you didn't tell Peter you thought you were pregnant?'

Anna shook her head like a guilty schoolgirl.

'You thought he might be pleased?'

This time Anna nodded, then said: 'But I don't think in his heart of hearts he wants a baby. He's not quite sure about how *I* feel.'

Katie nodded understandingly again.

'Nevertheless, it is a very natural instinct to want your own children, the blood tie as it were.' She paused. 'But not you?'

Anna shook her head again, this time emphatically.

'Not me.'

'I see.' Katie got up and wandered to the window of her consulting room where she stood looking at the busy street below. 'Then why don't you opt for sterilisation?'

Returning to her desk, on which lay a sphygmomanometer which she opened, she took up her stethoscope and, asking Anna to bare her arm, bound the rubber cuff around it.

She looked thoughtfully at the instrument as the mercury rose and then fell and, removing the stethoscope from her ears, placed it on the table. 'Blood pressure OK. But last time it *was* a tiny bit up.'

'Oh?' Anna immediately looked anxious.

'Not enough for me to comment on. I know you lead a pretty stressful life and put it down to that. However, this missing two periods for no reason might indicate it's time you came off the Pill. Let me see, you'll soon be thirty-six,' she paused as she counted on her fingers again, 'what, sixteen, eighteen years?'

Anna nodded.

'Even with the low oestrogen dosage I give you I think it's long enough. I had my tubes tied two years ago.'

'*Did* you?' Anna looked impressed.

'There's nothing to it. A couple of days in bed, a tiny bit of discomfort. I can even do you as an outpatient and have you home the same day. However, I dare say, like me, you'd value a couple of days in the comfort of a nice private hospital room. How about the Princess Grace?'

'You're really serious about this, Katie?'

'Perfectly serious.' Katie sat down again and drummed her fingers on her desk. 'That is if *you* are.'

'But I'm not ill or anything?'

'I can assure you that you're not ill. I'll take another smear, just to reassure you before you go; but this is not uncommon with busy women who are not yet menopausal but are past the halfway mark of their reproductive lives. Sometimes the cycle starts to misbehave, or miss out altogether. I just thought it was silly to continue dosing myself with, what is, after all, a powerful drug — the long-term effects of which we frankly don't know. They're making new discoveries all the time. It *is* rather worrying. And if you are serious about not having children I would suggest you think about it.' She glanced at the clock on the wall. 'Do we have time for the ritual lunch?'

'Just a bite. I'm due at the magistrates' court at two.'

'And I'm due at the hospital at the same time.' Katie capped her pen and got up. Then she studied her friend who remained seated.

'Anything else worrying you, Anna? You look terribly anxious today. I thought you'd be relieved knowing the test was negative.' She leaned towards her and studied her closely. 'What else ails you?'

'Well,' Anna fidgeted with her rings yet again. 'I couldn't face a baby while Guy and Fiona present us with such problems.'

'Ah!' Katie sat down again. 'As you hadn't mentioned it, I hoped things had improved since I saw you last.'

'They haven't improved at all. They've got steadily worse. Fiona just took her GCSE exams and has probably flunked the lot. Guy does them next year with not much hope of success there either. Peter is really at his wits' end.'

'And you?'

'Obviously I'm very worried too; but you know although I love them and regard them as my own, I . . .'

'*Do* you?'

Anna seemed surprised at the sharpness of Katie's tone.

'Do I what?'

'*Really* regard them as your own?'

Anna examined her hands.

'Frankly, since you ask . . . not really.' Her face, when she looked up, was strained. 'I did when they were small and lovable, but now they seem to have grown away from me. I would only confess this to someone like you. Sometimes I feel I dare not even admit it to myself.'

'It's not a sin,' Katie protested. 'Biologically they are not your own children, and there's nothing quite like the blood tie.'

'But when they were young . . .'

'They were beautiful, vulnerable. They needed you. Teenagers are very different. Sometimes it's only the fact that I'm their mother that makes me tolerate my own children. Even though they're so much younger they're very demanding. I resent them.'

'Really?' Despite herself, Anna looked surprised.

'They irritate you, they annoy you. But some of my patients and friends with teenage kids are nearly demented. They seem to go out of their way to be as much trouble as possible. They don't know what to do with them.'

'Oh, I'm so *glad*.' A look of immense relief flooded Anna's face. She put her hand to her mouth. 'I mean. Oh I *don't* mean . . .'

'You mean you're glad that their biological parents feel as you do. My dear, most of the parents in this country would say the same if they were honest.'

'Yes.' Anna looked at her solemnly. 'Sometimes I confess I hate them. They are so uncaring, so thoughtless. They cause so much grief to Peter, and they make me feel guilty. Peter wanted them to go to private school, but I was a keen supporter of State education.'

'It *is* a mess, isn't it?' Katie looked sympathetic. 'But, believe me, others pay a fortune in fees for them and their problems are exactly the same.'

'Drugs?' Anna whispered.

'If you mean pot, yes, I suppose so. Frankly, I'm not really against pot; but I don't think encouraging drugs or any other form of narcotic at their age is a good thing. I'd say the same about drink and cigarettes, but after the age of eighteen . . . well, people will do it anyway.'

'We found Guy and Fiona smoking pot in Dorset in the half term holiday. The tiny little hamlet where we have our cottage is just about the very last place you'd think of. There was a group of them including the mother of the girl Fiona was friendly with.'

'Doesn't surprise me.' Katie glanced at her

watch again. 'I wonder it surprises you, with all your experience.'

Anna rose, shook herself. 'Perhaps because it touches me, impinges on my private life.'

'If we're going to have that sandwich we'd better hurry.' Katie opened the communicating door between her and her secretary, had a word with her and then, gathering up her bag and briefcase, joined Anna by the door. 'Anna, I'd think very seriously, if I were you, about being sterilised. I mean at the moment you seem to me to be a bit unsure of your role as a mother. Maybe in your heart of hearts you actually do want a child of your own?'

'That's ridiculous.' Anna's reply was immediate as Katie closed the door and they waited for the lift.

'Anyway, it can't be done this summer,' Katie said. 'I'm going to America for a conference. Donald is joining us, and bringing the children for an extended holiday. We'll be away about a month. If you still feel the same, come and see me in the autumn.'

It was Peter who opened the buff envelope as Anna stood by with a sinking heart. He took the enclosure to the window, studied it for a few moments and then wordlessly passed it to Anna.

It was as they feared. Fiona had got hopelessly bad grades in all of her subjects except English and History, which could possibly be interpreted as a scrape pass.

She placed the letter down on the table and, going over to Peter, put her hand on his arm, pressed her head against his back.

'It's no surprise, is it? Maybe it will jolt her.'

'Jolt her into what?'

'Trying harder.'

'But she doesn't want to try. She will use this as a reason to leave school.'

As Fiona was already sixteen there was no reason why, if she wanted to, she shouldn't.

'What do you believe she will think she is qualified to do at the age of sixteen?'

'She won't think about it. She's opted out. She's trying to tell us that as clearly as anything.'

'Maybe that will bring her to her senses. She will realise you can't get anywhere without qualifications and then . . .'

'Oh, Anna, don't deceive yourself. You know Fiona as well as I do. She's telling us by her attitude that she hates our middle-class lifestyle and all it stands for. We've failed her.'

'She's failed *you*.'

'Why me especially?' He looked up at her.

'Because you care so much.'

'But you care too.' He appeared anxious to convince himself.

'Of course I do, but you, as her biological father, care more.'

'I often wondered,' Peter paused and studied the floor, 'if you really did care.'

'I *do* care.' Anna sat opposite him clasping her hands between her knees. It was a Thursday morning and, knowing the results were due and Peter would probably need her, she had arranged to be late at the office. 'But I'm not quite as torn apart as you are . . . Darling, it's better that way. Same as I can sleep at night when they aren't in, and you can't.'

'You should have a child of your own, Anna,' Peter said with uncharacteristic sharpness, 'and then you'd know.'

Anna rose and, without replying, went over to the door.

'I'm sorry,' Peter called out, but by that time the door had shut behind her and he didn't know whether she had heard him or not.

Peter felt like crushing the paper containing the exam results into a ball and hurling it out of the window, or tearing it into tiny fragments and stuffing it into the wastepaper basket.

But no. Fiona was on a school trip to France — how convenient to arrange it when the exam results were due — and he had to keep it for her. He wondered if he should go after Anna, but at that moment he heard the front door shut and seconds later her car started up.

She had stayed home specially to be with him and he had behaved like a pig. It was at times like this that, subconsciously, he thought about Nancy and his guilt became acute, because Nancy would have been far less use, help, or support to him than Anna was.

Nancy had never taken herself or her responsibilities seriously. She was not an especially good or doting mother to the children. She was a spoilt, beautiful woman who only really cared for herself.

Yet he had adored her and had never loved Anna in quite the obsessional way that he had loved Nancy.

Nancy was the sort of woman who besotted men. Despite her many failings, her selfishness and idleness, they fell recklessly and helplessly, illogically in love with her. She was fascinating, a charmer. She had only been thirty when she died and he had never forgotten her.

Of course he loved Anna, but in a different way. He loved her, but had never been 'in love'. She was the sort of sensible, practical woman even at the age of twenty-five — five years younger than Nancy — who he had known would be a support to a man, someone he could lean on; a conscientious hardworking stepmother to the children.

She had been clever and ambitious in a way Nancy never was; smart, well groomed, whereas Nancy never felt it necessary to adorn her beauty, could hardly have been less interested in clothes and slopped around all day in jeans and loose sweaters. People said that Anna and Nancy were alike but they weren't. It was true they resembled each other slightly, physically and in colouring, so that people said he had fallen in love with similar types of women as men often do, but that was all.

It may have been that the children would have turned out better with Nancy as a mother just because she would have been less caring. Left to their own devices, they might have tried harder. Whereas with Peter and Anna, concerned parents who read all the books and knew all the rules about development and awareness and so on, they seemed to leave everything to them as though asking themselves what was the point of making an effort when their parents were so hard-working, successful and, inevitably, wealthy?

Peter had also trained as a lawyer, but after being called to the Bar he joined a huge oil concern and had been with them ever since. Now he was head of the legal department, a member of the board and a man with a six figure salary, one who could easily have afforded the priciest public schools in the country for his children's education.

Nancy, ill-educated herself, would have left it to him to decide. But Anna had very firm ideas about equality of opportunity, fair shares for all, and there was never any question but that the children went to the local comprehensive and mucked in like everyone else.

It was easy to relate the kind of effect this had had on the children to the kind of person that Anna had become. She had firm ideas about everything. She seldom wavered or changed her mind. She was so busy that she believed in plan-ning well ahead, thinking that if she didn't, in-evitably everything would fall apart.

She was well organised, meticulous to a fault. Yet no one could call her uncaring or accuse her of lacking compassion and, in effect, he had.

Peter sank into a chair and put his head in his hands. He felt his life and his children's were a mess. But without Anna he could hardly begin to know how to handle it.

The firm of Robertson, Askew & Cole was nearly a hundred years old. It had been founded at the end of the nineteenth century by Andrew Robertson in the very premises it still occupied. Only then it had been in one room and now it occupied not only the whole house but the one next door. Cecil Askew had joined it in the thirties bringing his own clients and considerable expertise of litigation, and after the Second World War it merged with the respectable City firm of Cardew Cole.

It was extremely prestigious and well regarded, yet it still maintained an air redolent of an earlier age: leisured, civilised, unhurried and compassionate. Despite its upmarket West End address, it accepted Legal Aid and a number of its lawyers were, like Anna, engaged in voluntary work.

Anna, a clever student with a first-class law degree, had been accepted by Robertson, Askew & Cole as an articled clerk. Although full of bright promise, after completing her Articles and on her marriage she resigned to look after Peter's young children, returning to work at the age of thirty. Her old firm were glad to have her back; she was well thought of by her colleagues and highly regarded by her clients.

She was considered typical of that breed of women who successfully combined running a home, a family and a career. Little was known about her private life, and it never intruded on her work.

But did it? Anna gazed out of the window above Wigmore Street from which she could just see the trees in Cavendish Square and propped her chin on her clasped hands.

Even if she conceived now she would be well into her thirty-sixth year when her baby was born.

With a jolt she looked at the calendar and realised that Katie Ward would soon be back from her extended trip to the US and expecting a call from her.

Somehow she knew it was crunch time. A time for decisions. If they had a baby, perhaps it would take their minds off the problems posed by Fiona and Guy. On the other hand, was it fair, either to the new child or its elder half-brother and sister? Did not Guy and Fiona need *more* help now in their difficult adolescence rather than less, and what would be the effect on them of a young sibling in the home? Also, how would it affect her own career? Would she abandon it, or simply take maternity leave?

The intercom buzzed, rudely disturbing her reverie, and she pressed the button.

'Anna, I wonder if you could come into my office? Could you spare a few moments?'

'Of course. Is there anything I should bring with me?'

'Just yourself, Anna.'

David Dugdale Cole, the grandson of Cardew Cole, senior partner and the only descendant of any of the original families still to be with the group, sounded quite jovial. Maybe he'd got back from a good lunch, though she knew him to be abstemious in all things, and he ate and drank sparingly.

Although possessed of considerable charm and impeccable good manners, David was rather dry and remote. He didn't socialise with the staff, although there was an annual Christmas party, usually at Brown's Hotel, to which he brought his attractive upper-class wife, June. He had two children whom Anna had never seen, didn't even know how old they were. It suited her that the relationships among the staff were business-like. Few of them knew much about one another's lives out of the office; she didn't have one person she confided in, but as they were mainly men that was perhaps understandable.

She put her head into her secretary's office to tell her where she was going, and then descended the two floors to David's spacious office on the first floor. She tapped on the door and he called out inviting her to enter.

Before she could turn the handle the door was flung open by Henry Atherton, also one of the partners, and standing next to David's desk with a smile on his face was Michael Norden, yet another.

'Come in, come in, Anna.' Henry genially

reached for her hand and then, standing back for her to enter, closed the door after her.

'Welcome, Anna.' David got up from his desk to greet her, and Michael nodded. It struck Anna that the welcome was unusual. Something, decidedly, was up.

She felt a flicker of alarm but said nothing and, returning their smiles, took the chair indicated by David just to one side of his desk. Henry sat in the other and Michael, his hands clasped, perched on the side of David's imposing desk which, legend had it, had once belonged to the founder, Andrew Robertson.

'Well, Anna.' Resuming his seat, David, too, joined his hands together on the desk, and gave her a smile, the kind that must have reassured many an anxious client, or nervous junior barrister. 'I imagine you're wondering what this reception committee is in aid of?'

'I did wonder.' Anna tossed back her head and stared him straight in the eyes.

'Well, Anna,' David looking earnest, leaned forward, 'the object of this meeting is two-fold. As you know, we have been in these premises for nearly a hundred years. Although we have expanded and our space has increased — we now have two houses whereas in the days of the founder he had one room — we still haven't enough space for all the work we have to do and the staff we need to take on. We therefore propose to move.'

'Oh!' Anna's heart sank. If they were relocating

out of London, and firms bent on enlargement usually did these days, there would be no question of her moving with them.

That might provide the solution to several troubling domestic questions. More time to give the difficult adolescents and perhaps, at last, to have that baby whose possible existence always seemed to lurk at the back of her mind, however much she denied it.

She began to feel more relaxed and crossed her legs, her expression attentive.

'But,' Michael, head of human resources, leaned across the desk, 'there is another reason for our decision to move. We're increasing our corporate business. It has quadrupled since we've been in the EC, and we therefore propose to move to the City, which will give us more space and, at the same time, put us nearer some of our major clients.'

Mystification set in. Was she to get the sack? Made redundant? Well that would still give her the opportunities that had been at the back of her mind, but maybe with ignominy, which she didn't exactly relish. To get the push wasn't quite as heroic as giving up work voluntarily. But that's what it looked like. Her specialty was civil, family and divorce cases. She never touched corporation law.

Michael stopped talking, and she wondered if he was finding the next part of his task difficult.

'Seems like I'll be expendable,' she prompted him. 'Is that what I'm here for?'

The men looked at one another and simultaneously burst into gruff, clannish laughter. Michael rubbed his hands together as though in glee that his teasing approach had paid off.

'On the *contrary*, Anna,' David too gave a self-satisfied smile, 'we are hoping to keep these premises, for which we have the freehold, for our family and civil cases and we would like *you* to be the person in charge. We are thus offering you a partnership and making you a full member of the firm.'

'Wow!' Anna exclaimed, and they laughed again as if in self-congratulation. There really was something quite childlike about grown men.

'What about Arnold?' Anna asked before the laughter had subsided. Arnold Webster was the partner in charge of the civil and family division, her immediate boss.

'Arnold is nearly sixty and wants to retire. He will remain as a consultant to help you settle in. That is, if you agree.'

Anna remained silent for a moment and then said quietly: 'I don't think there's any doubt about that, except of course I'll want to consult Peter.'

They nodded in understanding, but David asked: 'Is there any reason why Peter should say "no"?'

'Oh, no. I don't think so.'

'He's not near retirement, is he? No plans to move?'

'Not at all; but we are a partnership. We do

consult. He consulted with me before taking up his new position a few years ago, and I feel I should do the same.'

'Naturally.' The urbane David Cole stood up and held out his hand. 'The plans do not come into operation until the New Year so take what time you need. Please accept my congratulations, Anna. We shall hope your acceptance is a foregone conclusion, shan't we, gentlemen?' The others nodded and moved forward to press her hand. 'I think if you do accept, and naturally we hope you will, you'll be the youngest partner we have had for many years.'

'And the only woman,' Michael interposed.

'So far,' Anna said smiling.

'Yes, I do believe we must move with the times. Oh, and Anna,' David called out as she turned and walked to the door, 'my wife and I would be delighted if you and Peter would have dinner with us. Just a small party you know, to get to know one another better.'

Anna shut the door behind her, leaned on it for a second and then sped upstairs, two at a time.

A full partnership, a private dinner with the boss. Barriers falling down, horizons expanding, the future unlimited.

Anna left the office earlier than usual, scarcely able to contain her excitement. She realised as she never had before that she was truly ambitious, she wanted to get to the top, she valued the respect the partners held her in, the chances they offered her.

They had no garage, and she parked the car outside the house as usual, noticing Peter's on the other side of the road. He had got home even earlier than she had, and then she remembered, and a curious little chill clutched at her heart dispelling her euphoria.

Of course. Fiona was due home from the continent, and she in her excitement had forgotten all about it.

So much for being a good mother.

Tomorrow she would ring up Katie Ward's office and make an appointment to get her tubes tied. She couldn't be a partner *and* have a baby as well. No question now of that.

That decision, if Peter agreed — and of course he would — had been taken out of her hands.

She put the key in the lock, and the front door swung open. She paused for a moment and knew immediately, from the unnatural stillness in the house, that something had happened.

No sound of the TV, no voices. It was as though someone had died. In place of the chill, fear seemed to grip her heart, and her mouth felt dry.

She stood in the hall and called out in as natural a voice as she could muster: 'Hi! Anyone at home?'

There was no reply, and then she thought that perhaps she was silly and that the silence was because there *was* no one at home. She was in a hyper-sensitive mood. Peter must have taken a taxi to meet Fiona because of the difficulty of parking at Victoria.

But the door of the sitting room, usually open, was shut. She turned the handle, and as it swung away from her, she could see Peter sitting in the chair next to the TV, his face sullen and angry, his hands firmly grasping each arm as if to give him added gravitas or, maybe, simply more support.

The door was wide open now, and then Anna saw Fiona, her face white, her eyes red with weeping, sitting opposite Peter. Her body was squeezed up into the chair in embryonic fashion. Like her mother, she was petite, and the large armchair dwarfed her. Her hand was pressed into her mouth as though she were sucking her fingers like a baby.

Anna crossed the room in silence, put her briefcase and bag on the floor and flopped into a vacant chair.

'Hi!' she said looking across at Fiona. 'Welcome home.'

Fiona didn't reply.

'Hi, darling!' Anna turned to Peter who gave her a wintry smile. 'Did I interrupt something?'

'No, you didn't.' Fiona uncoiled herself from the chair looking as though with one bound she would spring out of it. Yet she hesitated as though uncertain now what to do.

'Have a good time?' Anna tried to keep the tone of her voice natural.

Fiona still didn't reply.

'Fiona, Anna asked you a question.' Peter looked sternly at his daughter.

'I'm not deaf,' Fiona said.

Anna rose and reached for her bag and brief-case. 'I think maybe I did interrupt something. Call me when the conference is over.'

'Anna, please stay.' Peter pointed to the seat. 'I think this is something you should be in on. Naturally it's about Fiona's results. Her future. As her mother . . .'

'She is *not* my mother,' Fiona said angrily. 'How many times do I have to say that?'

'As your stepmother then.' Anna was deter-mined not to provoke Fiona. 'I am that, I think.'

'I wish you wouldn't take this attitude of rude-ness and hostility towards Anna,' Peter said peevishly. 'She has always been a support and help to you. Yet now you seem to want to exclude her from the family counsels entirely.'

'Look, if I'm not wanted and can't help, hon-estly I don't mind.' Anna remained standing, uncertain whether to sit down again or go. Peter's eyes seemed to implore her to stay, but Fiona's remained implacably hostile.

'I *want* you to stay, Anna,' Peter insisted. 'Please sit down again.'

Anna sat, feeling foolish but also rather angry. Sod Fiona, on this day of days, *her* day. The day she was offered a partnership.

'You'd better give me a résumé about what's being said. And I'll see if I can help.'

'Well, you can't!' Fiona spat at her. Anna ignored her and looked at Peter.

'I gave Fiona her results. Naturally she's upset.'

'But hardly surprised, I'd have thought. She did absolutely no work and unless you're brilliant you can't expect to pass, so she didn't.'

'Not brilliant like *you*,' Fiona said. Anna ignored her. Useless to argue with someone in this mood, this frame of mind.

'Is that all this is about?'

'No.' Peter studied his fingers. 'I've told Fiona that you and I had discussed the matter and we thought she should go to a crammer for a year and retake.'

'Yes, we did think that, Fiona.' Anna, despite her feelings, managed a smile, trying to remember that, although this girl was not the daughter of her body, she did have a long and close relationship with her, claimed that she loved her. Could she *still* say she loved her? No, not at the moment. Did Peter? Probably, because his was a blood tie. If she and Peter had a baby that would be a blood tie too.

Then she remembered the partnership and she knew that the challenge of running her own division, the opportunity to succeed and maybe, above all, the chance to be away from this place all day was irresistible. Yes, maybe that was it. She couldn't bear the possibility, with all its concomitant irritations and responsibilities, of being at home all day long.

As no one answered, Anna looked over to Peter, and spoke as though her stepdaughter were not there.

'What did Fiona say, Peter?'

'Well, naturally she's confused.'

'I am *not* confused.' Fiona's tone was louder and more forceful than was necessary. 'I am quite clear about it. I am sixteen and I want to leave school.'

'And what do you want to do?' Anna tried to sound relaxed, friendly, cheerful, but it was very hard. She guessed the truth was that she sounded artificial and insincere.

'Dunno,' Fiona shrugged.

'You don't want to do anything?'

'What is there to do?'

'You think you're going to be kept by your father?'

'Why shouldn't he? He has plenty.'

'That's not the point, Fiona.'

'Lots of people do it. Before the War, girls never worked.'

Anna could hardly believe her ears. 'Did you say "before the War"?'

'Yes, I did.' Fiona's expression was defiant.

'But that was over fifty years ago.'

'Even I can't remember it.' Peter's laugh was relieved as though somehow the ice had been broken.

'It does seem a bit daft, Fiona, if you don't mind me saying so, to quote what happened many years before you were born.'

'Maybe it was a good age. All this emphasis

on work. Why can't everyone relax and be themselves? What's wrong with me staying at home if Dad can keep me?'

'Because the idea of your selfishness appalls me, that's what.' Peter's tone was brusque. 'Even in the thirties women wanted to work, unless they were married with children.'

'And that happens now,' Anna nodded. 'Many women with children have no choice but to stay at home. Most people want to work.'

'But why?'

It was a good point. One, actually, she'd never thought of.

'Because work is fulfilling,' she declared after a while. 'Also, these days, most people need the money.'

'But you and Dad have got plenty.'

'Yes, but we didn't say we wanted you to live on it.'

'But I do live on it while I'm at school, and if you send me to a crammer it will cost a bomb, and you will also have to keep me, whereas if I stayed at home and didn't go to the crammer it would save a bomb.'

There was logic in her argument.

'What a day.' Peter sat wearily on the edge of the bed, tugging at his shoelaces. He had taken off his tie but not changed when he came home.

'Exhausting!' Anna, looking by contrast fresh and pretty, emerged from the bathroom in her robe, rubbing moisturiser into her face.

The argument with Fiona had raged well into the evening, whereupon exhaustion, also repetition, set in, and they had all gone into the kitchen for something to eat. During the meal Fiona unexpectedly called a truce and told them quite animatedly about the holiday. She'd obviously had a good time which made her mood of hostility when she returned home all the stranger.

They sat round the supper table for some time and the discussion about her future began again, only with less heat. It was decided that they would talk about it at the weekend when they intended to have a few days together before term began.

Fiona had assumed anyway, and so had her parents, that she would be starting back at school in the normal way.

At the end of the evening, to their surprise and gratification, Fiona announced that she was going to bed. She came and kissed them both, and went upstairs to her room.

Anna had anticipated a drama about her going out to see her friends. So, for the time being, there was a temporary respite.

It could only be a respite, a truce.

The emotions of the evening had taken all the gloss off her news, and she was in half a mind as to whether to tell Peter about it or not. On the other hand, David would be sure to ask her the next day and she could hardly say it hadn't been mentioned.

'Darling,' she perched on the bed next to him, 'I have some rather momentous news.'

He turned to her immediately and his face had a curious expression on it — a kind of expectation that she had no difficulty interpreting.

'Not that!' she said, putting a hand on him. 'You thought I meant pregnant?'

He nodded.

'Of course I wouldn't have done anything like *that* without consulting you. No, Peter, I've been offered a partnership, a full member of the team with my own department. They're relocating to the City, but I'm to stay in Wigmore Street in charge of the Civil and Family Law side of the firm.'

'What's happened to Arnold?' Peter mumbled as if either unable to, or disinclined to assimilate the news.

'He's close to retirement. Staying on as consultant to see me in. Peter, I haven't accepted, but you'd want me to say "yes" wouldn't you? I mean,' her voice faltered, 'I mean I said I'd discuss it with you, but I thought it would be a foregone conclusion.'

Peter sat staring in front of him, silent.

'Peter,' feeling suddenly anxious, 'aren't you *pleased?*'

'If it's what you want, yes.' Peter rose slowly from the bed. He got out of his City trousers, took off his shirt and went into the bathroom emerging almost immediately in his robe.

'Well, it's what I want, and I'd have thought

it was what you wanted.'

'Why should I want it?' He scratched his head as if the whole thing perplexed him.

Anna felt astounded.

'Well, why *shouldn't* you want it? I mean I wanted your promotion. I was glad for you. Why shouldn't you want me to be a partner?'

Peter slumped down on the bed again and an arm encircled her waist.

'Because I think I wanted you to have a baby,' he said.

Anna looked at him incredulously.

'Peter, you *can't* want to begin this whole ghastly business again.'

'What ghastly business?' He sounded hurt. 'You loved the kids when they were little.'

'Yes but "little" grows up. I don't want this drama in another sixteen or so years with our son or daughter.'

'Times change.'

'Peter, you aren't serious are you? I mean the last time we talked about it we agreed . . .'

Peter lay full length on the bed, his head resting on his arms.

'I think that was *quite* a long time ago.' His eyes fastened on the ceiling.

'Soon I'll be thirty-six.'

'Yes, I know.'

'If I had a baby . . .'

'You'd still be thirty-six. It's not very old. Lots of women do it.'

Anna ran her hands through her hair.

'Peter, I feel horribly, terribly confused. I really don't know what to do.' She looked at him wildly. 'This is all so unexpected.'

'Can't you be a partner and have a baby?'

'Not really. I don't think it would be fair.'

'Why is it unfair?'

'Because I'll have to take time off.'

'We could have a nanny.'

'I'd have to take a lot of time off! Don't be absurd. Anyway, I think David and the partners would feel cheated, offering me a partnership and departmental headship and then finding that I'm pregnant. It's just not on, Peter. It's one thing or the other. And we must decide. Quite soon.'

Peter clasped his head suddenly with both hands as though he had a headache. Anna, overcome with love, pity, sympathy, and remorse, bent over him to kiss him. As she did, one hand flew away from his head and he grasped at the belt of her gown which fell open to display her nudity. Undoing the cord of his bath robe, he drew her to him kissing her there, just where she stood above him, arousing in her immediate feelings so intense, erotic and overwhelming that she straddled him quickly as, her hands straining against his chest, the moment of intense mutual pleasure overwhelmed them both.

She lay upon him, savouring him, listening to the steady pounding of his heart, licking, with swift darts of her tongue, the sweat that trickled down his neck.

After a while she rose, went into the bathroom, washed herself, slipped on a nightie and tiptoed back into the bedroom.

Peter still lay where he was, eyes closed, and as she approached the bed, he held out a hand for her.

'I want you to do what you want,' he said, drawing her on to the bed beside him.

'How do you mean?' She turned towards him, stroking his hair back from his damp forehead.

'You know what I mean.'

'About the baby or the job?'

'Both.' He opened his eyes and passed a hand over his brow again. 'If you're sure you don't want a baby then I'm content. Frankly, starting it all over again at my age would be traumatic. I hadn't thought it through.'

'Getting up at night . . .'

'The screams, the tantrums.'

'Babies are beautiful, but they're a tie. Besides, we love Fiona and Guy.' He turned sideways to look at her. 'Don't we? Despite everything?'

'We do. And they'd be terribly jealous of a baby. As they are now, it would cause all sorts of confusion and probably hostility. Frankly, I don't think I could cope.'

'I never thought of that.' He hesitated, looking at her. 'If you're *sure*.'

'I am.' She paused and ran a hand along his arm. 'It means having my tubes tied. Sterilisation. It's the sensible thing to do.'

'It seems very final.' His voice was flat, unemotional. Then, doubtfully, 'I *suppose* I could have a vasectomy.'

'You don't sound very happy about that.'

No reply.

'Besides,' Anna continued, knowing Peter had gone into his shell, 'I've discussed all this with Katie. She's had her tubes tied. Says there's nothing to it.'

'I feel it would . . . might, damage my masculinity. I mean one doesn't know. Vasectomy, I mean.'

'Whereas if I was sterilised, we could have an abandoned, carefree sex life.' She paused and smiled wickedly at him. 'Better than ever.'

'Better than ever.' He began to caress her. 'I don't believe you.' His voice sounded sleepy. 'If you don't mind, and you're sure . . . Besides, in a year or two we'd be able to go away for long, sexy holidays all by ourselves. Do it.'

And on those words he fell asleep.

How like a man. Changing their minds every two minutes, and yet they said women were the changeable ones.

Anna lay on her back, head propped in her hands. It was terribly final, but she knew it was what she wanted. How frightened she'd felt when she thought she might be pregnant. How trapped, unable to concentrate, terrified. It was so unlike her, even Katie had commented on it. *And* she had never told Peter. Even in marriage there were certain things one kept from one's spouse, and she thought that if she told him, Peter might be hurt she'd been so positive, so relieved, that his sperm and her egg hadn't fused to produce their child.

Anna drew the duvet carefully over them as Peter, fast asleep, turned on his side, his back to her; she pressed herself against him knowing that the ache, the longing she had for him would never pass.

CHAPTER 4

The comprehensive had been built in the sixties and, nearly thirty years later, it had already undergone extensive repairs. Even then it looked a jerry-built affair, a sort of concrete blackboard jungle, badly planned and of shoddy construction. It had two macadam playing grounds interspersed with patches of lawn, trees and an attempt at a garden which was invariably vandalised from the spring onwards. It was pathetic how regularly the attempts of the authorities to beautify this depressing place went unappreciated.

The school had about eleven hundred pupils, a tiny number of whom, due to a false Socialist Utopian idealism, went on to higher education.

Jessie Clark remembered very well the long and earnest talks she'd had with the Livingstones when first Fiona, and then Guy, came to the school. Anna had been a diligent member of the parent/teacher association and at first, as an eleven year old, Fiona had done well. She began to drop out when she was approaching thirteen, started bunking off and mixing with a crowd from one of the broken-down housing estates in Paddington, on the periphery of the school's catchment area.

No one's fault really, a case of mistaken, misdirected educational policies which were engendered by a Tory politician, Rab Butler, in the famous 1944 Education Act, with the best of motives: equality of education for all. But Fiona was one of the victims of this optimistic and impractical policy which didn't suit everyone. The bad, invariably, drives out the good. It had to be admitted that some pupils reacted best to discipline, an ordered society and a structured curriculum, even a uniform.

The comp had none of these things, and even its curriculum had been devised by its own staff to suit its own individualistic and, in the opinion of some, idiosyncratic, ends. It was unique; a few thought it was wonderful, but most thought it was dreadful and ill-equipped the children for a decent, even adequate, education. The gulf between private and State education was seen at its widest here.

Jessie felt a flutter of apprehension as the time for the interview with the Livingstones drew near. She looked out of the window at the traffic rushing up and down the busy arterial road out of London, at the stragglers in the playground, who should have been at their lessons, and wondered if she, a devoted educationalist and upholder of egalitarian principles, had contributed to that fundamental failure of the school to bring out the best, not only academically but socially, in those committed to her care?

Her secretary popped her head through the door.

'Mr and Mrs Livingstone are here.'

'Do show them in,' Jessie said with dogged cheerfulness and, hands in the pockets of her jersey suit, she went to the door to welcome them. Anna, who came in first, seemed her usual confident self, but Jessie thought Peter looked tired. She remembered, with a stab of guilt, how reluctant Peter had been to send his children to the school, but egged on by a determined Anna and given assurances by Jessie that a better, all rounded education could not be found elsewhere in the kingdom, he had agreed.

The three shook hands, and as the Livingstones sat down Jessie retired behind her desk, as if retreating behind a protective barrier.

Before her were Fiona's GCSE results which were, indeed, awful. Outright failure in most subjects, a scrape through in English and History. But that was not the only thing. Beside it was a report from her form teacher, and those who dealt directly with her, which was every bit as damning as the examination results. Was it also a judgment on the school which had produced such an unsatisfactory pupil or, she studied them for a moment as they settled themselves into their chairs, the parents? Good, affluent, middle-class home it might be, but was it also a caring one? Above all, a perceptive one? Those with the most money were not necessarily the best parents. Had it in fact been the best environment for someone of Fiona's rebellious and unorthodox disposition? Did a stepmother *really* provide the love a vulnerable and sensitive child required? Was it actually possible? Especially with someone as hardworking and ambitious as Anna undoubtedly was.

'Well,' she braced herself as she began to speak, 'these results are very disappointing . . .'

'But not unexpected.' Peter, adopting an aggressive tone, shifted uncomfortably in his chair.

'No.' Jessie bowed her head in agreement. 'We *did* rather expect them. Nevertheless I'm still sorry they're *so* disappointing because Fiona did no work. Never once handed in written homework on time, if at all.'

'For years she didn't have any,' Peter interposed. 'I really blame the system, Mrs Clark.'

'Too late for that now.' Anna's quiet voice betrayed her unease. 'We didn't know at the time the children wouldn't have homework . . .'

'Well, they do in the fourth form . . .'

'But it was too *late,* Mrs Clark.' Peter struck the edge of the Head's desk with the palm of his hand. 'They should have been trained in the way of home study from the beginning and they were not. You don't just pick up these things. You have to learn them, be disciplined into them, get used to them. This sloppy attitude towards homework and the general uncompetitive nature of the school has worked to the detriment of Fiona and, if you ask me, most of the others like her. I take it the results as a whole weren't good?'

'Well, they *were* disappointing.' A flush stole up Jessie's cheeks.

'Then what are you going to do about it in

future?' Peter's tone was growing more aggressive, and Anna slipped him an anxious sideways glance. 'Are you going to change anything, Mrs Clark? Are you going, for instance, *now* to introduce hard work and the competitive spirit? We have a son here too, you know. This year he begins to work for GCSE and the following year, if you ask me, we shall be sitting here having the very same discussion and hearing the same sorry tale about *him*.'

'I hope not.' Jessie knew she was projecting an air of defeat.

'You know it's very likely.' Peter leaned forward, aware of having gained the upper hand. 'Because Guy too has done *no* homework up to now, has had *no* annual exams as well, and he is to enter the fourth form with a lack of knowledge almost as complete — or should I say as incomplete — as Fiona's.'

Jessie by now was reduced to silence. Guy certainly was not a promising pupil. He seemed destined to follow the path set by his sister.

'There is absolutely *no* point,' Anna said, putting a restraining hand on Peter's arm, 'no point at all in getting overwrought about something that's in the past.'

'We're talking about the *future*,' Peter said.

'I know, I know,' Anna soothingly stroked his arm, 'and, yes, we should start thinking about the future and what to do about Guy. But for the moment we're here to discuss Fiona.'

'That is the question.' Jessie nodded thoughtfully, looking up. 'Fiona I understand doesn't want to stay on at school?'

Jessie and Anna had spoken on the telephone that morning to try and prepare the ground before the meeting.

Both parents nodded.

'We would like her to go to a crammer,' Anna swallowed, 'and retake her GCSEs.'

'And what does Fiona say to that?'

'She doesn't want to. Consequently, we would like her to stay on here and resit.'

Jessie neatly joined her hands in front of her, her expression grave. 'I really think, Anna, she would be wasting her time, and I think you and your husband agree in your heart of hearts, don't you?'

'But what are we to *do?*' Peter burst out as if prompted by some inner agony. 'She has no ambition, no motivation, nothing.'

'She expects us to keep her,' Anna went on in a level tone, trying hard to calm the proceedings. 'She knows we have the means. Peter and I have talked it over, and we really think, Jessie, that if she came back to the school that *would* be the best, if not the only thing to do.'

Slowly, regretfully, Jessie shook her head from side to side.

'I'm terribly sorry to say this, Anna,' she included Peter in her remarks with an inclination of her head, 'but I think it would be completely futile to send Fiona back here. In fact I would not *want* her.

'Furthermore, as she is already sixteen, I have no statutory duty to educate her.'

'What do you mean you have no statutory duty?' Peter spluttered, almost out of control.

'What I say. There is no obligation to educate anyone beyond the age of sixteen, especially if, as is clearly the case here, the person in question does not wish to be educated. Fiona obviously doesn't. I can't force her. What is more, with her attitude she is extremely disruptive and a bad influence in class. She unsettles people and makes them discontented, rebellious like herself.' Jessie reached out for a sheet of paper that lay beside the school report and exam results. 'I have here an account of Fiona's visit to France with the school. I'm afraid that her behaviour *there* was anything but satisfactory. She never came in at night when she was expected, and was considered a very bad influence on others who slavishly followed her. Moreover, I am sorry to report that there was a suspicion of drugs. Some substance, possibly Ecstasy I believe it is called, being ingested in the company of some others, including a crowd of local French boys and girls in the town where they were staying. They were all considerably the worse for wear and lacking coherence . . .'

'And *where* was the teacher in charge at this time?' Peter demanded, standing up and leaning threateningly over Jessie's desk. 'Tell me that!'

'Mr Livingstone,' Jessie leaned back in her chair folding her hands in her lap with an air of one whose patience is extremely tried, 'these were mostly boys and girls fifteen or sixteen years of age, some older. I am not saying that Fiona was a ringleader or even procured the drugs; but she did seem to play a very prominent part and her particular cronies were concerned to protect her, cover up for her. After this episode a member of staff did insist on accompanying the children everywhere, but of course it was extremely difficult. They enjoyed giving the poor harassed teachers the slip. The members of staff have returned completely exhausted, one close to a nervous breakdown, and a similar visit will not be repeated next year . . .'

'You mean *my* daughter has been taking a number of drugs?' Peter's voice could surely by now be heard on the other side of the door.

'It seems like it, Mr Livingstone.' Jessie's clasped hands pressed closer together. 'Believe me, I am very sorry to say it, but the staff are convinced she was no novice to the drug scene either, was, indeed, an instigator. Frankly I would not have Fiona back in the school even if requested to by the Education Authority. Were she here, I should probably expel her. I consider her a totally bad, pernicious influence and, sad though I am to say it, because I know you both to be devoted parents, I shall be very glad to be rid of her.

'As for Guy,' she reached wearily for another document and held it up, 'his report was terrible too. He did not do well in his end of term assessment, as you know. I believe him to be of a higher intellectual calibre than Fiona, and he has more discipline because of his devotion to sport, but if you would like to try and place Guy elsewhere, since you have the means and can afford it, I should strongly be inclined to do so.' She rose to her feet.

'I feel we at the school have failed you and I am humiliated; but I have nearly eleven hundred other children to think about and the more disruptive and unruly elements I can weed out the better.' She nervously straightened her skirt, and pulled her jacket closely around her hips. 'Believe me, I'm terribly sorry. But we at this school have done all we can. I consider myself to be an enlightened, caring educationalist. I have been in my profession for nearly thirty years and the principles we have in this school are ones I strongly believe in and adhere to. I think Anna does too. But they don't work with everyone, and they haven't worked either for Fiona or Guy. But then many parents consider themselves let down by the private sector too.' With evident pride she pointed to her desk. 'I have an application here from the parents of a boy at one of the very top public schools.'

'God help them,' Peter murmured as Jessie held out her hand, but he turned away. 'I shall be making a report to the Education Authority,' he said stiffly. '*And* about the destructive and malicious influence this school, and its barmy ideas, has had on my son and daughter.' He stood by the door, his hand on the handle, and looked back. 'Don't think for a moment you've heard the last of this matter, Mrs Clark.'

Sal, happening to be passing, saw a light on in the cottage owned by the Livingstones and hesitated by the garden gate.

Then, as if suddenly making up her mind, she opened it and walked up the path and knocked on the door.

As Anna answered, Sal noticed she was still in her dressing gown.

'Oh, I'm terribly sorry,' she said. 'I hope you're not ill?'

'No, not at all.'

'I'm Sal, you know, from down the road.'

'Yes, of course,' Anna said frostily. The memory of the last time she'd seen her was not easily forgotten. They hadn't met since, and she really didn't much want to ask her in. But Sal was not easily put off.

'Are the family with you?' she enquired chattily.

'No, I'm here by myself.'

'Everything alright?'

'Fine. I had a minor operation and just came for a few days' break before starting work.'

'Oh!' Sal nodded understandingly. 'Everything alright?' she asked again, clearly wishing that Anna would spill out the gory details.

'Fine. Look,' Anna found it very difficult to bear a grudge, to be rude. The woman was obviously trying to make up for that evening. 'Why don't you come in for a few moments? It's cold outside. You must think me terribly rude.'

'Oh, no,' Sal waved a hand in the air, 'I wouldn't dream of intruding. I just wanted to be sure that everything was alright. Not often you're down this time of the year.' She shivered. 'Do you have enough logs?'

'Plenty, thanks.' Anna flung the door wide open. 'Do *please* come in. I'm just about to have a coffee.'

'Oh, well, if you're sure.'

'I'm quite sure.'

Sal entered rubbing her hands, then held them out towards the fire.

'Oh, it's so lovely and *warm* in here.' She looked round. 'You've central heating too, I see.'

'Yes. My husband's first wife had it put in. She lived down here for quite a long time. Nancy. I don't know if you knew her.'

Sal shook her head. 'I've only been here a couple of years.'

'And your daughter,' Anna paused, recalling that night in the summer, 'Honey, is it?'

'Yes, Honey.' Sal nodded and moved nearer the fire as if mesmerised by the flames.

'How is she?'

'Oh, she's *fine*. Left school now. Works in a shop in Blandford, for how long I don't know. Fingers crossed.' Sal held up crossed fingers and smiled cheerfully.

'She must be the same age as Fiona.'

'Sixteen, going on seventeen. How are your children, Mrs Livingstone?'

'Do call me Anna. And please sit down.' Anna pointed to the chair next to the fire.

Sal settled into the chair and crossed one leg over the other. She wore leggings and a long warm cardigan that looked as though she might possibly have knitted it herself. She had on a rather cheap pair of boots, and it could have been quite a while since her hair had had the attention of a comb.

She was not an unattractive woman, nor quite as unprepossessing as Anna had thought her the night of the pot smoking episode. She had a fresh, open face, devoid of make-up. Yet her skin was incredibly good and she looked in her early thirties, though it was reasonable to expect she was older if she had a daughter of nearly seventeen.

Anna went into the kitchen to make the coffee, and emerged after a few moments with two cups on a tray and a plate of biscuits. Sal seemed hungry and Anna wondered if she had enough to eat. She suddenly became curious about this odd woman whom she had reluctantly allowed into her life.

'I was *ever* so sorry about that night.' Sal bit eagerly into her second biscuit before she had swallowed the first. 'I haven't had the chance to explain since. I know how upset you were; but you know you shouldn't be.'

'Oh?' Anna, her hands clasped around her coffee cup, eyed her companion. 'You approve of drugs? I gather you take them yourself?'

Sal bristled immediately. 'How do you "gather" that? Did Fiona say anything?'

'Fiona said nothing about that evening, but from what little I saw of you I felt you were smoking in the company of the young people.'

'And you think that's bad?'

'To be honest, I think I do.'

'Well, I don't agree with you, Mrs Livingstone. Pot isn't a *drug,* you know. It's a harmless substance, much better for you than alcohol or cigarettes.'

'Possibly.' Anna nodded. 'Expert opinions seem to differ.'

'Oh, you *do* think that then?' Sal looked interested.

'No, I do not think it necessarily; but I accept that there is an argument. The argument against is that marijuana and allied substances might lead to harder drugs, and in Fiona's case that seems to have happened.'

'Oh, dear.' Sal looked crestfallen.

'She certainly had taken Ecstasy and probably hard drugs on a trip abroad in the summer.'

'Oh, *dear.*' Sal reached for a fourth biscuit. 'She's not at school then now?'

'No.'

'Working is she?'

'No.'

'Oh!'

'She's at home, probably in bed, where she spends most of the day. Then she gets up, and after an elaborate, almost ritualistic washing and dressing ceremony, goes out at night. We hardly ever see her. Even her father isn't as worried about her as he used to be.'

'And you don't worry?' Sal looked at her keenly. 'I thought you were ever so worried that night.'

'Yes, I do worry, but in a different kind of way. I don't know if you know this, but Guy and Fiona are my husband's children by his first wife.'

'Oh!' Sal looked thoughtful. 'No, I didn't know.'

'I wonder Fiona didn't mention it to Honey.'

'Well, she might have. But Hun would keep it to herself. They do, don't they, at that age? Very secretive.'

'Oh, yours is secretive too?'

'Very.'

'Is she living at home now?'

'Oh, yes. She has a friend who collects her every morning to take her to Blandford and brings her home again. Of course she's bored to death here. There are so few things for young people to do. She would like to get a room in Blandford and I have said that when she is seventeen she can.'

'Aren't you worried about what she'll get up to?'

'Look, Mrs Livingstone,' Sal reached in her pocket and drew out a packet of cigarettes and a lighter. After asking Anna if she minded and

104

being told that she didn't, she lit a cigarette and blew a long stream of smoke towards the fire. 'Look, Mrs Livingstone, I mean, Anna, what I say is this: kids are not like they were in our day, are they? I mean I don't know how old you are, but I guess about my age. We were bad enough, but not as bad as they are today. Don't ask me the reason: affluence, too much welfare, a lapse of moral standards. Don't ask me because I don't know. I reckon young people have got to sort their lives out as we had to.'

'But the drugs scene *is* very worrying.'

'Oh, very worrying. And so is Aids, and of course the two are related if they inject. Dirty needles, I don't need to tell you. But what I say is that it is up to Honey to make what she can of her life. She didn't like school. She didn't *pass* any exams. A lot of them don't. Tough. Let them find out for themselves that it's a hard world. It's their responsibility.'

'Don't you think that at sixteen a young person still needs guidance?' Anna asked, thinking it rather ironical that she should be valuing the opinion of this odd young woman.

'No, I don't frankly.' Sal finished her cigarette and threw the stub in the fire. 'When Honey leaves home she can lead her life and I'll lead mine.'

'And what do you do?' Anna asked tentatively. 'Do you do anything?'

'No. Just please myself. I'm on benefit, single parent. I like to read and watch the soaps on TV.

Frankly I don't really like it here, Mrs Living-stone — too quiet — but I didn't have much choice. It was either this or a council flat in Gillingham which frankly did not please me. You work, don't you?'

'I'm a solicitor.'

'Oh, I see.' Enlightenment appeared to dawn on Sal's face. '*That's* why you were so worried about the children smoking pot.'

'I'd worry anyway.'

'But why if they're not yours?'

Anna flushed.

'They *are* mine. I've had them since they were very small. I do worry about them.'

'But still it's not the same, is it?'

'Yes,' Anna stared at her boldly, 'it is.'

'Sorry.' Sal lowered her eyes. 'Didn't mean to offend.'

'I'm not offended, but it's an assumption people make and it's not true.'

Sal was anxious to change the subject. 'Ever think of having any of your own?'

'I did.' Anna paused. 'But I decided not to.'

'Very wise.' Sal got up and stretched her arms. 'Given my time again I would never have kids.'

'Oh, you've got more than one?'

'Yes. I've got a boy of nearly twenty.'

'And what's he doing?'

'He's at Bristol University learning to be a vet. Loves the country which is really how we came to be here. His father, my husband, was a farmer who got mangled in a tractor accident and was killed, silly bugger.' Sal's voice sounded gruff.

'Oh, I am sorry!' Anna put her hands to her face. 'How terrible.'

Sal looked solemn.

'It *was* terrible at the time; but it happened a long time ago. I've been a widow ten years, Anna. Ten very *lonely* years, really. I can't think I've made as much of a success of my life as I suppose you have of yours.'

Anna ran her hands through her hair. 'Not really.'

'Oh, I'm sure being a solicitor in London must be terribly important. Fiona did say you were clever. She spoke of you quite admiringly. I would never have thought she wasn't your real daughter.'

'Really?' Anna felt gratified, surprised.

'I think she's *really* fond of you.'

'You could have kidded me.'

'Seriously, I do. Why don't you ask her down? A spot of country air would do her good.'

'As a matter of fact, I think they're all coming down here for the weekend to take me back to London. Why don't you come over and have dinner with us on Saturday night? You and Honey.'

'That would be lovely.' Sal looked at the clock on the mantelpiece. She didn't wear a watch and gave the impression that time would not really be of much concern to her. She seemed such an urban creature that it was difficult to imagine her as a farmer's wife. 'I bet you want to get on with what it is you're doing, or maybe go back to bed.' She looked at her with concern. 'Feeling alright now are you?' Once again the hint that she'd like to know more.

'Oh, yes. It was just one of those things.'

Sal nodded understandingly as if to say: women's problems. Weren't they all the same?

Anna saw her to the door and stood on the threshold watching her as she walked back down the road to her cottage. Sal stopped at the gate of her own home and waved, and Anna waved back. Then she shut the door and went back to her chair by the fire, sat down feeling suddenly weary.

It was very funny how one had one's preconceptions shattered, one's prejudices excised. She knew that *she* had assumed that Sal was an unmarried mother with a difficult teenage daughter. That she would milk the system for all she was worth and get all the benefits to which she was entitled. She, Anna, would never have guessed that she was a widow whose husband had been a farmer and whose life had been blighted by tragedy. She would have assumed that Sal was comparatively uneducated, and perhaps she was, but not that she had a son clever enough to read veterinary science at a university.

In a way she herself was a woman of prejudices and presumptions, the traits she tended to condemn in other people.

Anna decided then that she rather liked Sal; that she was open, plain speaking and honest.

She was pragmatic, a realist for whom life would hold few surprises. An engaging sort of woman.

In a way, Anna felt she had shown herself to be a middle-class moralist of the type she professed to despise; a champagne socialist who buried herself in her work because she could not really face up to the reality of an unsatisfactory home life, two appalling step-children and a husband whom she loved but who was becoming increasingly unreasonable and remote.

She climbed slowly upstairs to her room and lay on her unmade bed.

She had in fact felt dreadfully tired since the simple operation of sterilisation. She had spent two days in a private clinic. The operation was carried out by Katie and pronounced one hundred per cent satisfactory. She could now never have children. She could have sex without worry.

At first Anna felt elated, free from a great burden, a solution to a dilemma. She expected to feel totally free and happy, but to her surprise she didn't. She felt tired and rather depressed.

Katie said she thought this was a natural reaction, one many women had after a similar operation, or an abortion. Only there was no need for Anna to suffer from any kind of guilt. She had not killed anything. She was now free to enjoy her sex life unfettered by fear, either of ill-health, brought on by the Pill, or of an unwanted pregnancy.

But Anna felt neither of these things. She just wanted to be alone, and so she took a week off from work and had come down to the country in order to try and work things out.

But all she felt instead was muddled, depressed, angry. She didn't even look forward to the new job starting in January. The family were planning to spend Christmas and New Year skiing in Switzerland. Oh, and she was going to allow her name to go forward for election to the Council.

So why didn't she feel great? On top of the world?

She put her head on the pillow and wept.

CHAPTER 5

Peter thought Anna looked surprisingly well, a little pale but cheerful as she greeted them on the doorstep the following Friday.

Peter had taken the day off and they arrived in time for lunch, earlier than Anna had expected.

'I haven't got anything to eat,' she said, flinging her arms round his neck.

'Never mind, we brought plenty of stuff with us.' Peter encircled her waist with his free arm and kissed her, murmuring, 'How are you?'

'I'm fine,' she whispered back.

'Really?'

'Yuk.' Guy screwed up his face.

'What's the matter now, Guy?' Peter disentangled his arms from Anna's waist and turned to his son.

'All this lovey dovey. Yuk.'

'Sorry if it displeases you,' Peter said. 'I'm just glad to see Anna.'

'Oh don't let's *start* a row, for God's sake.' Anna bent swiftly to kiss Guy on the forehead, taking him by surprise, but she wouldn't have dared attempt any such gesture, not at the moment, with Fiona. Instead, noticing her usual sulky expression, she squeezed her arm.

'Hi! OK?'

Fiona grunted again and Anna's heart plummeted a little more. If only Peter had been able to come alone. The children had been told the reason for Anna's visit to hospital and why. They'd received the news without any comment, although their faces spoke volumes. Sex between old people was disgusting. The thought of babies . . . 'Yuk' as Guy would have said.

'Let's go to the pub for a sandwich,' Anna suggested, 'then you and I, Peter, can run into Blandford for some provisions for the weekend.'

'I tell you we've brought everything. Everything you can think of.'

'But we're having guests for dinner tomorrow.'

'Oh?' Peter looked surprised. 'Who?'

'Sal and her daughter Honey.' Anna glanced at Fiona. 'I thought you'd like that, Fiona.'

Fiona grunted and reached into the car, evidently searching for her Walkman.

'Is Honey home?' she asked, emerging from the car.

'I don't think so. She's working during the day. Martin will be home from school later,' she added, addressing Guy. 'You'll be able to walk up to the farm and wait for him after we've been to the pub.'

'There's really no need to go to the pub.' Peter began unpacking the stuff from the car. 'We've brought enough for an army.'

It was true, there was more than enough food for the weekend. Peter seemed relaxed, glad to be at the cottage, and Fiona appeared to have decided to make an effort to be civilised, going so far over lunch as to ask after Anna's health.

'Did it hurt?' she enquired.

'What, the op? I had an anaesthetic. It didn't hurt at all. It hurt a bit after, a vague pain.' She gently massaged her lower abdomen.

'What do they *do* exactly?'

'They tie the Fallopian tubes, so that the egg can't get to the womb to be fertilised.'

'What happens to the egg?' Guy wanted to know.

Anna looked at Peter, hunched her shoulders and burst out laughing.

'I don't know, what *does* happen to the egg?'

'Or all the eggs,' Fiona said loftily. 'There are millions of them.'

'They're so tiny.' Anna squinted up at a small aperture made by her two fingers. 'I guess they shrivel up and die. I'll have to ask Katie next time I see her.'

'And you don't have any regrets?' Fiona looked searchingly at her.

'Why should I? Why should I want children when I've got you?'

There was a rather embarrassed silence as if they didn't know whether she was being sarcastic or not. Finally Guy spoke: 'Why didn't you do it before? Weren't you sure that you didn't want a baby?'

'No, I was sure.' Anna put down her knife and fork, tucked her hands under her chin. 'It just seems rather a final step to take when you're in your thirties. But I do feel committed to you, to your father, my work and,' she took a deep breath, 'I *have* decided after all to stand for the Council.'

'My God, now you'll *never* be at home.' Peter stared at her in dismay. 'I'll see even less of you than I do now.'

'Why don't *you* do something, Dad?' Guy looked questioningly at his father.

'Like what? Don't you think I have enough to do?'

'You don't have any hobbies,' Fiona said slyly. 'You don't collect stamps or garden. You're not very keen on sport. You don't ever watch TV, except the news, you don't read except the papers. If you had an interest you wouldn't be so jealous of Anna.'

'I am *not* jealous of Anna.' Peter's expression was indignant.

'I never thought your father was jealous of me,' Anna concurred, trying to conceal the awful feeling she had that Fiona was up to something again. Always stirring things up, always making trouble, never a moment's peace. 'Your father is absorbed in his work. He brings a lot home. Always writing reports . . .'

'I garden when I'm here,' Peter protested. 'I like it very much. In London I don't have the time.'

'Yet you're always sitting around moaning about when will Anna be home. You ought to get yourself sorted out, Daddy,' and without asking permission Fiona jumped up and left the table.

' 'Scuse me,' Guy said and, wriggling off his seat, followed her. The door slammed behind them as they both went into the garden.

'Well I'll be . . . jiggered.' Peter, hardly concealing his irritation, also rose from the table and stood in front of the kitchen range. Peter was a tall well-built man, with a rather craggy, bluff featured sort of face and a receding hairline. He had a long nose and rather thick tufted eyebrows and looked as though he might have been a sailor rather than a lawyer. Anna gazed at him with love.

'I wish you could have come alone,' she said getting up and laying her head on his shoulder. 'I know I'm not supposed to say this, but I do. I can't help myself.'

'Why aren't you supposed to say it?' Peter said tenderly, beginning to stroke her hair.

'I'm always supposed to be so *nice* and *understanding* but I find it terribly difficult.'

'Darling,' he nuzzled her hair with his chin, 'they are very difficult children. I always try, you know, Anna, to concentrate on having a happy home. I *long* for it; but just recently it's been so difficult. And who is Fiona, I ask you, to talk about having nothing to do! She never gets up until three in the afternoon! What does *she* know about what I do with my life? Sometimes,' Peter tightly clenched his fist and punched the air, 'sometimes I feel like throwing her out. I really do.'

'You *don't*. You'd go mad if you didn't know where she was. I'm afraid, Peter, that for the next few years, or for as long as it takes, we'll have to accept Fiona as she is; helping her, tolerating her but, basically, putting up with her rudeness, her selfishness and her spite. It will take its toll but we'll win in the end. I'm sure we will, darling.'

'It makes *me* so hateful,' he said. 'The horrible things I've said to you.'

'I understand,' she murmured. 'I say horrible things back. Neither of us means them.'

'Does it hurt?' Peter tilted her chin to look at her.

'Does what hurt?'

'The tummy?'

'Why?' Her hand gingerly pressed the place where there was a little scar.

'I thought we might take a little nap.'

'With the children here running about?'

'They'll have gone off. They won't be back.'

'Oh!' Doubtfully Anna looked at the table. 'Shouldn't we do the dishes?'

'We can do them after,' Peter said and, with his hand tight round her waist, he pushed her gently towards the stairs that led to the bedroom.

It was late afternoon when Anna woke, and she lay for a moment trying to orientate herself. She had fallen into a very deep, relaxed sleep after the gentle caressing, the mutual stimulation, that hardly amounted to lovemaking but was pleasing in itself. Besides, it did hurt, and the

116

last thing she wanted was to have to explain to Katie that the scar had burst open because she had behaved like an impetuous teenager.

Peter looked so peaceful asleep, the tired lines round his mouth and eyes had vanished, and for some time she lay contemplating him, the face that she loved, thinking what a perfect partnership they had, or would have, were it not for the children. How easily they forgave each other and overcame their misunderstandings.

Yet it was true that Peter had no hobbies, but neither had she. They were both workaholics and, apart from that, they enjoyed dinner parties with friends, occasional trips to the theatre or opera, and holidays abroad.

As for Anna, politics was work rather than a hobby because it involved ensuring, or trying to ensure, that people had a better life.

Peter didn't have her belief in or commitment to politics. He was an analyst rather than a believer. He voted Labour because she did, but she suspected that, at heart, he was probably an enlightened Tory. He believed in competition and the operation of a market economy.

Peter opened his eyes and stared straight into hers.

'Penny for them,' he said.

She reached out and touched him.

'Just thinking.'

Peter turned and looked at the clock by the bed. 'It's nearly four o'clock,' he exclaimed, sitting up. 'No sign of the kids?'

'No sight or sound. They'll be OK.'

'Remember last time you said that you found them smoking pot.'

Anna wriggled herself into a comfortable position, propped up against the pillows, her body touching his.

'Peter, we can't keep track of them all the time. You know that and I know it. Fiona, particularly, is independent, her own person.'

'She's still a child.'

'In your eyes, yes. In hers, no. I'm quite amazed, actually, that she came down with you.'

'She wants to look at her mother's things.'

'What things?' Anna turned to him sharply.

'Her paintings. She says that she wants to paint.'

Anna tried to conceal her astonishment.

'But she's never shown any interest before in painting or drawing, has she? Or any talent for them, as far as I know.'

'Well, I think drawing was her best subject.'

'No, that was English. If she had a "best" subject it was English. At least she passed in that. History too.'

'Well maybe it's been dormant. Maybe she has some of her mother's talent, who knows? Personally I'd be delighted if she got any inspiration from Nancy's work. If she wanted to train. It would be ideal, don't you think?'

'Ideal.' Anna snuggled down in the bed beside Peter. 'If we could get her focused on something it might be a whole new ball game.'

'If we could get Fiona interested in something and Guy concentrating on his work,' Peter slid an arm round her bare waist, 'it would be a whole new ball game for *us*.'

'How do you mean?' Anna felt a flicker of apprehension.

'We could have more time to ourselves.' He planted a kiss on the top of her head. 'We could really begin to enjoy life which, let's face it, we haven't for some time while concentrating on the kids. There'd be no need for you to stand for the Council.'

Anna didn't attempt to hide her concern.

'How do you mean, no need? I don't "need" to. I want to.'

'But, darling, *I* don't want you to.'

'You never said as much before.'

'But you must have realised it. Well I'm saying it now. I haven't been keen ever since you first brought it up.'

That was true. All the time she could detect a strong undercurrent of disapproval from Peter, a disapproval she hadn't wanted, perhaps because she lacked the courage, to challenge him on.

'We always agreed we wouldn't dictate to each other about our lives, Peter,' she said quietly.

'I never realised you'd grow so far away from me.'

'But I *haven't* grown away. Any division,' she paused to try and get her words just right, 'any split, if there has been a split, is because for some time you and Fiona, and others, keep on empha-

119

sising the fact I'm not her real mother. That is quite new, and frankly, I don't like it. It's hurtful.'

'I never . . .'

'You never *meant* to but you did,' Anna said firmly. 'Remember, I remarked on it? It made me feel that I was not part of the family. That somehow I was on my own.'

Peter shifted so that he lay on his back, hands on his stomach, and stared pointedly at the ceiling. 'I'm beginning to believe, Anna, that your work *has* superseded the family in your affections. It is of overriding importance to you, and standing for the Council is just part of it. Maybe that's really why you wanted to be sterilised.'

'That's ridiculous! And very unfair.'

'But,' he went on relentlessly, 'now that you can spend more time with me you want to spend less. I shouldn't think you'd ever have a night in if you're on the Council.'

'I think if *you* had any interests of your own you'd understand.' Anna thrust back the duvet and began to get out of bed. 'If the boot was on the other foot and you were the one thinking of standing for the Council, I'd be expected to support you.'

'No, you wouldn't.'

'Yes, I would. Look at all these MPs whose wives, though victims, are willing supporters of their husbands' ambitions. And usually men *are* more ambitious because they want power. I'm ambitious because I want to help people and now, as I have no children of my own and none are now possible, I feel free to do just that.' She got out of bed and put on her robe. '*And,* Peter Livingstone, I would be very glad if you would support me as you can be certain I should have supported you.'

And with that she went into the bathroom, seething with a rage, a sense of indignation, a ferocity she hadn't experienced for years.

The next morning after breakfast, which to Anna's surprise she had eaten with them, though Guy remained in bed, Fiona said: 'Has anyone seen the key to Mum's studio?'

'It's behind the door I think.' Anna looked up from the washing up, Peter drying and carefully putting everything neatly away. On his best be-haviour. He was taking a lot of trouble to be nice to Anna and she was taking care to reciprocate. The place was too small for tension, and it would never do to let the children sense this new feeling of unease between their parents. Peter didn't usually help in the house, regarding the garden, his province, as a more manly diversion. He found messing about in mud with thick wellies and producing a lot of sweat a gratifying occu-pation, especially if it was followed by a couple of pints in the pub.

'Not here,' Fiona said, after inspecting several keys on the back of the door.

'Maybe in the dresser.' Anna, with soapsuds up to her elbows, jerked her head in the direction of the large pine dresser that occupied a whole wall at the back of the kitchen.

Fiona went over to rummage in the drawer and, after letting out the plug and drying her hands, Anna joined her.

'We can't have lost it.'

'It's ages since anyone went in there,' Peter said. 'Maybe we have.'

'Is there anything in particular you want?' Anna kept her tone casual, offhand.

'I want to look at Mum's paintings. That's really why I came down here.'

'Fiona thinks she might like to paint.' Peter gave Anna a warning glance.

'What made you feel that?' Anna asked politely.

'Well, I was drawing something one day at a friend's and he said he thought I had some talent.' Anna noticed the 'he'. Who Fiona's friends were or where they lived was a complete mystery.

'Did you ever feel that way before?'

'No.' Fiona was immediately on the defensive. 'But it's never too late, is it?'

'I think it's a splendid idea if you have talent and it's what you want to do. Maybe we could break open the lock, Peter?'

'Oh there's a key,' Peter said. 'I know,' and he disappeared into the larder and emerged with a handful of keys tied to various pieces of string. 'It's one of these. Let's go to the shed to see, Fiona.'

Fiona looked excited, happy, even relaxed, for a change. She wore her pretty fair hair plastered in fashionable spikes and the inevitable leggings and Doc Martens boots. At home she wore no make-up but when she went out she did herself up to the nines, purple lipstick, purple eye shadow and eyes deeply ringed with kohl. She'd had her ears pierced and talked about having a ring through her nose as well.

Anna was by now accustomed to the sight Fiona presented when she left the house to go wherever it was.

She saw it not as an expression of individuality, but as a uniform too often presented by those clients she saw either at the Law Centre or in Court.

The hair spikes had taken some getting used to because Fiona had soft, pretty hair with a deep wave. She must have gone to endless trouble to sleek her hair back with the thick gel and train it into sharp points like the caps of Swiss mountains.

Anna remained by the kitchen window looking out as Fiona crossed the garden with her father, who began to try the assorted keys he had in his hand, one after the other. They appeared to be almost on the verge of giving up when one Peter had inserted turned and, with a cry of exultation, Peter pushed the door open and entered.

Anna went over to the vegetable stand and began to do the vegetables for dinner, plenty of potatoes to peel, cabbage to cut up. They were having beef that Peter had brought down, with smoked salmon to start, red and white wine. Anna filled the sink with fresh water and soaked the muddy potatoes in it, her eyes going from time to time to the shed at the other side of the garden. She could never recall Fiona ever expressing the slightest desire to visit it in all the years she had known her.

Fiona with a talent for art? Anna frowned in an effort at recollection as she began to peel the potatoes. If so, it was a light she'd kept hidden under a bushel, but if it was there by all means let her develop it.

After a while Peter came out, recrossed the garden and came back into the kitchen.

'I thought I'd leave her alone.'

'Good idea.' Anna nodded, but went on with her work.

'She seems happy.'

'I thought she looked happy when she came down to breakfast.'

'Shall I call Guy?'

'Let him sleep if he wants to. Doubtless when Martin appears he'll get up.'

She felt Peter's hand on her shoulder and involuntarily she stiffened. His lips brushed the nape of her neck.

'I do love you,' he said. 'Sorry about last night.'

Anna turned, potato and potato peeler still in her hands, and leaned against his chest.

'I won't stand for the Council if you don't want me to.'

He looked into her eyes, touched her nose gently with his finger.

'Let's wait and see, shall we?'

'Wait and see what?'

'What happens. You never know. Right now I'm going to go on with my digging and then a pint, or a couple of pints and a pub lunch.'

'Good idea.'

'I think I should be putting potatoes in for the spring.' Peter, a gardening amateur, looked unsure. 'Do we have a book?'

'Not here, but you can ask Fred at the pub at lunchtime if we see him.'

Fred was the local horticultural expert.

'Good idea.' Peter reached out and ruffled her hair. 'I love you.'

'And I love you too.'

Anna enjoyed the trivia of life in the cottage, so different from her usual daily routine. At home she had her daily, Paula, and was not much into cooking, but in the country she and Peter reversed their normal roles. He became transformed into a gardener and walker, a swiller of pints of Badger Beer, whereas in London he always drank wine, gin or whisky. Anna became the domestic animal she had never been, planning and cooking large meals in between washing up, making beds and keeping the cottage tidy.

It was a bit like Marie Antoinette and her court playing at being milkmaids in the opulent surroundings of Versailles because they had little else to do.

No, that was a bit far-fetched, Anna thought to herself with amusement as she straightened the duvet on her and Peter's bed, fluffed up the pillows and then turned her attention to tidying out one of the wardrobes, half of whose contents could go to Oxfam.

She wore a jersey and blue jeans, a smear of lipstick, no other make-up except foundation cream. For a moment she carefully studied her face in the wardrobe mirror and then, putting her fingers up to her eyes, smoothed out the creases underneath. She had good skin, she knew that, and a good figure. Her thick hair was in tip-top condition, well cut, and sprang back from her head, falling into a thick, neat bob halfway to her shoulders. Her clear blue eyes looked back at her appraisingly in a rather detached manner, as though she were measuring up a stranger, comparing herself to someone she didn't know.

Anna had always been at ease with herself. She supposed it would not be egotistical to say that she liked herself, and that this self-approval was not vanity or self-aggrandisement, but a genuine feeling of being at home in her body. Thus when people disliked her it worried her, and the gradual alienation of her two stepchildren had disturbed her profoundly and she sought for a cause, even though she knew that the experience of most people of the troublesome teenage years was similar to her own.

Her early years with the children had, she supposed, fulfilled her needs as a mother, stifled any natural biological urge she might have had to have children of her own. She used to do the school rounds, walks in the park, children's tea parties, outings to the zoo. They had been well behaved, good looking children, polite and well mannered, and in no time at all she came to see them, feel them as her own.

Peter was away a lot and she and the children were thrown together. She had to entertain them and care for them, supervise their activities and devise games for them, and when Peter came home it was like an endless celebration. There were special treats all round, holidays abroad or in the country. Very seldom, in those days, at the Dorset cottage because it still reminded him of the wife he had lost. It had been too sad a place to be too close to, the scene of Nancy's death.

When both the children went to junior school Anna resumed work part-time. An au pair was engaged to help in the house but Anna always made sure she was home on time to be with them while they had tea, bath them, put them to bed and read them a story.

Very slowly, only gradually, did it all change. Peter stopped travelling abroad so much, as he was given a senior position in the legal department at home, and Anna felt free to work longer hours and take on all the voluntary work she believed in.

She threw all the clothes on the bed and began briskly sorting through them. Jackets, old anoraks, jeans, tweed skirts which nowadays she never wore in the country — heaps of these.

She put the ones she knew they would never wear again into black plastic sacks. When it was all done she looked at her watch and was amazed to see that it was nearly twelve. She tied the tops of the bags, rearranged what was left in the wardrobe and shut the door. One day she would start on the spare room, but not now.

She looked in the mirror, ran a comb through her hair and glanced out of the window. The spade was stuck upright in the middle of the vegetable bed, but there was no sign of Peter. He'd already gone to the pub to slake his thirst or seek the advice of Fred, or maybe the two were not incompatible.

Anna smiled to herself. How Peter loved playing the role of the country gent, far from the tortuous and complex legal negotiations of his demanding job in the City.

Then her eyes travelled across to the shed and there was no sign of life there either. The door was shut. Probably Fiona had abandoned her examination of her mother's work and gone with her father. Well, in that case she'd join them.

Anna went down to the kitchen and into the pantry to check again that they had everything for the dinner with Sal and Honey that night. She slipped on her anorak, wound her scarf round her neck and put a woolly hat on her head. Gathering up her gloves she went to the front door and then stopped. Just as well to make sure that Fiona had gone, otherwise she would feel neglected and make a big deal out of that.

She unlatched the back door, walked quickly across the garden and turned the handle of the door to the studio, which yielded immediately.

Anna paused. The shed held a strange dread for her. She had never been in it, never wanted to see the canvases that Nancy, her predecessor, had left behind. It was not that she tried to avoid mention of Nancy because she never had. In the early days she had encouraged the children to talk about their mother and her photographs were scattered round the house.

It was not that she felt jealous of Nancy or resented her, yet inevitably over the years her memory had receded.

Why now, then? Strange.

Finally she pushed open the door and found Fiona on her knees in a corner, crouched over one of her mother's paintings, whimpering softly like a kitten.

In a second Anna too was on her knees by Fiona's side, an arm round her shoulder.

'Pet,' she said using an endearment she hadn't used for years. 'Whatever is it?'

Fiona didn't reply but, her body shaken by sobs, she leaned against Anna who, gratified by this unaccustomed reaction, pulled the stricken girl close to her.

'Pet . . . Fiona. What has upset you so much?'

Fiona shook her head, buried her face in her hands.

'Mum-m-y's pictures,' she blubbered, 'they brought it all back.'

'Brought all *what* back?'

' 'Bout Mummy, 'bout missing her.' Fiona began to talk in a babyish voice.

'Oh, Fiona I'm so sorry.' Anna felt that unreasoning chill, rejection, like an abandoned child herself, pushed away to the corner, far from contact with the family.

'All Mummy's pictures *neglected*,' Fiona pointed towards them, 'lying here covered with dust as though we had forgotten all about her.'

'Well we haven't. We have her photos all over the house. You've talked about her quite a lot recently. Look,' Anna leaned forward and gently brushed the dust off one of the pictures, 'why don't we spend the afternoon dusting the pictures, going through them and then deciding which ones we'd like to frame? Would you like that?' She looked around. 'We could tidy the whole studio up and, look here, there is an easel, some unused canvases. Why don't you see if you really can follow in your mother's footsteps? Maybe you really do have a vocation to paint?'

If one had to be honest, the paintings done by Nancy so many years before really weren't up to much; blobs of paint on a canvas, a few wishy-washy country scenes, mostly in pastel colours. Swirls of mist merging with cloud, patches of sunlight streaming through branches. But then she had never pretended to be a professional artist, made no claims, and no one said she had.

130

But in Fiona's eyes they were perfection, and now the most attractive ones stood around the kitchen propped up against the dresser, the walls, the kitchen units, as the dinner party progressed.

Nancy was very much the main topic of conversation, and Anna bore it all with determined good humour, encouraging Fiona to talk about her mother and her feelings about her mother's art.

Sal and Honey had enthused over them too, Sal confessing that she didn't know much about art but she knew what she liked and she liked these very much, all of them, apparently.

Peter joined in the acclaim, saying the best ones would go to be framed and hung in the London house, and Sal wondered if a local art exhibition could be staged? Fiona assented to this with enthusiasm and said she would help Sal look into it. Anna was rather relieved to be able to say, truthfully, that she had absolutely no contacts in the art world and wouldn't know where or how to begin.

Sal and her daughter were an honest, engaging couple, and Anna felt her prejudices melting, until they dissolved altogether in a torrent of goodwill and bonhomie. The meal was plain but good, and so was the wine, of which a tolerable amount was drunk.

Fiona, all animation now that her tears were forgotten, said that she would spend all the next day doing out her mother's studio, tacking the canvases, and sweeping out the cobwebs so that she could start work on her own.

Peter, gratified at his daughter's show of interest in something positive at last, however, demurred.

'Darling, we're going back to London on Monday. Couldn't you wait until the next holiday?'

'Oh, Dad *do* I?' Fiona pleaded. 'Do I have to really?'

'But you can't stay down here, darling, on your own.' Peter looked at Anna for support. 'Can she, Anna?'

'Well,' Anna was again being cast in the role of villain, always having to sound negative, to dampen ideas, always the fly in the ointment. There was no earthly reason really why Fiona should be doing something, or at least attempting to do something, here as doing nothing in London. Yet Fiona was young and really too irresponsible to be left on her own. But how to put it without alienating her?

'Won't you be *lonely* on your own, Fiona?'

'Lonely is not the point,' Peter said heatedly. 'Heaven knows what Fiona will get up to . . .'

'You don't trust me,' Fiona burst out petulantly. 'You treat me as a baby . . .'

'Couldn't *we* help?' Sal said in a quiet, authoritative voice. 'After all, we're practically next door. Here to reassure you. To keep an eye on Fiona if that would help. We all *know* she's not a baby, wants to spread her wings. Perfectly natural. I'll certainly keep an eye on her if that will help. I mean, I know she can look after herself, but if she needs anything, you know what I mean? Then Honey will be here in the evenings and at weekends. Frankly, I'd like the company for Honey. She so misses people of her own age.

'Besides we can get to work on trying to arrange an exhibition for Fiona's mum.' She looked around expectantly, but there was only silence. Suspense seemed to hang in the air as Peter and Anna each searched silently within themselves for a reason to refuse, wishing that they'd been offered the question in advance, allowed time to think.

'Oh, Dad,' Fiona, face plaintive, infinitely appealing, leaned towards him and grasped his hand. 'Please, please say "yes".'

PART 2

Horizons New

CHAPTER 6

Anna stood looking at the gaunt warehouse building which had been part of the derelict site beside the railway bridge since the nineteenth century. It was in that run down part of north London which had escaped development for some reason or another: bureaucracy probably. Or maybe it was lack of interest on the part of developers looking for prime sites to which to attract the high flying yuppies of the eighties, who had begun to find parts of London north of Euston and King's Cross attractive.

Some of the windows of the building were without glass, like sightless eyes, and part of the top storey was missing. All around in the yard were pieces of broken machinery, upturned crates, empty boxes, rubber tyres and cases of empty bottles. A few dogs ran around relieving themselves when and where the fancy took them, a couple of wild-eyed cats threatened war from the vantage position of the high, broken fence.

In the background, the noise of a goods train trundling past made conversation temporarily impossible. When it had passed, the young man beside her, eyes gleaming with an enthusiasm she found, in her heart of hearts, hard to understand, waving his arms about with an air of ill-concealed excitement, continued: 'You see, Mrs Living-stone, this site has *endless* possibilities.'

'For what?' Anna looked searchingly at him.

'Why, for all kinds of things. The yard could be a play area for children; we could house work-shops which would give employment to our members inside; some we could let. We could have sideshows, happenings, you name it.' As he stopped, his expectant gaze seemed to invite an enthusiastic response from her.

He was an engaging young man with his blond shoulder length hair, tuft of beard and mous-tache. His brilliant eyes were of an unusual tur-quoise colour, and in his long hessian robe and sandals he almost resembled the popular image of Jesus Christ: vibrant, alert, alive.

'How old were you when you left school, Damian?' she asked, abruptly changing the sub-ject.

The man's smile vanished. 'Why do you ask that, Mrs Livingstone?'

'I just wondered. You're such an intelligent man . . .'

His expression turned swiftly from pleasure to derision.

'You've already made up your mind about us, haven't you, Mrs Livingstone? Like the others.'

'I don't know what you mean, Damian.' Anna perched on one of the upturned boxes and gazed earnestly at the man beside her.

'All you people, you "do-gooders", councilors and the like,' he went on, 'come here either to condemn or patronise us. You think we're all hippies, drug-addicts, layabouts . . .'

'No, Damian, I don't think that at all.' Anna stood up, and putting on her sunglasses again, surveyed the scene around her. 'You have asked for Council planning permission to develop the site and I am the Councillor on the Planning Committee. I'm here to help you. Believe me.'

He stared at her solemnly for a moment or two, and then lowered his eyes.

'I'd like to believe you, Mrs Livingstone. In fact I like *you*. I liked you when you first came. We all liked you and thought you were straight. Unpretentious and straight.'

'I'm flattered by your verdict, and I like you. I just wondered if you personally had any form of higher education. If, for instance, if need be you could teach. That was all I was getting at.'

'Oh!' He blinked. 'As a matter of fact I've a degree in Maths.'

Now it was Anna's turn to blink.

'Oxford,' he said. 'Magdalen.'

'Did you have difficulty getting a job?' Anna asked, wondering why and how this alert, obviously intelligent young man had ended up as the leader of a group of squatters who called themselves the Pilgrims.

The Pilgrims were a motley collection of people, of both sexes and all ages, who had somehow got together and formed themselves into a collective. For the last six months they had been illegally squatting in this disused warehouse, doing no harm to anyone, it was true; but maybe for this reason causing considerable irritation to their neighbours who lived either on the high-rise Council estates or in the neat rows of Georgian houses which had exchanged hands for large sums of money, due to the late eighties boom in the housing market.

It was also true that the Pilgrims did occasionally give loud and persistent voice to the sense of euphoria their freedom gave them. They chanted, banged drums, blew trumpets and bounded through the streets, flinging their arms in the air to the accompaniment of wild, enthusiastic shouts, hops, skips and jumps. There were several binges induced by drink, drugs, or a combination of the two, which also caused offence and, of course, no one doubted that a considerable amount of drug abuse went on which gave the Council its most powerful lever to try and evict them. That, and the fact that the Borough Surveyor had condemned the building as dangerous. The task of sorting out this knotty problem had, unfortunately but, perhaps, understandably, fallen to Anna, in view of her legal expertise and experience in these matters. It was one of the first jobs she'd been given since her election to the Council in May.

She had a great deal of sympathy with these people. She knew a lot about them, not as individuals but as a type of semi-vagrant, an offshoot of the gaps in the Welfare State, eroded increasingly now by various kinds of punitive local authority and Government action.

She would like them all to have had homes, families, jobs. Most of them had none of these things. Families who were either non-existent, who didn't want them or whom they didn't want; homes because they had not the wherewithal to buy, rent or otherwise pay for them, and as for jobs . . . well, one went with the other.

Some dropped out voluntarily, and she guessed that Damian was obviously one of those. Probably somewhere in London or the home counties there was a family rather like hers and Peter's, who bitterly regretted the waste, in their eyes, of a talent he undoubtedly had: the ability to be a useful, productive, wage-earning member of society. Criteria that in middle-class eyes were of such overwhelming importance.

Damian and Anna had continued their tour of the yard and they now went inside to a large, dark hall, welcomely cool after the heat outside. The atmosphere seemed, in many ways, like a very busy railway station, with people scurrying about on their various tasks, and every now and again an announcement being made on some kind of hailer. There were perhaps forty people in the hall, including several children, some toddlers and babes in arms. Their busy mothers were working in a space which had been set aside as a cooking area, obviously preparing the noonday meal. Others were working among the neatly laid out mattresses on the floor, making up the beds or sweeping the floor.

Several older men and women sat about on makeshift chairs or boxes, and one of indeterminate age and sex was sitting against the wall curled up, his or her face pressed against bent knees. Several animals were to be seen wandering around, or scavenging where the cooking was being done. Everyone looked reasonably happy and well fed. One or two came up to greet her, obviously sensing a meal ticket.

Yet withal it was very sad, certainly a condemnation of society. However at the same time it was somehow heartwarming, that this gathering of disparate people from all circumstances and walks of life should be brought together by common need.

The cooking was done on butane gas and paraffin stoves, none of which looked too safe. There was electric light, but no apparent heating and it must have been freezing in winter, a fact which made it pleasantly cool in summer. The upper floors of the warehouse were derelict, and a chink of light could be seen at the far end, approximately under the spot Anna had noticed from outside where the roof had given way.

'I think the Council want you out of here because the building is fundamentally unsafe,' Anna said, pointing to the chink of light. 'That is right under the broken roof. The water must come in in the winter. In fact, in the winter,' she put both hands round her shoulders involuntarily and shivered, 'it must be horrible. Frankly to rehouse you will be more costly than keeping you here; but it can't be done. The building is unsafe.'

Where to put them? That was the problem, particularly as, having formed a community, they now wished to stay together.

A few people had risen to greet them as they entered the warehouse, and they stood studying Anna as though she were a being from another planet. They registered various degrees of emotion: hope, anxiety, fear. One or two regarded her with loathing. Clearly, neatly dressed and well turned out, she was Authority, representing for them that section of society they had come to hate.

'You know Councillor Mrs Livingstone,' Damian gestured towards her, and one or two nodded.

'You see it's got such *potential*.' A young woman with scraped back hair and a ring through her nose came eagerly to the front of the group. 'You must see that, Councillor. We could make little cubicles and here,' she inscribed a wide circle with cupped hands, 'the communal area. Crèches,' she pointed to the far corner where the chink of light came through, 'for the children and,' another sweeping gesture with her arm, 'the kitchens over there.'

'Where are the toilets?' Anna asked.

'Well, at the moment . . . we have to use the public toilets up the road.'

'How *very* inconvenient.' The men and children, she suspected, probably used the yard. 'And washing?'

'There's a tap in the yard.'

'And you *all* use it?' Anna tried to conceal her amazement.

'We can go to the public baths.' The woman sounded defensive. 'They're not far away. Usually when we go to get our benefit.'

Once a week they would go to the local office of the Department of Social Security and collect the various benefits to which they were entitled: probably, in most cases, the maximum: family allowance, income support, the lot.

'What do you think, Mrs Livingstone?' The young woman joined her arms and stood beside Damian. Maybe she was his girlfriend.

'I think . . .' Anna hesitated, 'I would be deceiving you, I honestly would, if I said I thought you had any hope of convincing the Council to let you stay on here. The costs of repair would be enormous.'

'But the potential . . .' the young woman's face darkened.

Anna nodded vigorously.

'Oh, I agree. What's your name by the way?'

'Hope,' she said with a self-conscious giggle.

'I agree, Hope, that the potential *is* huge, but it would cost an awful lot of money and that,' she screwed up her face, 'we ain't got.'

'But we could raise it.'

'How?'

'All kinds of ways.'

'You could raise it, or attempt to, if you had all the facilities you want: the workshops, and so on. I have no doubt that between you all you have enormous talent: a great range of skills that in the end would bring in money. But, you see, first of all this . . .' she gestured around with a broad sweep of her hands, 'has to be changed. I should think the place would have to be *gutted* quite honestly, pulled down and a fresh start made. Then again in the eyes of the Council it has valuable potential for development into industrial premises, or houses that could bring in much needed income.'

'You mean if it's sold?'

'Yes.'

'To rich developers . . .'

'Well,' Anna hesitated, 'developers certainly, people who would want to build something on the land.'

'But *we* want to build something on it, Mrs Bloody Councillor Livingstone,' a woman hissed from the back, stabbing a finger at Anna. 'We the meek, the fucking poor, want to make something of it. But we ain't nothing.' And she spat on the floor.

'Please don't swear at Mrs Livingstone, Rosie,' Damian said in the sharp, authoritative tone of a leader. 'It's not helping our case.'

'Sorry,' Rosie mumbled. 'But you know what I mean, Mrs Livingstone. I get carried away.'

'I know, of course I know.' Anna smiled sympathetically. She wanted to put her arms round her and assure this woman of the streets, who looked only in her early or mid twenties, that she was her friend; that she believed in her cause, her freedom to please herself, and wanted to help her as well as everyone else.

But she couldn't. Why? Just because she was who she was: a member of the Council, a qualified solicitor and, she had to face it, a member of just those middle-class forces of society whom Hope, Rosie, Damian and their friends were retreating from and revolting against.

Anna got home very late that night. She'd gone from the squat to her office where the rest of the afternoon passed in legal business including a complicated matrimonial case where the parents were fighting to the death for custody of their so very vulnerable young children. That, too, was an agonising business, even though the parents lived, or had before the split, on The Bishop's Avenue, and had more money than Croesus.

She'd seen both parties separately — the father with his solicitor, as she was representing the mother; but she knew already, and so did the husband's solicitor, that neither parent was prepared to compromise.

Weary from this ordeal, she had thrown down a cup of instant coffee, made hurriedly in the office, and then gone to the Town Hall to report to the Chairman of the Housing Committee the result of her inspection of the warehouse squat at noon that day.

The Chairman was frankly unsympathetic towards squats. He thought that they did the image of the borough, and the Party, no good at all, and that they should be broken up and their members forced to find refuge elsewhere.

'But where?' she had urged.

The Chairman had shrugged his shoulders, said that was really up to the people concerned who milked the state enough as it was — well, didn't they?

Anyway, it would come up at the next meeting of the Council and no doubt an eviction order would be served.

As usual, Peter was in bed and, as usual, Anna crept into their bedroom, conscious of his bulky back turned to the door as if to emphasise his disapproval, his distance from her.

A solitary light burned on her side of the bed.

Whacked, Anna sank into the chair in front of the dressing table and gazed at herself in the mirror. Tired, very; lines . . . she peered more closely. Surely they had *increased,* especially the crows' feet by her eyes? She raised her fingers in a fruitless effort to try and smooth them out, perhaps even to erase them, but was left with the sinking feeling that no amount of anti-wrinkle cream would disperse the ravages of age.

She found herself wondering how old Damian Bradley, the Pilgrims' leader, was. Twenty-five, twenty-six? He didn't look any older. He could even be younger by a year or two. She was at least ten years older than he was. And if so, so what? And what precisely was she doing thinking in this absurd manner about a young, unem-

147

ployed man who seemed to be going nowhere?

Yet he intrigued her. He had breeding, class. She hated the terms — of course, they were against her principles — yet they were here, nevertheless, at the back of her mind. He was extremely good looking, charismatic. He walked with a kind of languid elegance, and from his accent his family were certainly middle, possibly even upper, class.

Damn. There she went again. Labels, which, as an egalitarian, she abhorred. She tugged at her earrings feeling angry with herself — a successful, contented, happily married woman indulging in such fantasies.

Anna removed her rings, except her wedding ring, and undid the bow of her tie blouse. She took it off, rose and stepped out of her skirt and then went into the bathroom to complete undressing, did her teeth, cleansed and moisturised her face, brushed her springy hair.

Tired, exhausted, but at the same time mentally awake; the events of the day racing through her brain. She thought she'd go downstairs and watch some television to try and divert her mind from the myriad of things that seemed to possess it; but it was nearly midnight, and perhaps a book would do the trick instead. She crept into bed beside Peter and picked up a volume of political memoirs she seemed to have been reading for months. Just a few pages whenever she got the time.

She put on her reading glasses and turned to

the bookmark. She knew Peter was awake, but his back remained turned to her and she felt too tired, too keyed-up, for a confrontation, the usual question and answer, reproach and defence.

Maybe they should have separate rooms? It didn't mean the end of the marriage, as some people thought or assumed, just practical good sense when one partner came in later and left earlier than the other. Usually it was the man, and the woman was meant to understand and be more accommodating. Besides, in those circumstances the woman wouldn't move out of bed; wouldn't dream of it. It was her place, and if the tired-out, overworked husband wanted sex to send him off to sleep it was her job to provide it.

Sex didn't send Anna to sleep. It was, anyway, the last thing she wanted at the moment.

Peter stirred.

'It's nearly a quarter to twelve,' he murmured peevishly.

'I know.'

'I suppose you don't really consider me.' Back still turned. Anna put down her book, the bookmark carefully in its place.

'Peter, would you like us to have separate rooms?'

Now he turned, his expression dumbstruck.

'Did you say separate *rooms?*'

'I didn't say separate *lives*. I simply thought it might be better, as I'm so busy at the moment.'

'At the *moment*. You're always busy, but since you've been on the Council. Well . . .' he puffed his pillows up behind him and lay back with an exaggerated sigh, 'I told you it would happen.'

'Peter, what if *you'd* gone on to the Council, or stood for Parliament?'

'I would never have dreamed of it. You know politics don't really interest me.'

'I'm speaking hypothetically. Supposing you were a political animal — as I confess I am — and you decided to combine civic duties with your work?'

'What are you getting at, Anna?'

'Whether I wanted to or not, I would have been expected to be your helpmeet, provide meals at any time, welcome you home at all hours; maybe sex last thing and then again first thing in the morning. Be a proper woman, in fact.'

'You are a proper woman.'

'You know what I mean. I'm acting out what has, for centuries despite women's lib and all, been considered the male role, and you are be-having like the wounded female is meant to be-have: touchy, brittle, uncooperative, petulant, uncommunicative, and you've been like that for some time, Peter.'

'We used to go to the opera, the theatre . . .'

'It will all settle down. After all, I've only been a councillor for a few months.'

'And you threw yourself into it with almost indecent enthusiasm, *and* so soon after becoming a partner and taking charge of the Wigmore Street branch.' He looked across at her. 'Tell me,

Anna, is there something missing from our life, honestly? Maybe you should have had a baby. Maybe all this . . .' he waved a hand in the air, 'desperate search for something to do, filling in every minute of your time, is a kind of substitution for the baby you should have had, the maternal role, now that Fiona has left home and Guy appears to have settled down a bit.'

Anna lay listening to him, conscious of a rising feeling of anger, wondering if, in fact, she should make the move to the bed in the spare room that very night.

Flounce out of bed, seize the pillows and march to the door? No, far too dramatic. Not her style. Throwing down a gauntlet instead of offering an olive branch?

'I think to throw this back at me about the baby is unworthy of you, Peter. It's cruel and unnecessary. It's not as if we didn't discuss it well and truly at the time.'

'It was obvious you didn't want one. You were determined to have the sterilisation.'

'I was not. All things considered, it seemed the best thing to do, you *know* that. Then the opportunity of the partnership came up . . .'

'And that swayed you, didn't it?'

'No, it did not.' Her tone grew more heated. 'It brought it to a head. It was time to think about horizons new.'

'You'd been talking about the Council before that . . .'

'Fiona fluffing her exams and leaving school

was a big worry . . .'

'You can't blame it on her.'

'I'm not blaming it on *anyone*, Peter, can't you see that? I'm just saying that, at the time and in the circumstances, I thought what I did was right. Anyway it's done and can't be undone.'

'You can't have them untied?'

'No, I can't,' emphatically, 'most certainly can't, and wouldn't want to if I could. And it's not just the practice and my Council work. The children are still unsettled. Guy is not preparing for his exam year with much enthusiasm and we really don't know what Fiona gets up to in Dorset, do we?'

'How do you mean?' Peter looked at her anxiously.

'As far as we *know* she's OK and she's painting, but what influence does Sal have on her? Honey? We don't really know. Perhaps we'd rather not because we haven't faced up to the dope business. In a way we've shut that aspect of our lives away, put it in a corner.'

'I thought of going down this weekend.' His expression became critical. 'You really haven't been much of a mother to those kids you know, Anna.'

'Peter,' she sat bolt upright and stared at him, 'how *can* you say such a thing?'

'It's true.'

'You said once upon a time that I was a wonderful mother. The best they could have had.'

'That was when they were young. As soon as

they began growing up and you went back to work and they became more difficult, you kind of opted out.'

'I did *not*. I was very concerned and I said so.' Her tone grew more and more heated.

'But you only said recently that you didn't feel the way I did. You said it several times.'

Anna was silent, her sense of outrage quickening her heart rate until she thought it would burst. Finally she said: 'I was being honest. What I meant was that it was hard for me, for any non-biological step-parent, to feel the tug at the gut that a biological parent feels. I understand other step-parents feel it too. You know the thing about blood being thicker than water? Well that's how I interpret it. I worry about them, I love them and I agonise over them, but in not quite the *same* way as you . . . but to say I was an uncaring mother . . .' She felt unwelcome tears prick against her eyes and then Peter's hand stole comfortingly around her shoulders.

'Sorry.'

'You're always saying that, Peter.'

'I mean it. I shoot my mouth off. I thought this weekend we might both pop down to Dorset just to see how Fiona is getting on.'

'You mean *tomorrow?*'

'I know,' tone of resignation, 'you've a lot of things to do, a fête to open, a . . .'

'No,' firmly, 'I can come. I can put everything off. I will put everything off.' Features drawn, she glanced sideways at him. 'Despite everything you say, I want you to know how much you and the family really do matter to me. How they come before everything else.'

They reached the cottage at about eleven, having left after an early breakfast. First of all Guy said he didn't want to go and then he changed his mind. When they pulled up outside the cottage they sat for a moment looking at it as if each was wondering, a little guiltily, a little too late, whether they should have forewarned Fiona. It had seemed a good idea at the time to spring a nice surprise on her.

'She'll probably be at the back, painting.' Anna jerked her head in the direction of the silent house.

'She'll probably be asleep,' Guy said more prosaically.

Guy was right. The front door was locked and the shed round the back was deserted, though an easel was set up in a corner and a number of half-finished canvases lay around.

They went in by the back door and the kitchen was, as usual, in an appalling state: dishes stacked in the sink, on the draining board, the remnants of a half-eaten meal on the table.

Anna's heart sank. Well, it had been Peter's idea. If anyone was to blame, he was.

'This was rather a stupid idea after all,' she murmured, thankfully putting the two bags full of food she'd been carrying on the floor. 'We should have warned her. She's not going to change overnight you know.' Anna saw that Peter was making an effort to conceal his disappointment. He nodded; no words came.

They all looked at the staircase as if wondering who should be the first to go up.

'You put on the kettle, I'll go and see if she's awake.' Anna flashed Peter and Guy a cheery smile and gingerly mounted the stairs.

She stood outside Fiona's door for a moment, aware of that old familiar feeling of dread rearing its ugly head.

Fiona had been living on her own for over six months and, so far, things seemed to have gone well. Peter gave her a modest allowance. They came down occasionally to see her — they'd all, for instance, spent Easter together. She came up to London, not often but ostensibly to buy paint and materials, see friends. No one really knew how she was getting on as she was so secretive about her work but, to all appearances, she was well and happy, happier she said than she'd been for a long time.

Anna realised now that they *had* been fools not to forewarn Fiona they were going to visit her, and her courage nearly deserted her. Finally she braced herself and knocked firmly on the door.

'Fiona,' she called, 'it's us.'

Silence. It then occurred to her that Fiona might not be there. She was, after all, a young woman they didn't really know, and now, since she'd left home, how she got on or whom she met. Truth to tell, and if Anna had reason to feel guilty about anything it should have been this: they'd been so glad to get rid of her, to have that awful disturbing presence out of the house, that they didn't enquire too much. A terrible abnegation of the parental role but true nevertheless. They simply didn't really want to know.

She tapped again and, turning the handle gently, pushed open the door. She saw immediately that the curtains were drawn and in bed, fast asleep, was Fiona. Anna breathed a sigh of relief and was about to leave the room when Fiona's eyes flickered and opened. For a moment she stared incredulously at her stepmother and then reached up and rubbed her eyes.

'What . . .' She sat up in bed and gaped at Anna. 'Is something wrong?'

'No.' Anna gave a rather fake, pseudo laugh, and perched on the end of the bed. 'We simply decided we wanted to come and see you. The weather forecast was good.' She clicked her fingers in the air. 'Did it on the spur of the moment.'

Fiona looked at her suspiciously without smiling.

'Checking up on me, I suppose.'

'Oh, Fiona!' Anna got up and walked over to the window, drawing aside the curtains. 'Why *must* you always be so suspicious? I tell you it was an impromptu, friendly gesture. No ulterior motive at all.'

'The place is in a hell of a mess.'

Anna said nothing.

'I'd have tidied up if I'd known you were coming, I know you hate it. Hell,' she sat up in bed, tossed back the duvet angrily and sat with her feet on the floor. 'What a *hell* of a thing to do, arrive unannounced, just like that.'

'It really was well meant. Dad wanted to come and see you. Guy's here too.'

Fiona stared at her.

'*You* didn't want to come and see me, I suppose. You were dragged here?'

Anna decided to make a last effort and sat again on the bed next to the angry girl.

'Fiona. You are now seventeen and I've known you since you were four. For most of that time I've been married to your father. When I married him I took you as well as him, you and Guy, and I loved you and still do. Sometimes, I'll admit, it is hard. In recent years it hasn't always been easy; you haven't made it very easy for me . . .'

Fiona suddenly put her head in her hands.

'For Christ's sake I don't want a bloody lecture! I've only just woken up. Give me a chance to sluice some water on my face, clean my teeth and I'll be down.'

'Right.' Anna got up. Once again she felt rebuffed, but when had she really felt anything else when it came to trying to have a heart to heart with Fiona? Better really not to try at all.

When she came downstairs there was no sign of Guy. Peter still stood in the kitchen looking bewilderingly about him as if he didn't quite know what he should be doing. Well he could have done the dishes for a start, started to tidy up, Anna thought angrily, but decided to say nothing.

'Is she there?' He looked up as she came into the kitchen.

'Of course. Where did you think she would be?'

'Well,' Peter scratched his head, leaving a volume of words unsaid. 'Is she alright?'

'She was asleep. Didn't seem very pleased to see me. That's nothing new though.'

'I'm sorry we came. We should have rung.'

Anna moved over to the sink, biting back more words. She'd had three weekend engagements to put off, making what sounded like lame excuses to the disgruntled organisers on the other end of the phone first thing in the morning.

She'd put a lot of people out, upset a great many. For what? She tugged on the washing-up gloves with more strength than they required. For what? For this!

'Could you make the coffee, Peter?' over her shoulder as she began to tackle the mound of dirty dishes.

'I'd rather have a beer.'

'I dare say you would, but you did come down to see your daughter. I'd like a coffee, please.'

'Well, is she coming down or did she go back to sleep?'

'She said she'd have a wash and be down in a few minutes.'

'Does she seem alright?' She could feel Peter's breath on the back of her neck, his voice a mere whisper.

'Yes, she seems fine.' Not turning round. 'Only tired.'

'Tired at noon, for God's sake! We should have rung.'

Anna plunged her hands into the soapsuds. 'Peter, we should have planned this, say, for next weekend or the weekend after. That way I could have got out of my engagements and not offended so many people. As it is I had to lie. I know it sounded like a lie and I felt awful about it.'

'You didn't *have* to do it.'

Anna straightened her back and gazed out of the window.

'I think I did have to do it.'

'What do you mean?'

'I had, was forced to show you that I loved you and Fiona and Guy. That I was the wife and mother, part of the family. Somehow by your saying that I wasn't a very good mother, you made it essential for me to do this. Well I've done it and I've made the best of it, so let's get on with it. Let's try, really, once Fiona has come down, to make the best of it, and if we possibly can, have a really good time.'

CHAPTER 7

When Fiona came downstairs she was in a better mood than she had been half an hour before, not surprisingly perhaps, Anna acknowledged to herself as Fiona kissed her father and gave her a fleeting smile, a fluttery wave of the fingers, nothing too intimate. It had been rather stupid to descend on her unannounced. Few people, when it came to it, liked surprises, and Fiona was not one of them. They should at least have telephoned.

But then, when you came to think of it, it was Peter's fault. He had formulated his plans almost at midnight the night before. It was once again a case of men doing and women following. One had supposed that all that sort of thing was in the past.

Anna decided to let the children go off with their father to the pub for lunch while she made the excuse that she had a lot of odd jobs she wanted to do. Such as? Doing out the spare room which, she thought, could be made into a more comfortable studio for Fiona, a proposal that found favour with Fiona who contrived, from that moment on, to be more pleasant to her stepmother. Moreover, the spare room faced south and there was the possibility that they could put in a decent sized window to give it more light.

Anna assured them that she only wanted a snack anyway, and the three of them went off happily in one another's company. She stood at the window of the spare room watching them walk down the road, Fiona's arm linked through that of her father. A family togetherness. Did she fit in there? Had she ever? Would she ever?

She turned from the window with a heavy sigh and surveyed the rather unprepossessing sight: the spare room which had an unmade single bed in it but which was also a sort of glory room, a junk room.

It was really the fourth bedroom and would have made a nice guest room except that they had always made a point of never inviting guests to the cottage. It was a place where they went to get away from it all; where they wanted to be alone. There was enough entertaining and excitement and socialising, after all, in London. Here one wanted a rest.

Not that it was very easy for someone of Anna's temperament to rest. She scarcely knew the meaning of inactivity, of repose. She was either rushing from one appointment to another, attending meetings, committees or conferences and when she sat it was either to eat, to read legal documents, counsels' opinions, judgments and, of course, endless Council reports.

She was someone who, like Peter, could be said to have no hobbies. Maybe that's what had made her a bad stepmother. Had it also made her a bad wife?

She flopped on the side of the bed and gazed around her. This had been Nancy and Peter's room. Their bed had been sold and the decision was made to move to another room when she and Peter married. It wasn't so much that she would have minded using either Nancy's bed or Nancy's room, but Peter had. Now the room was very much as it had been when Nancy died. She, Anna, was sure that the children had completely forgotten it was their father and mother's bed-room, the room where she had died.

Anna tried to visualise Nancy as she must have been, the kind of person she was. How much of her was in the children? Certainly her looks were reflected in Fiona. But was her talent, or did she even have any? What of her temperament, her charm? The first certainly possessed by Fiona, and the second by Guy who could get away with a lot of things because he exuded it.

The striking of the church clock nearby jolted Anna from her reverie. It chimed for one o'clock, and Anna realised that it was a lovely day outside and once she had finished her self-appointed chore a number of pleasurable things could be done in the afternoon. Doubtless Peter would want to garden and she thought she might stroll down to see Sal, maybe invite her and Honey to supper. Or would they consider that always being asked at the last minute was patronising? Should she have telephoned first? But the whole visit had been arranged in such a hurry . . . Decisions, decisions. Always decisions.

Anna bounced off the bed and flung open the double doors of the wardrobe which was literally stuffed with clothes. They were mostly country clothes: jeans, shirts, anoraks, a couple of jackets that clearly belonged to Peter, but which she never remembered seeing him wearing, and several dresses which had belonged to Nancy. It was odd that no one had considered going through this cupboard for over a dozen years — maybe Peter did from time to time, but she suspected he didn't and that Fiona had no interest in it either.

Anna gathered most of the clothes into her arms and threw them on the bed, hangers and all. Then she began to sort through them. She'd make a pile of Nancy's things and then the family could decide what they wanted done with them. She would ask Peter if he wanted any of his things, and if he didn't, they could bundle them up and send them to Oxfam.

Nancy had been much smaller than Anna: petite, fine-boned, and beyond colouring and superficial facial characteristics there was no resemblance. Nancy, it was agreed, was lightweight, a scatterbrain. If Peter was to be believed, and there was no reason why he shouldn't be, she took very little interest in her children. Conversely, they adored her for it, venerated her memory more than ever now, since the passage of time seemed to have eclipsed the years.

Anna found the process of sorting through and folding the clothes oddly satisfying. There was something soothing, she decided, in the sameness of domestic routine.

She liked peeling potatoes, preparing the simple food they ate in the cottage, even washing up. In London it was all microwaves, precooked and frozen food usually made in advance by her excellent daily who doubled up as a housekeeper. But so many meals were eaten out, or not eaten at all.

She liked making beds, dusting, hoovering, tidying. She felt at one with the chores of the house while Peter preferred the manly role of digging and muck-spreading. Of course, it was all fantasy. She would hate it all the time. But, for a while, to play Marie Antoinette and the milkmaids was kind of fun.

At the bottom of the wardrobe was a selection of boots and shoes of various shapes and sizes, male, female and unisex. Nancy had small feet too, and her taste in shoes seemed unexceptional. Apart from casuals they were mostly sensible court shoes, such as one would wear with a good dress for a dinner party in the country.

There were few signs of the artist; nothing outlandish or bizarre, like her daughter wore now. Just unmistakably middle class, in good taste with, perhaps, a liking for bright colours: blue, turquoise, shocking pink and leaf green which would give her the sort of bright, bird-like effect Anna imagined Nancy had.

She left the footwear where it was and went down to the kitchen to get some black bin liners in which to put the clothes. To her surprise she found that Fiona had returned and was ferreting in a drawer as though she'd lost something.

'Oh!' Fiona looked up sharply when she saw her. 'I didn't realise you were still here.'

'I was tidying the spare room. Have you had lunch?'

'I had a sandwich. Daddy and Guy are still in the pub. Daddy loves jawing away to farmers as though he knows what he's talking about. He and Fred can keep each other bored for hours.'

Anna grinned. This confidential, friendly tone was like the Fiona of old. She wondered if she dared hope that a rapprochement was taking place?

'I'm sorry I was rude to you this morning,' Fiona said, as if she could read her mind.

'That's OK. You were half-awake. We should have rung. It was your father . . .'

'I know. He said over lunch that you had cancelled any number of engagements just to come and be with us.'

'It's the least I can do.' Anna, mollified, perched on the edge of the kitchen table. 'I realise I haven't been a very good mother of late. I have taken too much on and . . .' she paused, not quite knowing how to proceed.

'But why should *you* reproach yourself?' Fiona sat down in the chair facing her. 'You've had a rotten time with us. I know I've been hateful,

165

and I so meant to be different this time, but I started out badly. I feel I've let you down and I let Dad down. We said horrible things to you about not being our real mother. After all this time it was a nasty, silly thing to do.'

Anna could hardly believe her ears. What had brought this on? Surely in such a short time it couldn't be due to anything Peter had said? As if answering her unspoken question Fiona rapidly went on. 'Sal thinks you've been a brick. She likes you.'

Ah, Sal, that was it.

'You mean you confided in Sal?'

'Sal's a mixture of youth and maturity,' Fiona said thoughtfully. 'She can be as young as us and as old as you. She can do the things we do and understands us. She and Honey are more like sisters than mother and daughter. In a way she's a teenager herself. She knows she can be irresponsible and lazy. She looks up to you and admires you enormously.'

'Really?' Anna felt gratified. Also surprised.

'You know I was beefing about you always being busy and not understanding, and she said that you also had the right to your own life. She said you had done a lot for us and obviously loved and believed in us even to the extent of foregoing having babies of your own. I never thought of it like that.'

'Look,' for a moment Anna felt almost overcome by emotion, 'I wasn't a martyr. Don't think that for a moment.'

'Oh, I don't. Neither does Sal. But you see there are things I never thought of. Then I know you persuaded Dad to let me stay down here, and it's been great. It really has.'

Anna thought it was not quite the best moment to ask this stepdaughter, who was acting as though she had undergone a Damascus-like conversion, to come and decide what to do with her mother's old clothes. It would break the bond, rather the fragile thread that drew them together. So she said: 'Why don't you show me what you've been doing? I'd love to see your paintings.'

'Oh, would you? Really?' Fiona's expression suddenly reflected the self-doubt and insecurity she'd often had as a little girl.

'Yes, I would. And then we can go up and have a look at the room. See what it would be like as a studio.'

'You're very good to me really, Anna.' Fiona reached out for her hand, pulling her off the table and towards the door like the excited, trusting little girl of old.

Anna followed Fiona across the garden, standing aside as she threw open the door, the expression on her mobile face suddenly registering not excitement but doubt.

'I don't *know* exactly if you'll like them.'

'I'm sure I shall.'

'They're not much good.'

'Well, let's see.' Anna smiled at the excited girl and pushed her inside.

Whatever their quality, there was no doubt that

Fiona had not been idle in the months she'd had to herself in the cottage. Canvases were stacked around the wall in various stages of completion, and there was a half-finished painting on the easel by the window. The place was in Fiona's usual state of clutter, and it was obvious she didn't go in for cleaning paintbrushes which must have been rather expensive. Many of them lay congealed on the pallets as if Fiona had carelessly thrown them down, too impatient to clean them.

Casting an eye swiftly around the assorted canvases, Anna saw at once that Fiona's untutored talent was even less than her mother's. The pictures were of a uniform chocolate-boxey effect, simple subjects amateurishly executed, in wishy-washy colours. Yet there were dozens and dozens of them and it was obvious that Fiona painted feverishly, probably mostly all the time, dashing them all off with little consideration given to perspective or style.

It was very difficult for Anna to dissemble, even more so as she knew that Fiona almost breathlessly awaited her verdict.

'You *have* been busy.' She began thoughtfully to walk around, examining each one carefully. It was rather like looking at the work of a class of untrained young artists such as one would find in the average school. There was no real evidence of natural ability, of talent at all. But why, after all, should there be?

The whole enterprise had been one of Fiona's whims in order, Anna suspected, to stay down in the country. It was rather like people who wanted to write or act without any real vocation whatever.

Anna knew that Fiona was watching her, so she took as much time as she could on her tour of inspection while turning over in her mind what she could possibly say. Finally, standing in front of the unfinished canvas on the easel she said: 'Fiona, I like very much what I see, but,' she turned to study the anxious face, 'it seems to me you could do with some training. I mean you haven't had any, have you?'

'You mean to say I'm no good?' Fiona's features recomposed themselves into the familiar mulish stubbornness.

'No, I don't mean that at all; but most artists, even the best, have trained for many years. I think if you had a teacher you would learn more about form and colour . . . and perspective,' she finished knowing very well how lame and unconvincing she must sound.

'You just don't like them. Don't pretend.'

'I do, really. I like them. I'm simply saying that if you want to go on doing this, you can. No one's stopping you. Your father is prepared to support you, to help in any way. Having seen your work I feel personally that it would be better all round, and more productive from your point of view, if you studied with a teacher, and I'm sure someone can recommend one. Or you might try art school.'

'You're *saying* I'm no good,' Fiona insisted.

'Fiona, I am *not*. But you don't want me to lie to you.'

'Just when I was trying so hard to be *nice*.' Fiona petulantly stamped her foot. 'Just when I tried so hard for us to be friends you have to be horrible and negative about my paintings.'

'Fiona . . .' Anna's outstretched hand went instinctively towards her, but instead of taking it, Fiona slapped it away from her, her face contorted in that familiar frenzy of anger, loathing and, perhaps, fear. 'You know you don't like me, Anna. You don't like anything about me. So why do you *pretend?*'

She then turned her back and ran out of the door, across the garden, round the house and out of sight. Probably on her way to try and get comfort and reassurance from Sal, or her father, or both.

'You could have pretended you liked them,' Peter said later when, in the seclusion of their bedroom, they could discuss the events of the day; the exhausting events of the day: Fiona's renewed tantrums, her outburst against her stepmother, her threat to destroy all her canvases and make a bonfire of them in the garden. (It was so tempting to say 'let her'.)

Finally Fiona disappeared without saying where she was going, but they were determined that her behaviour would not be allowed to spoil the day. After all, there was Guy, who appeared unusually subdued, to consider as well. They ate dinner virtually in silence, and at nine Sal rang to say Fiona had been with her and Honey, and was on her way home.

She had gone straight to her room where, eventually, Peter was allowed in. He now relayed the results of his talk to a more than usually exhausted Anna who would rather have had any number of events to open or committee meetings to attend than this.

'I didn't say I *disliked* them.' Anna, already undressed, lay on the bed longing for sleep. 'I suggested she might like to have proper training.'

'Well, she misunderstood.'

'She said I'd never really liked her,' Anna said bitterly. 'She uses every excuse she can to make the thing personal. Look,' Anna propped herself up on her arm on the bed, 'I don't honestly think the paintings *are* very good, but what do you expect? She has had no training, given no indication ever that she liked art and suddenly she decides she wants to be a painter and expects us to say she is a genius. It's not reasonable. It's not fair.'

'It's true though, you *are* rather critical of her. After all, the poor girl is trying to do something.'

Anna turned over, reached for the pillow and thumped it hard, wishing it was someone's head.

'Oh, Peter, you make me so angry. I am not *saying* that Fiona can't paint. I am just suggesting that, if it is what she wants to do, she might go to an art school, take lessons, learn more about the techniques and craft of being a painter. Oh, for God's sake . . .' she thumped the pillow again, and then kneading it into a ball climbed beneath the duvet and buried her head in it.

Peter remained for a long time by the window staring into the darkness before he joined her. He felt Anna's body stiff and unresponsive beside him, and knew that another idea he'd had was doomed to disappointment. A relaxing, rather sexy weekend in the country.

'What a day!' he murmured as he put out the light. He lay still for a while and, realising that Anna wasn't asleep, his libido still charged, his hand tentatively moved across the space between them and landed on her thigh. She didn't move.

'Anna?' he whispered. 'You awake?'

'You know I'm awake.'

'Let's try and relax.' He moved closer to her. 'It will do us both good.'

'For God's sake, Peter,' she turned over, 'you can't solve *everything* with sex you know.'

'It helps.'

'Well, it doesn't help me.'

'It used to.' The tone of Peter's voice changed, and he removed his hand. 'I thought that having your tubes tied was supposed to make our sex life better?'

'No, it wasn't. It was so that I could come off the Pill and possibly avoid an unnecessary and premature death.'

'Don't be so dramatic.'

'I'm not being dramatic, but that was the reason. Anyway,' she paused and he could feel her gazing at him through the gloom, 'you never complained about our sex life before.'

'I'm not complaining now.'

'You said "it was supposed to make it better".'

'Well it was a silly thing to say. I didn't think. I suppose I meant . . . more spontaneous.'

'Peter, our sex life was always spontaneous while I was on the Pill. It had nothing to do with spontaneity.' Pause again. 'What are you trying to say, Peter?'

'Nothing. Oh forget it.' He pulled the duvet over his shoulder, turned his back on his wife and closed his eyes.

'Peter, you can't just go to sleep and pretend this never happened.'

'I can try.'

'You make a pretty insulting remark and then . . .'

'It was *not* insulting, nor meant to be.'

'You said you thought our sex life was supposed to be better. Better than what?'

'I got my words wrong.' Peter turned restlessly in the bed again, ran his hand over his face. 'Look, Anna, I'm tired. Forget it, for God's sake. Anyway look, it isn't very good now, is it? I mean at this moment. I feel like relaxing, making love to try and unwind. You don't.'

'Is that a sin? Or do you want me to pretend?'

'Look, Anna. Let's face it. Since you had your tubes tied, since you got promotion in your job and, especially, since you joined the Council, our sex life has been pretty non-existent. Pretty lousy.'

'If you mean it's not as frequent, I say that's just because we're getting older. You can't go on fucking like rabbits when you've been married twelve years. I think it's quality not quantity that counts.'

'I think having your tubes tied has taken the fun out of it.'

'Oh, don't be absurd. What fun?'

'The fun of making love, the danger . . .'

'You mean pregnancy? The danger of pregnancy?'

'Yes, I suppose I do. It's silly, but there it is.'

'But there was no danger of pregnancy with the Pill, you idiot. That is what it is all about. Women taking the Pill can't get pregnant.'

'They can if they forget.'

'Oh, I see. That's it.'

'Well, it makes sense, Anna, doesn't it? Something's changed. Something's happened.'

Anna was not going to be talked into doing something she didn't want by childish and largely unsubstantiated arguments and now she turned her back to Peter, but as he settled she was aware that something had happened between them. It was not only sex, not Fiona or Guy. It really was the state of their marriage. Peter was trying to tell her something. Many of their friends were getting divorced or contemplating it. She saw it every day, several times a day, in her office. Divorce was increasing, especially among their age group. People with a mountain of worries, busy lives and careers, difficult children.

It seemed to her that if a man's wife didn't support him he'd just get another wife. It seemed to be the nature of the beast.

With women it was different.

Sal popped her head round the door.

'So sorry we couldn't make it last night. I should have rung.'

'That's OK. We always leave things until the last minute.' Anna dried her hands on a towel and pointed to the chair. 'I was just going to make coffee.'

'What time are you off?'

'Well, now we're not going until tomorrow. Peter and I are so exhausted that we feel we need another day.' Anna shrugged. 'We shall both have to ring our offices, but there you are.'

'Busy lives, uh?' Sal lit a cigarette.

'Very busy.'

'Had a long talk with Fiona yesterday,' Sal said chattily, taking the cup of Instant Anna held out to her. 'She really is very sorry.'

'Sorry about what?' Anna faced her, sipping her coffee.

'Well, she's been trying so hard. She knows she flew off the handle. Didn't mean to.'

'She could have apologised.'

'She finds it very difficult. You must know that. Besides she feels you and she always get on the wrong side of each other. She really is very fond of you, you know.'

'Frankly, Sal,' Anna paused and swallowed a mouthful of coffee, 'I find that very hard to believe.'

'No, I think she is. She talks about you a lot when you're not here, I don't just mean now. Says you were very good to her as a child and she loved you like a mother.'

'I notice you use the past tense.'

'She thinks you don't have time for her, that you're so busy. I think she also envies you a bit your success.'

'Envies me?' Anna looked incredulous.

'Yes, jealous in a way. She feels an utter failure, and here you are: successful law practice, local councillor. She's sure you'll stand for Parliament.'

'Well, I won't.'

'No, but she's proud of you. She just feels so inadequate, and then when you attacked her paintings, my God,' Sal paused to light a fresh cigarette from the stub of the first, 'that girl has worked her little butt off painting away. She loves it . . .'

'I did *not* attack her paintings, Sal,' Anna said heatedly. 'I merely *suggested* that she might be better if she had proper training. I was trying to be constructive. Look, I don't give a damn if she goes on painting for the rest of her life, if that's what she wants to do. I was thinking of Fiona, of her own satisfaction, her success . . .'

Sal looked at her shrewdly, head on one side.

'You don't really think they're very good, do you?'

How to reply? Pondering the dilemma Anna gazed at the woman across the table. Then she did what she might have done in her law office, answered one question by another. It was a useful ploy.

'Do you?'

Sal smiled. 'Well we both know, don't we, to be honest? Not much. I mean there's nothing to them, and when you look at Nancy's they weren't up to much either.'

'The idea of the exhibition came to nothing?' Anna, too, put her head on one side.

Sal shrugged. 'It seemed to go off the boil. Fiona's not much of an organiser. Frankly,' she gave a fleeting, nervous smile, 'neither am I. It gave Fiona a reason at the time to stay on here. She never really referred to it again. Maybe she realised they weren't much good, but we all have to *pretend*, don't we?'

'Do we?' Mentally Anna pictured the scene between herself and Peter the night before.

'I think so.' Sal reached out to flick ash into a makeshift ashtray, as no one else in the house smoked. 'I think we have to compromise in life and, yes, that involves a lot of pretending, a good deal of the time anyway.'

'So in other words we should have said that we *liked* her pictures very much and left it at that?'

And I could have made love to Peter last night

and pretended it was because I wanted to, Anna thought to herself, bitterly regretting now that she hadn't. When she'd woken in the morning Peter was already up and had gone for a walk.

'Maybe,' Sal shrugged and got up. 'Then let *her* bring up the fact that she'd like training. Now that you've put the idea into her head I think you'll find her willing if you suggest it again. If you could bring yourself to do so, that is.'

Anna leaned across the table and reached for Sal's hand. 'Thanks, Sal. I think you've been an excellent go-between and I'm grateful. You know I have a large office and I do legal aid work and run an advice bureau and I'm a councillor; but I still think I've a lot to learn.'

'I think that too.' Sal suddenly looked serious, vulnerable. 'About myself, I mean. I'm nearly forty. I've got two grown-up children, but sometimes I think when it comes to human relationships I don't know a thing.' She returned Anna's firm handclasp. 'It's always much easier to deal with other people than your own family. It's the blood tie . . . Oh . . .' her hand flew to her mouth, 'sorry, that was stupid.'

'Think nothing of it.' Anna also got up, but in that instant the feeling of hope and euphoria she'd had while Sal was speaking evaporated.

There it was again. The blood tie.

Anna saw Sal out and began the preparations for lunch, thinking about what Sal had said. Somehow, between now and tomorrow, she had to bring up, or get Fiona to bring up, the subject of training. Maybe Sal had been sent as a sort of emissary, and it would happen anyway.

They were going to have a late lunch; Sunday roast, Yorkshire pudding (from the freezer), the lot. She went to the larder and got out the beef, sirloin with the fillet which she and Peter had bought in Blandford the previous day, presumably while Fiona was pouring her heart out to Sal.

She shook her head as she carefully spread lard over the beef and peppered it before putting it in the oven. The blood tie. It would never go away, and Peter was trying to tell her that she had destroyed her chance of being linked to the family by blood by not having a baby. Her and Peter's child would have been linked to Fiona and Guy by blood, and thus they would all be related.

No chance of that now.

She looked up as the door opened and Guy sidled into the kitchen, a shifty, rather untypical expression on his face. Immediately she wondered what he wanted.

'Hi!' she called cheerily. 'Want a cup of coffee?'

'No, thanks.' Guy shook his head and sat opposite her, watching her carefully as she placed the partly boiled, floured potatoes round the joint in the baking tray.

'Why do you do that?' he asked.

'Do what?' She looked up at him.

'Put flour on them?'

'It makes them softer and crunchy.'

'Do you like cooking?' Guy put his face between his hands and stared at the tin. Anna thought he looked pale. In fact, he had been particularly subdued all the time they'd been here.

'Sometimes.'

'But you don't have time at home, do you?'

'Guy, I do a fair amount of cooking and put it in the freezer. Just because we have a defrosted meal doesn't always mean I haven't cooked it.'

'I'm not criticising you, Anna,' he said carefully. 'I mean I think you're a very good cook.'

'Thank you, Guy.' She smiled, and taking the roasting tin carefully between her hands, popped it into the oven. Then she shut the door, adjusted the heat and, returning to the table, sat opposite him. 'That's that, then. Is Daddy in the garden?'

'I think he went to the pub.'

'You haven't seen much of Martin this weekend.'

Guy stuck a finger in his mouth and seemed to be struggling with some sort of inner battle or dilemma. Anna began to feel concerned.

'Anna,' he burst out removing the finger, 'supposing a friend of yours had done something awful, what would you do?'

Taken aback, Anna waited a second or two before replying.

'Something awful, like what?'

'Something that was really bad.'

'You mean, should *you* tell somebody?'

'Yes, or keep it to yourself. I mean if others got into trouble?'

'Oh, I see what you mean.' Anna's unease increased. 'You mean somebody, your friend, say, has done something wrong for which others might be punished?'

Guy nodded, and Anna noticed the high colour in his cheeks.

'And you feel your friend should tell the authorities?'

Guy nodded again and the blush deepened.

'What is it, Guy?' Anna leaned over towards him. 'What is it your friend did . . . or was it you?' She rose swiftly from her chair, went across to him, putting a hand on his shoulder. 'And if it was, and you tell me what it was, I'll do my best to help . . .'

'No scolding . . .' Guy faltered, his body tense.

'Promise. No scolding.' Her grasp on his shoulder tightened as his head touched the table and he burst into tears.

'Oh, Guy!' Anna said, gently massaging his back, pressing his face close to hers and, finally, enveloping him in her arms.

Guy sat on the edge of his chair, hands clutching the sides, head bowed. Although he was tall, he seemed somehow to have diminished in size as he sat between Anna and Peter under the baleful gaze of the Head.

'I do very much appreciate your honesty, Guy, in owning up; but what you did was very terrible,

181

very serious, and could have resulted in someone being killed.' The Head paused while the words sank in.

Anna closed her eyes involuntarily, visualising the scene, as she had several times since the extent of Guy's misdemeanour had become apparent. Together with two other boys he had thrown an old radiogram belonging to the school out of a fourth floor classroom window, regardless not only of the damage caused, the wilful destruction of property, but of who might have happened to be passing underneath on what was normally a busy walkway. Thankfully, no one had.

'I'm afraid I have got no option but to expel Guy from the school together with the two other boys he was involved with. Their parents have also been informed.'

The verdict was not unexpected. Nevertheless Anna felt a sharp sense of shock.

'But, Jessie, if Guy hadn't owned up . . .'

'Someone else would have been expelled instead of him. We had some idea who the culprits were, but we did not include Guy. Young people being what they are, loyal to the tribe, they would not have betrayed him. As it is, we can't keep Guy and let the others go. It wouldn't be fair.'

'But Guy wasn't in the same position as the other two,' Peter said. 'I understand they'd both just been released from young offenders' institutions.'

'One of them had,' Jessie corrected him. 'The

other was on probation. And in any case Guy should have known better. Both came from underprivileged families.'

'And what kind of company was that for my son to keep?' Peter's voice rose.

'You may well ask Guy that question, Mr Livingstone.' Jessie Clark turned to Guy. 'What should attract you to people like that? Hey, Guy. Can you answer?'

Guy hunched his shoulders and said nothing.

'Guy?' His father looked at him, but Guy remained silent and, sensing he was close to tears, Anna shook her head at Peter and her hand groped for Guy's. To her surprise he gave it to her and let her hold it. She thought then of the number of pupils from the school who had appeared at the local magistrates' court and that if a fatality, or even injury, had resulted from the action of Guy and his friends, the committal proceedings would have been held in the same court. One of the things she had so often dreaded might, in fact, have come true. She could just see the smug expression on Mrs Bridges' face.

Peter broke the silence, the unnatural stillness, again.

'I might ask you, Mrs Clark, why disturbed youngsters like that are at a normal school at all. What were they doing here?'

'Mr Livingstone!' Jessie Clark's tone indicated that she was on the verge of losing her patience. 'This is a state school run for the benefit of all its citizens. Whatever you may or may not think

183

of it, the boys concerned had paid their debt to society and were entitled to receive an education. I may doubt the wisdom of this, but I have to obey the rules set by the Department of Education. As it is, they have now been expelled from the school and so, I'm sorry to say, has Guy . . .'

'Couldn't Guy have *one* more chance?' Anna squeezed his hand very tightly in hers. 'After all, it is a first offence . . .'

'Mrs Livingstone . . . Anna,' Jessie Clark sighed deeply. 'It may be his first serious offence, but there are a number of minor ones I have had to take into consideration. I have been very patient with Guy, as I was with Fiona. But I am sorry to say that neither of them have responded to my kindness and tolerance. Guy has not been a satisfactory pupil. He has been lazy, work-shy and has frequently been up for some sort of punishment in the time he has been in the school. We have found him a trial. Frankly, I shall be glad to see the back of him. And as this is nearly the end of the school year you will have plenty of time to try and find a new school for him.' She drew a line firmly under whatever it was she had written on the piece of paper in front of her.

'What about his sport?' Peter demanded. 'Captain of football, cricket.'

'If Guy could apply to his work and life in general the dedication he applies to football and cricket then I would have some hope for him. I would suggest that in looking for a school you find one which imposes very strict discipline, which places a great deal of emphasis on work . . . and,' she got up and joined her hands, 'which has none of the imperfections you have apparently found in us, if that is possible.'

She then looked pointedly towards the door, and as the Livingstones rose and filed slowly out there was no attempt to shake hands. Anna however remembered all the heart-to-hearts she and the Head had shared over the years and halted at the threshold looking back.

' 'Bye, Jessie,' she said.

Jessie smiled, winked and mouthed the words 'Good luck.'

CHAPTER 8

In a way, Anna's department almost ran itself. She had under her a team of good people, some of whom had been Articled to her as she mounted the firm's hierarchy. There were still, however, many things she had to do herself, and all the important decisions were made by her.

For anyone it was a full time job, but as the work of the Council encroached more on her time she sometimes had to leave essential work to others. She worked longer hours, left the office later and later to make up the time that she gave not only to Council and legal aid work but, increasingly, to the family.

Getting Guy into a school had not been easy, on two accounts. In the first place he had been expelled, so had a very black mark against him, and in the second his work was not up to the norm for a boy in the year before GCSEs. They had trundled him round all the London day schools because Guy deeply resented the idea of being a boarder. Valuable time was taken out, both by Anna and Peter, visiting these institutions, only to receive the discouraging news that nowhere was he wanted, not only because of his conduct but the low standard of his work. Even some expensive private schools, desperate for pupils, wouldn't take him.

Guy was a big problem, just now being tutored at home by a young man about to go up to university, to try and raise his overall standard of education before they tried again for the beginning of the autumn term.

A holiday was clearly indicated, but Anna considered it out of the question for her. Too many days off from the office, while she trailed round looking at schools for Guy, made her feel she was in danger of losing her position and authority at work unless she spent long hours making up for time lost.

There was a protracted row on the subject with Peter, but in the end he agreed to take Fiona and Guy to a hotel they'd stayed at before on the island of Rhodes, and on the whole it was a good holiday. Anna suspected not only that the children enjoyed the undivided attention of their father, but that they all got on better without her.

In the two weeks they were away she made up for a lot. Many cases were sorted out for the opening of the law term. Council work was largely in abeyance because councillors were on holiday, and Anna found that the problem needing her most urgent attention was the future of the self-styled Pilgrims: not only was their tenure of the warehouse almost at an end but, with the winter coming on, it would be impossible for them to live there. It was practically uninhabitable.

She found she had become very involved with

the Pilgrims, and the outcome of their difficulties was important to her. As a lawyer she knew they had no chance, but as a councillor she hoped to be able to help bend the law. She felt it was terrible that so many lives were dependent on what was basically an unfair, uncaring and increasingly greedy society. Too many years of Conservative rule had provided a greater gap between the rich and the poor, the haves and have nots. She realised what little room there was for people who would not, or could not, conform, and she suspected that her experience with her two step-children gave her more insight into misfits than she had even a year before.

Peter, Fiona and Guy returned in the last week of August looking fit and rested, lots of tales to tell about the good time they'd had on Rhodes. Fiona produced some paintings she'd one, rather pretty, simple watercolours, and Anna felt that she'd made some progress, fancied she saw the shimmerings of talent.

Moreover, Fiona had decided that she would, after all, apply for art school, and Guy had agreed to the idea of being a boarder if a school could be found to take him. So progress had definitely been made.

Anna began to hope that the autumn would finally see a resolution, at least, to the problems of the family. There remained a tolerant yet disciplined school to find for Guy, and an art school for Fiona which would encourage her fledgling talent.

Anna was tired. Very. She had spent a long day in the magistrates' court and began to think she'd been short-sighted not to take a holiday. Maybe at Christmas a couple of weeks in the snow, or perhaps some sun in the West Indies? Anyway, it was something to look forward to.

It was nine o'clock. She'd phoned to say she wouldn't be in, but the answer-machine was on. Peter and Guy had been to see another school in the west country, one which specialised, discreetly, in adolescents with difficulties and charged accordingly, and Fiona had an interview with an art school in central London.

Anna expected no one to be in and was surprised to see a light in the living room. She called out, but there was no reply. Silence. She looked in, saw that it was empty and went into the kitchen to make herself a snack. She was starving. Her heart sank when she saw the usual messy pile up of supper dishes, the open fridge door. Fiona was back with a vengeance, and if she got her place at art school it would be as though she'd never left home. In her heart of hearts, Anna knew nothing would change.

She saw the back door was open as well, and went to close it. Something was stuck between the door and the outside path where the dustbins were kept, which meant it was unable to close. Anna put out a foot to remove the impediment and then stopped to look at it closer. She opened the door wider and gazed with some astonishment at a pile of junk that overflowed the dust-bins and blocked the path.

Canvases, through which someone had put a fist or a boot or both. She had no need to examine them to know that they were the works of art produced by Fiona who, doubtless, lay now on her bed upstairs. The vandalised canvases seemed to tell the whole story.

Anna's hunger promptly evaporated and, with the greatest reluctance, she dragged herself back into the kitchen, across the hall and slowly upstairs to Fiona's room.

She didn't knock but gently turned the handle.

'Go away!' Fiona shouted, as Anna pushed open the door. Something was hurled at it, but Anna sidestepped the missile and stepped inside. Fiona lay on the bed. Around her were crumpled pieces of paper, probably the watercolours she'd brought back from Rhodes.

'Go away!' Fiona bellowed again, louder, and turned her face to the wall. Anna sat on the bed beside her, and put a hand on her shoulder.

Fiona tried to wriggle away but Anna wouldn't budge. 'I guess the interview didn't go well,' she said.

'I said go *away*,' Fiona shouted again. 'You are a pig and I hate you!'

Anna flinched but stayed where she was. Despite the fact that Fiona was now seventeen, Anna had to remember she was still a child.

'Tell me why I'm a pig,' she said after a moment, her hand on Fiona's shoulder firm, reassuring.

Suddenly Fiona, face streaked with tears, rose up on the bed. She'd made herself up heavily for the interview at the art school and the result now was terrible. She looked like a victim of war with black, red and purple blobs all over her face, her spiky hair, thick with gel, looking like a toppled blancmange. Anna felt infinite pity. Pity and love.

'Tell me why I'm a pig?' she asked again.

'Because,' Fiona pointed a trembling finger at her, 'because *you* should have told me the truth instead of pretending . . .'

'Pretending what?'

'That I was any good.'

'I thought you accused me of saying that you weren't any good, that was why you needed tuition?'

'No, no!' Fiona thumped her knee. '*You* said you thought I had potential . . .'

'Anyway what happened? They turned you down?'

'They said, the Head of the art school said I had *no* talent at all and it would be a waste of time admitting me. He said . . . she said,' Fiona's lip trembled and she began to cry again, 'she said I was an *amateur* and no amount of tuition would do me any good. I had *no* sense of perspective, *no* idea of line or form, no talent at all. I was wasting my time, and hers.' Fiona flung herself face down on the bed again and her body heaved with heart-rending sobs.

Anna went on patting her back and then got up and wandered to the window, stepping care-

191

fully across the mangled balls of paper. It was almost dark outside and the lights of the houses all round were on, houses full of happy hopeful people. Or were they? Maybe everyone had problems like theirs. One always assumed one's own were the worst.

So she should have told Fiona the truth. But what did she really know about art? And was it fair to discourage someone when there was something they desperately wanted to do?

'There are other art schools,' she said without turning around. 'But I guess you destroyed your portfolio.'

'I'm hopeless, utterly *useless*. She said so. She was a hateful pig.'

'She certainly doesn't *sound* very nice.' Anna returned to the recumbent form. 'I am so very sorry, Fiona; but I'm sorry you destroyed your work.' As Fiona didn't seem to be rejecting her, she sat on the bed again. 'I think the trouble with you is that you give up too easily. I mean, who's to say this woman is right?'

'She is the Head of one of the top schools.'

'So, there are other schools.' Anna looked down at the floor. 'And now you've destroyed everything. I saw the mess outside the kitchen door. I wish to God I'd been here when you got back.' She bit her lip thinking of all the advice she'd given at the Law Centre to people who probably wouldn't take any notice of it anyway, whereas here was someone close to her whom she could actually have prevented

192

from doing herself harm.

'I know this woman was right.' Fiona shook her head. 'I know I'm no good. I just liked to pretend . . .'

'But you do enjoy painting, don't you? I mean you did all that stuff in Rhodes? Frankly, Fiona, I liked it. I thought it was better than the water-colours I'd seen in the country and that you'd progressed.' Anna reached down to the floor and taking one of the pieces of paper began to smooth it out over her knee. It was a simple seascape with brightly coloured sails in a harbour setting. It had the air of an amateur Dufy, with stronger colours than before. As she studied it she was aware that Fiona's tears had ceased and she was looking over Anna's lap at the picture on her knee.

'Yes, I *do* like painting,' she said in a different, less whining tone. 'I love it. It helps me to lose myself.'

'What the Head of the art school meant was that you were not yet up to professional standard. There's no reason why, if you really have a strong urge to paint, you shouldn't have tuition of some kind, and then maybe try an art school later on if that's what you want to do. Or . . .' she looked at the girl now lying quietly beside her, finger stuck in her mouth like a baby, curled up, indeed, in rather a foetal-like position, 'maybe you'll just remain an amateur painter all your life like your mother; but it will be something that you enjoy doing, as she did, and which you'll gradually get better and better at. The main thing is that at last you've found something you really want to do. You hated school. You hated study, but you like to paint. I think you should stick at it and, please,' she smoothed the picture with her hands again, 'no more destructive urges like this. You want to start a portfolio otherwise no one will have any idea at all what you're like.'

She gazed down at Fiona who, in her foetal position sucking her thumb, reminded her more than ever of the fair-haired, little girl she first knew and came to love. The blue eyes gazed so trustingly up at her, and the expression was so innocent and adorable that she forgot the brittle confused unhappy young woman Fiona had become and remembered only the child she'd loved, loved like a mother. And still did. She stooped suddenly and, still afraid of a rebuff, planted a kiss on Fiona's cheek and, to her surprise and gratification, Fiona flung her arm round Anna's neck and hugged her close.

The school was an undenominational one whose principles were based on a spirit of Christian toleration and understanding. It had been founded by an enlightened educationalist in the thirties who realised that children's learning problems often stemmed from mysterious forces that were not necessarily to do with parents or their upbringing or environment, but probably went back to the womb.

The present Head, Dick Preston, was a man

in the mould of the founder who had produced from the poor fodder that was sometimes sent to him, successful and happy citizens who not only prospered and did well, but went on to lead happy and fulfilled lives.

He wasn't sure about Guy Livingstone because, in so many ways, he did seem well adjusted. Yet the confidential report from his previous school told him differently. He was a youth whose looks and behaviour belied his age, and he felt that, perhaps, in the environment of an inner city comp with both a mother and father who were apparently workaholics, had high-powered jobs, he had matured too quickly. Some children, especially those living in cities, missed out on part of their childhood and grew up too fast.

The school offered a complete contrast to that of the city. It was set in fifty acres of green Wiltshire countryside, part of which was farmed and worked by some of the pupils, all of whom were encouraged to develop the skills they were good at or attracted to. This didn't mean that they were allowed to neglect academic work, but the principles of the school, although it was not Roman Catholic, were modelled on the ancient monastic foundation that divided the day into physical work, study and prayer. There was also ample time for recreation, which included plenty of sport.

The school itself had been the country house of a noble family which, like many of their kind, they had been forced to sell in order to meet debts or death duties. The house had been bought in the thirties by the school's founder with the help of backers who had faith in his educational methods and had turned the enterprise into an educational trust. It took both boys and girls and all of them had to board.

After the interview with the Head, Guy was set a number of tests which took up a couple of hours of his time, during which Peter wandered round the school and its grounds, which had made an immediately favourable impression on him. Term had not yet started, but there were a number of resident staff going about their various tasks, mostly domestic staff preparing for the new term or gardeners or farm workers who lived there all the time.

There was an atmosphere of peace and relaxation about the place, of order, routine and structured discipline. There was a chapel where prayers were said every morning and evening, and the pupils had small bedrooms instead of sleeping in large dormitories. The sixth formers had study-bedrooms to themselves in a specially built sixth form block behind the main house. Unlike some buildings in other schools they had seen which had grown up higgledy-piggledy in an assortment of styles, the new architecture here had been blended into a harmonious whole, with a neo-classical facade masking all the modern amenities of bathrooms, lavatories and central heating inside. Throughout, there were shiny parquet floors and a smell of fine old beeswax; well-polished furniture, maybe a few antiques among them, that had once belonged to the noble family. In the public rooms were comfortable chintz-covered sofas and chairs. The dining hall had long tables with benches, and various trophies of the school, and a war memorial for those who had fallen in the Second World War adorned the walls.

The outside of the house was covered with rust coloured vine, old rambling roses and ivy. While Guy did his tests, Peter stood for some time on the gravel in the drive looking up at the mullioned windows imbibing the sense of peace, and he wished Anna were there with him. He was sure she would approve. Now, more than ever, he wanted Guy to pass his tests because he knew the Head liked him and thought that Guy liked the Head, the staff he had met and the place — everything so unlike the inner city concrete jungle he was leaving.

Peter walked along the drive, past urns full of roses, petunia, lobelia and geranium now mostly past their best, and then he took the path across one of the lawns to a copse full of old yew trees, beech and oak, which framed the building.

Anna had nearly come, had wanted to come, but at the last minute, inevitably, something had turned up, a court case urgently needing her personal attention. He knew that Anna felt the opposing tug of two duties: one to family, one to her work. He knew that now in particular she would give preference in this war of opposing loyalties, to the family; but they had been to see many schools together. Then there was the problem of Fiona and trying to keep her on an even keel, her morale shattered by rejection of the art school, the cruel dismissive words of the Head, fatal to someone like Fiona, constantly in need of encouragement, who gave up all too easily. Anna had been trying to find another school or a tutor for Fiona, determined to build on that precious rapport they'd briefly shared and make it into a new and deeper understanding.

Peter was a worrier; he fretted, always imagining the worst. At these times he slept badly; he had an ulcer which modern medication now kept under control. He needed Anna's calm which he knew that he, and others, sometimes mistook for coldness, indifference, a kind of almost ruthless efficiency. This was what really had happened between her and the children recently and, to some extent, between her and himself.

He knew that in her heart she was a warm and caring person, but it was this iron will of hers, this control, that could mislead. She was a complex person who, in all the years he had known her, he felt he never completely understood. There was always that air of remoteness about her that could repel, but also intrigued.

He knew that in the year she'd been sterilised he'd felt a sense of ineffable loss that he and she had never had a child of their own, but it would be useless to try and make Anna realise it. This decision of hers, as well as many other things about Anna, he really failed to understand.

He was about to turn towards the school again when he heard a voice calling him and, in the distance, he saw Guy running towards him. He hailed him and quickened his step and when Guy caught up with him he was breathless.

'Hi, Dad!'

'Hi! How did you get on?'

'I think I was OK.' Guy stuck his hands in his pockets. 'Aptitude, intelligence tests really, a bit of maths.' He grimaced. 'I don't think that was so good.'

'Well, what do you think, son?' Peter put an arm paternally round his shoulders.

'I like it, Dad,' Guy nodded vigorously.

Peter's heart leapt. 'I like it too . . .'

'You don't think somehow,' Guy hesitated screwing up his face, 'it's too remote, too far from the real world?'

'Well,' Peter looked around him towards the beautiful old house in its lovely setting, the gracious lawns and colourful gardens, the well-stocked fish pond with an antique fountain in the middle. 'Well, it *has* got enormous charm. What's wrong with that? You've had quite enough of the real world, my son. At the most you'd only have three years here, one in the fifth, two in the sixth.'

'I'd have to work jolly hard. Mr Preston told me that.'

'I think you want to work jolly hard now, don't you, Guy?'

'I want to try and make up for the way I've messed things up. The misery I've caused you and Anna.'

Peter felt a strange emotion as though a great weight had been lifted from his heart.

It was nearly six o'clock and Anna shifted restlessly in her chair. But what her client was saying was important, important for her anyway to get the trauma of her impending divorce, her resentment against her husband who had gone off with his much younger secretary, and her anxiety about her children, all of whom were under fifteen, off her chest.

Sheila Jones was a smart, attractive woman, a buyer in a London store, a high flyer like Anna, and they seemed to understand each other well.

Anna had urged her to go for a clean break; not to be too vindictive, not to make the man suffer too much. After all he had gone, he wanted to marry the woman he was living with, they were expecting a child and she had absolutely no hope of saving the marriage. It had broken down irretrievably. He had offered a generous settlement and allowances, the family home, the children could continue their private education. What else did she want? Revenge. Mrs Jones wanted revenge.

This was where one could see the unattractive side of Mrs Jones, the reason, perhaps, why her husband had left her not only for a woman who was younger but who was also probably his intellectual and social inferior. She had obviously reached her position because she had just that extra degree of ruthlessness needed for a woman to succeed in a hard, competitive business.

Anna started, shocked more by her own thoughts than by what Mrs Jones was saying as she went on about getting her pound of flesh, squeezing until the pips squeaked, not letting him forget, making him pay, all that kind of thing.

What shocked Anna was the fact that she was thinking in terms of stereotypes, and her opinions about Mrs Jones could so easily apply to herself. Just that extra ruthlessness needed to succeed in a competitive world . . . like the law, a male profession if ever there was one, or the Council where he or she who shouted loudest was the one who got most attention and, inevitably, what they wanted. If she had to think in terms of men's and women's worlds, then she and Mrs Jones stood with a foot in each camp. If she called Mrs Jones hard then, perhaps, she was hard herself?

She had, after all, given up thought of having a child of her own not only because her step-children were so difficult, but because the idea of a small baby at her age was somehow frightening. What really was the truth about that decision, taken now a year ago? Whatever it was it had had unforeseen effects on her life, on Peter's life and that of the children.

'Mrs Jones, I really must go now,' she said looking at the clock. 'My husband has been away all day with our son looking at a new school and, well,' she smiled, 'it *is* rather important.'

'Oh, you've children of your own then?' Mrs Jones looked interested. 'Somehow I didn't think you had. You gave that impression.'

'Two,' Anna said with a firm smile, 'a boy and a girl.'

'Well, you know what it's like then.' Mrs Jones's tone changed and Anna knew that she was about to become chatty, to confide as one mother to another.

'We could make an appointment for later on in the week.' Anna rapidly turned over the pages of her diary, her heart quailing as she saw how full it was, meetings all day, every day, going on into the evenings. A Council meeting on Thursday, a visit to one of the deprived area schools on Friday. 'I'm *afraid* it will have to be next week,' she said, flipping over the pages and seeing how full that week was too. She frowned. 'Look, I'll get my secretary to call yours tomorrow and try and find a time.' She closed the book, her expression rueful. 'You know how it is.'

'Busy, busy,' Mrs Jones gave her a conspiratorial smile. 'I suppose *your* husband's jealous too?'

'I don't think he's jealous. Sometimes he gets a bit irritated.'

'You'd better hang on to him . . .' Mrs Jones was about to return to her favourite tack, but Anna steered her carefully, firmly to the door. Any minute now and she knew that Mrs Jones, a hurt and bitter woman, would start insinuating things about her own marriage, if she didn't take care.

Perhaps Mrs Jones would be right.

Peter looked up as Anna came in, arms flung out in apology.

'Sorry,' she said rushing over to kiss him, 'got held up by a client.'

'As usual.' Peter grimaced, returning her kiss.

'As usual.' She put bag and briefcase down and sat on the edge of the chair opposite him. 'How did it go?'

Peter leaned back in his chair, arms behind his head. 'It went well. It's a lovely place and the news is that they'll take Guy. Guy thinks he wants to go.'

'Thank *God* for that.' Anna also leaned back, sighing deeply. In the dreary rounds of the last few weeks she was so used to schools either which Guy didn't like or which didn't like him. Then she looked at Peter. 'What do you mean "thinks"?'

'He's thinking about it. He's gone out to consult with some of his friends. He feels it's too elitist.'

Anna groaned. 'In that case he'll come back . . .'

'No, I think he really liked it. He genuinely seems to have undergone a change of heart. He said he wanted to try and make up for the bloody awful mess, the misery he's made of our lives.'

'Guy said that?' Anna looked incredulous.

'He specifically mentioned you. "The misery I've caused you and Anna." His very words.'

'Well, I *am* impressed.' Anna got up. 'Did you eat?' She looked guiltily at her watch.

'I had a snack with Fiona.'

'Is she in?'

'No, she went out with her friends. I'm afraid she's getting more depressed again.' His voice became reproachful. 'She said you said you'd help her find another school or a tutor. Have you done anything?'

Anna rounded on him. 'For Christ's sake, Peter, you really should see my diary. I can't even fit in a woman I'm divorcing for at least another *ten* days.'

'But still you said you'd help her, Anna. It's important. Look,' Peter rose and went over to her, 'I know you're very busy and the kids take up a lot of time . . .'

'Peter, I've trudged all round the country looking for schools. I've taken days off I'm not entitled to, and now you both seem to have got on very well without me. Maybe you could do the same about art schools?'

'Anna, it was simply coincidental that we found a school when you weren't there. It could have happened at any other time.'

'No, I seriously think that you and the kids get on better when I'm not there. With each one of us individually it's alright. Fiona is fine with me. I mean when I see her, when we have a chance to talk.' Seeing the look of exasperation on Peter's face she sat down again. 'Peter, what is it you want me to do? Give up work?'

'Of course not!'

'The children are almost grown up.'

'I know, but they still need help.'

'Help I'm giving them, you're giving them. What else can we do?'

Peter rose and stood looking down at her.

'Look, Anna you've got to face it. Neither of these kids is much of a success. Both were expelled from school, well, virtually. Guy *was* expelled, and they wouldn't take Fiona back, which comes to the same thing. How do you think I feel as their father? I feel a failure, that's what. I'm trying desperately to overcome this feeling of failure. Anna, I need help too.'

Peter sank on to a chair and put his head in his hands. Watching him, Anna was aware of that feeling of anger and frustration she experienced so frequently with the children. She felt in a way that they were all children — Peter, Guy, Fiona, all needing her, all needing help.

She was not going to give Peter the sympathy he so obviously was agitating for, indulging in an orgy of self-pity really, so she picked up her bag and briefcase, dumped them in the hall at the foot of the stairs and went into the kitchen, which was in the usual chaotic state after Fiona, Guy, and even, Peter, had finished with it. There was no earthly excuse she thought angrily as she opened the dishwasher and started to stack, no excuse at all. When they'd finished their food they could put the dishes in the dishwasher instead of leaving them piled in the sink with remnants of food stuck to them. No one was actually asking them to wash anything.

Was it because they knew how angry it made her? Or was it simply because they didn't care? Or were they trying to tell her something?

She paused in the act of scraping the leftovers into the bin by the side of the sink and gazed out of the window into the dusk. Sometimes, really, she felt she'd like to leave home, strike out. Start all over again.

CHAPTER 9

'God save the world,' Arizona said. 'Joy to all.' She extended her arms over them as if in benediction as her rapt audience responded 'Joy to all,' and then, at the end of her homily, split up into small groups chattering animatedly.

Anna stood at the back of the room watching them wondering, as she always did, at the impact this small, fat, friendly woman seemed to have on the members of the Pilgrim community. For if Damian was the acknowledged leader, Arizona was the mother. Maybe because of her diminutive height, Arizona favoured flowing robes, large hats — with bells, tassels or feathers bobbing precariously about — long dangling earrings and pointed shoes with extremely high heels on which she managed, with difficulty, to teeter along. Above all, there was her long pretentious name which was almost certainly assumed: Arizona Washington.

No one knew her real name, or where she'd come from. She had been at the squat ever since it was formed. She had simply turned up one day with all her worldly goods in a bag slung over her shoulder, and a small, ugly, extremely pugnacious and snappy Jack Russell called Waffles at the end of a long piece of string. She was, and remained, devoted to the dog, giving him all her best scraps. Arizona had a vaguely transatlantic accent, was obviously well educated, had presence and charm and was a great asset to the community. In age she was between thirty and forty, it was impossible to be more accurate. She had an unlined, ageless face, an expression of calm that probably had more to do with drugs than religion.

'Hi!' Anna went over to Arizona as, her little homily finished, she lit a cigarette and perched on an upturned box. Waffles, snarling at Anna, jumped on to Arizona's knees and she kissed him fondly before setting him down again.

'Hi, Anna!' Arizona looked pleased to see her, and lifting her hand waved it about vaguely. 'Peace and joy.'

'Peace and joy,' Anna dutifully replied.

'Did you like my sermon?'

'Oh, it *was* a sermon?' Anna sat on the box next to Arizona and shook her head as she offered her a cigarette. 'I often wonder.'

'We always have a little gathering on a Sunday,' Arizona said piously. 'Of course I'm not religious, strictly speaking.'

'But you said "God save the world"?'

'I mean in the sense of the One, the Great Creator. The Other. There has to *be* a giver of life; but formal religion makes me puke.' Arizona made as if to spit on the floor. 'What did they ever do for the poor? What did *Jesus* do, for Christ's sake?' Anna felt inclined to agree, but she was not here to discuss polemics or matters theological. She was aware however that Arizona was gazing at her keenly. 'What brings you here on a Sunday, Anna?'

'It was the only time I could find,' Anna admitted. 'I'm already cast aside by my family.'

'In that case you must join us,' Arizona replied enthusiastically, her attention deflected by the approach of Damian who too raised his hand as he saw Anna.

'Love and peace.'

'Love and peace,' Anna replied. Whatever they thought of organised religion, the community was curiously ritualistic.

'Love and peace,' Arizona repeated, picking Waffles up and hugging him. 'Jump for joy.'

It really was amazing the way this bedraggled and disadvantaged group of people kept their spirits up, Anna thought, not for the first time. With few worldly goods, no place to live that gave them any security, comfort or stability, constantly harassed by the authorities, they maintained an outward show, at any rate, of joy, though what they really thought when lying on their makeshift beds in the cold and dark was anyone's guess.

'Do you know,' Anna hugged her knees, 'I just thought the other day I'd like to give *everything* up, run away . . .'

'Flee, flee, sister,' Arizona's head turned as though watching a bird in flight and then she looked anxiously at Anna, 'but don't forsake us, sister, for God's sake.'

'If Anna joined us she wouldn't forsake us.' Damian, perched next to Anna gazing at her with a similar expression to Arizona's, a semblance of serenity that in his case once again made her think of the Biblical representations of the Christ figure. 'We could certainly do with a lawyer in our midst,' he said invitingly.

'You have a lawyer in your midst,' she replied.

'But one to share our life.' And Damian leapt up and gave a little twirl, hands in the air, before settling down again. Surely there was a double entendre now in every word he uttered?

Anna experienced that slight frisson in Damian's presence that was a kind of attraction. Again she felt that sense of disquiet, of unease whenever her thoughts, however brief, lingered on him. She lowered her eyes to avoid his gaze, conscious of him, angry with herself for reacting like this.

'I've never actually seen *you* skip or jump, Anna,' Arizona said reproachfully. 'Do you really experience joy? You can't share our life unless you do.'

'I promise I'll give it my attention.' Anna suppressed a smile. 'But seriously, brother and sister, I am not here with good news.'

'We have to move?' Damian's expression showed resignation rather than surprise.

'You *do* have to move,' Anna looked around her, 'for health reasons as much as anything. It will soon be winter and this place will be damp, dark and rat infested. Now look, there are a couple of houses that I think the Council will grant you strictly on a temporary basis.'

'*Houses!*' Arizona looked aghast. 'How can we all fit into *houses*, sister? We are a community . . .'

'Yes, well . . . some of you will have to split.'

'The community cannot split.' Damian shook his head emphatically. 'We are indivisible.'

'But you keep on growing,' Anna wailed. 'I'm sure there are several people here today I haven't seen before.'

'So the Council absolutely refuses to let us do up these premises?'

'It is far too costly. They have to be demolished. Basically they are unsafe and, Arizona, as the mother, I think you should be concerned about the welfare of your children.'

'All my children.' Arizona looked at her gravely and lit a fresh cigarette. 'All are one.'

It was a terrible problem, but sitting there with the September sunshine outside, winter seemed very far away. There were at least forty, maybe more, people including three children who ought to be at school, five toddlers, two babes in arms and assorted animals — dogs, cats, a goat and three gerbils, one of whom was pregnant.

'I'll see if I can get another house.' Anna got to her feet. 'But it's *not* a long-term solution.' She gestured around her. 'Arizona, this is really no way to live.'

Arizona regarded her through heavily kohled, half-closed eyes, puffing away on her long expensive filter cigarette. 'Is that so? You just said yourself you longed to get away. Well we have. Don't you think we've got responsibilities we've left behind? People, problems? We've abandoned the lot. This life we live, though apparently uncomfortable as far as you are concerned, is freedom; we have put aside material things for the life of the spirit. We are pilgrims looking for the Promised Land, are we not, Damian?'

Damian seemed to agree, but his attention was caught by a tall, solemn looking young man dressed incongruously in a pale coloured double-breasted business suit with a black roll-top sweater, who was strolling casually over towards them. Anna's first impression was that he might be a Council official or a welfare worker, even though the designer stubble, long pony-tail and pearl earring dangling from his left ear might possibly, though not certainly, preclude such an occupation.

'Greetings, brother,' Damian hailed him, arm raised.

The young man too raised an arm, though he said nothing.

'Joy and peace,' Damian continued. 'Do you know Anna?'

The young man looked gravely towards Anna, and shook his head.

'This is Errol,' Damian said with an unmistakable note of pride in his voice. 'Our artist.'

'Artist?' Anna looked interested.

'He's very talented.'

So far, Anna realised, the young man had not uttered a word. It occurred to her to wonder if he was dumb, but just then he spoke in a very low, quiet voice with a pronounced northern accent.

'How do you do, Anna?' He reached out to shake her hand.

The members of the community gave many gestures of greeting including hailing, skipping, jumping, hugging and kissing, but shaking hands was seldom one of them. The handclasp was firm and cool, authoritative. Errol was decidedly different.

'How do you do, Errol?'

The introductions over, Arizona offered Errol a cigarette which he took, lit and sat opposite Anna on one of the upturned boxes. His scrutiny was rather unnerving.

'I know it's rude, but what sort of art?' she asked.

'I trained at the Slade,' Errol said, as if that explained everything.

'Really?'

'He has exhibited at some important London galleries, haven't you, Errol?' Arizona said proudly. '*And* he has drawn all of us for posterity.'

'I see. You keep a record of . . .' Anna looked around.

'When I feel like it.' Errol shrugged. His hand trembled slightly, he had a deep sadness in his eyes, and his shoulders drooped.

'Errol gets depressed,' Damian explained. 'That's why he joined us. No will to go on living.'

'I'm very sorry,' Anna said sincerely. 'Is it better here?'

Errol said nothing but went on smoking moodily, staring at the ground.

'I have a daughter who wants to paint,' Anna heard herself saying. 'She feels she hasn't any talent.'

'Perhaps she hasn't,' Errol said prosaically. 'Not everyone who wants to paint can.'

'Exactly.' Arizona addressed Waffles who wagged his tail in obvious ecstatic agreement.

'I wonder if you'd like to . . . I mean, well, it would be nice to have your opinion,' Anna heard herself saying.

'Oh, Errol will give you an opinion, won't you, Errol?' Arizona spoke encouragingly. 'Anna is *the* lawyer trying to help us to keep the warehouse.'

'Oh!' Errol momentarily brightened. 'What is it you want me to do exactly?'

'Fiona, my daughter, would really like some coaching . . . a bit of encouragement . . .' Anna tapered off. She wondered what had made her suggest this — Peter was sure to be furious. For once in her life she had acted with thoughtless spontaneity. Too late, now, to retract.

'I don't mind looking at her stuff,' Errol said offhandedly. Obviously he was not a man anxious to please. 'But don't expect me to say I like it if I don't, or to say she has talent if she hasn't.'

'She's got very little left to show,' Anna said,

wishing now that she hadn't spoken. 'She destroyed most of what she'd done.'

'Oh! Why was that?'

'She also got depressed about her work. She hasn't had a very easy time.'

A glimmer of interest suddenly flickered in Errol's dull eyes. 'Now that I understand,' he said.

Errol looked round the large room and thought how nice it would be to live in a place like this. It had blue walls and a white ceiling with a plaster cornice. Town houses built early in the nineteenth century to house large families. Now they housed the small families of the rich.

The furniture was old but good; some was even shabby. There were books everywhere, from floor to ceiling, piled on small tables, on the floor. Books that were used, read, not just there to be seen. There was a fireplace, but he imagined no real fire was ever lit in this part of London where they had long gone out of fashion, and a tall window about thirteen feet high from floor almost to the ceiling looking out on a long, well-stocked garden. There was a decent carpet on the floor, again old, but of the quality which endured for years, and rugs on top of that. Perhaps a bit threadbare but good. The whole place was good, solid, monied.

In the corner was a large TV set with a video underneath, and a good supply of tapes, a stereo in the corner with speakers on either side of the room. Tapes here too, doubtless Bach, Mozart, Beethoven, perhaps Tippett and Benjamin Britten. The girl would have her own stereo upstairs and her own CDs, probably her own TV too. She would have been born here, or at least lived here for years, used to a room of her own, this kind of style, not realising how luxurious it would seem to someone who came from the backwoods and lived on the streets.

Errol turned from his inspection, his thoughts racing, as the door opened and Fiona came in, her mother behind her. Fiona no longer had spiky hair; it was short, fair and cut close to her head. She had on a dress to her knees over leggings, a flowered waistcoat unbuttoned. She wore pink eye shadow, mascara and a heavy blusher on her cheeks, her lips coloured magenta. He thought she was startling, but not unusual.

'This is Fiona,' Anna said. 'Fiona, Errol.'

'Hi!'

They shook hands. Errol realised his palms were slightly sweaty because he was anxious. The cool sang-froid he had adopted at the squat was gone.

It was the weekend after Anna and Errol had met, and in the meantime Anna had managed to get a stay of execution about the eviction from the squat. Only it was near the end of September and the weather, benign at the moment, would soon be turning from autumn to winter.

Peter, having been briefed to stay away while the introductions were made, came in and met

Errol. By that time, Errol and Fiona were chatting quite happily, both smoking, and Anna said she had to go to a very brief meeting in Hampstead but would soon be back. Would Errol like to stay on to supper later? Errol thought he might.

She said goodbye and surreptitiously jerked her head to Peter who, mystified, followed her into the hall.

'What the hell?' he said.

'Leave them alone, for God's sake. It's awkward enough. Why don't you run me up the hill and go for a walk while I have my meeting? That will give me an excuse to get away.'

'Why don't you give up the blasted meeting and come for a walk instead with me?'

'I'd love it, but you know I can't. They already delayed the meeting until three because of me.'

'But who the hell *is* he?' Peter slipped on his jacket and followed Anna to the car.

'He's an artist. I haven't seen his work but they say he's a good one. I thought he might help Fiona.' Ashamed of her impetuosity, she hadn't dared tell Peter the whole truth.

'Oh!' Peter seemed cheered by the news as he slid into the driving seat beside Anna and drove away, Anna glancing at the notes she'd produced from her bag. There was a campaign to section off part of the Heath, merely to build some very expensive houses and, of course, she was on the committee opposing such an act of vandalism. Once you began these things there was no knowing where they would stop.

Peter drove up Haverstock Hill and asked her where she wanted to be dropped off. 'But *why* on a Saturday afternoon?'

'There was no other time.' She leapt out, peeped through the window. 'I promise. Be back here in an hour, say, an hour and a half and we'll go for a cup of tea?'

She smiled brightly and walked quickly away.

'Big deal,' Peter said to himself and drove along the High Street, thinking that perhaps after all as the weather was nice he would take a walk on the Heath. Blow away some of the cobwebs.

Errol and Fiona sat looking at each other rather awkwardly as Peter and Anna left, Peter having popped his head round the door to say that he was going too.

'They seem rather nice, your mother and father.'

Fiona nodded.

'Get on, do you?'

Fiona nodded again, suddenly tongue-tied and wishing that Anna and Peter had stayed or, at least, one of them.

'Just you, is there?' Errol was making all the running which for him was unusual. Usually he waited for others to speak.

'I've got a brother. He's away at school.'

'Boarding school?'

She nodded.

'That fits.' Errol nodded too.

'What fits?' Fiona looked defensively at him.

'Well, all this, you know,' he looked round, 'the set-up. Rich people.'

'It's not like that at all.'

'Shall we look at your paintings then?'

Fiona coloured, the moment she'd been dreading.

'They're not very good.'

'Still, let's have a look. That's why I'm here.'

'And there aren't very many.'

'I know. Your mum said you tore them up.'

'Oh, she told you?'

'It's the only reason I agreed to come.' He looked at her. 'I fancied you were some rich, privileged kid, and then she said you had difficulties. Otherwise I wouldn't have bothered.'

'Where do you live then?'

Errol gave a half-smile, cupped the match in his hand, while he lit another cigarette.

'She didn't tell you?'

'All she told me was that you were an artist, not how or where she met you.'

'I live in a squat.'

Fiona's mouth fell open.

'Not *the* squat?'

'The one she's trying to save.'

'By the railway line?'

'That's it.' He looked sullenly across at her. 'Does it matter?'

'Of course it doesn't. I think it's very exciting and I hope you win.'

'I don't.'

Fiona expressed amazement.

'What, you don't *want* to win?'

'Have you ever seen the fucking place? The trains keep you awake all night. There's a hole in the roof, and it's going to leak in the winter. It's either perishing cold or too bloody hot.'

'Can't you sell your paintings?' Fiona's voice sank to an awestruck whisper.

'It's not that. It's other things. I don't want to talk about them really.' Errol got up and wandered across the room, turning sharply to stare at her. 'Well, am I to see those paintings or not?'

'You'll tell me *honestly* what you think?' Her expression was anxious, vulnerable, like a small child's.

'I'll tell you honestly what I think.'

Errol then suddenly smiled at her and Fiona thought that, although he was sexy, moody, had a lot of charm, he was full of hidden hurt like she was.

They were back by six. Anna's meeting had of course gone on longer than expected, and she had some shopping to do for an extra mouth at dinner. Peter thought they might all go out but Anna felt it was better the first time . . .

'First time what, for God's sake?'

'He may be able to help her. We'll see how they get on.'

'They're not getting *married*, Anna.'

Anna looked at him disparagingly.

'Of course they're not.'

'One thing leads to another.'

'Don't be silly. She's far too young.' All the same, she had felt it especially important to get home sooner rather than later. You couldn't chaperone young people these days, and they would do their own thing no matter what. But, still, maybe she had been idiotic to introduce Fiona to someone from the squat. A young man she knew nothing about; she didn't even know if he could draw, if he was an artist at all. God Almighty. In any case, how stupid to introduce one depressive to another.

She was appalled by her lack of judgment in her enthusiasm to get some sense of purpose into Fiona's life, and could hardly wait to get out of the car and rush up the path to the house, a heavy carrier bag in each hand. Peter watched her with some bewilderment, locked the car door and followed her.

The house was silent. No sound of voices. Anna stood in the hall and listened. Nothing. She glanced into the living room. It was empty. The kitchen looked as though no one had been there since she'd left. No empty teacups.

My God. She went into the hall and called: 'Anyone at home?'

No reply.

She climbed up the stairs two at a time and halted outside Fiona's room, took a deep breath and knocked.

'Come in,' Fiona called, and, before Anna even had time to turn the handle, the door opened in her face. Fiona all smiles. Errol, looking relaxed, was lying on her bed propped up on an elbow, his jacket off but otherwise fully clothed. In front of him were Fiona's still rather crumpled sketches which she'd tried to iron out and mount on thin board. Then a few of the canvases that had been thrown out had been salvaged and repaired with Sellotape. These stood on the floor, displayed in front of them. The stereo in the corner played quite softly for Fiona, and there was a very faint sweetish smell in the air.

'They're good,' Errol said bluntly, not bothering to get up as Anna walked slowly into the room. She would ignore the sweet smell because she knew quite well what it was. Pot. Her keen eyes took in every detail of the room and she was pretty sure they hadn't been to bed, or at least not in bed, and in a way she was more worried about that, though even in these enlightened times would people leap into bed *that* fast? That didn't mean they hadn't kissed or fondled, but somehow she didn't think they had. The atmosphere didn't exude sexual tension but relaxation, leisure, friendship, maybe — was it too much to hope for? — a mutual appreciation of art?

Fiona was looking pleased, her face flushed.

Anna perched on the bed beside Errol, and saw to her surprise that those doleful eyes actually seemed more alive.

'Do you *really* think they're good?' she asked.

'Oh, I do.' He held up one of the ironed-out

paintings, one she'd done in Rhodes. 'I think she has a lot of talent. I'd like to help her.'

Now Anna knew she'd made a mistake, but it was too late to go back. 'You really could help her?' she faltered.

'Oh, sure. I think so.' Errol smiled conspiratorially up at the beaming Fiona looking admiringly down at him. 'I think I could help her, and that we'd get on.'

Fiona looked around her with awe. She had never seen anything like it in her life except on the TV or in the cinema. To one end of the large shed were rows of mattresses. Beside each one were a few possessions: bundles, boxes, clothes sometimes thrown on the bed, sometimes on the floor. There were one or two cots and, what struck her most, a total absence of privacy.

In the centre of the room was a long trestle table filled with bowls, plates, various cooking ingredients. Behind them were butane or paraffin stoves on which were a number of bubbling pots. A jolly hoard of women and one or two men were stirring the pots adding ingredients to them all the time, tasting, adding more seasoning. They all looked in high good humour.

In front of the trestle table were smaller tables with rickety chairs drawn up to them. The people sitting at the tables were mostly older, both men and women, some in groups, some solitary. Several small children ran about, watched over by the younger women, and there was an assortment

223

of dogs, cats and small furry animals in cages at the far end.

Fiona felt that all that was needed was for someone to stride forward with a megaphone and cry 'action'.

From the grimy windows high up in the walls a little daylight struggled in, but although there was a curious atmosphere of cheerfulness mingled with resignation, when one paused to consider that here was a mass of breathing, living humanity who had nowhere to live, it was pretty awful.

Errol stood to one side of Fiona, closely watching her reaction. He hadn't wanted her to come, but she had insisted.

Finally she turned and looked at him.

'Which is yours?'

'Which what?'

'Where do you sleep?'

'Oh, come on,' he began to feel agitated.

'No, I want to see . . .'

They made their way through the people scattered about, some of whom greeted them, some ignored them. Errol's patch was a neat mattress on which was a pillow, a duvet and two boxes, a chest of drawers. Fiona stood looking about her. Not far above the place that apparently contained all Errol's worldly goods was the corner where the ceiling had started to fall away.

'You couldn't live *here* in the depths of winter,' she said aghast, pointing to the ceiling. 'And it's nearly winter now.'

'That's what your mother says.'

'But why can't it be repaired?'

Errol shrugged and began to roll a cig
using tobacco from a tin he kept in his po

'I mean,' Fiona looked around, 'it *could* ve a
nice place with a bit of imagination.'

'But you see we don't own it. It belongs to the
Council.'

'But Anna's on the Council.' Fiona looked
indignant. 'She could *easily* . . .'

'No, she can't. She's tried.' Errol shook his
head. 'She . . .'

'Joy to all. Greetings, brother.' He was interrupted by the arrival of Arizona who had been
surreptitiously watching them ever since they had
come into the building. She paused and stared
with frank interest at Fiona. 'Who have we here?
Another recruit for our community?' Arizona
shook her head slowly from side to side. 'No.
Somehow I don't think so.'

'Why don't you think so?' Fiona challenged
her.

'I simply don't think so.'

'This is Anna's daughter, Fiona,' Errol said,
and then to her, 'meet Arizona, she calls herself
the mother of the community.'

'Don't scoff at me, Errol,' Arizona said reprov-
ingly and then to Fiona: 'Anna's daughter?' Arizona examined her closely. 'I don't see the
resemblance . . .'

'She's not my real mother. My mother died.
Anna is my stepmother.'

Ah!' Arizona nodded. 'I remember now. She asked Errol if he would look at your paintings.'

'Yes.' Fiona felt confused.

'Is she any good?' Arizona looked towards Errol.

'Very good,' Errol replied. 'She has talent.'

Fiona laughed in embarrassment.

'Oh, I don't think I really have. Errol's simply being very nice about me but . . .'

'So what happened?'

'He's tutoring me. Every day for the past week.'

'And now she wanted to see where you lived?'

'Exactly.'

'And what do you think of our little home?' Arizona got out a packet of cigarettes and lit one.

'I think it could be terrific. I can't understand why the Council won't do anything about restoring it.'

'The Council want to turn it into offices and homes for the rich,' Arizona said derisively. 'You know how it is near the canal? It could be just as swanky round here.'

'They want to take the area upmarket.' Errol's tone was equally sarcastic.

'But Anna doesn't believe that!' Fiona looked enraged.

'There's not a lot that Anna can do about it. She's tried. She has been very good. Some of those so-called "socialists" don't want to know, do nothing about it; but Anna has done all she can. The truth is we will have to leave in a few weeks and our community be split up. Just now we're trying to do all we can to keep it together, find a place big enough.'

'I think it's lovely,' Fiona said wistfully. 'I really do.'

'Join us, daughter.' Arizona piously raised a hand. 'See how the other half lives. Skip and jump for joy.'

'Don't talk nonsense, Arizona,' Errol said angrily. 'Fiona doesn't want to "play" at being poor, at having no home.'

'But think of the publicity for the cause. "The daughter of Mrs Councillor Livingstone . . ." '

'No, I wouldn't like that at all,' Fiona said quickly. 'And Anna would hate it. Besides, Errol's right. I have no real place in this community. I would be pretending, and people would despise me, but I assure you I will do all I can to help Anna to find you somewhere proper to live.'

'Very well. Then why not join us for lunch? Nothing wrong with that, is there?' Arizona extended a hand graciously as though she were showing Fiona to a table at the Café Royal. 'I think you will find that the fare we have to offer is excellent. Plain but wholesome.'

An orderly queue had formed at the trestle table and three women were doling out what looked like thick soup or stew into earthenware bowls. The children pushed eagerly up in front of their mothers, and another cheerful soul was handing out large chunks of bread.

'Don't you think I am taking food from people's mouths?' Fiona whispered anxiously.

227

'Oh, there is plenty for all,' Arizona said expansively.

The smell was good and the food did, indeed, look nutritious, chunks of meat and vegetables in a thick broth.

'Where does it all come from?'

'Local shops and markets.' Arizona and Errol took their places in the queue with Fiona. 'People are very good to us. They give us stuff that no one wants to buy. Oh, don't worry,' she laughed at the suddenly anxious expression on Fiona's face, 'there is nothing *wrong* with it. It would pass inspection, the vegetables are sometimes bruised but we make sure that the meat is always fresh. There are many good people locally who help to keep us fed and want nothing except a word of thanks in return. The baker will always give us bread left over from the day before, which means there is nothing wrong with it.' Arizona sniffed disapprovingly. 'Just that those with money like it fresh out of the oven. Spoilt brats.'

The woman who gave Fiona her bowl had a friendly smile for her.

'You new here, dearie?'

'This is Anna's daughter,' Arizona said with a proprietorial air, pushing her forward.

'Oh, Anna's *daughter*.' The word went round the group, heads nodding approvingly. Yet above the voices one suddenly rose stridently. It was the woman giving out the bread. She looked no more than about twenty-five, yet three small chil-

228

dren, fingers in their mouths, hovered near her. 'Anna's *daughter*,' she said scathingly. 'What need has *she* of our food?'

Fiona flushed, and was about to return the bowl she'd been given, when Arizona snatched it from her and put it firmly back in her hand.

'Who do you think you are, mean minded slag?' she said, roughly addressing the speaker. 'Anna has been goodness itself to us. Can't we give something to her daughter in return?'

'You think you'll get preferential treatment, don't you, Arizona?' the bread woman replied, unabashed. 'By sucking up to her daughter . . .'

'If you don't take care I'll slap you across the gob,' Arizona threateningly raised her hand. At that moment, fraught with tension, Damian appeared and stood between Arizona and the bread woman, who happened to be Rosie.

'What's going on here?' he demanded. 'I can hear your shrieks at the back of the yard. Do you want a riot, the police called? What will happen to us then, do you suppose?'

Rosie's children by now had run up to her and were clinging to her long woollen skirt.

'I don't see why this rich bitch . . .' Rosie began and Damian thundered at her: 'Silence! Do you hear?' He then turned to Fiona with a smile of great charm. 'Did they say you were Anna's daughter? How do you do? I'm Damian.'

'Greetings.' Fiona, into the lingo by now, extended her hand.

'Fiona wanted to see where we lived,' Errol

explained. 'Nothing wrong with that.'

'Nothing wrong at *all*,' Arizona chipped in, 'for all that *we* owe Anna.'

'I really am sick of the way you all kow-tow to Anna,' Rosie said in a tone of heavy sarcasm. 'Anna this, Anna that, Anna is so good and now we have *Anna's daughter*. What did Anna really do for us? Nothing. We have been under the death sentence for months, and we still are. The mighty Mrs Councillor Livingstone with a nice house in Hampstead . . .'

'Belsize Park,' Fiona said quickly.

'The same thing,' Rosie snarled. 'A nice *big* house, I hear, with a garden and two bathrooms, perhaps three. Everyone has their own bedroom. The children go to the best schools. I hear our champion councillor is a successful lawyer with a practice in the West End. She must make a mint of money. *And* her husband . . .'

'Oh, do shut up,' Damian commanded.

'Rosie *does* have a point,' a diminutive woman standing nearby piped up. 'We don't like being patronised by the children of the rich. We have our dignity. We have our pride. Does little miss here realise that? We'll have the TV cameras here next and an article in the *Big Issue*. We . . .'

Fiona put her bowl back on the table and looked at Errol.

'I really think she's right,' she said, and turned sharply on her heels towards the door. Arizona walked swiftly after her, teetering on her wobbly high heels.

Errol and Damian followed.

'Daughter . . . Fiona . . .' Arizona called after her, 'please don't go just like that.' Fiona paused and Arizona caught up with her.

'She is right,' Fiona said earnestly. 'I *do* see what she means. I mean we may have the best intentions, and we do. I know Anna does; but compared to what little people here have just what do we know? We know nothing and I feel bitterly ashamed and she,' Fiona pointed in Rosie's direction, 'is absolutely right and I'm sorry.'

Fiona continued to walk quickly to the corner of the yard where she'd parked the car her father had given her for her seventeenth birthday just after she'd passed her test. She had been so proud of it, but now she saw it through eyes blurred by tears. She felt ashamed of it as a symbol of affluence, and herself. She would like to have gone right past the car and have pretended that she had nothing to do with it. It had been really crass to bring it here, a trendy Volkswagen Beetle, a real yuppy design car in hectic psychedelic colours. She was aware of footsteps next to her, Errol, the first to catch up with her.

'Take no notice . . .' he began.

'But I *do,* Errol.' She stopped and looked at him. 'I feel ashamed . . .'

'*She* should feel ashamed.' Angrily Errol looked behind him. 'She shoots off her big mouth and she knows *nothing*. Believe me, she knows *nothing*. She is a slag, she has a child by every man

231

she meets and expects the State to look after her and them. She can't keep her legs together. She's a whore. Seriously, Fiona, she's a prostitute. We have to look after her kids at night while she skips off to King's Cross.'

'I still think she was right,' Fiona's eyes smouldered, 'and personally I'm sorry she has to do that.'

'Look,' Errol opened the car door for her and closed it after she had got in, 'don't waste your sympathy on these people. You know . . .' he darted round to the passenger's side, opened the door and slid in, 'most of them are here because it is their *own* fault. It's *my* fault I'm here. We've given up. We're defeated by society. Others aren't. They go out and lick it. We've allowed it to conquer *us*. We all have something wrong with us, that's why we're here, Fiona. We're bums. Not worth wasting your tears over. Nothing to be ashamed about, honestly . . .'

Fiona was looking at him uncomprehendingly as she switched on the ignition and slowly let in the clutch before reversing the car out of the yard. Errol stopped speaking as she manoeuvred, anxious because she was such a new driver; but she had been well taught and passed her test on the first attempt. She came out of the yard and turned carefully into the main road, heading north towards home. She clutched the wheel firmly, her eyes on the road in front of her. She drove slowly, carefully, making the right steady gear changes because she knew that Errol was nervous. Then half way up Haverstock Hill she pulled into the kerb and stopped, switched off the engine and turned towards him.

'Why are you telling me all this, Errol?'

'Because I saw how upset you were. Honestly, no one there gives a shit. They are all on benefits, they scrounge off the State. They are jealous and envious. No one can help them because they're a load of bums, beyond help.'

'But *I* thought you identified with them?'

'Me identify with them?' Errol laughed loudly. 'I despise them. I'd give everything I could to get out of there. I'm ashamed of myself for living there, for taking someone like you there.'

'You didn't want to take me.'

'I didn't, and I was right. But I didn't dream that what happened would happen.'

'Then why are you there?'

'Because I gave up. Gave in. Look, I have a problem. I'm a depressive. There are times when I can't cope and everything caves in. I couldn't sell my paintings. I got a bad review for a show. Someone said I couldn't paint, so I knew how you felt when you were told you couldn't. I'm not as successful as Anna thought I was.' He put a hand on her shoulder. 'I feel ashamed, Fiona, that I've involved you with this world, with me. Your mother will never forgive me for taking you there and she will be right. It's spoilt everything.'

'What has it spoilt?'

'Our relationship. It was coming on good.'

'Don't be silly,' impulsively she seized one of

his hands. 'Of course it hasn't spoilt our relation-ship. It is good. Look I have an idea . . .' she put her other hand to her head and closed her eyes. 'I don't know how this sounds to you. It might sound mad, but you see I thought you *believed* in the squat. I thought it was a matter of principle and you identified with everyone there. Now I see that you don't, and that what Anna is trying to do is pretty futile. Maybe it is. I mean she has given much of her life to help the helpless, most of whom, according to you, don't need or deserve help . . .'

'Not everyone,' he said quickly.

'No, not everyone. I agree but,' she looked at him with her open, honest large blue eyes. 'If you really don't like it there you don't have to stay there. I've a cottage in Dorset. It belongs to me and my brother. I was working there for six months before I came back to London. London has made me depressed, made me destroy my work. Obviously you hate it too. What do you say, Errol, to life in the countryside?'

CHAPTER 10

'Young homeless people have no place in our increasingly materialistic and greedy society.' Anna paused and looked round at the faces of her fellow councillors listening attentively to her in the chamber at an emergency meeting of the Council. She was a good speaker — she had had a lot of practice — and she usually captured her audiences' attention and held it. Today was no exception, except for the handful of Tories who, acting as though they had heard it all before, and far too often, shuffled their papers, yawned, or simply stared at her with bored expressions, eyes sometimes half-closed, arms folded across their breasts.

'But it is not only the young who suffer. People of all ages are roaming the streets because they fall between the nets the increasingly hard-stretched Social Service Departments throw to them. They . . .'

She knew it was hopeless. Sympathetic though most of her audience was, the building occupied by the squatters was unsafe, the Council couldn't possibly vote enough funds to repair it. However she would go down fighting, which she did.

There were many who spoke in her support, people who genuinely wished to help the Pilgrim community but who would be accused of gross abuse of public funds if they did. The alternatives were in place: two derelict houses had been repaired for the most needy in the community, places in hotels or hostels for mothers with young children. Yet temporary accommodation was not a real answer to their needs. The problems of the homeless in inner London were insuperable.

The Council voted almost unanimously to close the squat, only Anna and a handful voting against as a protest rather than because they thought it would do any good.

Afterwards many of her fellow councillors came up to her and offered commiserations.

'First rate speech, Anna.' Jim Crowther was a supporter and a close colleague. He did a lot of work for the homeless and disadvantaged in all walks of life. He was also a journalist on a local newspaper and had written many articles in support of the Pilgrims. 'You should stand for Parliament where we can do something to change these disgusting laws which cap councils like ours trying to bring a little sanity to society.'

'I think my husband would really take off if I did.' Anna gathered her papers together and put a hand on Jim's arm. 'Thank you so much, Jim, for your support as always. To me now falls the ghastly duty of telling them they really have to get out. You wouldn't like to come with me, would you?'

'Of course I will. Gladly.'

'It will have to be first thing in the morning. I

have a court case, but I think my deputy can hold the fort until the afternoon, or we could get an adjournment.'

'Would you like me to tell them for you?'

'Oh, no.' Anna looked gratefully at him. 'I must do it. After all, this time they'll think I've chickened out if I don't.'

'I think you'd better take the police with you, Anna.' Dorothy Singleton, the deputy-leader of the Council came up to her, 'They might turn nasty.'

'Oh, I wouldn't dream of having the police,' Anna said coldly. 'That really *would* be provocative.'

'Well,' Dorothy looked grim. 'Don't say I didn't warn you.'

Anna slept very badly that night and was up early to prepare herself for what would be a harrowing day. She crept out of bed, leaving Peter still asleep. It was so early that the central heating hadn't come on, and even the bath water was cold. Well it was nothing to what the people she had to talk to had to endure and, indeed, after the move most of them would be better off. The new premises had recently been put in good order, were newly decorated and passably furnished. There was electric light, running hot and cold water, gas fires and a proper kitchen. She herself had been several times to make sure the renovation was being carried out to acceptable standards.

However there were still those in the Pilgrim community who would say she had let them down, and others who would never fit in because they would never assimilate into any ordered existence, nor had they any desire to. Anna found it very hard to understand people like this, like Arizona and Damian, Rosie, Maeve, Hope, Biff Cassidy and others whom she knew would not want to live in an orderly society with decent accommodation and nearby schools and amenities, however much one tried. They were the vagabonds, the modern gypsies who also lacked the freedom of the road, being harassed by the authorities from pillar to post as their pathetic processions of unserviceable, unlicensed and uninsured vehicles made their way from county to county, only to be roughly moved on by unsympathetic councils and outraged local residents.

Anna quickly emerged from her tepid bath and dressed with care. By seven she was sitting at the kitchen table drinking black coffee and studying her brief for the law case that afternoon which concerned a woman trying to avoid being sent to prison for prostitution. She was an habitual offender, and the chances seemed slim as there were also several charges of breaking and entering for the purposes of theft to be considered. Yet another person whom Anna had spent many weeks desperately trying to help. But the woman needed the money. She had one child whom she adored and was bringing up alone. But it was not the answer, so one could only assume that, as she spurned other assistance, she rather enjoyed her job. She was also on drugs. In many ways prison might be the best place for her, but Anna didn't see it that way. She thought prison was to be avoided at all costs. The trouble was that there were not enough rehabilitation centres for people like her client, who would probably end up in some sort of squat until inevitably the drugs she pumped into her frail body killed her, and left the daughter she worked so hard to rear to fend for herself.

Anna poured herself another cup of coffee and popped two slices of bread in the toaster. She wasn't hungry, but she didn't know when she'd next eat. The squat situation was bound to be an ordeal and then straight from there to court which would recommence at about two. Then when the court closed back to the office to see what additional work had accumulated during the day. In the meantime there would be a number of calls to make on her mobile, and she would want to keep in touch with what progress, if any, was being made on arrangements for the orderly dispersal of the Pilgrims. A court order would be obtained this very morning ordering their evacuation by Saturday. Many officials thought that the sooner they were out the better, before part of the building collapsed and there was an even greater scandal for which they would be sure to be blamed, Anna prominent among the accused.

It was rather eerie in the house in the quiet of

the morning. Around her everything gleamed, and remained that way. Although it was curious to have no children in the house after all these years — the first and only time unless they had been on holiday — it was at the same time welcome and unwelcome. Above all she loved the order, the feeling that when she came home the place would look as it had when she went out, or even better as the cleaner would have been and would have met no opposition from Fiona or Guy about the state of their rooms or the kitchen or wherever else they chose to make their messes. This part was lovely, so was the absence of tension. But also Anna missed the presence of young people in a way she never thought she would, friends going in and out, and she knew Peter missed them too. Well, they might soon be back. There was no knowing how long Fiona would remain in Dorset, and Guy would be home first for half term and then holidays, of which private schools had a lot that seemed to go on for an awful long time.

It was getting light outside and Fiona finished her toast and marmalade, drained her coffee and then made a pot of tea for Peter which she put on a tray and took upstairs.

Peter was awake, lying in bed gazing at the ceiling.

'You're up early,' he said.

'I've got to go and tell the Pilgrims they have to leave,' she looked grim, '*and* I have to be in court this afternoon. I should be there this morning but Roger is holding the fort for me.'

'Another busy day, Anna.' There was a hint of sarcasm in his voice as he reached up and took the tea from her.

'I'm afraid so, dear.' She bent over and lightly kissed his brow. 'I'll try and make it back in time for dinner.' And before he could begin the customary whinge about how much she had to do, she fled downstairs and out of the house collecting her raincoat and briefcase on the way.

When she got to the warehouse Jim was already there. So too, to her irritation, was a policeman standing guard at the gate.

'We said "no police",' she hissed.

The policeman touched his helmet respectfully. 'I'm sorry, Councillor Livingstone, but we have instructions. It is just for your safety, ma'am. We will not enter the building unless it becomes necessary.'

'But it won't, and they are not being asked to leave today.'

'I know that, madam; but I have my instructions. I am here on duty by myself with orders to call my colleagues only if and when it should become necessary.'

'But . . .'

Jim Crowther put his hand on Anna's arm.

'You can't argue with him, Anna. It seems that the news may have got round.'

'But how?'

Jim shrugged.

'You know what the grapevine is like. Can't

stop it, I'm afraid.'

By now the rain had started to fall steadily, so Anna returned to her car and drove it into a corner of the yard where Jim joined her after a further word with the constable on duty who had closed the gate after them.

'Let's hope this won't take long.' Jim put his umbrella over Anna's head as she emerged from the car. 'What a day.'

'A bloody awful day.' Anna gazed up to the skies. 'However it might make them realise that a move would be the best thing. The roof is sure to be leaking.'

And indeed it was. The first thing she saw as she and Jim quietly entered as inconspicuously as possible from the rear door was a collection of buckets, pots and pans under the portion of the ceiling where daylight usually came in.

Only today it was so dark that no light came, just a steady stream of rain not only from that corner but other parts of the ceiling too.

Some members of the community had not bothered to get up, but others were at the portable stoves making breakfast. The main lighting, which was not very good, was by paraffin lamps and candles, a hazard in itself. The Council had refused to pay for any more electricity and it had been disconnected two weeks earlier. Anna noticed several vacant spaces and guessed that some had already moved on. There was an air of palpable dejection and gloom in the building, and from the stares that greeted herself and Jim, she realised that everyone knew.

Having their meagre breakfast, heads close together in earnest discussion so that they had not noticed their entrance, were Arizona and Damian. Anna and Jim walked across the room to them to be greeted in stony silence.

'I gather you heard.' Anna sat in one of the rickety chairs next to Arizona who was feeding Waffles on slices of buttered bread, thereby probably depriving herself.

'You might have told us,' she said reproachfully without looking up.

'The vote was only taken at nine o'clock last night. I didn't think you'd know. Besides I couldn't have come here at that time. The gate is always locked.'

Arizona and Damian exchanged glances, ignoring Anna and Jim.

'I came as soon as I could.' Anna glanced at her watch. 'It is only half past eight now, and Jim has come with me because he has all the details about the move.'

'We're not going to go, you know.' Arizona passed Waffles another choice slice of bread and butter, and licked her fingers.

Anna leaned forward.

'Arizona, you know you *have* to go. It is your duty to go and lead your children to a better style of accommodation. I have seen, you have seen, what we're offering. The Council has done its very best.'

'Anna made a marvellous speech.' Jim's voice

was full of admiration. 'I was proud of her. Many councillors had tears in their eyes.'

'How very touching,' Arizona sniffed disdainfully. 'Wish I'd been there to hear it. The only tears I would have had in my eyes would have been for those with nowhere to live, not for those who live in posh houses and have the gift of the gab.'

'I do get so irritated when you speak like this,' Anna interrupted angrily. 'You *know* you can't continue to live here. It's falling to pieces around you. Look at the rain coming through the ceiling. Half the people here have got colds, and God knows what the effect on the children will be. They'll develop rickets.'

'You should have got somewhere for *all* of us.' Arizona gazed at her accusingly.

'Look, I'm going to talk to them now and explain. I can't guarantee you, no one can, *purpose*-built accommodation for a community that is largely composed of a group of itinerant people who have joined together to form themselves into a loose bond . . .'

'Loose!' Damian exploded. 'How do you think Christ's disciples came together?'

'I didn't think we were talking religion.' Anna looked surprised. 'You always told me you were an atheist, Damian, despite the fact that you call yourselves "The Pilgrims".'

'Pilgrims looking for a better land, as our forefathers did in the seventeenth century. Here we are talking of a so-called "Christian" society that treats people like outcasts.'

'But, Damian, as a qualified mathematician you know perfectly well that you could get a job, and probably a very good one. The fact that you don't happen to want to, that you prefer to live like this, is your decision entirely. As far as I know, you are neither an alcoholic, nor are you drug dependent. Your parents are ready and willing not only to help you financially but to give you a home. And this you have rejected to become leader of a band of people without direction in their lives, some through their own fault, others not. If you like this lifestyle, and I know you do, so be it, but please don't tell *me* about treating people like outcasts. *I* too could be an outcast if I wished, but I prefer instead to work from within society for the betterment of those outside it. I think you do it so that you can manipulate people, Damian. It satisfies some need for domination you can't find elsewhere . . .'

'Anna, please,' Jim interrupted, grasping her arm. 'Don't get yourself so worked up. It's not worth it.' He gestured towards the centre of the room, to where the rest of the community had gathered, slowly advancing towards them. 'Look: make it short and positive.'

'Right!' Anna stood up and faced the concourse of hostile faces gathering around her. Rosie was there, a contemptuous smile on her face, her children clustered, as usual, round her skirt. Merrylee, the mother of one of the babies, stood with the baby slung on her hip drinking

245

contentedly from her exposed nipple. Biff Cassidy leaned nonchalantly against one of the tables and most of the others stood, squatted on the floor, or perched on the end of the table. Quite a few, mostly the older ones, remained in bed. It was bitterly cold and Anna felt she had never faced such a situation in such a depressing location in her life.

'Right,' she said again, 'I gather you all know why Jim and I are here.'

'*And* the policeman at the gate,' someone shouted.

'I specifically asked there should be no police,' Anna said. 'Jim will bear me out on this.' She glanced at Jim who nodded his head vigorously. 'But there is just one policeman at the gate, and although I asked him to go away he wouldn't.'

She paused and took a deep breath. Used as she was to making speeches, this was one of the most difficult.

'Last night the Council voted to seek an order to have the squat evicted. There is no appeal. The last day will be Saturday, that is in four days' time. In the opinion of the Council you have had plenty of notice and plenty of time to prepare. Other accommodation is available for you.'

'Not for us all,' someone shouted.

'For most of you.' Anna swallowed. 'Mothers with young children will be put in Bed and Breakfast accommodation, hostels or hotels until they can be rehoused. They will have priority. In the meantime . . .'

'Rich bitch,' someone yelled from the back.

Anna paused, her heart pounding.

'If you mean *me*, I am not rich and I am not a bitch. I have done all in my power to help you. I tried desperately, both as a lawyer and a borough councillor, to enable you to stay on here, to try and persuade the Council to agree to do the place up; but the estimates ran into millions, money which the Council felt could be better used elsewhere.'

'In the pockets of the fucking capitalists,' Biff Cassidy bawled in his rich Irish brogue. In his time he had worked as a builders' labourer, so he knew all about those who soaked the poor.

'This building will be demolished and the site redeveloped.' Anna felt her throat drying up. 'That I can do nothing about. We are not a rich council and we have an undue preponderance of people in need in the city as a whole. Others might object very much had we lavished millions into making what would in fact have been a sort of squatters' hotel. I spoke on your behalf to the very best of my ability; but the vote went against me by a large majority. I am,' as murmuring began around her she was forced to raise her voice even higher to make herself heard, 'I am very, very sorry. Many of you have become my friends. I have the welfare of you all very much to heart. The places we have got where most of you will be accommodated are of superior standard.'

'Good enough for *you?*' The woman's voice

was shrilly accusatory.

'Only *temporary*,' cried someone else.

'They, too, are due ultimately to be demolished, but no time has been set.'

'What sort of way is *that* to live?'

'No way at all, I agree . . .'

'Not like the nice place you have got for your daughter and Errol.'

Anna stopped, momentarily winded. 'I had a lot of problems with my daughter . . .' she began.

'Yeah, and you'll have a whole heap more with Errol . . .' screamed someone, and a general gust of ribald laughter swept the building.

'Please, friends . . .'

Anna suddenly felt a sharp sting on the side of her face and something smelly and horrible started to slide down her cheek. This was followed by another missile which hit her shoulder, another her hair. One hit Jim, another Arizona, for whom it certainly was not intended. Anna's eyes began to stream but she could still see that, from several parts of the hall, rotten eggs, fruit and vegetable were being hurled at them, obviously gathered early that morning or perhaps late the night before from the market.

Jim got one straight in the eyes, another landed squarely on her face. The smell was appalling. Suddenly Damian jumped up on the table and bellowed through cupped hand: 'Comrades, brothers and sisters, friends, I *beg* you do not . . .'

'Go and fuck yourself,' jeered a woman, and

then, 'put it up your mother's . . .' Then Biff Cassidy ran forward like a rugger scrum half, and threw a violent punch in Jim's midriff, causing him to buckle.

'Judas!' Biff cried. 'Filthy, rotten, stinking swine in league with the capitalists . . .'

Some women began to scream in frenzy and the children, scattered to the far corner of the room, took up the refrain with gusto. The din was indescribable. The situation indeed looked menacing and Anna thought of the policeman at the gate and wished fervently that he were here. Suddenly a melee began in which Damian and Jim seemed to be the victims, and shaking from head to foot, trying her best to rub away the horrible egg and mess from her face with a handkerchief, she stumbled through the fracas towards the door and eventually found herself out in the yard where she raised her face for a moment to the life-giving rain.

At that moment the gates swung open and a number of police cars sped into the yard disgorging their personnel who headed towards the door.

'Are you alright, Councillor?' She recognized the bobby who had stood at the gate, and looked at him with stricken eyes. 'I *knew* you'd have trouble, Mrs Livingstone.' He put an avuncular arm around her shoulder. 'You should have listened. You can't ever trust people content to live like animals. In time they come to resemble them, madam.'

And to her shame and horror Anna rested her

head on the policeman's shoulder and wept.

Anna hardly ever rested, was never, or seldom, ill, and to find herself in the middle of the afternoon still in bed was an unusual, almost an extraordinary occurrence. One that hadn't happened since she'd had her sterilization the year before. Then she'd had an excuse, but this time she felt she didn't, really, that she was merely indulging herself.

The house seemed incredibly silent, still, except for the distant sound of traffic racing up and down Haverstock Hill. It was odd, but it was not unpleasant to be in bed surrounded by the papers, the TV in front of her if she wanted to watch it, which she didn't. Daytime television seemed almost as sinful as staying in bed when there was nothing physically wrong with you.

The police had brought her home the day before and, despite her protestations, Peter had been summoned from work. The doctor too appeared and gave her a sedative. He said she should rest, take some days off yet not brood. Peter suggested that when she felt fit she should pay a visit to her mother in the north, a woman she loved deeply but felt she neglected.

Anna felt a bit of a fraud lying in bed, plucking at the bedcovers like some nineteenth-century damsel suffering from the vapours. Paula had been, cleaned, done some washing, brought her a light lunch and the latest editions of the newspapers and left.

The story had made national headlines: Tory supporters naturally cackling with glee.

Labour councillor pelted with rotten eggs

The members of the self-styled 'Pilgrim' squat in north London, whom Mrs Anna Livingstone had tried so hard to help, had a surprise for her when she went to see them yesterday: they pelted her with rotten eggs, cabbage and tomatoes.

Mrs Livingstone, thirty-seven, one of the most selfless, committed and respected Labour councillors, who devotes her spare time entirely to good causes, had tried to stop these people from being evicted from a condemned warehouse. This is the sort of reward she got. They have now been dispersed to alternative accommodation, at the taxpayers' expense, to other recently renovated quarters in the borough. Mrs Livingstone, who also has a successful private practice as a solicitor, was seen to be in tears as she left with a police escort. At her express request, no charges have been preferred, although two men and a woman who assaulted police officers were arrested.

Mrs Livingstone was unavailable for comment.

Mrs Livingstone was certainly unavailable for

comment, but Mr Livingstone had appeared, reluctantly, at the garden gate to address reporters not only from the papers but from radio and television news. He'd made a short, dignified statement appealing for calm, denying that his wife would press charges ('Foolish', David Cole had remonstrated on the phone) and that was that.

Well, for the time being, though soon the story would be superseded by another disaster, a happening in another part of the city, and all attention would be focused on that.

It was after three, but Anna wasn't sleepy. She felt she should get up, but she didn't know what to do. She'd telephone her mother, arrange to go north in a day or two, return the call Fiona had made while the daily was here and Anna was in the bath. Nice. Gratifying that Fiona was concerned.

The strident sound of the doorbell interrupted her reverie. She stiffened involuntarily, plucking again at the bedclothes, aware that the pace of her heart had quickened. Really, her nerves were shot to pieces. This was ridiculous. She lay where she was and listened. Maybe it was the press. The doorbell rang again and she got out of bed and, running lightly along the corridor, looked gingerly down towards the front door from the first floor window. She saw the brilliant, variegated tops of a large bouquet and, smiling to herself at her foolishness, returned to her bedroom, put on her gown and ran downstairs ridiculing her fears. Another bunch of flowers. The house was full of them already.

She opened the door, ready to take the present and then she stopped, the welcoming smile vanishing.

Damian was wearing jeans and a shirt, his hair tied at the back in a pony tail, his beard neatly combed. His expression was one of concern, contrite, difficult to fathom. He thrust the flowers towards her and she held out her arms to take them, not knowing what to say. For one who was so articulate she was momentarily lost for words.

'I just wanted to say . . .' he began as the flowers passed from his arms to hers.

'Come in,' she said tersely, stepping to one side and pointing the way indoors.

'Oh!' He scratched his head and looked uncertain as to what he should do.

'There's no one at home,' she added, wondering why she bothered to reassure him, and he nodded as if with relief and stepped inside looking round at the large airy hall towards the open door of the living room.

'Do go in', she said, gesturing towards the room, 'and I'll pop these into the kitchen. It's very kind of you.'

'Anna,' Damian hesitated, stroking his beard. 'I just don't know what to say . . .'

'I'll make us some tea,' she said, propelling him gently towards the living-room door. 'Don't say anything.'

She went quickly into the kitchen, aware of the overpowering scent of the flowers. Beautiful roses, carnations. They must have cost a fortune. No question that these had fallen off the back of a lorry.

She realised she was trembling and her face was hot. She had been so totally unprepared to see him, here, in her home. She felt like a schoolgirl caught in some misdemeanour. She realised her hands were trembling as she filled the kettle, got out the cups and saucers, searched around for the teapot.

Why hadn't she told him to go away?

Biscuits. There were biscuits somewhere. In the tin. Where was the tin? Why, in the usual place, on the kitchen table.

The clock in the hall struck four. Supposing Peter came home early? What would he do if he saw Damian *here*? Silly. She wasn't doing anything wrong. But all the same she'd give him his tea and tell him to go.

Stupid to let him in. She should just have taken the flowers and . . .

'The flowers are really beautiful,' she said, kicking the living room door wider with her foot and bearing the tray towards a small occasional table as Damian jumped up to take it from her.

'Here, let me. You shouldn't.'

'They're just gorgeous. I love roses. Must have cost a bomb . . .' She halted. The implication was 'where did *you* get the money?' How tactless.

What a stupid thing to say. She realised she was gabbling and that her gown had fallen open, a lock of hair hung across her brow.

She stooped, straightened up and looked at him.

'I must look a sight,' she said and she saw he was looking at her in that way, smiling.

'You look very nice,' he said. 'I've always thought you looked nice, from the moment you walked into the squat.'

She fastened her gown, tucked the lock back behind her ear and began to pour.

'Do sit down.' She jerked her head in the direction of Peter's chair, but Damian remained where he was, looking round.

'Nice place you've got here, Anna.'

'It was Peter's house before we married. Milk and sugar?' She looked up to see him still looking down at her with that curious, enigmatic smile. 'I mean, he lived here with his first wife.' She felt a bit calmer now, more in control, and passed him his cup. Of course she'd been taken unawares, she'd been silly, childish. Her hand no longer shook. She took up her own tea and sat down, indicating he should sit opposite her. But Damian remained where he was, cup and saucer in his hand, still gazing down at her.

'Anna, I can't tell you how awful I feel. I personally should have done something to stop what happened. I feel very responsible for it all. It was a terrible experience for you. I shall never forgive myself . . . Anna.'

She couldn't stop the tears. They just flowed spontaneously, burst out as from a great underground well. It was all the pent-up emotion, resentment, fear.

'I'm sorry,' she murmured, shaking her head. 'I'm in a stupid emotional state. I shall be perfectly alright.' She groped in the pocket of her gown for her handkerchief and blew her nose hard. 'I guess the doctor gave me some drug. And . . .'

'Anna, Anna, it's perfectly alright.' He was on his knees beside her, grasping her hand, stroking her brow, his touch so cool, tender. 'Relax, unwind, Anna.'

'Oh, *Damian*.' She put her head on his shoulder, as she had on that of the policeman, and once more gave herself up to unrestrained tears.

Damian' s arms were around her, his lips, also cool, on her forehead. He slid one of his hands inside her gown and felt for her breast. She knew her nipple became instantly erect to his touch. She felt as though she had absolutely no willpower, that she was made of rubber. She raised her mouth and he kissed her. His lips were very firm and the feel of his beard and moustache was odd, prickly yet sexy. She had never kissed a man with so much facial hair.

She moved off the chair on to the floor. He took off his jeans and knelt beside her, raising her gown high over her hips and gazing at her, his hand very cool as it touched her flat stomach.

She knew that what was to happen was inevitable and she gave herself gladly to him.

Gladly and, at that moment, without guilt.

CHAPTER 11

The light filtered in through the tiny mullioned windows of Anna's mother's cottage on the outskirts of Leeds. Anna guessed it must be about eight, and she lay for some time gazing at the light, trying to guess the hour, too lazy to look at the clock. Then she made herself tea and got back into bed.

It was good to be out of London and away from the repercussions of the aftermath of the squat. But, more than that, she had had to put distance between herself and Damian as fast as she could, and to try and come to terms with what was a glorious adventure but, at the same time, an incredible folly.

It was glorious, reckless, total abandonment producing the deepest moment of orgasm she had had for years, perhaps ever. The others seemed like tiny tremors rippling on the surface. This time, the earth really had moved.

He had knelt over her when they had finished, staring into her eyes, and she had taken his face between her hands, kissed him and released him. She had told him matter-of-factly that he must go, her husband would soon be home. She had become the one in control of the situation, and it was he who was confused and trembling.

She'd felt utterly in command, asking him to take the teatray back into the kitchen while she straightened the room, opened the windows wide. The smell of sex seemed to her as pervasive as the chaos inside her own body. They'd stood briefly in the hall, arms linked, farewell kisses on the cheeks.

'I *must* see you again,' he said but she bundled him towards the door and shut it quickly after him, not even seeing him to the gate.

Then she'd gone slowly upstairs and had a long, long bath. She'd felt wonderful.

But the feeling didn't last. She felt less wonderful when Peter came home and a bit shabby. But her emotions varied. She kept on savouring the moment, that gigantic upheaval of the flesh, wondering if she could ever repeat it. But it was, after all, a sensation, and it passed. She'd known she had to get away, and the next day she pronounced herself fit and, despite Peter's misgivings, had driven north.

What to do about Damian on her return? Well, time, she guessed, would take care of that, but an affair was impossible. Besides, she wasn't sure she wanted one. She had too many messy marriages in her practice to contemplate one of her own.

She loved Peter. Just now there was a bad patch, but it would pass. What had happened between her and Damian was purely physical; in a way like dogs copulating in the street or the park only, she supposed, with more emotion, more cerebral pleasure, but just as quickly. She'd never had anything quite like it.

Anna took another sip of the hot tea, relishing the warmth from her electric blanket. It was a pretty room with white furniture and white-washed walls, chintzy curtains. It was not a house associated with her childhood, for her mother had moved here a few years before in order to be nearer the countryside which she loved.

The house where Anna had grown up was semi-detached, also on the outskirts of Leeds. It was in a row of similar houses, all with a neat patch of garden in front, and a bigger one behind. It was not Council and it was not working class. In so far as people thought in stereotypes, and unfortunately they did, it was lower middle-class suburbia where bikes leaned against the railings, dogs ran about and children played in the streets.

Anna had not been born there either, although she had indeed been born in Leeds. Her father had left her mother when she was little, and the smaller house was part of the divorce settlement. Anna had never seen the house she had been born in, where she and her parents had lived before the split. Nor had she ever particularly wanted to. She was not a sentimental person which was, she supposed, the reason why she had chosen law as a profession. But she had heard it was a big house. Her father had been a suc-cessful businessman, like Peter, but he left her mother for another woman and subsequently showed very little interest in his daughter, even though he had no more children. Not long after his remarriage he died in a motor accident which left her mother financially rather badly off.

Anna and her mother had been close, but the relationship was a difficult one. They were very different kinds of people. Sylvia Wood was hurt by her husband's desertion and also diminished by it. She blamed herself, her lack of personality and attractiveness. It reinforced her low self-esteem, her basic lack of confidence.

For all that, she was an extremely good mother to Anna. She encouraged her and fostered her ambition, and Anna rewarded her by being a good and dutiful daughter, serious minded, devoted to her studies and, ultimately, successful.

Sylvia Wood had worked most of her life in the shoe section of a large department store in Leeds. She was one of those women who try hard to please, neatly dressed, self-effacing, efficient, rushing about with boxes of shoes, squatting on their knees to try them on the feet of sometimes capricious customers who spent more on footwear in one session than Mrs Wood could earn in a week.

Maybe it was her mother's unremitting air of sacrifice that had made Anna determined to succeed where her mother hadn't.

Sylvia always said Anna was like her father. She had a hard edge.

Yet, needless to say, Sylvia was extremely proud of her successful daughter, her first-class law degree, her subsequent success, her election to the Council, her marriage to a man so like her father, in many ways. She had one sorrow, one rarely-voiced complaint: that she had no grandchildren and now she never would.

Anna turned restlessly in bed, gazed at the clock and was surprised to see that almost an hour had advanced since she woke. Her mother, who now worked part-time, didn't start work until the afternoon and she could hear sounds of stirring downstairs. She'd be laying the table in the little breakfast room, cutting bread, making tea, maybe watching the last few minutes of the breakfast programme on television.

Suddenly feeling guilty, Anna jumped out of bed, put on her gown, brushed her teeth and, taking the tray with the dirty teapot and cup, went downstairs to the kitchen where, as she thought, Sylvia, elbow on the table, was watching the nine o'clock news.

'Anything interesting? Morning, Mum.' Anna kissed her on the nape of the neck, and Sylvia turned, a smile of welcome on her face.

'Nothing much, dear.' She reached for the remote control to turn off the television. 'How did you sleep?'

'Fine.' Anna gently ruffled the top of her mother's hair and, going to the fridge, poured herself a glass of orange juice.

'Sure?' Sylvia looked at her anxiously.

'Sure. I didn't wake until nearly eight.'

'Oh, that's good.'

Sylvia always had this air of excessive concern

for Anna, as though she were incapable of looking after herself, which her daughter found irritating. But she was so kind, so goodhearted, that she was careful not to show it.

Anna had driven up the day before, taking a few days off on David's advice to get over the publicity engendered by the squat, reporters at the door of her home, at the office. Peter had also taken time off and had gone down to Dorset to see Fiona, so the house was empty. Like many victims of the tabloid press before them, and doubtless many after, they hoped the fuss would die down. And it would. After all, no one had died.

'I thought I'd take you out to dinner, Mum. Anywhere nice you'd like to go?'

Sylvia thought, named a new restaurant not far away that she'd heard was good but, needless to say, had never tried. She only really ate out when her daughter and son-in-law came to see her. Ate out in style, that is. If she and a girl-friend went to see a film or a show, a preview of a London run in a Leeds theatre, they'd eat at a Burger King or a McDonald's, just have a snack.

Sylvia was very careful about money and always had been. She not only managed to live within her means, but also to save. It was a matter of pride, she felt, not to be a burden on her daughter and, hopefully, to leave her something when she died.

She made the toast, brewed the coffee, and mother and daughter sat facing each other across the breakfast table.

'I shan't be able to get away until six,' Sylvia said, continuing to look anxious. Being of a nervous disposition, she was always expecting something to go wrong, of giving offence or causing pain, ruffling feathers.

'That's OK.' Anna reached out an arm. 'Mum, do you still have to work at that place?'

'But what else could I do?'

'Do you have to work? You always told me you'd saved and saved, and you are nearly sixty.'

'I rather *like* work,' Sylvia said defensively. 'I can't think what I'd do with myself all day alone at home. In fact, I don't know what I'll do when I give it up, and there is talk of redundancies being made to make way for younger women.' Momentarily Sylvia looked indignant. 'They don't value the experience of older people who have been fitting shoes for thirty years; how important it is to the customer. I have some ladies who have been coming to me for years, and their daughters too. What will they do when I go?'

It did indeed seem sad, unfair that, in order to make way for young people who probably couldn't care less about a good fitting and wouldn't stay long anyway, the older, more reliable and loyal people had to go.

'I hope you're not brooding about the squat, Anna,' her mother said, anxious to change the subject. 'It wasn't your fault, you know, that those people behaved so badly.'

'No.' Anna sat back nodding her head. 'I'm not thinking about that, Mum. I'm thinking about you.'

'Me?' Sylvia proffered surprise.

'You've worked so hard all your life for, really, very little. *That* doesn't seem fair.'

'You can't compare my life with yours, you know, Anna. I never wanted very much. I was never ambitious, which was probably the trouble.'

'How do you mean the "trouble"?' Anna looked at her curiously.

'As far as your father was concerned.' Her mother lowered her voice, as though someone might be listening. 'You know. I think he thought I was rather dull. Pretty, but dull.'

'Mum, you *underestimate* yourself! You were *not* at all *dull*. You brought me up, gave me a good chance.'

'And you made the best of it, darling.' Her mother reached out to touch her hand. 'I'm so proud of you, Anna.' She removed her hand and gave a deep sigh. Immediately Anna knew what was coming, and braced herself. 'I only wish . . .' Sylvia began.

Anna interrupted her immediately. 'Well I didn't, Mum, and that's that.'

'But stepchildren are never like your own. I always wished that I'd spoken to you in the early years of your marriage, but somehow it didn't seem my place.'

'Spoken about what?'

'About having your own children; but at that time I didn't think you wouldn't. I mean, you were young. There was plenty of time. The years seemed to slip by. There still would have been time if you . . .'

Anna was beginning to regret the impulse that took her up the M1 to see her mother; partly guilt because she hadn't seen her for so long and partly because of a desire to get away. She in one direction, Peter in another, in order to throw what lingering press hounds there might have been off the scent. There would be a sad little homily now from her mother about no grandchildren, the loneliness of old age, etc., etc.

She got up from the table and went to stare out of the kitchen window.

'It's a bloody awful day. I think I'll go back to bed and read.'

'That's a good idea. I'll go shopping. You wouldn't like to come with me, dear?' She paused, looking a little wistful.

'I think not, Mum.' Anna nervously ran her hands through her hair. 'I'd just like to take it easy, mooch about.'

'Of course,' Sylvia said with forced cheerfulness. '*Must* you go back tomorrow?'

'Yes, I must. The heat will be off. These things are always a two-day wonder, and then something else of interest happens.'

After Sylvia had gone, Anna felt guilty that she hadn't gone with her. She'd set off with her shopping bag and a brave face. Stoical as usual. It would be nice to have a shopping companion but she wouldn't insist. Anna needed her rest.

Anna watched from the window of her bedroom as she got into her little car and drove away. It really wouldn't have been too much trouble to have a quick bath, throw on a sweater and jeans and go with her mother. It would have given her so much pleasure to be seen with the daughter of whom she was so proud.

Too late now. She'd make it up to her that evening. She also decided she would make an effort to see her mother more often, ask her to London, to Dorset. She'd never even seen the Dorset cottage. But then, at the moment, Anna wasn't terribly keen to visit it herself. She could imagine the state of the place with Fiona and Errol; but apparently they were getting on well, not only as far as the tuition was concerned, but personally.

It wasn't what either Peter or Anna would have wished, and Anna felt that had she not been so busy, so rushed, she would have stopped to think of the consequences of introducing Fiona to a personable needy young man. Fiona had acquired both a cause and a lover: a purpose in life.

Fiona had finally pronounced herself 'in love'.

Anna didn't go back to bed, but had a long leisurely bath and washed her hair which was the easy, thick, slightly wavy sort that set itself naturally. She was reading the Guardian when the

267

phone rang and, cup of coffee in her hand, she answered it.

'Hello?'

'Hello, Anna?'

'Peter. Hello, darling. How are you?'

'I'm alright.' She thought his voice sounded strained and her brow puckered in concern.

'How are you, *really?*'

'Really, I'm fine. How's Mother?'

'She's fine. Peter . . .'

'Yes, Anna?'

'You don't sound quite yourself. Is everything alright? Those awful hounds of the press . . .'

'No, it's not them. Anna . . .'

Now she felt really anxious and put her coffee cup down on the table.

'What *is* it, Peter?'

'Fiona's pregnant.'

Silence.

'Anna, did you hear me?'

'Yes, I heard.' Anna bit her lip. 'Well, it's not the end of the world, darling.'

'But she wants to keep it. She wants to have a baby. She actually seems thrilled.'

'And Errol?'

'I think he's a bit bemused by the whole thing, as far as I can tell. He hardly says a word. I really don't *like* that fellow you know, Anna.'

Anna knew Peter didn't like him because he was the very opposite to the sort of man Peter would consider suitable for his daughter. He was a working-class northerner with a strong north-country accent. He had never worked and even his talent as an artist was suspect. He certainly painted, large abstracts whose worth it was impossible to evaluate. No one was even sure if he'd *been* at the Slade, if he'd ever really exhibited in London, or anywhere else. In short, he was possibly a con man who knew a good thing, a vulnerable girl with her own home, when he saw it.

Peter had wanted to have him investigated but Anna had stopped him saying what, after all, was the point? What was the point of investigating a past they both agreed, in hindsight, was probably made up anyway?

'If only you hadn't got involved with that squat, Anna, this would never have happened.'

'Well, I did and it has. We could never have known. She might have met someone else.'

'But not like *him*.'

His tone sounded outraged, accusatory.

'The point is, Peter, they're happy, or seem to be.' Even that was doubtful. Fiona was ecstatically happy, but Errol gave little away.

'And the place is the most awful tip.'

'I can imagine. Are you there now?'

'Oh, no!' Loud laugh. 'I'm at the pub, getting drunk.'

'That won't help matters much. How far gone is Fiona, Peter?'

'She says about three months.'

'It must have happened immediately.'

'I think he was her first man, Anna, you know. She knew absolutely nothing.'

'Probably.' Though with these worldly-wise young people of today, using make-up and smoking at thirteen, you never really knew.

'It's a hell of a mess, Anna.' He did sound rather drunk.

'I'm sorry, Peter, we'll discuss it next week.'

'Well, what are we to do?'

'We can't do anything. If Fiona really does want to have the baby and keep it, we must help her all we can.'

'Oh, hi!' Anna heard Peter say from the phone in his social voice, then to her, 'Anna, Fred has just come in and I'm going to buy him a drink. Will you be home tomorrow?'

'If I can. Yes.'

'Why? Is there anything wrong with your mother?'

'She just misses me, that's all. She makes me feel guilty.'

'But I miss you too. And I damn well wish you were here.'

'I'll see you tomorrow, darling. 'Bye.'

' 'Bye.' Kisses down the phone.

He did love her and he needed her.

Momentarily she felt quite dreadful about Damian, and sorry now it had ever happened. Really sorry. Anna sighed and brewed fresh coffee, looking anxiously at the clock. Just as well she hadn't gone with her mother. Just another problem, too, to solve.

She was not sure whether Sylvia would come home or go straight to work after shopping. Probably have a solitary cup of tea and sandwich in a snack bar. She could have taken her for lunch as well as dinner, helped her with the shopping. Guilt. Guilt all round. It was awful, in a way, to have so many people depending upon you, to be responsible for so many lives.

It was a small restaurant near Wetherby, and Sylvia was obviously enjoying herself, tucking in with gusto. She was very thin, even gaunt, a woman in whose life the pleasures of the table had never predominated. Really there had been very little pleasure in Sylvia's life, apart from the justified pride she felt in Anna's career. She'd chosen a pretty dress for the evening's outing, and a few pieces of costume jewellery to go with it. Anna wore the trouser suit she'd driven up in, but it was smart, a tailored black suit, the sort of thing that looked nice anywhere, and she'd chosen a red shirt to go with it. It became her tall, slim figure. But still she felt her mother was critical. She should have worn a dress.

However, Sylvia had the good sense to say nothing, and after they'd chosen and Anna ordered wine, Sylvia told her about the events of the day, nothing very exceptional apart from so and so she'd met in Marks & Spencer and they'd had a busy afternoon in the store. Suddenly she broke off the patter and looked at her daughter.

'I *wish* you didn't have to go back tomorrow, Anna.'

'I wish I didn't too, Mum.' True and also not

true. Divided loyalties. Divided worlds.

'I so love having you here. I feel I don't see enough of you. You're all I've got.'

'I know, Mum.' Anna reached out and put her hand over her mother's. 'I've been thinking that I don't see enough of you too, and I promise I will come up more often, and you must come and see us. Really, Mum, I want you to start enjoying life more, and to consider giving up work. We can always help out financially, you know, if . . .'

'But, Anna, I really would *hate* giving up work. I'd miss having something to do. I have my friends there. The store is a kind of family. As it is, as I said, I might have to give it up anyway, and then I'd feel lost, I know I would.'

'But, Mum, you could travel. Go on a cruise. Maybe meet a man.' She smiled at her mischievously. 'Have you really never met anyone in all the time since my father left you?'

Sylvia shook her head and Anna was rather alarmed to see the suspicion of tears in her eyes. She always said 'my father', never 'Daddy' or 'Father'. She could never bring herself, never felt the need, to speak so intimately about a man she could scarcely remember. All Roger Wood was to her was a fuzzy face in a photograph.

They said a woman's relationship with her father affected her whole life; but she had never cared to delve too deeply into how it had affected hers.

'By the way,' she said quickly, in an attempt

272

to forestall the tears, 'Peter rang this morning.'

'Oh, did he?' Sylvia liked Peter, good solid successful Peter. 'What did he have to say?'

'Fiona is pregnant.'

'Oh!' Sylvia put her knife and fork neatly side by side on her plate. 'I didn't know Fiona was married. Isn't she still at school?'

Fiona's dramas had always seemed too complicated to explain to her mother, who wouldn't understand anyway. She had always shown a kind of indifference to the welfare of her daughter's stepchildren who she scarcely knew.

'Well, no, she's not at school. I think I told you she left in an attempt to become an artist.'

'Oh, yes, you did say something.' Sylvia picked up her knife and fork again, attacked her chicken suprême à l'estragon with vigour.

'Well she met, or rather I introduced her to a young man who we thought could tutor her. They went down to Dorset and . . .'

Sylvia put down her knife and fork again and her lips formed in a disapproving arc. 'I see. That was a bit risky, wasn't it? A big short-sighted? Of course, in my day and age such a thing would be unheard of.'

'Well today it's very common, Mum.'

In these days too there would be less of a chance of making the mistake of marrying a man like Roger Wood when you were also too young and ignorant about the facts of life. It was obvious that her mother and father had never been compatible, but that the then youthful apprentice engineer was at the time temporarily captivated by the good looks of Sylvia Marsden, who worked in the office, and in those days the thing to do was to marry and no nonsense.

Sylvia, who was thoughtfully chewing her food, paused and said, 'I still think it's wrong. Is she going to have the baby? These days they get rid of them, don't they?'

'Apparently she doesn't want to.'

'Something else for you to bear, Anna. Another responsibility, as if you haven't enough already.' Her mother went on chewing thoughtfully, swallowed, and took a sip of her wine.

'On the other hand she *is* Peter's child, not yours.'

'Mum, you know I never thought that way.' Feeling stung, Anna put down her knife and fork and leaned across the table.

'Anna, you can't tell me you've thought of those children as your own all these years? I know you tried, and when they were smaller it was easier. But since they've been teenagers it seems to me they've been nothing but trouble to you. And this doesn't surprise me in the least. Young girls given their head, no discipline. How different it would have been, Anna, if *you'd* had children of your own. You could really have cared for them then. And I,' Sylvia's voice became tremulous, and Anna braced herself for the inevitable, 'I would have had my very own grandchildren I could love and care for. I don't think you know, Anna, how much I wanted grandchildren, what joy they would have given me, a purpose in life. How I could have *loved* them and done things for them, and what pain it gave me when you had that senseless operation last year and finished for ever your chance of being a real mother.'

There, it was out, in a torrent of words towards the end. Sylvia put down her wine glass, and leaned across the table saying in a hiss that reverberated with spite, 'In many ways you think of no one but yourself, Anna. Sometimes, although you pretend to care for others, there's a very selfish streak in you. You're very like your father. He was a very selfish man.'

And for the first time Anna saw in her mother's eyes an expression of bitterness and rancour she had never seen before, and she felt shocked to her very core.

PART 3

The Blood Tie

CHAPTER 12

The corpse's sightless eyes seemed to stare re-proachfully at Anna who gazed at the swollen, distorted face for a moment as though willing it back to life. Then, abruptly, she turned away feeling, somehow, that as she did the eyes fol-lowed her. But, of course, they didn't. The young woman had been dead for hours.

The governor put a comforting hand on her shoulder and propelled her towards the door which she opened and shut behind them.

'It's not our fault,' she said as she led Anna away from the infirmary block and along the corridor to her office.

Once inside the room, Anna sat down and gratefully took the cup of coffee offered by the governor's secretary. The governor sat opposite her, also with a cup in her hand.

'I thought I should call you, Mrs Liv-ingstone, in case there was any more press comment. I know you've had a lot of it recently.'

'I don't see why there should be.' Anna looked curiously at her. 'If anything, I think it will focus on you.'

'It may come out that you failed to defend her because of the business with the illegal squat which, after all, wasn't so very far away or long ago.'

'That was extremely unfortunate, but my deputy was quite up to the job of defending Jansie.'

'Still, she felt you would have got her off. She brooded on it.'

Anna had brooded on it too ever since the telephone by the side of the bed had rung at seven that morning, and the governor had told her that Jansie Dicks, the prostitute she should have defended on the day of the riot at the squat, had been found hanged in her cell. The awful thing was that, with so much on her mind, Anna had hardly thought about the poor woman from that day to this. Events had seemed to follow one another in such rapid succession that the fate of a woman sent down not only for prostitution but other offences had entirely escaped her mind. Well, not entirely. From among the mass of papers waiting her perusal in the office each day she knew an appeal was being lodged which Jeremy had in hand. After all you couldn't, no one possibly could, keep all the problems of all your clients to the forefront of your mind.

'The point was,' the governor crossed her ankles, 'that you seemed to take such a personal interest in her. She totally relied on you.'

'I did. I did take an interest in her, and we are now very definitely considering an appeal.'

'If only she'd known . . . I mean, how much you'd cared.'

The governor was rubbing it in, Anna decided.

Maybe trying to put the blame for the prison's lack of supervision on to the hard-pressed lawyer, probably with a possible enquiry in mind. Cheek.

'Really, Governor, I can't be *everywhere* at once,' Anna said with a touch of asperity. 'I can't see all my clients simultaneously, and thank heaven most of them do not think it necessary to take their lives if I don't. This is terribly unfortunate. But please don't put the blame on me.'

'Of course she was mentally rather unstable,' the governor conceded. 'I think however that she felt an attachment to you. But one does, Mrs Livingstone,' the governor smiled sweetly, 'you are so very persuasive, you *do* seem to care, I can quite understand your popularity and your success.'

'Well, I don't appear to have been very successful recently,' Anna admitted ruefully. 'The squat was a miserable failure and everyone ended up hating me there. I was pelted with rotten eggs and vegetables. Red faces all round, especially mine.'

The governor uncrossed her ankles and rose to pour more coffee.

'No, thanks.' Anna put out a hand and rose from her seat. 'Well, there'll be an inquest and, of course, I'll give evidence. We were considering an appeal. We had not realised just how much her mental state had deteriorated.' Touch of criticism of the governor there.

'I don't think *any* of us had,' the governor said firmly, accompanying her to the door, 'otherwise we'd have put her in a secure wing. Such a *pity* about the little girl.'

The governor's words rang in Anna's ears as she drove from the prison to her office. 'Such a *pity* about the little girl.' Jansie had been a devoted mother. Anna had visited her in the high-rise where they lived in Highbury. The place was clean, the child well cared for. The only thing was that this was from where Jansie had plied her trade. How much had the poor child known about that?

And the fact that they were black and that their neighbours had informed the authorities, probably just because of that, didn't help at all.

Anna parked the car in the garage in the mews behind the offices reserved for senior staff and hurried round to Wigmore Street. The receptionists were busy at their computer screens in the hall, one or two clients sat waiting to keep their appointments. As Anna entered and proceeded to the reception desk to check her mail, a figure rose from a chair and called in an unnecessarily loud voice: 'Ah, *there* you are, Mrs Livingstone! I've *only* been here two hours.'

Anna turned, clapped a hand to her mouth.

'Oh, Mrs Jones, I'm so *terribly* sorry. An unexpected emergency . . . you could have seen my deputy. Didn't he . . .'

'I didn't *want* to see your deputy, Mrs Livingstone.' Mrs Jones's tone grew shriller by the second. 'I came here to see *you*. I do *not* expect to be kept waiting when I pay astronomical fees to have you, and you personally, to represent my interests. Now, see here, Mrs Livingstone,' she put a hand on her hip and stuck out a finger until it came within an inch of Anna's face. The gesture enraged Anna who felt as though a blood vessel was about to burst.

'And see *here*, Mrs Jones,' she retorted pointing her own finger at her obnoxious client before she could say another word, 'don't you suppose I have enough to think about without people like *you* making my life an added misery? Don't you think I have enough to do without rich, spoilt women thinking they have an exclusive right to my time when others are far more in need of it? I've just seen the body of a dead woman, Mrs Jones, a dead woman. I should have been in court to defend and wasn't because of people like *you*,' she concluded, stabbing her finger with each word again and again at the astonished woman.

Anna could hear the blood drumming in her ears. If she wasn't careful she'd give herself a stroke or a heart attack. Dead before forty. Why? What was the point? She was aware of Jeremy at her side saying quietly into her ear: 'Anna, maybe behind closed doors?'

'Do please come into my room, Mrs Jones.' Anna, visibly making an effort to control herself, lowered her voice and pointed the way upstairs.

'Thank *you*, Mrs Livingstone,' Mrs Jones drew herself up, 'but I shall be taking my business elsewhere. I wouldn't dream of remaining with this firm for another second. I shall also be making a complaint about your disgraceful conduct here today to your supervisors. Make no mistake about *that!*'

And Mrs Jones swept towards the door which a startled Jeremy rushed to open.

'Golly,' he said, following Anna as she climbed the stairs two at a time to her room and shut the door behind them.

'That's blown it.' Anna tossed her briefcase on her desk. 'And she will. What with the squat, this and now Jansie Dicks has topped herself.' Jeremy screwed up his brow in an attempt at recollection. 'The black prostitute you defended on the day of the squat riot. The day I couldn't make it because I had to go home and get squashed tomato out of my clothes, to say nothing of trying to restore my emotional equilibrium.'

'You were treated abominably,' Jeremy said earnestly.

'Well that wasn't too much.' Anna reflectively fingered the side of her face. 'A few scratches really.' In fact she'd had to have an injection in case any of the putrid substances that had been thrown at her might have entered the bloodstream through the scratches caused by the egg shells exploding in her face. There was also the shock. It was easy to forget about that. She had indeed been very, very shocked, and there had been absolutely no possibility of her returning to court that day.

Jeremy sank into a chair, a hand to his face.

'I should have gone to see her.' Anna sat down in the chair behind her desk. 'I personally should have told her we were appealing, made an application for bail. I shouldn't have forgotten her. That's why I'm here. Everything recently has happened *so* quickly.'

'You can't take the blame,' Jeremy said loyally. 'I made a botch-up of the case.'

'Not your fault, you weren't properly briefed.' Jeremy, in fact, although talented, was a newly qualified solicitor, completely lacking in court experience. They should have asked for an adjournment. 'Sometimes I think this job is getting me down,' Anna said, staring at the wall. 'I've taken on too much.'

'Nonsense.' Jeremy rose and went over to her desk, picked up a bundle of legal documents bound with pink tape. 'About the squat incidentally, Damian Bradley is claiming police harassment. He has launched an official complaint.'

Anna sighed. The troubles with the squat were by no means over yet, even though, as she'd passed the site from the prison, she had noticed that where the warehouse had stood there was now a large piece of waste ground. The authorities had lost no time. What, she wondered, had happened to Damian?

For once, Anna spent the day at the office dealing with matters that were mainly routine but also important. The day that had started badly and had gone downhill thereafter, improved by

285

degrees into one of normality and routine. She even had a sandwich lunch at her desk and found time to call Katie to fix a lunch appointment for the following week, and to say 'hello' to her mother before she left for home.

Anna had a handful of close women friends, some scattered around the country, others abroad. Most, like her, led busy lives and one tended to lose touch with them. With Katie, although there was a semi-professional relationship, she felt at ease, able to bare her heart and be sure of an experienced and sympathetic response.

Just now she felt problems, both personal and professional, were multiplying, partly to a lack of judgment and partly to bad luck. She hadn't realised how much her mother, although proud of her success, also perhaps resented it because Anna imitated her father rather than her. And so had come the dreadful — and Anna thought unfair — accusation that, beneath her apparent concern for others, she was basically a selfish person who had deprived her long-suffering and resentful mother of grandchildren.

Yes, Katie would be a good one to talk to. Anna looked at her watch. Nothing else dreadful had happened during the day; just routine conferences with her assistants, clients and, for once, she thought she'd leave early, surprise Peter by having a meal ready for him when he got home, usually about seven. It was a very long time since she'd done that. If she left now she could shop in the fancy delicatessens and smart butchers' shops on Marylebone High Street. Surprise Peter for once with a slap-up, gourmet meal.

Her telephone rang and she picked up the receiver, an eye on the clock on her wall.

'Anna, there's a call for you,' her secretary said in an unnecessarily furtive whisper. 'Damian Bradley.'

Anna felt her heart lurch, put a hand on her chest.

'I'll take it,' she said in a brisk, practical manner. 'Put him through,' and as she heard the phone click she said in a bright, artificial voice: 'Hi, Damian!'

'Hi, Anna.'

Pause.

'How are you?' they both said at once. Then laughed. Another awkward pause.

'Damian,' Anna realised that the nervousness she thought she had under control was showing, 'I hear you're taking action against the police.'

'The bastards.'

'Is it wise?'

'You mean it could involve you?' She was aware that his tone had hardened.

'I'm not thinking of me, actually; but yes, it would involve me. I'd be called. Is that why you rang?'

'I rang because I want to see you, Anna.' His voice softened. 'I haven't forgotten.'

The blush stole up Anna's neck, suffusing her cheeks. She visualised vividly how it had been that day: herself spread on the floor, Damian kneeling above her, bearing down on her like some Nordic god. She closed her eyes involuntarily seeing it now as from a distance, from a long long way. But almost sensing again that cataclysmic upheaval that had penetrated her belly, engulfing her entire body.

'Have you forgotten, Anna?'

'Of course I haven't. I think we'd better meet and have a talk, Damian.'

'But I want you . . .'

'Please,' nervously she glanced around as though someone was watching her. Her hands riffled swiftly through the pages of her diary. 'Look, can I give you a call? Where are you staying?'

'I'll have to call you. No fixed abode at the moment, as they say. My dad's not well and I may have to go home.'

'Well, give me a call next week.'

'You sound terribly impersonal. Please don't say you're going to end it, Anna?'

End what? It had hardly begun. 'Look, I'm in the office. Call me midweek,' she said. 'I must go now. 'Bye, Damian.'

She replaced the receiver without waiting for his reply, and sat for a long time with her chin in her hands staring at the phone. Supposing he said something? Tried blackmail? It would be his word against hers, but the effect on Peter would be shattering. She felt however that there was something good, almost noble about Damian;

that he wouldn't stoop to such behaviour. She hoped she was right. Then she sighed and drew one of the many files awaiting her attention towards her.

Anna finished making the last notes on a file in preparation for tomorrow's load and packed her briefcase. She examined her face in the mirror of her compact and applied fresh lipstick, a quick dab of face powder to take the shine off her nose, put on her jacket, when there was a tap on the door and before she could call out David Cole put his head round it.

Anna's heart sank. The vision of the gourmet meal and Peter's pleasure on seeing it somehow receded.

'Hi, Anna!' David sidled round the door while she tried to rearrange her expression into one of welcome.

'Hi, David!'

'You were just leaving, I see,' he said, closing the door behind him. 'Well, I shan't take too long.' But the way he eased himself into her most comfortable armchair seemed to indicate that he would in fact be staying for quite some time.

'Well, I did think that I would leave and maybe make Peter dinner for a change.' She glanced at her watch. 'Shop in Marylebone High Street on the way home.'

'Excellent idea.' David too consulted his watch. 'I shan't detain you. Peter and the family well?'

'Very well, thank you.' There was something unusually strained about David's manner and Anna felt a flutter of apprehension. The day had begun badly. Maybe it was going to end badly too.

David joined his hands together like a church steeple and stretched his long legs, encased in dark blue pinstripe, before him, looking at his most avuncular, almost judicial. He peered at her over the tops of his fingers.

'Things haven't been going too well for you lately, Anna, have they? I'm so sorry.'

Anna felt immediately on the defensive. She resumed her seat at her desk and rested her chin on her hands. 'In what sense, David?'

'Well, all these problems you've had to cope with.' David raised his hands above his head and cracked the joints of his fingers one by one. 'That dreadful business at the warehouse. The woman who just killed herself and now, today, I had a very irate call from Mrs Jones who accuses you of bullying and shouting at her in reception.'

'Oh, did she?' Anna, strengthened by a feeling of indignation, rested her hands on her desk and looked up at him defiantly.

'She was extremely upset,' David went on. 'We have been her solicitors for a number of years and,' he paused, looking at her levelly, 'apparently are not going to be any longer.'

'She is the *most* obnoxious woman,' Anna said heatedly.

'Nevertheless she's a very important client, and

a very wealthy one. Her father deals with us too, and no doubt will follow her lead. He is Sir Harry Carter of the shipping line.' David paused ominously.

'David, am I supposed to be blackmailed by an angry and capricious client acting over my head? After all, I *am* in charge of this section and all complaints should come to me.'

David opened his hands in an eloquent expression of bewilderment.

'But if you, the head, have offended, to whom can one complain? Naturally she came to me who she has known for a very long time. Whether you like her or not, Anna, is beside the point. We're in this business to make money.'

'I realise that.' Momentarily Anna studied the shiny surface of her desk. 'But I am in it primarily to serve justice. However I *am* prepared to concede that I may have acted hastily. But as soon as I came into the building, Mrs Jones launched herself at me, shouting and bawling, poking me in the face with her gem-laden finger. Frankly, I almost lost control.'

'I realise that and, especially, why. I understand one of your clients had committed suicide and you had just come from viewing the body.'

'*That* has got to you very quickly. It only happened this morning.'

'These things do,' he replied urbanely, and Anna could somehow visualise the always polite but similarly urbane Jeremy getting quietly on the phone to his master. 'Anna's cracking up,' he might have whispered. Hence the visit.

'Naturally, Anna, when I heard about the scene I made a few enquiries and learned what had happened, and why you were in a state.'

'Did you by any chance learn why *she* was in a state?' Anna was aware that her voice was rising by decibels.

'My dear,' David languidly eased his lanky form out of the chair and, hands in the pockets of his trousers, strolled across to the window and gazed on to Wigmore Street, 'she is in a state because her marriage is breaking up. Her husband is trying to get as much of her money as he can . . .'

'I am aware of all this, David, and it is, or was, under control.'

David turned round and looked at her. 'She is also holding down a most important job, and if you feel your work is suffering, so does Sheila Jones.'

'I see.' Anna, hands in the pockets of her jacket, sat back. 'This is a reprimand then. Is it an official one?'

'My dear Anna,' David came over to her desk and leaned both hands on it, his face now very close to hers, 'it is *not* a reprimand. I am simply stating the facts, as I know them, to suggest that you may be overworked. You do look, if I may say so, desperately tired. Much much more tired than you have in all the years I've known you. What I am suggesting, Anna, is that the reason for this apparent exhaustion, unwise behaviour towards a client, is that you are taking on too much voluntary work in this firm's time.' The emphasis in his voice changed imperceptibly. 'The whole business about the squat, which got so much unwelcome publicity that you and your husband felt you should disappear for a few days . . .'

'I had leave due. Lots and lots of it. Besides, *you* suggested it.' She gazed at him accusingly.

'I am quite well aware of that, and I think you did the right, indeed the only, thing. But this firm was mentioned in the papers several times despite the fact that the incident had nothing to do with us at all. Nothing whatever, and now I am quite sure there is going to be an enquiry into this business of the death of the prostitute in custody . . . again work undertaken outside this office yet I believe Jeremy, your deputy, was asked to act for you in your absence. Again quite understandably; but . . .' David hunched his shoulders expressively and grimaced, 'hardly fair on *us,* is it?'

She had never, of course, thought anything of it. But she should have. Formerly, she would have trusted Jeremy. Now she knew better.

'I considered it good experience for Jeremy,' she said, aware how lame she must sound. 'Legal aid would, naturally, have come to this firm for the time he appeared in court,' she went on, 'as it would if I'd represented Miss Dicks.'

'Legal aid,' David sniffed. 'Legal aid, you say, and then you saunter in this morning and lose us one, maybe two, of our most valuable clients. I'm sure having got divorced once, Sheila Jones will again. She's not the sort who will ever keep a man.'

Anna winced. David Cole was a closet chauvinist, and usually she would have remonstrated with him. They knew each other's political views and amicably disagreed about them. But at this moment she dare not. She felt her courage, her confidence, evaporating.

'Are you by any chance giving me notice, David? Asking me to leave?'

David looked horrorstruck.

'Oh my dear, Anna, by *no* means. Not at all. We value you highly. But I am going to ask you — and I have discussed this with the partners before I came — if you could give up some of your voluntary work or, at least, curtail it in the interests of the firm you work for and which pays you a very high salary. I'm also suggesting that we think of appointing a partner to *share* your duties with you and ease some of the burden you are under.'

'And who is this partner?' Anna felt a high colour rush to her cheeks.

'It's only an idea. Naturally someone you will like and approve of.'

'When you say "share" do you mean on an equal basis?'

'Well,' David studied the ceiling, 'it's all to be decided. Nothing's fixed.'

'If that were the case, it amounts to demotion.

I will no longer be in charge.'

'That we shall have to think it out further, Anna. It is suggested we leave it until we see the response you make to my suggestions.'

'In other words it's a sort of blackmail?' she said bluntly.

David suppressed a shudder. 'That is a word I never thought I'd hear used against me, or any of my colleagues.'

'You're just saying "toe the line or else". That *is* blackmail.'

'We are *suggesting* that you are overworked, and I think you'll agree you are, and we're trying to help you in your own best interests. We value you, I assure you, Anna. You've a fine legal brain.' David resumed his seat and looked appealingly across at her. 'Anna, you're a young woman with a husband and family. You are not yet forty. Surely you don't want to burn yourself out yet. Do you?'

Anna put her key in the lock, dead tired, exhausted. She'd hardly been able to climb up the steps as a sudden overwhelming weariness had set in. As the key turned she pushed open the door.

The house seemed quieter than usual, empty, sepulchral. It was also cold as though the central heating had not yet come on. Seven-thirty. In the winter it usually came on about five. Perhaps something was wrong, and as it was a particularly cold evening they'd freeze.

Anyway, the meeting with David had dragged on and when she left it was far too late to shop in Marylebone High Street. Maybe they'd go out, except that now she wasn't hungry.

She knew Peter wasn't in. The house was too cold, too dark. Peter liked light and warmth. She went into the kitchen, switching on lights as she went. She checked the boiler and then she looked at the thermostat on the wall. It had been turned right down for some reason; probably by the daily by accident.

She flicked it to a higher number and she could hear the boiler spring to life. Relief.

She went back through the hall to the sitting room and glanced round. Peter definitely hadn't been back. The curtains weren't drawn and it was the first thing he always did on a winter's evening.

She thought maybe he'd come in and then gone out in a bad temper because she had promised to be home early and, once again, had broken her promise. But no, he hadn't come home. On the mat, just inside the door, was the local 'freebie' and some leaflets and he would have picked those up. He would never have left bits of paper lying around.

Anna switched on the answer-machine and played over the messages. Nothing important. Nothing from Peter. She sat down, head in her hands, feeling dejected, dispirited, close to tears if the truth be told.

Anna was not a woman who had ever been

prone to tears. She was not emotional, and they had seldom been necessary. Her slight depressive outburst after the sterilisation, and weeping on the policeman's shoulder the day of the riot at the squat, had been two rare occasions in recent years. And yet here she was again, ready to blub. She felt so lonely, isolated. She craved Peter, needed Peter and he wasn't here. No, she was too resilient, too self-controlled to cry. She shook herself, got abruptly to her feet and drew the curtains firmly together.

Beware of pity, especially self-pity. She had had a lousy day and had been looking forward to telling Peter all about it — especially the conversation with David, and he wasn't here. No need to behave like a child on that account. But she did feel curiously empty, purposeless, rootless. She felt she had no props as other people had to get through the difficult spots in life. She didn't smoke, hardly drank, wine with a meal perhaps, but never spirits, and certainly never alone. That would somehow offend against the canons of the middle-class Protestant ethic in which she had been raised: hard work, abstemious in all things.

Had her father drunk, she wondered? And she realised again, as she had ever since she returned to London from her visit to her mother, that she knew so little about him, what sort of man he was. She had always taken her mother's side, believed that her mother had been wronged and her father was to blame. Girls must stick together.

She didn't have a pet to stroke or fondle, an animal whose welcome, unquestioning love and obedience would be, if not as good as human contact, the next best thing.

It was absolutely useless getting maudlin. Peter was probably dining out, thinking maybe that, just for once, he would get his own back. It was, after all, a natural human desire to show his male assertiveness. Anna had never really thought of it that way.

She made a sandwich, watched the nine o'clock news and then read a brief for the next day. This time she was in court on behalf of one of the firm's clients; but it was a Crown Court case for which a barrister had been briefed, and she would be sitting on the sidelines, watching, helping. It could take several days.

At ten she put out the lights downstairs, except for the ones in the hall and the sitting room, and went upstairs, ran a bath and had a long soak.

She felt vaguely apprehensive, worried about Peter. She always left a message reporting on her whereabouts and so, usually, did he. Had he had an accident? Impossible. If he had there were any number of documents he carried about with him that would identify him. If he'd been taken ill, the same would apply.

Then where was he?

The idea slowly crossed her mind that he might be having an affair. Peter? Why not? She knew from her legal experience that it was just the people one least expected who had affairs; seemingly faithful husbands' eyes suddenly began to rove in their late forties or fifties, just the age that Peter was now.

She and Peter had had a tough time recently. She knew he was worried to death about Fiona, and there was fresh anxiety about Guy who initially appeared to settle into and like his new school, but now wasn't so sure. Maybe Peter had gone out on a blind with some men friends and got drunk, but that seemed about as unlikely as him having an affair.

Anna knew she wouldn't sleep until he came in, so she settled down to read a book.

But by one o'clock Peter had still not returned and Anna began to become seriously anxious. She didn't think he would want to upset or frighten her and the conviction grew steadily that somehow he'd had an accident which had as yet been unreported.

What did one do? As a lawyer she should know. She put her book down and swung her legs over the bed. One rang hospitals, the police? But supposing, while she was ringing, Peter was trying to get hold of her? It was a dilemma. Supposing also he was in the arms of some woman while she was making a hysterical fool of herself?

She lay down on the bed again, took several long deep breaths to try and relax. Unlike her to panic. Very. She picked up the book, held it in her hands for some moments before she realised it was upside down. She righted it, put on her reading glasses and made a determined effort to concentrate. But it was useless.

She had an extremely busy schedule the next day, an appointment in court, a Council meeting in the evening and goodness knows how many other things to do. She'd planned on getting up at six, even earlier maybe, put a couple of hours in the office before rushing off to court. If Peter was doing what he was doing deliberately it was wicked and irresponsible of him.

By two o'clock she began to feel drowsy, the book slipped in her hands. She reached for the light while she was still somnolent and let the book fall on the floor.

Suddenly the phone went. Her heart began to pound wildly in unison with the rings. She knew that her hand trembled as she picked up the receiver and said in a hoarse voice: 'Hello?'

'Anna?'

'Peter! Where in God's name are you? I've been worried sick . . .'

'I'm terribly sorry, Anna,' his voice sounded abnormally tense, strained, 'but I couldn't ring you before. I'll tell you why in a moment.'

'Are you alright, Peter?'

'I'm fine, really fine. Let me explain. I had a call from Fiona just as I was leaving the office. I knew we'd planned an evening in, but when I rang your office there was no one on the switchboard.'

Anna knew an involuntary plummeting of the heart. Fiona, of course, it had to be Fiona again.

'And believe it or not the phone at home was

engaged. Your mobile wasn't working either.'

'I switched it off in the office. But please go on, Peter. Is Fiona alright? The baby . . .'

'Well she's in a fearful state. It's nothing to do with the baby, thank God; but Errol has left her. She came back from a day's outing with Sal and Honey and found he'd cleared out. Taken the TV, video, the hi-fi and all the money she had in the house. You know how careless she is. She had quite a lot lying around.'

Anna was aghast. 'Did he leave a note?'

'Nothing. But she knew he'd gone. He'd rifled through all the drawers, cupboards, for anything of value. The place was in a terrible mess,' he paused, 'I mean worse than usual.'

'Poor Fiona. I am sorry. But you could have rung when you got there . . .'

'Darling, I know I should have tried, made more effort, but Sal rang me and made me seriously worried about Fiona. Said she was hysterical, she had to get the doctor. That wasn't easy because her phone was out of order,' he lowered his voice as if afraid of being overheard, 'as a matter of fact it's been disconnected. So when I got there . . .'

'OK, OK.' Anna ran her hands through her hair. 'I understand. Peter I'm so terribly sorry . . .'

'Anna, we need you here. We really do. Can you come down first thing in the morning?'

After all she had been through in the past few hours Anna felt a sudden surge of anger.

301

'Peter, please be reasonable! I have work to do. I can't just drop everything . . .'

The silence on the line was wary and palpable and then Peter's voice, sounding subdued.

'Anna, I thought this family meant a lot to you . . .'

'It does! Of course it does . . .'

'And that you felt as a real mother to Fiona and Guy . . .'

'Yes . . .' tremulously.

'Well then, I think a real mother would have wanted to be with her daughter, and a good wife with her husband at such a difficult time.'

'Peter, I know what has happened must have upset Fiona dreadfully, and I am truly very sorry, but it isn't as though anyone had died.'

'Someone might die. She might lose the baby.'

'Is it as bad as that?'

'It's a possibility, I suppose. She's still at Sal's. The doctor said she must be monitored for twenty-four hours. That's why we need you, Anna.'

'Peter, normally I'd be down at once, but this has come at a very unfortunate time. Please *try* and understand. David Cole told me today that he thought I was doing too much, and that he might appoint a joint head of the office.'

'Sounds like a jolly good idea.'

'Peter, how can you *say* that? It will mean loss of seniority.'

'Well, that's very important to you, isn't it, Anna? And you *are* doing too much as a matter of fact. The only thing that surprises me is that you don't have some kind of breakdown. It's dehumanising you, Anna, and as far as the family are concerned it's making you seem very selfish, thinking only of yourself.'

Selfish. There it was: that word again.

'I'll have a word with David first thing in the morning,' Anna said stiffly, 'and I will try and come down. Otherwise it will be the weekend. I'll let you know. Give Fiona my love . . .' But from the sound of the tone at the other end she already knew that Peter had rung off.

Fiona did indeed look very ill. By the time Anna got down early the following afternoon the doctor had visited her again and didn't want her to be moved from Sal's. Peter had paid Sal's outstanding telephone bill and the company had promised to reconnect the line as an emergency.

Anna went straight to Sal's where she was rather relieved to find her alone, with Fiona asleep upstairs. Peter had gone into Blandford to do some shopping.

'He'll be delighted to see you,' Sal said, leading Anna into her sitting room. 'Men don't know how to cope, do they?'

'Seems not.' Anna sank on to the sofa.

'You'll need a cup of tea I expect?'

'I do.'

After hardly any sleep the night before and an acrimonious conversation with David when she rang him at home that morning ('I can't under-

303

stand *how* you can do this, Anna, when we only
had the talk we had yesterday. It's not as though
she's your own daughter'), she felt shattered.

While Sal busied herself getting the tea, Anna
crept upstairs to look at Fiona. Even in sleep she
was pale and exhausted, one hand clutching a
handkerchief to her mouth like a baby would its
comforter. Anna had stood for some time gazing
down at her, but Fiona didn't move. Emotionally
exhausted she was genuinely fast asleep, probably
under the influence of a tranquilliser.

When Anna went downstairs there was a pot
of tea, cups and a plate of biscuits on the table
drawn up to the fire. It all looked cosy and
inviting.

'You look as though you could do with a sleep
yourself,' Sal said, passing Anna her cup as she
sank back into the sofa.

'You can say that again. I was so worried . . .'

'Well, yes . . . it was too bad about the phone.'

'He could have gone to the cottage. So unlike
Peter not to let me know. He's never wanted to
carry a mobile. Thinks they're pretentious. I
couldn't do without mine.' Anna thankfully
sipped her tea.

'You've no idea how *worried* we were, Anna.'
Sal's face creased with concern. 'Everything was
chaotic. We thought she'd lose the baby.'

'Was she having contractions or anything?
Pain?' Anna the lawyer wanted the rather woolly
statement to be substantiated.

'Well, no; but she was that upset. The doctor

had to give her a sedative.'

Anna sat staring at the fire, thoughtfully biting into the biscuit she'd taken.

'It's all my fault, really . . .'

'Oh, Anna, you can't blame yourself . . .' Sal looked shocked.

'Not this, but that they ever met at all. I introduced them. Peter never liked him from the start, but I thought that was just middle-class prejudice. Did you like him, Sal? I feel I hardly knew him. I just so hated the mess the place was in, that in the relatively brief time he was here I kept away.'

'Well with young people like that you feel you want to leave them to themselves, don't you?' Sal nodded understandingly. 'I *quite* liked him myself. I mean, deep down he was an ordinary kind of bloke. A bit sullen, not a great personality, not educated like you and Peter. But then Fiona's not educated, is she?'

'Well, not very.' Anna was aware of indignation rising again at the implied distinction, on the grounds of class, which she found offensive.

'I mean she didn't get GCSEs or anything, did she?' Sal, blissfully unaware of Anna's inner torment, pursued her point.

'Apart from scraping through English and History, she didn't.'

'Then perhaps they were quite suited? I mean everyone's the same these days, aren't they? No difference really. Did she ever meet his parents?'

'I don't think he had any.' Anna shook herself

from the state of somnolence induced by the fire. 'I mean, I always assumed he had left home under some cloud, or perhaps he was an orphan. We knew very little about him.'

In that case how *ridiculous* to have introduced your stepdaughter to a man you knew nothing about, a social reject who was part of a squat. Would she have done that if Fiona had been her natural daughter? Did it seem like carelessness, almost criminal in fact, to behave as she had?

If so, no wonder Peter was angry.

She ran her hands over her face. 'Did he give Fiona no inkling that he was going to do a bunk?'

'None at all. They seemed so happy. He even seemed pleased about the baby, that he was going to become a father, that he had a home and that this would give him the chance to settle down. I mean he had everything going for him, didn't he really? She kept him, yet he still got all his benefits. Not that I begrudge people their benefits because I get as many as I can myself. I mean I think we deserve them, don't you?' Sal's tone grew defensive. 'I mean that's what they're there for. For people to claim.'

Anna nodded.

Sal's eyes narrowed. 'Except that, for people like him who are being kept *and* leading the life of Riley, it doesn't seem fair, does it?'

'I suppose the social security system would have caught up with him sooner or later. In fact, it may be one way that we can find him again.'

'Would you want to find him?' Sal registered surprise.

'Of course.' Anna turned to her in astonishment. 'He's a thief. He has taken property that doesn't belong to him and, anyway, in a few months he will have a child he is one half responsible for. I'll certainly do everything I can to find him.'

'I don't think Fiona would like that,' Sal said quietly.

'How do you mean?'

'I think she still loves him. Silly I know. But I think she really does. Whatever he's done, if you ask me, she's crazy about him.'

CHAPTER 13

Mrs Hanson opened the door a crack and then, seeing who it was, flung it wide. Behind her lurked Martin, looking rather furtive as though he were anxious not to be seen. Maybe he was bunking off from school, or maybe it was the instinctive distrust of strangers that seemed to categorise the whole Hanson family, as though there were two distinct categories of people: locals and foreigners.

However today Mrs Hanson seemed initially friendly as Anna told her she had come to settle the bills run up by Errol and Fiona and collect more eggs.

The news seemed to please Mrs Hanson. Errol and Fiona had, indeed, run up rather a large bill: eggs, milk, bacon, pork, vegetables — anything, it seemed, they could get their hands on.

'I'm terribly sorry,' Anna said gaping at the amount as, after laboriously totting it up, Mrs Hanson presented her with a bill of over £100. 'I'd no idea they spent this much.'

'I dare say you hadn't.' Mrs Hanson looked sideways at her as Anna produced her cheque book.

'You don't mind a cheque, do you, Mrs Hanson?'

'Anything so long as it's legal,' Mrs Hanson replied. Then she turned abruptly to the boy behind her who had been surreptitiously watching the proceedings.

'Now don't stand there gawping, Martin. Get back to your work.' She shook her head wrathfully. 'I can't get him to do anything. Moons about all day.'

'Why isn't he at school?' Anna asked curiously.

'Woke up with a migraine, he *says*, but you've got to believe them, haven't you? Normally I would fetch him one and send him off to school, but today he really seemed quite poorly.'

Martin Hanson did indeed have the white, pasty face of a town boy rather than a country lad. Anna suspected that he spent quite an amount of his spare time in a smoke-filled room smoking pot, and that the rest was spent in front of the telly.

'How's your Guy doing?' Mrs Hanson inspected the cheque and popped it on the sideboard behind her.

'He's fine.' Truth to tell Anna still felt ashamed and embarrassed about the private school, a betrayal of her principles.

'Settled then, has he?'

'It seems so.'

'You're lucky you could afford to send Guy to private school. Something like that is just what Martin needs. A strict boarding school to discipline him.'

'I wouldn't say it was a "strict" school. In fact

it's rather liberal. As a matter of fact it's something I feel rather ashamed about.'

Mrs Hanson looked puzzled. 'Ashamed?'

'I'm really dead against private education. It goes right against my idea of equality.'

Mrs Hanson's expression remained unchanged. She was not much over fifty but she had the careworn face of a woman overburdened with worries; of the family, the farm, the hard grind which was life.

'What's happening to Martin at *his* school goes against *my* idea of equality.' She paused sensing that the matter was a thorny one, as it emphasized the gap between the Livingstones, who could afford to send their children to private schools and didn't want to, and the Hansons who wanted to but couldn't afford it. 'How's Fiona?' she asked. 'I'm terribly sorry to hear what happened. You can't trust people, can you?' She looked over her shoulder to be sure that Martin was out of earshot and then leaned conspiratorially towards Anna. 'I hear he ran off with everything?'

'TV, video, everything that he could put his hands on.' Anna gestured helplessly.

'He must have had an accomplice, someone to help him. Would you like a cup of tea, Mrs Livingstone?'

Anna felt honoured. She never remembered being invited to have a cup of tea by Mrs Hanson before. To have refused would have appeared rude.

'That's very nice of you,' she said.

'Come in and sit down.' Mrs Hanson led the way from the big hall to a sitting room that Anna had never seen. It was a lovely room, even a gracious one, overlooking a lawn that sloped down to the river upon which a family of ducks were now cavorting. It was a high-ceilinged room with an original plaster cornice, and had windows that ran from the ceiling almost to the floor. Anna had never been further than the hall, or the larder behind the big farmhouse kitchen at the back.

'What a lovely room,' Anna enthused as Mrs Hanson invited her to sit down.

'We like it.' Mrs Hanson sighed deeply. 'We shall miss it when we go.'

'Go?' Anna looked at her in concern. 'You're leaving?'

'Well we would *like* to leave. The farm isn't paying. We'd like to sell up. Ted's health is not good, bronchitis last winter turned to pneumonia and it took him weeks to recover. Martin is hopeless about the farm and the girls aren't interested. It's a big burden.'

'It must be. I didn't realise. I'm so sorry. Can't you get help?'

'No one wants to work on the land these days.' Mrs Hanson sighed wearily again and Anna felt she was glad to unburden herself to a virtual stranger, someone not local or a part of the family. 'I shan't be a moment,' she said pointing towards the door. 'I'll just get the tea, Mrs Livingstone.'

311

'I wish you'd call me Anna.' But Mrs Hanson had gone.

Anna stood by the window gazing at the river as it idled by. On the other side were water meadows, land which was subject to flood in winter and its lush greenery seemed to bear this out. It sloped gradually up to a coppice crowning the brow of the hill opposite, growing thicker towards the east and becoming sparser towards the west.

It was a scene of beauty, harmony and tranquillity, so different from the clutter they'd found in the cottage, the misery and chaos surrounding them there.

Anna knew she would always hate the cottage not only for its recent bad memories but for something that went much further back: because it had once belonged to Nancy and she had never truly felt happy or at home there.

She turned as Mrs Hanson laid the tray on a round mahogany table. All the furniture in the room was good, possibly antique, though the heavy red flocked walls would not have been to her taste. The carpet was well worn, but the great fireplace obviously saw service in winter; logs were piled up on one side and a brass coal scuttle stood on the other.

'When will you be leaving?' Anna asked as Mrs Hanson poured the tea, gave her her cup and proffered a plate of home-made cake.

'When we can sell. It's on the market, but so far no offers. Times are hard, aren't they, Mrs Livingstone?'

Anna knew she would never call her by her Christian name. There would always be that chasm sanctified by the formality of social address. She didn't even know Mrs Hanson's Christian name. It was the way they had of politely keeping strangers in their place.

'It will be dreadful without you. Whatever will we do for eggs and milk?'

Mrs Hanson gave a brittle laugh.

'Do the same as everyone else. Go to the supermarket. On the one hand we can't sell our produce because it's either too expensive or it falls foul of these daft European Community regulations. Our eggs for instance . . . well, you know, we're not supposed to sell those.'

Lovely big brown eggs fresh from the hen. It seemed ridiculous.

'Well, I hope you'll let me have a dozen today.'

'I will, Mrs Livingstone. When will you be going back to London?'

'I should go back very soon.' Anna looked uneasy. 'I have a job to hold down, you know. I'm taking unpaid leave at the moment. My husband has already gone back. We would like Fiona to return to London with us but she doesn't want to. Until that's solved I can't leave her.' Suddenly, acting on instinct, she said: 'Do you think I could see the rest of the house?'

'Are you interested perhaps in buying it, Mrs Livingstone?' Mrs Hanson perked up.

'Oh, no,' Anna said quickly, 'but I might know someone who is. It could, of course, be sold apart from the farm?'

'Oh, we'd sell all the animals. There would be nothing to stop it being turned into a private dwelling.'

The same heavy flock wallpaper lined the hall and stairways, the skirting boards and paintwork were stained or painted brown. The place looked as though it hadn't been decorated in the lifetime of the present incumbents, though it was by no means dirty or uncared for. On the contrary, everything was neat, tidy and clean. The beds in the bedrooms looked as though they had been freshly made, waiting for the next occupants. It was well-aired and welcoming. From every window there were extensive views, and the higher one climbed the better they got. There were two bathrooms with old-fashioned baths and basins, lavatories with solid wooden seats, old-fashioned cisterns and brass taps. It was all redolent of a past age, as though the Hanson family lived in a time warp.

'Won't you miss it dreadfully?' Anna asked looking from the window of what was obviously the master bedroom with a solid double bed, a pretty painted porcelain jug and basin on a stand in the corner and a huge double-fronted wardrobe, its highly polished surface gleaming in the afternoon sunlight.

Mrs Hanson, arms folded, stood beside her gazing out but not speaking. Finally, in a low voice she said: 'We've worked hard all our lives, Mrs Livingstone, with little to show for it. Our children are not keen, the first generation of Hansons not to want to farm. We did so hope that our married daughter's husband, or Martin, would show some interest but they don't. All they are attracted to these days are the bright lights of the city. When Ted was sixteen and school leaving age he knew almost as much about farming as his father. He'd worked on the farm ever since he could remember, getting up as a small boy to help with the milking, bringing the animals in from the fields when he got home after school of a winter's afternoon. It was a hard life, but it was satisfying. It was a different age.'

'It's a lovely house.' Anna sighed. 'I hope whoever buys it is as nice as you.' She felt impulsively that she wanted to kiss her cheek, but she didn't dare. The reserved, undemonstrative Mrs Hanson would think it extremely odd.

Once downstairs again, Anna put the eggs in her basket, was warmly thanked for paying the bill, and prepared to take her leave.

'I hope everything turns out well for you,' Mrs Hanson said. 'A young girl like that having a baby and no father.' She shook her head. 'It's a terrible thing. Not yet eighteen, is she?'

Anna shook her head. 'Well it *has* a father.' Instinctively she assumed the lawyer's sensible practical tone of voice. 'The trouble is, we don't know where he is.'

She took her time going down the hill towards the village and the cottage nestling in the centre;

315

the place she so disliked. But her mind was on the farm, that house, the big, light airy rooms, the views which, as she entered the cottage, made it seem almost claustrophobic, its rooms so small and dark, and the sense of foreboding, the feeling of depression that now always seemed to go with it.

Fiona was a terrible problem, and Anna felt resentful that so much more pressure was being put on herself than anyone else. Peter had gone back to work. He said there were a number of knotty international problems that needed his personal attention. Anna was forced once more to get on the phone to David Cole, aware, more than ever, that her job, her career was in jeopardy. She was also missing meetings of the Council and the numerous committees she was on. The Law Centre had almost completely gone by the board. She hadn't been there for weeks.

There was the usual silence in the cottage as Fiona needed no excuse now to spend most of the time in bed. It was doubtless partly depression, partly her condition. She was pregnant, and she now had good reason to be depressed. Her partner had deserted her, and was she old enough, strong enough, to cope with motherhood?

Anna put the eggs in the larder and then climbed the stairs to Fiona's bedroom pausing with the customary feeling of tension before she knocked and went in.

Fiona was awake.

'Hi!' Anna said with forced jollity.

'Hi!' Fiona replied after a while.

'It's past noon,' Anna said, drawing the curtains and squinting at the wintry landscape. Since she'd left the farm the sun had gone in, which somehow seemed symbolic.

'I 'spect it is,' Fiona muttered, and Anna turned to see that she was curled up sucking her thumb, a child in a woman's body.

A child having a child. It seemed deeply, even morbidly, ironic.

With an assumed cheerfulness Anna went over to Fiona's bed and sat down on it.

'Fiona, do you feel up to talking?' She wanted to reach out and smooth her hair back from her sticky brow, but she didn't dare for fear of being repulsed. But in that crumpled figure before her she couldn't help seeing the Fiona she had known as a small girl: anxious, insecure, loving Anna to touch her, wanting her. Anna would reach out and smooth back her curls and then she would kiss her, hug her and perhaps sing to her until she fell asleep. They had once been very close, but it all seemed a long time ago now.

'Talking about what?' Fiona asked after she'd given it some thought.

'Things. The future.'

'If you mean am I going to have the baby adopted, no, I'm not.'

'No, I didn't mean that. I know you want it, and we want it.'

'Huh!' Fiona replied, eyeing Anna maliciously.

317

'We do really.' Anna's throat suddenly went dry and she coughed.

'How can you say that when only a year ago you got your tubes tied so that you could never have children?'

'It's different.' Anna coughed again, her throat feeling inexplicably tight and constricted. 'This is your baby. It exists. Mine didn't.'

'You can't have much of a maternal instinct to do a thing like that.' Anna realised that Fiona was sounding smug, implying in fact that she was one up on her stepmother.

'Fiona, please . . .' Anna struggled to find the right words. 'Just for once let's have a practical, sensible talk about the future. Let's forget about what happened in the past, or even a year ago, or why I did what I did which I thought at the time, and still do, was for the best. Look, I can't stay down here permanently with you. I have a job to do. Besides, you wouldn't want it, but your father and I would like it very much if you do come back to London. You'll be near the best hospitals, have the best care and treatment.'

Even as she spoke Fiona was shaking her head, eyes closed as if she didn't even want to listen.

'I don't *want* to come to London. You know I don't. I've said I don't, and I won't.'

'But, Fiona, isn't it more sensible? The weather . . . it's so remote out here.'

Fiona again stuck her finger in her mouth and went on shaking her head in that maddening way that made Anna feel she could cheerfully throttle her.

'You've got to think of the baby.'

'I am.'

'No, you're not, you're thinking about Errol.'

Pause. Then: 'What if I am? If he comes back he'll know where to find me.'

'If you're not here he'll know you're in London.'

Again the violent shaking of the head.

'He would never come and see me if you and Dad are there. You know that. He'd be afraid of what you'd say, or do. Being a lawyer, you might have him put in prison.'

'Which is something I'd dearly like to do,' Anna said savagely, and then, quickly, seeing Fiona's expression, 'only I shan't. But, darling,' instinctively she reached out and did what she'd wanted to do, stroked Fiona's brow and was pleased, and also surprised, to find that she didn't resist. 'Darling, Fiona, you must realise that it's unlikely Errol will come back.'

'Why?'

'Because he wouldn't have left as he did, especially,' curling her lip contemptuously, 'after pinching all the things he pinched.'

'They were no good to him. He'd want to sell them.'

'Obviously, but still it wasn't a very nice thing to do.'

'Nice,' Fiona burst out, 'that's all *you're* concerned about isn't it, Anna, with your horrible

319

snobbish middle-class attitude? Nice, being nice. A nice person doesn't behave like that . . .'

'*Most* people don't . . .'

'Errol didn't want a baby. He didn't want the responsibility. He told me that. He said he was a free spirit, but he also said he loved me and I believe he does — *that's* why I think after it's born he'll come back. I'm staying here, Anna. You can do what you like. You can't force me to return, and I shan't.'

Anna stood looking around at the canvases stacked untidily in the shed. It was quite easy to see which were Errol's bright, vibrant colours as opposed to Fiona's, which were still rather wishy-washy, despite his tuition.

Yet how much tuition had there been? Anna didn't think he had any real talent. But then it was hard to judge something quite as abstract as the canvases before her. She might well feel the same about works of art, so-called, in some London galleries.

'Do you like his stuff?' she asked Sal who shook her head.

'Neither do I. He said he was at the Slade. I've no reason to think he lied. If he was, he must have had talent to have got in. They don't take anybody. Still, I should have checked up on him. I should have been more careful. I did so *much* that was wrong.'

'It wasn't your fault.' Sal touched her arm, running her finger up and down it, a sisterly gesture Anna appreciated.

'Everything *was* my fault. I acted out of a kind of desperation. I was so anxious that Fiona should be encouraged to get on with something she seemed so interested in.'

'It's still strange he took off though.' Sal continued to look puzzled.

'Why?' Anna bent down and began to flick through the canvases. 'I don't find that surprising.'

'He had a meal ticket, a home.'

Anna went on sorting through the canvases, putting them in three piles according to artist. It wasn't very difficult to distinguish Fiona's from Errol's (it showed how much he thought of them that he had left them behind) and the ones with any slight merit were Nancy's.

Nancy's house. She looked around. Not only the studio but the whole house belonged to Nancy. Still did. It was as though, even from the grave, she clung on to it and those inside it; made them her own, as she did with her children, or Peter. It was as though, after many years, she was reclaiming them. Anna felt alienated, somehow not belonging. Nancy's ghost resented her. Involuntarily Anna shivered and got up.

'Cold?' Sal asked sympathetically.

'Cold and a bit scared.' Anna glanced over her shoulder.

'Scared?' Sal looked puzzled.

'I always feel the presence of Nancy's ghost when I'm here.'

'It's because you've been looking at her pictures.'

Anna nodded and, crouching again, turned them all to the wall.

'There,' she said, 'that's better.' She dusted her hands and grinned across at Sal. 'You think I'm crazy, don't you?'

'No, but for someone so practical I'm surprised you're so sensitive. I mean ghosts don't exist. We all know that.'

'I think "presences", for want of a better word, do. I think something of Nancy lives on here and Fiona knows it and uses it against me. But to return to the subject of Errol. It's not so strange he took off. He didn't want a baby. That was too much. Fiona says that's the reason he left and I believe her. I can just see someone like Errol seeing it as the most enormous problem. The responsibility too much for him. Sal . . .' she turned to her and clasped her arm, 'do you think you could look after Fiona for us? She won't come to London, and I can't stay down here indefinitely.'

'Of *course* I will.' Sal's eyes earnestly sought Anna's, reassuring her.

'And as soon as anything happens, you'll let us know.'

'The very minute the pains start. You can rely on me.'

All the way back to London Anna thought about the farmhouse, about how beautiful the scenery around was on that winter's day, stark and severe in the December sunshine. How much more beautiful would it be in the spring, the leaves burgeoning on the skeletal trees, the birds busy nesting, the dawn chorus announcing the mating season. It was a time of year when everything in the country sprang to life.

It was true that in her part of London, near the Heath, the trees were full of blossom and the gardens of the well-heeled also seemed to spring to life. Driving through the park, though pleasurable, made you yearn for the country. Further towards the West End where her office was, you forgot about it altogether except for a glimpse of the tops of trees in Cavendish Square or the sight of a few bedraggled pigeons risking life and limb frenetically chasing one another around the streets.

There, the only indication of a change of season was the weather, or the fact that it got lighter or darker in the mornings or the evenings, or the streets were too hot, too cold or slippery with rain and ice.

But she also thought, couldn't help it, how much nicer it would be in the country, far away from Damian and the trouble he could cause.

It was with a feeling almost of discontent, of dissatisfaction, that Anna drew up outside the house and unpacked her bags. As she opened the gate she looked up and saw Peter standing by the window. She raised her hand and waved. He waved back before disappearing and reappearing at the door which he flung open running down the steps to welcome her.

'Darling,' he exclaimed crushing her to him, 'it's wonderful to have you back.' He released her and, taking her bags, preceded her up the steps.

Inside, the house was warm and welcoming. There was the smell of something delicious coming from the kitchen.

'Paula did a casserole.'

'How nice of her. It smells wonderful.' Anna put down her things and looked around. 'Yes, good to be home.'

'How's Fiona?' Peter asked stooping to kiss her again.

'Oh, she's fine. I'm still not happy leaving her but you can't force her, and Sal said she really would keep an eye on her, make sure she saw her every day.'

Peter put an arm round her and led her into the sitting room. The curtains had been drawn and he had evidently been reading the paper, a glass of whisky on a side table.

'Well here we are.' Anna sat down hands on her knees. She looked round, aware of a feeling of unease.

'Yes here we are.' Peter flopped into his chair and took up his glass. 'To you my love.'

She nodded. He was being especially loving and welcoming.

'Would you like a glass of wine?'

'No, thanks, I think I'll go up and unpack. I'm

quite hungry actually.'

'It's ready any time you are, darling.'

In the hall Anna picked up her hold-all, which wasn't very heavy, and went upstairs to her room, shutting the door behind her. She leaned against it and looked around. Her own room. Her own, familiar room. She'd lived here since her marriage. Nancy had lived here too, of course, and yet she didn't feel about this house the way she felt about the cottage.

She realised that the cottage *was* Nancy; it had her studio, her work, her canvases still stacked around, her pictures on the walls. Her daughter Fiona, and soon there would be her grandchild.

Anna thought of the farmhouse with its large airy rooms, painted white, restored to its eighteenth century origins, or maybe in Georgian colours: pastel blues, yellows, pinks and greens. She could see period chandeliers hanging from the ceilings instead of the very basic lighting fixtures there now. The beautiful original doors would be picked out in white with gleaming brass handles and fingerplates. It was difficult to know what was under the carpet. Was it parquet, boards or concrete? If concrete it would have to be recarpeted in a soft grey Axminster or Wilton. If parquet or boards they could be restored and waxed, covered with rugs. She could visualise the great range in the kitchen, still with the original coal fire, freshly blackened, with brass pots and pans hanging above it. In the garden, with its lovely views of river and coppice, would be a bird table for the robins, the woodpeckers, the chiff-chaffs and goldfinch . . .

She pulled herself up sharply as Peter's voice called out from below: 'Grub's up, Anna. Are you ready, darling?'

'Ready,' she called, and quickly fluffed out her hair, glanced at herself in the mirror, and without even applying fresh lipstick bounded down the stairs, two at a time.

They ate in the kitchen, serving the meal directly from the stove. Peter had put a candle in the centre of the table and she knew there was also a special bottle of wine. She toasted him and he smiled at her. 'I have missed you.'

'Me, too.'

'And thank you so much for doing what you did. I can't tell you how I appreciate it.'

'Doing what?' She looked surprised.

'Staying with Fiona.'

'It's my job. I wish I could have stayed longer. We can go down every weekend.'

'Can we?' He looked pleased, surprised. 'Oh good.'

'Peter,' Anna began, then paused not quite knowing how to say what she wanted to say. For once she was lost for words.

It was important to get it right, not to be misunderstood, to have him on her side.

'Yes, darling?' He looked up encouragingly.

'It's simply that the Hansons are selling the farm.' In the end the words all came out in a rush.

'Oh, dear, that is bad news.' Peter leaned back and broke into his bread roll. 'We shall miss them.'

'That's what I said. It's a lovely farmhouse. I . . .' She didn't want to get it wrong. 'Peter, I wonder if we should buy it.' There, it was out and even now she was surprised by her own words.

'Buy it!' he said in the crushing, almost derisory tone she'd dreaded. 'Buy the farm?'

'Yes. But not to farm it. You know what I mean.'

'I don't think I do. Don't you think we've enough on?' Peter got up to restock his plate with casserole and vegetables and looked across at her: 'Anna?'

'No, thanks.' She'd been terribly hungry, but now her appetite had gone.

'Yes, we have enough to do. It's just that I saw the house really for the first time the other day. Went all over it. I never realised it was so lovely. It's Georgian. I bet at one time it was the manor. It's got glorious ceilings. Mrs Hanson gave me tea when I went to pay the bill — enormous by the way — and get some eggs. It's such a beautiful house and the views . . .'

'Yes, those views are lovely.'

'It makes the cottage seem so claustrophobic.'

'You never liked it.'

'I think it's because of Nancy.'

Peter looked at her. *'Nancy?'*

'It was her place. Fiona is always more difficult

when she's there. Somehow I think the presence, the memory rather, of her mother makes her irritated and dissatisfied with me.'

'Don't be ridiculous.'

'I'm serious. I always get depressed, frankly, when I go to that cottage, and it's not just because of the time we've had there recently with the kids.'

'Then why not move away altogether if that's how you feel? Get somewhere else?'

'We couldn't sell that cottage, not at the moment, not with Fiona the way she is. Anyway, doesn't it belong to Fiona?'

'Yes.' Peter screwed up his nose. 'Nancy left it in trust for Guy and Fiona. I haven't thought about it, actually, because I've always regarded it as ours, you know, that is belonging to the family. To all of us.'

'So you can't sell it anyway unless they want to. Fiona might well make it her home. She seems to love it and we would want to be near Fiona and the baby.'

'I really believe you're serious,' Peter said wonderingly.

'I am. I mean I've thought a lot about it. Become obsessed by it, in a way, especially in the last few days. Mentally I've been refurbishing it.'

'Did you tell Fiona?'

'Oh, no. I told no one; but I think if we are interested, and I am, very, we must get a move on. It is on the market and we don't want the

Hansons to sell it before we have the chance to inspect it properly, weigh the pros and cons and consider an offer. You see, darling,' she leaned earnestly across the table, 'I don't want to labour this point, but it will be hell on earth, once Fiona has had the baby, to keep on going there, expecting her to put us up.'

'You mean the place will be in a terrible mess.' Peter grinned and poured them each more wine.

'Well, that too. But it's her home. She can make it her home, and the farm is far enough away yet also near enough for us to keep an eye on her.'

'She'll move in,' he warned.

'If she did there'll be plenty of room. Six bedrooms.'

Peter whistled. 'It's a hell of an undertaking. It might mean changing your life.'

Anna smiled at him mysteriously and then abruptly left the table and went over to kiss him.

She felt like a little girl asking for a present, and offering something nice in exchange by way of a bribe.

Guy stood awkwardly, hands behind his back, as Peter and Anna shook hands with the Head.

'Oh, he's doing awfully well,' Dick Preston murmured, turning to Guy's form master who stood beside him. 'Isn't he, Tom?'

Tom Merton nodded.

'*And* he's a popular boy, too. The school seems to have brought out the best in him.'

Guy, in his neat blazer, striped tie, white shirt and grey trousers, well-polished black shoes, was hardly recognisable as the jean-clad boy from the comp who, only months before, had been expelled for hurling a radiogram out of a fourth floor window.

Involuntarily Anna's eyes closed at the memory. If he'd injured or killed somebody what a very different story it would have been. Incarceration, a life ruined, to say nothing of the person or people who had been maimed or killed.

Worlds apart. That's what came of having money. It enabled you to buy a new style of life, whether it was changing schools or swapping a cottage for a large country house.

It hadn't been easy, but it had been possible to transfer Guy to a fee-paying school where the classes were small and most, if not all, of the children came from well-off middle-class families like the Livingstones. Or from families who, if not well-off, had thought it best to scrimp and scrape, sell their homes, borrow from the bank, jeopardise their futures, to ensure that their child avoided the pitfalls offered in some parts of the country by state education.

Yet Anna still felt ashamed as she looked at the Bentleys and Jags in the drive, at the large hats worn by many of the mothers, the well-creased pin-striped suits of the fathers.

But then she and Peter were not so very different, though their car was a normal production model in the medium price range and she wore a woollen coat over a navy blue suit, while Peter wore tweeds. But it would be quite easy to tell that they were well-educated, affluent and that their son had his own room in a nice home and, possibly, a get-away place in the country.

Yes it would be quite possible to tell all of these things.

After chatting to the Headmaster and his form master, Guy took them through the school hall, along the highly polished corridors to his bed-room, which was small yet big enough for a bed, desk, chairs and a wardrobe, a basin by the window which looked out on to the fields at the rear of the school. There were posters of his favourite football team on the wall — Arsenal, of course — of the pop stars of the moment, of various sporting heroes.

The room was tidy but not suspiciously so. It still had the look of being Guy's room, and Anna guessed that if she opened the wardrobe or one of the drawers she would have found clothes tossed in any old how, crumpled shirts, creased underpants and socks with holes in them.

But she wouldn't.

'We're thinking of buying the farm in the village,' she said, unable to conceal her excitement, perching at the end of his bed.

'Which village?' Guy looked up.

'In our village, Little Halton.'

'Yippee!' Guy let out a whoop. For the first time since they'd arrived, he looked happy. 'Are you going to give up work and become farmers?'

'Not exactly,' Peter laughed. 'Anna's fallen in love with the house and the Hansons are selling up. Anna might work part-time, spend more of the week down there.'

'We want to be nearer Fiona after she has the baby. We feel she'll need help and support.'

Guy nodded, looked solemn, but also rather embarrassed. He couldn't see his sister, so near to him in age, in this unaccustomed role of future mother. Couldn't begin even to envisage it.

'Farming would be fun,' Guy said, and there was a sudden catch in his voice which made Anna look up.

'We're not going to farm, Guy. The Hansons are selling the animals and we'll buy the land to stop people building on it should the eventuality ever arise.'

'Oh!' Guy looked abashed.

There was something wrong with Guy. He was too quiet, too polite, unnaturally so. The atmosphere was awkward, strained.

'Is everything alright, Guy?' Anna asked looking at him intently.

'Of course.' Guy ran his finger along the side of his desk but avoided her eyes. 'Why shouldn't it be?'

'I don't know. It's just that you don't seem terribly at ease.'

'Oh, for God's sake, Anna,' Peter said irritably, 'don't encourage him, now that we've got him settled.'

'I hate this place,' Guy said suddenly. 'I loathe

it.' His expression was bleak.

'Oh, *Guy!* . . .' Anna leaned forward and caught one of his hands. 'We thought you were happy, settled down. Your letters were fine. The Head said . . .'

'I don't like anything about it; the staff, the boys and girls are all snobs . . .'

'*All* of them?'

'Most of them. They look down on anyone who hasn't got money, and they know. They know whose parents have asked for help with fees, who are on assisted places schemes and they're horrible to them.'

'Then it's up to you to counteract that.'

'I do. I try, and they call me Trotsky, or Trot, you know the one who didn't fit in, who fell out with Stalin. The people here just cover all this up. The ones who are victimised put up with it for the sake of their parents, the sacrifices they made. They really are the nicest ones of all and my few friends are among them. But they want to get out, and so do I.'

Peter sat dejectedly on the bed next to Anna, his hands loosely joined in front of him.

'I knew it was too good to be true,' he said. 'I knew it was unbelievable.'

It had been hard to tell from Guy's letters home, and when they visited him he seemed well, happy in a controlled kind of way. But Anna realised now that it hadn't been at all like Guy. He'd been fooling them all along.

'Can you just bear it until you've done your

exams?' she asked.

'Until the summer? Next summer?' He brightened at once, and the tears which had seemed to be lurking failed, after all, to flow. 'You mean I can *leave* in the summer?'

'We didn't say that,' Peter frowned at Anna. 'You might like it better by then.'

'Oh, I shan't.' Guy leaned against the wall, arms folded, and looked at them. 'I shall do as Fiona did and if you don't let me I shall still leave. I'd prefer to do it with your agreement. You know you can't make me stay here, but after all the trouble I've been I did want to try.' And then, suddenly, the tears came, first a trickle and then a flood cascading down his cheeks.

'Oh, *Guy!*' Anna leapt up and put her arms around him drawing him down on the bed. 'Really we didn't know. We wanted to do it for the best.'

'We wanted you to have a decent education, Guy,' Peter said tetchily, 'and you'd think that after what has happened to your sister that's what *you'd* want too.'

'I did. I do; but I just loathe it here.'

'But you loathed it at the comp.'

'I didn't loathe it.' Guy's tears dried up and his tone of voice became truculent. 'I just didn't like work. I had a lot of mates. Here I don't really mind the work but I don't like the people, and I don't like their parents,' he said viciously. 'A bunch of arty-farty snobs.'

'Well I don't know about "arty-farty" but I did

334

think one or two of them didn't look too bad,' Anna demurred. 'However I know what you mean. It's not the real world.'

'Anna, why do you *say* these things?' Peter began to look really angry. 'Why are you encouraging him to behave like this?'

'What's the use of pretending, Peter?' Anna rose and went to the window. 'It's a lovely place, a beautiful setting, but it is an expensive minor public school. It's the sort of place I guess I knew Guy would be unhappy in.'

'Well *he* liked it. Christ, we went all over the bloody country.'

'I know, Dad, and I'm sorry. That's why I didn't say anything before. I know I've upset you and you've wasted a lot of time and money. I will stay here until the summer and I will do my best in the GCSEs. But after that I want to leave. I shall be sixteen and there will be no compulsive reason for me to stay on at school.'

'And do what?'

Guy shrugged.

'I quite like the idea of farming.' His face brightened, eyes looked hopeful. 'I mean if you bought the house and kept the land . . .'

Peter was silent for such a long time after they drove through the school gates that Anna wondered if he should be driving; he seemed to seethe with suppressed anger beside her and once or twice made a rash move.

'Shall I take over, dear?' she asked after a while.

'Why should you take over?' He looked at her savagely.

'I can see that you're upset.'

'Of course I'm bloody upset; and who was it that mentioned farming?'

'I saw absolutely nothing wrong in saying we were thinking of buying the farm. I didn't suggest he should farm there but, Peter, if we did and he wanted to, what's wrong with it?'

'Because I want him to do something with his life. I want him to get As and go to university.'

'Farming *is* doing something with his life. I mean, if you're so keen on an academic career for him and he is serious about it he could go to an agricultural college.'

'He's never said he was interested in farming before. If you ask me, the idea just occurred to him.' Now that they were actually discussing the subject that so irritated him, Peter's driving seemed to have improved and Anna felt easier.

'I seem to remember he did mention it once. Anyway, I didn't know I wanted to do law until I was in the sixth form. Even then I wasn't sure. Look, between now and the summer is quite a long time. He has agreed to stay on and that's the main thing. He might change his mind again.' She put out her hand and lightly touched his. 'One step at a time, darling. Don't make it too hard for yourself.'

The Hansons had been surprised but pleased by the Livingstones' interest in the farm. They would have preferred to sell it to working farmers, but in these days of recession the property market was sluggish and they had their eyes on a bungalow by the sea with half an acre of land, just enough for the amount of gardening they wanted to do. Time to put their feet up and retire, take things easy.

At Christmas all the family — Peter, Anna, Guy and Fiona — went round the house. Guy again affirmed his interest in farming and to emphasise this, helped Ted all over the Christmas holiday. On the whole, apart from the usual rows, misunderstandings and silences it was a happy time, a traditional Christmas with a tree, lights, turkey and a party for the neighbours including the Hansons, Sal and Honey, Fred and many more. All of them were delighted at the prospect of the Livingstones rather than strangers buying Hall Farm. Finally, Anna and Peter put in an offer only marginally below the asking price, and after further negotiation and deliberation the deal was settled.

A man called Michael Lawrence had been appointed to run the law practice in Wigmore Street jointly with Anna. They were equal partners and at first Anna liked Michael and got on with him. She swallowed her pride and found, besides, that having someone to share the workload gave her more time for her Council work and her voluntary sessions at the Law Centre. But she also felt increasingly that her many duties had become irksome. The purchase of Hall Farm and its future was much on her mind, and so was the question of Damian who had started to telephone her again.

Anna knew she couldn't go on stalling for ever. Now was the time to do something about it.

McDonald's, off the busy Holloway Road, was hardly a romantic spot for a tryst. McDonald's at noon with people bustling in and out for an early lunch, a late breakfast, a snack.

Damian was already there when Anna arrived, having had difficulty finding somewhere to park her car. She stood for a moment in the doorway looking at him. It was not a large place, and had a back area, vaguely Art Deco, filled mainly with small tables and chairs. At one of the tables Damian sat staring moodily in front of him, hands clasped, fingers intertwined. He seemed bathed in a golden glow. His hair bleached by the artificial light, his beard full of red-bronze highlights, his earrings twinkling like tinsel. Anna remembered what kissing him had been like, and the supple firmness of his youthful body.

She swallowed and, as she did, he looked round, rose from his chair with the expression of an eager schoolboy and came towards her, one arm easily, briefly encircling her waist.

'Hi!' she said looking towards the counter. 'Sorry I'm late.'

'That's OK.' He removed his arm. 'Do you want something to eat?'

'Just a coffee. I'm between courts.' She moved

towards the counter but he said: 'Hey, let me get it,' and pushed past her, hands in his pockets counting out the change. 'You get a place.'

In the fast food restaurant few, of the tables were free, but she found one at the rear where she thought no one would notice them, busy metropolitans with no time on their hands.

She had deliberately chosen McDonald's because it was an impersonal sort of place in a busy part of town where they were quite unlikely to see or be seen by anyone they knew.

Anna sat down, loosened her jacket, placed her bag and briefcase on the floor beside her, gave a deep sigh just as Damian joined her, setting her coffee in front of her, taking his place opposite.

'Thanks,' she said nervously, immediately putting her cup to her lips. She felt awkward, and wished she hadn't agreed to his request for a meeting.

She was aware that his eyes had never left her, and as she looked up he put a hand over hers. He'd gone to some trouble to groom himself for the occasion. He wore jeans, a clean shirt and a sweater, and the ribbon round his pony tail looked new.

'Anna,' he said, speaking hesitantly, 'I fancy you something rotten.'

'I like you too.' She lowered her eyes and clumsily tried to withdraw her hand.

'You know what I mean,' he urged. 'You're really sexy, Anna. You try to hide it . . .'

'I don't hide it,' she retorted angrily, looking

up at him. 'But I really am in love with my husband, Peter. What happened was . . . well, a moment of aberration.'

He leaned forward as if he, too, were angry. 'You call that marvellous fuck a moment of aberration?' he hissed.

Momentarily she was speechless, and he grasped her hand again, his thumb and forefinger harshly rubbing against her rings.

'No,' she acknowledged, again avoiding his eyes. 'It *was* marvellous.' Then suddenly she looked straight at him, feeling liberated from her stupid middle-class inhibitions. 'Of course I enjoyed it.'

'Oh, *Anna!*' He squeezed her fingers so hard that the rings pressed into them and they hurt. 'Let's go on. I don't mind about Peter. Let's meet from time to time, do it again. I won't be around a great deal. My father is very ill. He's probably going to die. My mother says I've helped to bring on his illness, made his last years wretched, so I've promised to go home for a while. I've also,' he paused, 'called off the case of suing the police.'

'Oh, I'm so relieved.' She gave him a broad smile and returned the pressure of his hand. 'Not just for me. I think it's time for you to begin again, Damian. You haven't really got a squatter's mentality. You're a talented, educated man who could give a lot to society in other ways. Make a positive contribution. You could easily get a job.'

'You really *are* oriented to jobs, aren't you, Anna?' he said sarcastically. 'Success, money . . .'

'No, I'm *not*, but I think you're wasting your life.'

'Let's go on, Anna.' They had scarcely touched their coffee which was getting cold. Momentarily Anna thought that if anyone happened to be observing them they must have presented a strange picture: a woman in a black suit, white blouse with a briefcase and a man with a pony tail and three earrings through his ear, earnestly clutching her hand. 'Anna?' he said again.

'I was thinking we must look odd.' She smiled rather shyly. 'Look, we *can't* go on, Damian. Not only is it wrong, it's not sensible. Life is too complicated to do what you want to do. Let's just look at that day as something nice, memorable but unexpected that happened between us.' She touched his hand for a second, letting her fingers linger, and then her manner changed, becoming brisk and practical. 'Damian, do you know where Errol is? He left Fiona and we'd like to find him. She's having a baby.'

Damian whistled and shook his head.

'He just did a bunk,' Anna went on. 'I thought you might know. I always felt guilty, you see, that I never checked up on him properly: where he came from, anything about him. I mean he came from the north. Do you happen to know . . .'

Damian shook his head again and swallowed

341

the rest of his cold coffee.

'You know that we never suss people up, Anna; but Errol was a genuine artist. He was properly trained. He suffered from depression. I guess he couldn't cope with the idea of a baby. It doesn't surprise me. But you'll never get any support out of him, Anna. He'd never . . .'

'It's not just *that*. I think she pines for him. She loves him. I'd like to think that if we find him we could reason with him, maybe offer him support.'

'Patronise him,' Damian said bitterly.

'No, not patronise. You're so damn defensive, Damian.'

'That's what it's all about, isn't it, Anna?' Damian suddenly slipped off his chair. 'The haves and the have nots. Patronise them, offer them charity, screw them . . .'

'Oh, Damian!' Anna shook her head and realised she felt wretched. One or two people had interrupted their meal to stare at them. Strangely she didn't care. 'That's *never* the way I thought about you.' Briefly, her fingers reached out and stroked his face. 'Just the time, the place, the moment, if you like; but a future for us? Never. Only heartache.'

She, too, rose from her chair, picked up her bag and briefcase and, followed by him, walked to the door.

Rather shyly, they stood facing each other on the pavement outside, as if neither knew what to say.

342

'Happy memories, Anna?' Damian stooped to kiss her cheek. Then he turned abruptly on his heels and walked quickly away, up the Seven Sisters Road, leaving a confused, unhappy woman not a little sorry about what she'd done, but, even more, for the unworthy thoughts that she'd harboured about him just because he was a squatter.

CHAPTER 14

Anna drove slowly along the lane that led from the farm to the village feeling, despite the normal worries and preoccupations that were so much a part of her life, very happy. It was late June and the hedgerows were lush with a profusion of wild flowers.

As if the beauties of nature weren't enough, she had another reason for her spirits to soar. She was a grandmother and how she loved it, surprising everybody, not least herself, by her reaction to Fiona's lovely baby, Harriet, who had been born a little premature, it seemed, but healthy at the hospital in Yeovil. Anna had been at Hall Farm at the time, the purchase having been completed two months earlier, and was there for the birth waiting, just as anxiously as any mother, for news of her daughter's safe delivery.

Fiona and Harriet had gone back to the cottage and Sal was persuaded to work full time as mother's help. She was needed. Everyone expected Fiona to be depressed, but curiously she wasn't. Instead she displayed a worrying apathy towards the child, a kind of indifference as though she could scarcely believe, indeed doubted, that she belonged to her. With time, hopefully, that would change. Fiona had all the help and support she could want, all the love except that of her baby's father: Errol.

Anna frowned as she approached the village. Momentarily her feeling of joy abated. Fiona remained a problem; probably she always would. The really amazing thing was how protective she herself felt towards the infant, maybe as a way of compensating. Anna simply doted on Harriet. The boot of the car at the moment full of useful gifts. Every day there was a visit, sometimes two, despite all the work there was to do in the house. And how she hated going back to London, longing to return to the country, her house and the baby again.

There was so much to see to at Hall Farm. So much to sort out. Workmen and decorators to be consulted, and somehow it seemed mostly to fall upon her. Not that Peter disagreed; he simply rubber stamped everything she suggested and came up with the money when it was time to pay.

But nevertheless there remained that tug between two worlds: the world of the city and the world beyond.

Anna had spent the morning with the interior decorator who had decided views of her own. She had come up from Bournemouth with swatches and samples of this and that, and the inevitable argument had followed. The decorator had rather grandiose ideas about the heavy use of silks and satins as hangings and coverings, and four-poster beds, while Peter and Anna wanted a simpler style, a place where their friends would feel at ease, not forced to dress up, the atmosphere as informal as possible. Sometimes Anna wished she had done the whole thing herself but there really wasn't time, and expense on this scale could not be repeated every few years. It had to be got right.

She'd travel down on Friday afternoon, sometimes with Peter and sometimes without, and back on Monday morning thus, in effect, taking a day off work, which continued as stressfully as usual and had to be sometimes crammed in. Peter told Anna that if she wasn't careful she'd have a nervous breakdown, to which she had replied that if she was that sort of person, she'd have had one a long time ago.

Peter had a conference in Scotland this weekend which Anna was rather pleased about. It gave her the chance to spend time alone in the new house and time with Fiona to help try and sort out what she was going to do with the next, say, eighteen years of her life while Harriet grew up. The time it would take Harriet to turn from the baby she now was, into a responsible woman like her mother.

Responsible? Well.

Anna, armed with various samples of material about which she thought it would be nice to consult Fiona and Sal, alighted from the car and went up the path, stopping for a moment outside the front door before entering.

It was such a lovely day, the countryside around so beautiful, the air so balmy, so different from London that it was odd still to feel this sense of foreboding that she had so many times experienced outside Fiona's bedroom door, a kind of mental taking stock, involuntarily bracing oneself for something unpleasant.

As she opened the door and entered, Sal looked up from the baby's cot, a smile of welcome, almost of relief, Anna thought momentarily, on her face.

'Hi!' Sal said.

'Hi! Everything OK?'

'Fine.' Sal looked tenderly at the baby sleeping in her carrycot. She was adorable, cuddly but not fat. She had wispy blonde hair, almost white, great blue eyes and dimpled cheeks. Thank heaven she seemed to have very little of the dark, brooding nature of Errol. It would be extremely difficult not to love her on sight, and Anna had fallen an immediate victim to her charms. She fussed anxiously over her, making sure that her bedding was right and her breathing regular. There was so much more these days in the way of infant welfare, yet there seemed to be a disproportionate increase in the amount of anxiety. Surely mothers hadn't worried so much in the past? Yet, years ago, mortality among children had been common. In a large family everyone expected one or two children to die. How agonising it must have been to watch a young life snuffed out and not being in a position to do anything about it. What anguish.

Anna made baby noises and then looked up at Sal.

'Isn't she *adorable?*'

'Adorable. She's a picture-book baby.'

Anna sighed and rose from the cot, looking in the direction of the stairs, her expression changing.

'Is Fiona still in bed?'

'Yes.'

'God knows how she could do without you.'

'I don't think we could leave her on her own with the baby.' Sal also rose and lowered her voice. Anna looked at her in alarm.

'You don't mean . . .'

'Oh, I don't think she'd *harm* her. Not for a moment. I just don't think she'd look after her properly, change her regularly, even feed her. That sort of thing. She'd forget.'

Mentally, Anna once more braced herself for that walk upstairs that sometimes seemed to resemble the march to the scaffold.

'Well, I'd better go and see how she is. Did she have breakfast?'

Sal shook her head. 'She didn't want anything.'

'I'll take her a cup of coffee.'

'I think she'd prefer tea.'

'Tea then. Look at these bits of material and tell me what you think.' Anna indicated a mass of stuff lying on the table. 'The decorator's got such fancy ideas. These came from Liberty's.'

Anna made the tea, put cups and teapot and

milk on the tray and then, on impulse, toasted two slices of bread and added butter and honey as well. Honey was full of good things, vitamins, the nectar of the gods. Carefully she carried the tray upstairs and then outside Fiona's door she put it on the floor and tapped.

'Fiona?'

No reply, naturally.

Anna turned the handle, pushed open the door, picked up the tray, crept in. The curtains were still drawn and Fiona appeared asleep. Anna stood gazing down at her, her emotions the usual compound of irritation, anger and pity. She looked so vulnerable herself, scarcely out of childhood, someone who had never really grown up. Had she wanted a child because she herself was a child, wanted a companion to play with? Or had she thought, maybe subconsciously, that it would help her to hang on to Errol? That Errol would never leave her as long as she had his child?

'Fiona.' Gently Anna shook her and then realised from the rigidity of her body that she was awake. How long had she lain like that pretending to be asleep?

'Hi, you are awake!' Anna turned to the tray which she'd put on the chest at the foot of the bed. 'I brought you some tea.'

'I want my mummy,' Fiona said in a childish, little girl tone. She rolled her great eyes towards Anna. 'My real mummy, not you.'

Anna's heart froze. Even when you dread

something, expect it, it's hard to be proved right.

She turned her back on Fiona and poured out two cups of tea, buttered the toast and spread honey on it.

She took one of the cups and the toast over to the bed and put it on the table near Fiona's elbow. Then she retrieved her own cup and sat in a chair facing it.

'We seem to have been here before, Fiona.'

Pause, then: 'What'd ja mean?'

'All this business about me not being your mother.'

'Well you aren't.' Fiona surreptitiously eyed the food placed beside her, then stretched out a hand and, taking the toast, began to eat it hungrily. This convinced Anna, as if she needed any convincing, that most of Fiona's attitude was an act rather than any form of depressive illness. In short she seemed prepared to do anything to get attention.

Anna finished her tea, put down her cup, joined her hands and contemplated Fiona. She had quite abandoned her spiky hairdo. It was pretty hair with a natural springy curl and it now tumbled about her face, half obscuring her features. She was an attractive girl, had the makings of beauty, had so much. Still only eighteen.

Anna felt a pricking on her temples, a tightening in her chest, all the symptoms of tension that seemed to go with Fiona. Soon it would develop into a headache and she'd want to creep away and lie down. This was something fairly new, an extension of her apprehension to her physical well-being.

'Fiona, what is it you want me to do?' she asked wearily.

No reply. Try again.

'I mean, do you want me to take Harriet to the house for the time being? I can easily do that and let you rest or, if you like, you can both come up to the house. It's a bit like camping but there is room.'

Fiona shook her head, gazing at Anna with those large, reproachful eyes, still saying nothing.

'You don't want to do any of those things?'

Fiona shook her head.

Anna began to feel exasperated and the pain across her forehead gradually grew worse as she knew it would. Fiona's eyes suddenly closed. One piece of toast had been eaten, the other not. The tea had been drunk.

'Fiona, I wish I could help you.' Anna sat on the bed beside her. 'I realise you're unhappy and it makes me feel helpless. I am also worried on Harriet's account. She must suffer.'

'She is not suffering.' Fiona's eyes flashed open. 'You know I love her. Sal loves her. She is very well looked after thank you, Anna!'

'I'm not talking about love. I simply feel the tension might somehow affect her.'

'What do you mean "tension"?'

'You staying in bed all day and not acting like a normal mother.'

'You're always so critical of me.' Fiona

bounced around in the bed and buried her face in her pillow. 'I miss him so much.'

That was it. Errol.

'You haven't mentioned him for a long time,' Anna said gently. 'I'd hoped you might have forgotten him. Perhaps it will help to talk about him.'

'*How* can I possibly *forget* him?' Fiona, still with her face in the pillow, beat the bed on either side of her. 'He's Harriet's father. Don't you think . . .' she sat up, hugging her pillow as though it was her baby and looked pathetically at Anna, 'don't you think you could find him? You're so clever, Anna. You've got so much *influence* with all important people: the Council and so on. Couldn't you try?'

'My darling, what good would it do? Really, if we did find him? Would we be able to convince him to come here, to see you and Harriet? He would be afraid that the authorities would be after him to support the child, you know, the kind of thing you read about in the newspapers? Let's face it, basically, Errol has opted out of life with you. As long as he had it easy with you he was happy, but once you discovered you were pregnant then so many alarming speculations occurred to him.' Tenderly, gently Anna began to stroke her back. 'Dear, Fiona, and believe me, you are very dear to me, you must try and live for the present, for Harriet and yourself, and get Errol completely out of your mind.'

Anna looked round the house. What a wrench it was to leave it. Half-finished as it was, she knew that she loved it. It was her place. The walls of its high-ceilinged rooms were now stripped and painted in soft pastel colours. Some of the doors, accretions of a later age, had been replaced by eighteenth century originals found in antique shops, sometimes dug up in junk yards, restored and rehung. The floorboards too had been stripped and waxed and a collection of beautiful rugs had been assembled, some newly purchased, some brought down from the London house.

Slowly everything was beginning to take shape. Some of the rooms had a modicum of furniture in them. In the master bedroom there was a double bed, and beds in two of the other rooms. The rest remained untouched. Some of the rooms were curtained, others not. In theory, therefore, it would have been possible for Fiona and Harriet to have moved in with Anna, but in many ways it was better they stayed where they were. When Anna had seen her that morning Fiona was up, dressed and playing quite happily with the baby in the sunlit garden. A different person altogether from the gloomy teenager of previous days, a creature of moods and impulse.

Anna had had another week's holiday, unpaid. She knew that she was beginning to stretch the amount of leave she could possibly take and even the status of part-time was being abused.

She went through the house checking that

everything was in order; the last workers had left for the day and they would be there again at seven the next morning. The Livingstones had said they wanted the house to be ready by late summer. It was a tall order but with enough money you could get anything. Especially in times of recession people would work extra hard.

Anna went out into the sunlit yard and looked wistfully into the garden to where Peter, with the help of a part-time gardener, had already begun making inroads. The entire garden, which was a large one, was being redesigned. The Hansons had been practical people with a huge kitchen garden but with little time for herbaceous borders or ornamentation.

Looking around Anna realised that, for most of her life, she had in fact been starved of beauty, of the leisure time to enjoy the glories of nature. No time to stand and stare, to enjoy the hedge-rows, fields full of corn and maize, the bright yellow of rapeseed in the spring. In London one knew sparrows, pigeons — plenty of those — and the odd blackbird, but little else. Here bluetits, robins, chaffinches and greenfinches were common and now and again one saw the green or great spotted woodpecker, a goldcrest or tree creeper, the swift flight of the tiny wren with its upturned tail, maybe a majestic heron rising from the river bank with a fish struggling in its mouth.

Once they were settled in they could have domestic pets, cats and dogs. She had always been an animal lover, but thought that to keep a pet

354

in the London environment with its busy streets wasn't fair.

As Anna loaded the car for the drive back to London she thought that they would soon have to make the decision about what to do about the London house. They didn't really need a large house, especially if Fiona was going to stay in the country, and Guy wanted to farm. Perhaps a flat in the Barbican was the answer?

The idea of a flat wasn't very appealing, but the capital that would be released by the sale of the house would be a help now that Anna no longer worked full-time. However, she hardly felt part-time, what with all the toing and froing, and racing about she still had to do. She now gave Friday mornings to the Law Centre and drove down to Dorset in the afternoon. Coping with Fiona and the baby and the new house and its innumerable problems was hardly taking it easy.

She had an easy drive along the A303 and the M3, very little traffic about, and reached home at nine. The house was empty. Somehow she expected it would be and now, increasingly, Peter hardly ever left a note to say where he'd be. The thought uneasily crossed her mind again that he might be having an affair. After all, so many people did nowadays. If so, with whom? Would she mind? Well of course she'd mind terribly, but merely to speculate was a stupid waste of time, and she doubted that she would ever ask him outright.

She felt tired, a little headachy, and after playing the messages on the answer-machine and watching news headlines on the TV in the kitchen while she had a snack, she decided it was time for bed.

She rinsed the dishes under the tap, dried them and was in the act of putting them away when the phone rang. She quickly wiped her hands on the kitchen towel and, with a pleasant sense of anticipation, took the receiver off the wall phone.

'Hello?'

No answer.

She sensed there was someone on the line and she repeated herself.

'Hello? Peter, is that you?'

Still no response.

'Press the button' she said, beginning to feel irritated and remembering that these days people put the coins in the machine if they were calling from a call box. Or, perhaps they had a phone card?

It occurred to her that the caller was in fact calling from a private phone, and that he, or she, was there listening to her. It was an eerie, unpleasant sensation and she was about to replace the receiver when the line went dead. The person at the other end had done it first.

Thoughtfully Anna replaced her own receiver and slumped into a chair, leaning her elbows on the kitchen table.

This had happened before. Several times, now she came to think of it, but one often got wrong numbers, busy lines, and she hadn't given it another thought.

Supposing Peter did have a girlfriend? Some distraught woman who just wanted to hear the sound of his voice, know where he was or why he hadn't called? Or, perhaps, wanted to hear what his wife sounded like? A woman, maybe, she was crazily jealous of?

Anna rose abruptly, tucked the chair under the table, looked round to see everything was in place, though when Peter came in he would be sure to go into the kitchen. He always did. She put the light off and, leaving the one on in the hall, went upstairs, conscious of a dreadful feeling of depression, as though her body were weighted down with a huge stone.

Inside their bedroom she put on the lights at either side of the bed, went into the bathroom and turned on the bath taps, then back to the bedroom where she slowly began to undress. Well, supposing Peter *was* having an affair? Was she going to confront him or continue to torment herself with her suspicions? That green-eyed monster that denied peace of mind. How often had she counselled her clients to put it to one side and get on with their lives?

And what, if it came to that, of herself? Hadn't she had, well one could hardly dignify it with the name 'affair', but she had had sex here in this very house with a man she didn't love, hardly knew. She had been swept away in the crudest possible manner. It was quite outside any rational, sensible behaviour and, although it meant so little to her, knowledge of it would have devastated Peter, could possibly have ruined their marriage. But what about all these odd calls? If they *were* for Peter, from a woman, this was no casual fling. This was an affair and, yes, if so, it deeply worried her.

Anna returned to the bathroom determined to take the good advice she gave to others and put these, after all, very vague suspicions out of her mind. She would deliberately turn her thoughts to the country again, to the views from the house, the memory of changing seasons, the proliferation of colours, the sweet sound of birdsong and the peace and tranquillity it gave her.

She lay in the bath for a long time, ruminating. She felt the tug between the country and the town was unsettling her, almost, literally, pulling her apart. It was silly to lie there dreaming of lush green fields, of magpies on the lawn and squirrels chasing up the great oak trees in the fields when here she was in the heart of London with a very heavy schedule the following day.

After taking her bath and cleansing her face she got into bed wishing that, somehow, she didn't feel uneasy about Peter. Supposing he was having an affair and it was serious? Supposing he wanted to leave her, start a new life with someone else, a younger woman who would give him the baby he said she had denied him?

She had just picked up her book when she heard the key in the lock downstairs. She lay for some time listening to Peter moving around and then he came quietly upstairs and gently pushed the door open, looking at her.

'So you're awake? How long have you been in?'

'I got here at nine.' Anna put down her book. 'Where've you been?' She tried to keep criticism out of her voice. The last thing she wanted was to turn into the sort of nagging shrew, suspicious of her husband she met so often in her office.

'I had dinner in the club. Bumped into Matthew Thomson. I haven't seen him since university days.'

The name Matthew Thomson meant nothing to her.

'How nice,' she said.

'Anna?' In the act of taking off his shirt Peter paused and looked across at her.

'No, I mean, I just don't know the name.'

'It was the way you said it.'

'Sorry,' she smiled at him, 'I feel tired.'

'I bet you do,' he paused, 'you're doing too much. More than ever now.'

'That's what I think. Sometimes,' she hesitated, wondering whether or not it was wise to go on. 'Sometimes I wonder if . . . it would be nice to live in the country all the time.' She finished in a rush. Peter, sitting on the bed to take off his shoes and socks, stopped abruptly and looked at her.

'Are you serious?'

'No. I just wonder. It was particularly beautiful when I left today. All serene and peaceful. The house is coming along well and, of course,' pause again, 'there is Fiona. She's a worry.'

Peter sighed.

'The other day she said she wanted her real mummy,' Anna went on. 'Then last night we had a perfectly civilised meal at the pub while Sal baby-sat and she was as nice as anything. Full of plans.'

'What sort of plans?'

'Oh, for painting, for Harriet's future. She's a female Jekyll and Hyde.'

'She's still very young. We mustn't forget that.' Peter got off the bed, removed the rest of his clothes and went into the bathroom.

She watched him as he walked across the room naked. Were there any telltale signs? Bruises? Marks on the neck? Bites on the body? Lipstick on the collar? She would never have thought of looking, but maybe now she should. If he was sleeping with someone else did they use contraception and, as it was natural to suppose they would, what kind? Peter would hate the condom. They had never used it and, Anna thought, if he *was* in fact sharing her with someone else should she worry too? AIDS, Herpes, vaginal thrush, there were any number of things of which so far she had been free.

That was the worst of being a lawyer, of having an analytical mind. One could be objective about the most subjective, intimate things pertaining to oneself.

Peter came back, washed, teeth brushed, pyjamas on and climbed into bed beside her. He lay for a moment and then reached out gently, drew up her nightie, let his hand rest on her stomach and sighed.

'Nice,' he said closing his eyes.

Anna felt herself stiffen. Supposing, just supposing, in the past hour or two he had been having sex with someone else? It didn't mean, did it, that he wouldn't necessarily want her now, that he'd had enough? In fact, the more you had the more you wanted. It became like a drug.

'Peter,' she asked, gently pushing his hand away, 'are you having an affair?'

She could sense his reaction before she turned and looked at him. You had to see people's eyes, their faces to know the truth.

'Why do you ask me, Anna?' He seemed more curious than angry.

'I just wondered.'

'But why *should* you wonder?'

'Because,' she paused, 'you are out an awful lot at night. I know you don't have any hobbies or belong to any committees, and maybe you don't think our own sex life is full enough. I just thought . . . I mean I don't think I'd blame you.'

'Really?' Now he sounded amused. 'You mean you wouldn't really care?'

'I would care, a great deal; but it's illogical, isn't it? I mean I see enough of it in my practice. The wife who doesn't know really what her husband does, or didn't until he asked for a divorce.'

'Do you think I'd have an affair with all that

361

is going on in my life?'

'All what?'

'All this.' He spread out his hand. 'Moving to a new house, my teenage daughter with a baby, Guy about to do GCSEs and not knowing what to do with his life.'

'It might take your mind off it. You know, a fling, someone younger perhaps? *I* don't think you're the type, but one never knows. My work has taught me that the most ordinary people do the strangest things.'

'And I am an ordinary person?'

'Well you're not extraordinary. You're a nice, ordinary man. Yes.'

'Do you still love me, Anna?' He turned and looked at her with a sweet, sad expression.

'Yes, I do,' she paused, 'very much.'

'Because I, too, sometimes wonder.'

'You wonder about *me?*' She looked incredulous.

'Yes, I do.'

'You wonder if *I'm* having an affair? How preposterous.'

'No, I don't wonder, though of course one never knows. As you say you think you know someone and then find you don't. We're always being surprised by what other people do. You've always been a mystery to me.'

'How extraordinary.'

'You have. I always feel I never quite know you, understand you.'

She waited a long time before replying, because

in a way she knew what he meant. Know thyself: she did, others didn't.

'I think we're *both* too analytical,' she said turning to him. 'I love you. I do. Take my word for it.'

'I love you.' He raised her nightie again and re-established his hand on her stomach. It would either travel upwards to her breasts, or down to her groin where, already, she began to feel a delicious anticipatory sensation.

She would try not to mention an affair again. But she would never really know the truth about Peter because, as they had now established, one never really knew the whole truth about another person, even if one was married to them.

There was always that inner, secret place that no one could reach.

And maybe there was also that other person, silent, listening at the end of the telephone line.

CHAPTER 15

The optician rose from his stool and switched on the lights, smiling at Anna as she blinked at the unaccustomed brightness.

'Everything seems absolutely fine,' he said. 'Your eyes are in very good shape, except for the slight problem you have seeing close up and this we deal with very effectively with your reading glasses.' He held them up. 'The prescription doesn't need changing at all.'

'Well, that's good.' Anna prepared to get up too, and looked around for her bag, but the optician indicated that she should stay where she was.

'How frequent are the headaches, Mrs Livingstone?'

'Well, fairly frequent.'

'Every day?'

'Oh, no.'

'Once a week, twice a week?'

Anna screwed up her nose in an effort to remember.

'They're intermittent. Every so often.'

'Do they relate to anything specific? Any time, not the time of the month for instance?'

'I wouldn't say so.' Then again, spontaneously, at the back of her mind the picture of Fiona formed. Fiona frowning, Fiona having a tantrum, Fiona turning her back to the wall as though in rejection.

'No!' She shook her head emphatically. 'They just come and go.'

The optician tapped his fingers on his bench, gazing at Anna's card and frowning.

'You do lead a very stressful life, I suppose, Mrs Livingstone, don't you? Family commitments, work, the Council . . .'

'I've cut down,' Anna said firmly, getting her bag and standing up. 'I only work part-time. Everything fits in very well.'

'Pressure *does* cause headaches.' The optician rose too. 'There's no sign of anything serious in the brain, as far as I can see, but it might be a good idea to get your doctor to check you over too.'

Brain? Anna eased her car into the traffic that moved at a snail's pace along Wigmore Street. The lights by Cavendish Square seemed to be changing every two seconds, another rush of traffic would surge forward and she moved two more inches. She could feel the tension mounting. In her breast, the fear that, once again, she would be late for a Council meeting, the gnawing anxiety that she was letting not only herself but the Party down by missing so many debates.

It was a Thursday, late-night opening in the West End and the traffic was appalling. After her optician's appointment she had stayed late at the office because there was so much more catching up to do now that she only worked a three-day week.

The traffic stopped again, someone had decided to sit on his or her horn. Probably a 'him' because men were inclined to show their impatience whereas women just suffered and simmered, as she was doing now. She gripped the wheel hard between her fingers and felt that familiar knot of tension and anxiety right in the middle of her solar plexus. It would be the usual excuse as she slipped into her seat under the baleful stare of the Council leader.

'Sorry, the traffic was bad,' she'd murmur.

Of course the traffic always was bad, every Londoner knew that. It wasn't an excuse either, so the thing was to leave in time to allow for the traffic. That was what she told people who were late for work, and what she knew others would like to tell her though, of course, because of the seniority of her position, they wouldn't dare.

The debate was drawing to an end as she slipped into the chamber, glancing at the leader, the word framed on her lips: 'Traffic.' He barely glanced at her before looking away again. But she was aware all round of stares, heads shaken, almost a palpable collective sigh of relief. She only realised how serious the situation was, or could have been, when the vote was carried in their favour by one. If she hadn't made it they would have lost. She screwed up her eyes and clenched her fist, rigid with embarrassment as the vote was announced.

It seemed to her as the chamber rose with much murmuring and shuffling of papers, people crossing the floor to confer with colleagues, that there was an attempt to isolate her; as though an invisible barrier formed around her as she sat alone to one side of the chamber, a gulf separating her from everyone else. No one came up to talk to her as they usually did.

Finally, as she was about to rise she saw Jack Fishwick, the leader, approach her, his progress towards her halted by individuals or groups who stopped to have a word with him, or tried to catch his attention.

'Glad you made it, Anna,' he said at last, his voice heavy with meaning as, hands in his pockets, he stood in front of her. 'It was a vital vote.'

'Sorry, Jack. You know,' her hand fluttered vaguely in the air, 'traffic. One *should* make allowances but one doesn't.'

He leaned towards her, lowering his voice.

'Do you think we could have a word in my office, Anna? It's more private there.'

'Of course.' She finished putting her papers in her briefcase and rose, looking at him eye to eye, not afraid. 'There's also something I want to ask you about.'

'Oh, good,' and together, chatting, to all extents and purposes amicably, they crossed the floor of the chamber into the corridor and walked down to the leader's room.

'I guess there's no point beating about the bush, Anna,' Jack said as he shut the door. 'You probably know what this is about.'

'My attendance record. Sorry. That's all I can say.'

'You nearly let us down tonight, Anna. When you first came on to the Council you were so diligent.'

'Things were rather different then, Jack; but I have tried to lessen my workload.'

'But you've taken on a house in the country, I hear.'

'Oh?' She looked up sharply, aware of a flush slowly creeping up her cheeks. 'Oh, you know about that?'

'Well I did hear about a large house . . .'

'How, may I ask?' She joined one hand across the other, irritated at being the subject of Party gossip.

'I guess these things get out.'

'I guess they do, though I'd like to know how.'

'Was it a secret then, Anna?'

'No, of course not.'

'Well, then, are you intending to live there permanently?'

'No, we're not.'

'Was it something to do with your daughter's baby?'

'In a way; but really, Jack, personal affairs and those of my family are nothing to do with my work on the Council.'

'I think they are, Anna.' Jack Fishwick sat down on the other side of the desk as though to emphasise his status as leader of the Council.

'There is also the question of a son at private school. That hasn't gone down at all well when the Party so rigorously opposes private education.'

Anna bit her lip. Obviously gossip had been rife.

'You know, I think, that Guy was expelled from the comprehensive. We had no alternative.'

'There are other state schools . . .'

'Jack, is this really the Council's business?'

'I'm afraid it is. It is not only the fact you've two homes, a house in the best part of London, and a son at private school, both of which ill become the image of a Labour Councillor; but you have either missed or been late for too many important debates recently. The Tories are saying "we can always rely on Anna Livingstone to send her apologies". In a Council where the balance is tight . . .'

'I think that's *very* unfair, Jack,' Anna paused thoughtfully for a moment while his message sank in, 'or should I say that I hadn't realised that I had so many enemies.'

'Not "enemies", Anna,' he said quickly.

'Well, people who obviously wish me harm.'

'No,' he shook his head emphatically, 'they don't wish you harm. They just want you to do what you were elected to do, and many of them do think you've got too much on, too many personal problems to cope with, and the idea of buying a large country house . . . when the country as a whole is in recession and people are being repossessed, didn't go down too well,' he murmured almost to himself.

'It is *not* a large country house in the sense that it is a status home or anything like that. It is a farm and my stepson Guy, who takes GCSEs this summer, may well think of farming.'

'Isn't he *lucky* to have someone to buy a farm for him?' Now Jack's tone was openly derisive.

'Jack, I don't think I have to make explanations to you . . .'

'And neither would I, Anna, were it not for your attendance record, your voting record, the fact that you resigned from the Housing Committee after the fiasco of the Pilgrim squat . . .'

'Oh, that's really what this is about, isn't it?' she asked. 'Come clean, Jack. It's about the Pilgrims and the way it ended, with me being escorted off by the police.'

'It didn't go down too well then.'

'Even though I did *everything* I could for those ungrateful people.'

'Well, we don't expect gratitude on the Council.' Jack stood up abruptly. 'I have several other people to see now, Anna, but I thought I should report back to my colleagues that I've had a word with you.'

'And what are you going to report back to them?' Anna again felt that icy finger on the back of her spine.

'Well, I shall say that we've spoken,' Jack began sorting through his papers, 'that you understand the situation and . . . well, Anna, quite frankly, if things don't improve, and improve dramatically, over the next few months or so I'm afraid that I shall have to suggest to you that you might resign and create a vacancy for someone else who will perform the job better than you appear to be doing at the moment.'

Jack crossed the room and, opening the door, held it for her. She hesitated for a moment and then she went through, stopping at the threshold to say in a low voice: 'I really am very sorry. I will try to improve and, incidentally, do you happen to know what has become of all the members of the squat? That's what I wanted to ask you.'

Jack looked surprised. 'Well, some of them were rehoused and others . . . just wandered away.' He looked at her quizzically. 'May I ask why?'

'Just wondered,' she said. 'Goodnight, Jack, and thank you for being so frank. I appreciate it.'

'I thought you would, Anna.' He gave her a polite rather than friendly smile and closed the door gently after them. 'It's our reputation I'm thinking about as well as that of our Party. But above all, Anna, the tide in the affairs of Labour is turning and we can't afford in a crucial marginal London Borough like this to let the Party down.'

It was wounding and it was humiliating to be accused not only of letting the Party down, but oneself too. There was the implication that she wasn't such a good socialist, in reality a champagne socialist — of whom the Labour Party had a fair number — with a son at private school and a 'large house in the country'. There was the implication that, somehow, if you were like this you didn't care as much for your fellow men and women as you might, couldn't strictly identify with them. She thought how much she'd agonised about the fate of the members of the squat — and what sort of reward she'd achieved as a result; of the countless hours she'd spent in the Law Centre and at court defending those who had the misfortune to come up against the law.

Was she somehow less humane and caring just because they could, in fact, afford to take Guy out of a school where he wasn't achieving, buy a larger house, alright partly for selfish ends too, so that Fiona would be able to bring up her daughter in some comfort in a house of her own?

Anna drove thoughtfully along, looking for a spot to park in Wimpole Street, and seeing a car emerge from a space nipped smartly into its place.

Katie was specially staying behind to see her and already she was late. Looking guiltily at her watch she nipped smartly out of the car, stuck some coins in the meter and ran up the steps to her consulting rooms.

Katie herself let her in with a rather strained smile.

'Sorry I'm late,' Anna said breathlessly. 'You know, the traffic.'

Katie smiled sympathetically.

'Unfortunately I have a meeting at the Royal Society of Medicine in an hour; but it won't take long, will it?'

She ushered Anna into her consulting room and closed the door.

'Just as long as it takes to check I haven't a brain tumour,' Anna said, sitting down and forcing a grin.

'A *what?*' Katie was looking through Anna's file in front of her on the desk.

'I'm joking, at least I hope I am. I've been having bad headaches and the optician said I should consult you.'

'Oh!' Katie, brow furrowed, went on leafing through the file. 'You didn't mention headaches before.'

'They're pretty recent, actually. They're so bad I have to lie down sometimes.'

'That's not good.' Katie got up and, going over to Anna, drew back her lower lids and looked at her eyes.

'Look up,' she said, and Anna obeyed. 'Look right, left . . . look down. The optician didn't find anything?'

'He said I only needed reading glasses.'

'Let's take your blood pressure.' Katie hesitated for a moment. 'Look, you might as well take off your suit, keep your bra and pants on and I'll give you a quick once over.'

Anna went behind the screen at the far end of the consulting room and began to undress.

The examination took about a quarter of an hour: heart, lungs, blood pressure. Katie took blood to run some tests, and asked for a urine sample. Then she told Anna to dress and went back to her desk.

'I know your smear is OK because you only had that done a few months ago.' She sat down and began to scribble some notes while Anna completed her dressing and sat down at her desk. Katie looked up with a reassuring smile.

'Like the optician, I'm glad to tell you I can find nothing wrong. Blood pressure fine, heart and lungs fine. I don't expect to find anything in the blood or urine samples. Tell me,' she leaned forward confidentially over her desk, 'you've been overdoing it, haven't you?'

'No more than usual,' Anna said defensively.

'But there's the baby now, and Fiona does need a lot of care because she's a baby herself?'

'Yes,' Anna nodded in agreement. 'I suppose that's half the trouble.'

'*And* there's a big new house.'

'Oh, I love it . . . I love *that.*'

Katie leaned back and looked at her. 'In that case why don't you spend more time there?'

'Well, I do spend more time there. I go down almost every weekend now. I've gone on a three-day week at work and cut down on the Law Centre.'

'That's still quite a bit of toing and froing. And there remains the Council.' Katie tapped her pen on her desk.

'Good heavens, Katie,' Anna replied, 'look at all the work you do. You have a full-time medical practice. You're on the Council of this and the Council of that. You have a busy husband and two children.'

'Yes, but pressure takes us in different ways. So far, touch wood,' Katie tapped her desk, 'I don't have any symptoms of stress. The children are older and can look after themselves. Douglas has always been self-sufficient. I manage to juggle what I do reasonably well.'

'Well, so do I.'

'Yes, but you have these blinding headaches which have the effect of making you lie down. I think it is a form of migraine and that in your case, since you haven't had them before, it is a form of stress. Your body is telling you something and that seems to be saying "ease up". Do what you want for a change instead of what others want. You seem to love this house, and I suspect it's for you. It's your bolt hole, your security.'

'I still get headaches there.'

'Yes, but that's because Fiona is only a mile or two away. Couldn't you have moved, say, even further away?'

'I fell in love with the house and, yes, we did want to be near Fiona and the baby. The baby is quite adorable.' Anna's features softened for a moment. 'The baby I never had,' she concluded almost in a whisper.

'Are you sorry now?' Katie also lowered her voice.

'Yes, I think I am sorry now, just a little.'

'But you also know there is nothing you can do about it.' Katie got up and put Anna's file back in the filing cabinet. 'I mean, it is irreversible and frankly in the circumstances and at the time I think you did the right thing.'

'You really do?' Anna looked gratefully at her.

'Yes. It's all very well to moon over someone else's baby, but I think at the time you really didn't want one of your own. I also think there were contra indications to the Pill and these headaches may be a symptom. We *may* have avoided a thrombosis. Maybe you did come off just in time.'

'Oh, my goodness.' Anna clasped her hands to her face. 'You really think so?'

'So let *that* reassure you and cheer you up.' Katie glanced at her watch again and, patting Anna on the shoulder, handed her a prescription.

'I'm going to give you some medicine that you should take for a while to see if it eases the headaches. When you have a headache double the dose but they shouldn't be as bad.'

'Is it a tranquilliser?' Anna looked dubiously at the piece of paper.

'No, it's a new drug we prescribe to relieve migraine. I think you might find it helpful, and when that house is ready I'd love to see it.'

'You and Douglas must come down.' Anna got up and shrugged on her jacket. 'And thanks. I'm so sorry I kept you.'

'What are friends for?' Katie murmured as she

saw her to the door. 'Oh, and of course there will be a bill.'

They both laughed, embraced on the steps and then Anna went to her car while Katie, with a wave of her hand disappeared round the corner into New Cavendish Street.

Anna sat on the lawn with baby Harriet on the rug beside her. Chubby and strong, she was growing into an even more beautiful baby and Anna drooled over her. Anna and Harriet were alone. Peter was up in London, Guy on holiday abroad and Fiona and Sal had gone into Bournemouth on a shopping expedition.

Anna sat back on her hands, face raised to the sun. Little Harriet, strapped in her baby rocker, chubby fists beating the air, gurgled with laughter, bubbles running down her chin. Anna turned and looked at her and was suddenly aware of such a profound maternal urge, a totally unexpected flow of feeling that was so intense that she knew she envied Fiona her baby and wished that she had one too; that Harriet was indeed hers.

She leaned over to Harriet and gave her a finger. Harriet grasped it in her podgy little fist and tried to stuff it in her mouth. Anna rolled over on her tummy and, undoing the strap that fastened the baby in, lifted her out so that she lay beside her, Anna's arm protectively round Harriet.

In a way Harriet was hers, or almost. Fiona

seemed to have grown more and more distant from her baby, less interested in her, and had also taken to going up again to London while Sal was left in charge, or Anna or Peter came hurrying down to take over.

It was so awful that Fiona who'd wanted the baby had turned into such an indifferent mother, and Anna and Peter felt strongly the need to compensate. It was no chore. It was a pleasure but, still, it was a pity. There was no substitute for a natural mother as Fiona had so often pointed out to Anna. What an irony there was there!

Weatherwise it had so far been a glorious summer, at least in the West Country. But it had also been an anxious one, mainly because of the growing distance between Fiona and Harriet, the worry of what would happen if Fiona continued to be as bored with the country as she obviously was now and wanted to take her up to London. What rights would Anna and Peter have then if she did? Supposing they disappeared into a squat and Harriet ended up traipsing after her mother, if she adopted a hippy lifestyle?

It didn't bear thinking about.

One of the workmen called from the house and Anna looked up. It was almost finished and in record time. The rooms had been decorated, all the improvements made and the carpets laid. A lot of furniture had been brought down from the London house, which was now on the market, while Anna and Peter searched for a pied à terre.

They enjoyed in their spare time making forays to auction rooms up and down the county and emerging with some piece of furniture which they bore triumphantly back to Hall Farm like a trophy.

Anna stood up, and taking Harriet in her arms walked across the lawn to the workman who, a pencil behind his ear and a plank under his arm, asked her which way she wanted the door to open, inwards or outwards.

'What do you think?' she asked shading her eyes from the sun.

'I'd say outwards,' the workman replied. 'That way you have more room indoors.'

'Of course.' Anna agreed and accompanied him round the house to look at the half-completed conservatory.

'It has to be big enough to hold a vine,' she said, looking at it doubtfully.

'Oh it will, Mrs Livingstone,' he replied genially. 'You could grow a palm tree in here.'

'Doubt if we'd want that.' Anna shifted Harriet, who had reached out to try and grab the workman's hair, from one arm to another.

'She's a lovely little thing,' the workman, whose name was Jerry, chucked her under the chin, 'your granddaughter, madam?'

'Yes,' Anna nodded.

'She's like you.'

'Thank you.'

'Not that you look old enough to be a grandmother,' he said, regarding her thoughtfully.

'I'm a step-grandma,' she said. 'My husband was married twice.'

'Ah, I see.'

Jerry returned to his task and Anna, still hugging Harriet, who felt so natural, so at home in her arms, wandered through the garden inspecting the improvements that had been made, all the plants they had planted, the enlargement and development of several herbaceous borders, the beginnings of an arboretum, a fishpond being constructed in the middle of the patio that had been laid at one side and which caught the sun all day long. There would be a fountain in the middle which at night would be lit by spotlights at the side of the house. It was partly surrounded by a high wall which one day would be covered by honeysuckle, clematis and climbing roses already planted underneath.

In five years' time, Peter said, the place would be transformed. Anna hoped it would be very much sooner. She gazed for a while at the river and then, sensing that Harriet was sleepy, went indoors and took her upstairs for her afternoon nap.

Next to her and Peter's bedroom was a nursery where Harriet slept when Fiona was away. There was a room for Sal on the other side and then Guy's room beyond that. Guest bedrooms were on the top floor.

The whole house was light and airy. Sunlight flooded in from every aspect, and even on dull days its mellow, pastel-coloured walls and white paintwork dispelled the gloom. Anna had taken a month off work, though she had a computer, a fax, two telephone lines, and was able to keep in touch with the office, which anyway was slacker during the summer than at other periods.

Anna put Harriet in her cot and for a while remained with her, watching her eyes grow heavy, allowing her finger to be clutched in the little hand as a kind of comforter until Harriet fell asleep and the clasp slackened.

Anna loved her so much that she felt she was hers, a strange and dangerous feeling given the uncertainty, the precariousness of the situation. What would she do if Fiona took her away? Would they attempt to have Harriet made a ward of court? Better not to think, not to envisage such an awful situation which, anyway, might never happen.

Anna drew her finger away and, standing up, rearranged the bedclothes over the beloved baby's shoulder, not too tight and not too loose. To add to the anxieties of parents there was all this worry now about sudden infant death syndrome, something that had never been heard of twenty years before, though it must have been around for ever.

She tiptoed out of the nursery, switching on the baby alarm as she went which would take the sound of Harriet's cries, her lightest movement, to every part of the house. She went downstairs to her study where the fax and computer were installed. There were a couple of messages for her on the fax which she read and, discarding one, dealt with the other, faxing her London secretary back with the answer to the enquiry. She had chosen the room because of the view it had of the garden sloping down to the river, the fields with their grazing cattle rising on the other side. Even watching a cow chewing its cud could induce a soporific effect, and near her on her desk were powerful binoculars and a book to enable her to identify the many different birds alighting on the lawn.

In the background, but not obtrusive, was the sound of workmen banging, and outside the caw-caw of the crows and jackdaws, the cooing of the collared doves.

Anna closed her eyes and gently inhaled, as though she were breathing in the atmosphere of the countryside — no wonder it had inspired so many poets and writers, no wonder it had filled them with a sense of peace.

But how long would this peace last and what would happen if the restless Fiona took her baby to London, as she had every right to do, and one day disappeared? She could forbid them to see her daughter; she could in fact do anything she liked. The only hope was a judge, if it came to that, might be sympathetic. But what if, like Errol, she couldn't be *found?*

Anna cupped her head between her hands and stared out of the window. And what of her, Anna's complex emotions; the bond she had with Harriet? Was that natural, when she was not even related to the child by ties of blood?

She decided to abandon her profitless and futile line of thought and spent the afternoon in her office, resisting the strong temptation to return to the garden until she had finished her work. She was so used to keeping her emotions under control that she could achieve things that other people regarded as impossible: staying indoors on a hot day, refusing to be tempted out until the tasks she had set herself were done. Some people said she was inhuman, but she knew that for her a frame within which to work was essential.

At four she went to make a cup of tea for herself and the workmen, taking pleasure in the now completed and well-equipped kitchen with its huge stove, polished working surfaces, deep fridge-freezer, dishwasher and all the appurtenances of modern domestic aids that the Hansons would never have dreamt of. She took a tray to the men in the conservatory and then went into the garden, sipping her tea under Harriet's window so that she would hear if she cried out. The baby was sleeping for a long time today, the heat must have made her tired. Then, suddenly, a feeling of apprehension overwhelmed her and, leaving her cup, she dashed into the house and upstairs, threw open the door . . . Harriet, fully awake, kicked her legs in the air and, giving a deep-throated chuckle, seemed to hold out her arms to welcome Anna.

'Oh, my *precious*,' Anna cried, dashing over to

the cot and taking the baby in her arms. 'Oh, Harriet, I do so *love* you.' She smothered her face with kisses only looking up when she realised that she and Harriet were no longer alone in the room.

Sal stood in the doorway, mouth agape.

'Did something happen? Is she alright?'

'Yes, she's fine.' Anna looked at her foolishly. 'I was just sitting in the garden enjoying it all so much. I'd put Harriet down about two and I suddenly realised she'd been asleep for a *long* time, you know usually it's an hour and I thought . . .'

'Cot death . . .' Sal murmured.

'I dashed upstairs and oh . . . there she was,' Anna pressed her cheek to the baby's head again. 'Oh, Sal, wasn't I *silly?*'

'Very silly,' Sal said prosaically, taking Harriet from her and lying her on the table where her nappies and creams and powders were kept. She put on a clean nappy and handed her back to Anna who cradled her gently in her arms.

'You're so *sensible*, Sal.'

'So are you.' Sal busily put the tops on the cream, the lids on the jars. 'Or you were.'

'When it comes to Harriet . . .'

Sal looked as though she was unsure whether or not to say what was on her mind and then decided she would.

'Anna, take care. You're *not* her mother.'

'I *know* that, Sal,' Anna said in a subdued voice, 'and I would never want to be or pretend to be. Fiona's her mother and we all do what we can to help Fiona . . .'

'Well, Fiona has gone off to London,' Sal said abruptly. 'Asked me to tell you. Said she'd be in touch . . .'

'London?' Anna looked aghast. '*Again?* Where, when?'

'She went to Bournemouth to buy a new suitcase and some clothes. She seemed very excited, somehow not quite all there. Like she was on a high. Then we drove home and she dropped me off at the gate. She said she was going to the cottage to pick up some things and she'd give us a call.'

'Did she say for how long?' Anna asked.

'No. But I don't think it was spur of the moment. There was something odd about her today, couldn't quite put my finger on it, you know. But she took me quite unawares when she put me off at the gate. I mean what could I do?'

'I'm going to ring the cottage,' Anna said. 'She can't just take off like that,' and, hurrying to the telephone, she dialled the number, stood there tapping her feet impatiently while it rang. Finally she put the phone down.

'Not there,' she said.

'Oh, she'll have gone by now. My feeling is that she was in a hurry, as if she was going to meet someone. She was all excited. Oh, and she had her hair and nails done in Bournemouth. Looked really nice in her new clothes, really pretty. I suppose I should have asked, but I didn't. I couldn't stop her, could I?' Sal suddenly looked worried, as though stricken with a sense of guilt. 'I mean I hadn't the right, had I? There was nothing I could do.'

As Sal stared at Anna and Anna stared back it was as though something had fallen from a great height and dropped to the ground without making any disturbance, any sound.

Anna paused outside the house and looked up at the lighted windows. The facade had been freshly painted, the brickwork repointed. It could have been a yuppy-type house on the fringes of Camden Town and Islington, not far from the Holloway Road. The neat black iron railing with its forbidding spikes had been freshly varnished. She rang the bell for a long time before she realised it might not be working so, as there was a large brass knocker on the door, she gave it a good hard bang.

Someone upstairs threw open a window and looked down.

'Yes?'

'Is er . . . May I come in?'

'Who are you?'

'Anna Livingstone . . .'

'Oh, Anna Livingstone,' a voice said, and she could hear someone inside bounding down the stairs. Then the door was thrown open and a large, big-breasted woman she recognised as Maeve stood on the doorstep. Fortunately, she had a smile on her face. Anna hadn't known what the existing members of the squat felt about her now after the eviction.

'Anna, what are you doing here?' Maeve asked, her smile friendly enough, but she didn't ask her in.

'I just wanted a bit of help.' Anna tried to look past the vast circumference of Maeve, but it was difficult. 'I wondered if I might come in?' She looked over her shoulder. 'It's pelting with rain.'

'Come in, come in, Anna,' Maeve said briskly and drew her into the hall shutting the door behind her. 'We have to be careful who we let in. So many people just try and barge in. Squatters you know,' she sniffed derisively and led Anna up the flight of stairs to the first floor landing where she recognised another amiable face leaning over the banister.

'Hi, Anna!' the man said, and held out his hand.

Biff Cassidy had always been a charmer, an easy talker despite a string of convictions for theft, pimping and drug pushing. He was about thirty-five with long flaxen hair and a ring through his nose. He was clean-shaven and wore jeans, a T-shirt and sandals. It was Biff who had attacked Jim, butted him with his head, but his manner was amiable enough now.

Biff led the way into a large front room which was well-decorated and quite tastefully if sparsely furnished. It had a full set of curtains held back by a tie.

Some of the furniture looked quite good, and

in the corner was a large double divan with an attractive oriental throw-over and scatter cushions. There was a gas fire in the hearth and something cooking on a small Belling stove in the corner.

'Nice,' Anna said approvingly, looking round.

'Better than the warehouse, eh, Anna?'

'I think so.'

Biff pointed to a cane chair and Anna sat down on it.

'How many people have you got here?'

'About eight couples, four singles and some kids. Some are from the original squat and some are new; but we vet those we allow in very carefully. They have to be voted in and behave themselves, otherwise they get thrown out; we work very closely with the social services. They have to keep their rooms clean *and* help with the common parts. We take a great pride in the place and hope that once we can get jobs and pay rent the Council will let us keep it. We don't want people to think we're a bunch of hoodlums, because we're not.

'Though it's due for demolition,' Biff went on. 'The whole area is to be developed. A drink, Anna?'

'I'd like coffee or tea if you've got it.'

Maeve went over to the sink and filling the kettle with water plugged it in and switched it on. Then she got out three mugs from a rack over the sink and plopped a teabag in each. The room vaguely smelt of incense, or maybe it was hash. Old habits died hard, if they died at all, but there was a joss stick burning away in the corner.

'What help is it you want, Anna?' Biff lay on the divan, his eyes bright with interest.

'I want to try and find Errol. You remember him?'

'Errol?' Maeve turned from the stove, an expression of surprise on her face. 'I thought he went off with your girl?'

'He did. But he left her.'

'Oh, dear, that would be Errol.' Maeve chuckled, pouring water on the teabags and, after stirring and adding milk, brought Anna's over to her. 'Not what you'd call reliable.'

'An eye on the main chance.' Biff lit a cigarette and stuck it between his lips. 'Thought he liked the cushy life, so I wonder he left her. No, we've not seen him.'

'Would you know anyone who had?' Feeling dejected at the news, Anna looked at the people she had befriended and failed, but who obviously bore her no grudge.

'Why is it so important to find Errol?' Maeve joined Biff on the divan. 'Did he nick something?'

'Yes, he did when he left her. He took everything he could lay his hands on — TV, video, hi-fi. I suppose he wanted to sell them. But I'm not here about that. Fiona has now disappeared and we think she may be with him.'

Biff let out a whistle.

'Why would she want to do that?'

'She loved him I guess.' Anna found herself trying to avoid their scrutiny. 'Fiona had a child. Errol is the father.'

Biff whistled again.

'A dear little girl,' there was a catch in Anna's voice, 'called Harriet. Errol left Fiona before Harriet was born. She seemed OK at first and then she started to pine for him. She became moody and neglected the baby. First of all when he left she never mentioned Errol, but much later when she did we realised how much she'd missed him. I don't think she really wanted a baby, but it happened and she thought, wrongly, as it turned out, that it would tie Errol to her. It did just the opposite.'

'Poor kid.' Maeve, Anna remembered, had three children who didn't seem to be about.

'Where are your kids, Maeve?' she asked.

'Oh, they'll be with friends somewhere.' Maeve jerked her head towards the window. 'They're getting older now you know, Anna. The youngest is twelve, the eldest fifteen.'

'And doing very well at school,' Biff said proudly though Anna knew that Biff was a good bit younger than Maeve and the children weren't his.

'I'm very glad that things turned out all right.' Anna sipped her scalding tea and then carefully put the mug on the floor. 'It was an extremely painful business for me.'

'For us all in retrospect,' Biff said. 'We all behaved rather badly, especially towards you. It was a tough time. No hard feelings, Anna?'

'None at all.' She raised her head and smiled. 'What happened, by the way, to Damian and Arizona?'

Maeve snorted. 'They got married!'

'Married?' The statement amazed Anna.

'They went all respectable. Damian's father died and left him some property so he and Arizona moved into the family mansion and kicked out his mother.'

'Well, I don't know.'

'Stranger things happen at sea.'

Anna rose. 'No idea at all then where I could find Errol?'

'Do you really want to find him?' Biff leaned over to the table next to the divan and stubbed out his cigarette.

'Of course I do. Why shouldn't I?'

'What makes you think the girl is with him?'

'Because of the way she left. She had her hair done and bought a complete set of new clothes. She also had her own car. The friend she was with on the day she disappeared said she was excited, as if she was going to meet someone, and she never had another boyfriend except Errol. We think he'd got in touch with her, or she somehow found out where he was and went to meet him.'

Biff slowly shook his head and Anna, feeling suddenly apprehensive, looked at him.

'What's the matter, Biff?'

'Errol was very heavily into the drug scene you

know, Anna. There's no doubt that he couldn't do without the stuff. He would have nicked your daughter's property to sell to buy heroin or speed. I'm afraid that if your daughter has ended up with him she may be in trouble. Deep trouble.'

'Heroin?' Anna whispered.

Biff nodded. 'And he knew where to get the pure stuff. It's lethal.'

Anna put her head in her hands, her thoughts racing.

'Could you *please* help me find him?' she asked, raising her head. 'It seems absolutely essential that we do.'

'We'll do all we can. Leave us your telephone number. But we have lost touch. Mind you, one or two people may know. We'll ask around.' Maeve put a hand on Anna's arm and squeezed it. 'We owe you one, Anna. You did a lot for us and we were an ungrateful bunch of swine.'

CHAPTER 16

Anna looked up from her desk at the knock on the door.

'Come in,' she called, and then rapidly went on with writing her report ready to give to her secretary before she left. 'Shan't be a minute,' she said without raising her head. 'I've just got about five lines left to do.'

There was a distinctly masculine cough and she looked up sharply.

'Oh, David, I'm so sorry. I thought it was Joyce.'

'Carry on,' David said affably with a wave of his hand. 'We don't want to keep Joyce waiting.'

Anna glanced at her watch.

'As a matter of fact she's probably gone. I'll leave it in her "In" tray.'

It was Thursday and Anna's last working day of the week. So much had to be done.

'Do you mind if I just ring home?' Anna picked up the phone, smiling apologetically at David. 'It won't take a minute.'

'Go ahead, but I shan't keep you.'

'Sal,' Anna spoke to the person at the end of the line, 'everything alright? Good. Good.' Looking at her watch again. 'I should think about eight or nine,' she glanced across at David. 'The boss has just come in so . . .'

'It won't take a minute,' he hissed.

'Says he won't keep me long, but I know him. Good.' Anna listened to some more words from Sal at the other end. 'Give her a kiss from me. A big hug. Right. I'll see you.' She replaced the receiver and joined her hands, composed, smiling across the desk at David, inviting him to sit down.

'I'm all yours.'

'Everything well at home?'

'Everything is fine.' Anna sighed. 'As far as it can be. We keep the . . . tragedy of Fiona's disappearance as far to the back of our minds as we can, but of course it isn't easy. It's always there, like a wound.'

'Naturally,' David nodded sympathetically. 'How old is Harriet now, Anna?'

'She's just a year old,' Anna said with a sigh. 'We're having a party for her at the weekend. It seems incredible doesn't it?'

'How the time flies. Who would have thought, this time last year . . . Do you think Fiona will ever come back?'

'I don't know what we think, quite honestly. Of course we hope she will. We've done everything we can to find her. My old friends in the squatters' community are helping. It's possible she and Errol went abroad. Thailand, somewhere where drugs are easy to find.'

'Terrible for you and Peter.' David cracked his knuckles, raising both arms over his head as if in an effort to relax. 'All of which doesn't make this any easier to say, Anna.'

'Oh?' Immediately that little ball of lead lodged beside her heart, so familiar by now it was almost like a friend.

'Anna, you do *know* how much we appreciate all you have done while you've been with us and . . .'

'This sounds like the "goodbye", David.'

'No, Anna it is not "goodbye", emphatically not. At least we hope not.' He paused and looked at her. 'But the fact is, Anna, and it is *quite* understandable, that however hard you've tried, and I know you have, you have not been pulling your weight and Michael Lawrence has had a lot of the extra burden to carry.'

'I think that's unfair, David. I know I work part-time but I take work home. I am here sometimes at seven in the morning and don't leave until eight or nine at night. The fax and phone are going all the time I'm at home.'

'I'm sure of that, Anna; but it is the daily grind and it doesn't seem fair on Michael to have to take on much of your work as well as his . . .'

'That's quite untrue,' Anna interrupted heatedly.

'On the contrary, Anna,' David spoke quietly as was his custom when telling people unpleasant news, 'he had to appear at the Crown Court at the last minute last week because the little girl was ill.'

'That's true,' Anna bit her lip. They thought that she'd swallowed something that was making her choke and had to rush her to the Royal Free. 'I couldn't possibly have left Harriet . . .'

'Of *course* you couldn't, Anna.' His voice was very gentle now, 'that's my point. You're a woman standing in place of the baby's mother. I know how you feel about her, how much she means to you. We all are deeply sensitive of the trials you and Peter have been through in the last few years and think you have coped marvellously.'

'Come to the point, David.' Anna began to feel vaguely nauseous.

'I want to make Michael Lawrence head of the section and ask you to be a consultant, Anna. I know you wouldn't like to go into second place and this does seem the best way out.'

'Consultant?' Anna looked incredulous. 'I'm being kicked upstairs, is that it?'

'No, not at all, a consultancy is a most important position . . .'

'All the consultants in my experience have been people either well past their sell-by date, or who have committed some serious misdemeanour that nearly had them struck off the roll. Neither of which applies to me. I am not yet forty and remain in control of all my faculties.'

'Anna, *no one* is disputing that and, believe me, if the volume of work was not such and, above all, if Michael felt more amenable this wouldn't arise. But he doesn't. He's going to leave if he doesn't get overall control and I'm sure he means it.'

'I'm sure he does,' Anna said grimly and leaned her chin on her cupped hands staring in front of her.

The truth was really, in a nutshell, she and Michael Lawrence were incompatible. They respected each other but personally they didn't get on. Their relationship was polite but formal. She supposed it had been inevitable that Michael would use his position, his comparative youth, somehow to get her out of the way.

'Let me think about it,' she said at last standing up, getting her things together.

'It's no reflection on you personally, Anna.'

'Oh, but it is,' she said, her eyes flashing. 'I'm sure a lot of women would be able to keep down running a home, a busy law practice, a job as a councillor and so on.'

'But not many, Anna. Not without more support than you've got. Peter has his own busy job, and you have two rather difficult kids.'

Anna suddenly slumped back into her chair, feeling stupidly weak and vulnerable.

'I feel I've been a failure in my career, David, to be given the boot before I'm forty.'

David's expression was agonised, and she thought he was about to reach for her hand, then thought better of it. Instead he leaned forward, gazing at her earnestly. 'Oh, but you have not, Anna. You've been incredibly successful. You've made more money as an individual than anyone else in this practice.'

'Money isn't everything,' she said bitterly.

'Well, it helps. You have also combined with this a lot of voluntary work that only does you credit. Now you have the heartache of wondering what has happened to Fiona, the worry and responsibility of taking care of Harriet. As a family man, I know the toll all this has taken of you, and I think you coped brilliantly.

'But Michael Lawrence is young. He resents hanging about, referring decisions he is quite capable of taking himself, day to day routine matters, to you. You must appreciate his position and, believe me, as a consultant you will be very valuable to us indeed. Besides,' he looked at her slyly, 'apart from releasing you from the day to day trivia there is the money side. The fees consultancies bring can be quite substantial, and with your added responsibilities — a baby, a large home in the country, I'm sure that you'd want to feel the financial side as well taken care of. And it will be. Man cannot live on bread alone, Anna.'

Indeed man could not, nor woman. Anna turned off the A303 towards Shaftesbury and now she always felt she really was home, only a few miles and she would be there. Sal would have a meal ready and maybe Harriet would still be awake to greet her. The following day there was the birthday party with local babies. Peter was coming down in the morning and Guy driving over from the agricultural college where he was taking a course in farming after getting passable

GCSE results the previous summer.

If only Fiona could be there. But there had been no trace of her. In the months since her disappearance, they had done everything possible, besides Anna's visit to the squatters. The police had been alerted, the Salvation Army and various missing persons bureaux had been informed. There had even been an appeal on a missing persons programme on TV.

No one thought that Fiona was dead, but that she was alive somewhere and living with Errol. What they didn't know, couldn't know, was whether or not they would ever see her again or she would remain on the missing persons' list for ever.

When she arrived at the house Guy was already there, and Harriet had stayed up though it was past her bedtime.

As Anna came into the living room she stood at the threshold for a few moments, watching her playing on the floor with Guy who, despite his youth, was a devoted uncle. He had found it as difficult as anyone else to come to terms with Fiona's disappearance, and Anna knew that when he was in London he frequented old haunts they'd visited together to try and find news of her.

Harriet's demeanour changed when she saw Anna, and she tottered across the floor towards her outstretched arms.

'My precious one,' Anna said clutching her. 'How are you, darling?'

Harriet said, 'Mum, Mum,' and stuck her sticky fingers into Anna's face, eyes lit up with pleasure.

'Hi, Anna!' Guy held up a hand. 'Good journey down?'

'Very good. Any news from Dad?'

'He'll make it for the party. He's in Leicester.'

'Leicester? What's he doing there?' Really, they had so much to do now they scarcely saw each other.

'Some conference,' Guy shrugged his shoulders.

Sal came in, greeted Anna, said food was on the table and she and Guy should begin while she put Harriet to bed. This was a chore Anna enjoyed doing herself, but tonight she felt dead tired so she nodded and accepted Guy's offer of a drink while Sal took Harriet off to bed.

'Let's wait for Sal,' Anna said sitting next to Guy.

'Good idea. I'm not hungry anyway. How're things, Anna?'

'Well,' Anna gave a hopeless gesture. 'I don't suppose things will ever be the same until we find Fiona. If only people who do this sort of thing realised the suffering they cause.'

'They do. She must know, not only to Dad and me but you too. I don't mean,' he blushed, 'that you should care less. Oh, you know what I mean.'

The blood tie.

Anna nodded. No need to be reminded about the blood tie.

'Dad's terrifically cut up about it. He seems to be working flat out.'

'Yes, doesn't he?'

Always away. It never used to be like this. Maybe he'd taken comfort with a woman who could give him just that extra special bit of attention that Anna, with all she had to do, denied him.

'Oh, I've got a bit of news,' she said suddenly, and then seeing the expression on Guy's face said apologetically, 'no, I'm sorry, it's not about Fiona. That I would have told you immediately. David Cole wants me to give up being the joint head of the Wigmore Street practice. They've offered me a consultancy.'

'Oh!' Guy looked perplexed. 'Is that good or bad news?'

'Well, at first I thought it was bad. It's a kind way of giving me the sack. I've never got on especially well with Michael Lawrence. But he is a very capable lawyer and he's rather sick of having to consult on things with me. He's told them he'll leave if he can't take over complete responsibility.'

'And how do you feel about it?' Guy got up to refill her glass.

'At first I felt rather sick. But on the way down here — it only happened today — I thought maybe a consultancy is not such a bad deal. We're changing our lives, anyway, by selling the London house. When you've finished your course we'll start buying animals and restocking the

401

farm. I *like* country life you know, Guy. Sometimes I feel I've had it up to here,' she drew an imaginary line across her forehead, 'with the city, office problems, the traffic, the noise, the rush. Maybe Fiona would not have gone off if I'd given her more time.'

'You can never know that. No one can.'

'I introduced her to Errol. I feel responsible for that.'

'Anna, it might have happened anyway. You can't go back and say what might have been. You, above all people, should know that.'

Guy was right. He'd grown up so much suddenly, as if the absence of his sister made him more mature. Maybe, severally, they all felt responsible for Fiona, and if they never saw her again they would each spend the rest of their lives blaming not her but themselves, wondering where and how they'd gone so badly wrong.

Anna was up early the following morning anxious to make the best of her time in the garden before the final preparations began for the party.

Anna had found herself surprisingly adept at dealing with babies, not only Harriet. Sal, of course, was marvellous but when Anna had to cope by herself, cope she did. She knew it was this one-to-one relationship, especially at an early age, that made the bond between parent or, in her case, carer and child, so vital.

Maybe if she had been able to establish it with Fiona and Guy when they were babies the outcome might have been different. There would not have been the vague memory of Mother, producing a residue of bitterness and suppressed hostility which flared up during their adolescence.

What would Nancy have made of Fiona, had she lived, Anna wondered as she studied her plan for the border running south along the side of the lawn towards the river which allowed for a colourful display of lupins, delphiniums, pink and scarlet peonies, marguerites, dahlias, a splash that would be visible from the house and road alongside the river alike.

Trowel in hand, trays of bedding plants by her side, packet of blood and bone fertiliser at the ready, Anna sat back on her haunches. She wished she could have an instant garden full of these tall, brilliant flowers like those people who exhibited at the Chelsea Flower Show managed to produce. Instant gardening; but really to do that sort of thing one needed a full time gardener, and with all the expense of the house, Harriet, Guy's education and now her lack of a full-time job, they were going to have to rein in a bit and watch the money. The bright rays of the sun shining above the tall trees at the far side of the house began to burn her back, even at this early hour. It was going to be a hot day. Better to get everything in before the sun rose too high. Although most of the preparation for the party was done there was still the setting out to do, balloons to festoon round the house and hang at the gate.

Happiness. Anna felt herself slowly being infused by a sense of pure joy, and she closed her eyes momentarily to savour it. A slight breeze blew in from the river and the landscape seemed enveloped by an ethereal haze that made the moment a unique, almost mystical experience.

A life of solitude in the country would not mean abandoning London altogether. A consultancy would bring in some money and she could continue to give a few days a month at the Law Centre. But she decided she would resign from the Council. They wanted her to anyway — better to resign than be pushed — and all the other voluntary bodies to which she gave so much time.

She was already part weaned from the city, used to the slower pace of life in the country, the time taken in, say, the butcher's shop while one waited for ages while Mrs so and so explained what cut she liked and how she liked it and how much it should weigh and what it should look like. Then the butcher would disappear, the sound of chopping would be heard from his board around the corner out of sight and he would reappear with the joint that might, or just possibly might not, be what Mrs so and so wanted. If it was, there followed a discussion about how it should be cooked and some mention would be made, in passing, about the state of their various families, usually numerous and including children and grandchildren if they had any. If Mrs so and so did not like the joint the butcher would go back to his chopping block and try again.

It all took so much time that was both incredible and annoying to the person brought up in the city and used to the frantic pace of supermarkets, convenience shopping, traffic jams and city life.

Anna looked at her watch and jumped up. Harriet would be stirring if she wasn't already. She rushed indoors, washed her hands and then, two at a time, up to Harriet's room. But the infant, perhaps because of her relatively late night, was still asleep, although showing signs of stirring. Anna sat quietly by her side gazing at her, and then she knew how grateful she was to Fiona and Errol for giving her Harriet, a child of her own bound to her if not by blood then by a more invisible but precious commodity: love, pure and unadulterated.

Peter arrived just before lunch, his car boot packed with parcels and presents which included a large bunch of flowers for Anna.

A guilt offering? Could he have a mistress tucked away in Leicester, London, wherever? She'd looked into his eyes but saw only tenderness and love.

'How was Leicester?' she asked in the bedroom as they changed for the party.

'Very boring. We had a conference of all our overseas legal executives.'

'A likely tale,' she said doing up the buttons of her pretty cotton dress, and looking at herself in the mirror.

'But true.'

'I often do wonder if you're having an affair,' she heard herself saying, although she knew she hadn't meant to.

'Say again.' She saw him behind her looking at her in the mirror.

'You heard.'

'Don't start that again, Anna.' Peter put a hand on her shoulder. 'You know it's like in a film or novel. It's not true.'

'You wouldn't say if it was.'

'I'm not,' his nails dug into her shoulder, 'and if you like I could ask you the same question.'

'Me?' She turned around, speechless. 'When have *I* the time for an affair?'

'I could say the same about myself.'

'Or the inclination?'

'Exactly!' He took her by both shoulders, spun her round and kissed her hard on the mouth.

Some people said that if you didn't desire your spouse you thought no one else would either. So maybe a little mutual suspicion was a good thing?

They finally came apart and, hand in hand, ran downstairs together to the lawn where already the party guests were foregathering.

Everyone knew that children's parties were exhausting. They'd hired an entertainer, but there was still a lot to do. There were the other parents to entertain as well with alcoholic refreshment after five when no one seemed to want to leave. One of the children was sick and had to be taken home, another had what was either an asthmatic attack or a spasm brought on by over-excitement and had to lie down. There was an anxious consultation about whether or not the doctor should be called but the child, one of the eldest who had had a previous attack, recovered and later rejoined the party.

By seven everyone had gone, and leaving the kitchen in a state of considerable disarray Anna, Peter, Guy and Sal collapsed on the terrace drinking white wine, while Honey went round the garden picking up the leftover bits. After a moment she was joined by Sal and Guy, leaving Anna and Peter alone on the terrace.

The swifts rose higher in the cerulean blue sky or dived low towards the trees, uttering their shrill reedy cries, while from the woods came the coos of pigeons or collared doves. Later a nightingale would start its song and later still the owls would begin their night-long dialogue as they hunted their prey.

Anna leaned back in her chair, briefly closing her eyes as Peter's hand stole into hers.

'Happy?'

'Very,' she gave him a warm, reassuring smile. 'You were wonderful.'

'So were you. So was Sal. I could lead this kind of life always,' Anna murmured.

'Could you really?' Peter's clasp tightened.

'Yup.'

'Or do you just say it and you'd miss the city?'

'No.'

'Well . . .' Peter paused, 'why don't you do it?'

'Are you serious?'

'Yes, perfectly.'

'All the time? But what about money?'

'We'd manage.'

'I was going to tell you later but I'll tell you now,' Anna said. 'They want me out of the office.'

'Who wants you out?' Peter looked indignant.

'David wants me to be a consultant so that Michael Lawrence can run the place.'

There was silence for a moment.

'Sounds great,' Peter said eventually.

'You really think so?'

'Ideal.' As she turned her head their eyes met. 'Don't you think?'

'I'm gradually getting used to the idea.' Anna stretched out her legs and slipped off her sandals, rubbing her feet together, realising how tired she was. 'Trying not to feel kicked out, insulted, you know.'

From the house came the shrill sound of the telephone.

'Damn!' Anna said, opening her eyes.

'I'll get it.' Peter began to rise.

'No, I'll get it,' Anna pushed him back, 'it's bound to be some mother whose child has left a

408

vital article of clothing.'

She almost danced to the phone. Happiness. Yes, it was within her grasp. She realised she was humming a tune sung by the kids that afternoon as they danced round in a circle.

The farmer's in his den, the farmer's in his den
Hey ho daddy oh the farmer's in his den . . .
The farmer picks a wife
The farmer picks a wife
Hey ho daddy oh the farmer picks a wife . . .

'Hello?' She lifted the receiver to her ear. For a long moment there was silence, and her heart suddenly skipped. Could it be . . .

'Anna, is that you?' a man's voice, kind of familiar, said.

'Yes. Can you speak up, you're rather faint.'

'Anna, it's me, Damian.' Anna then realised that the voice was not so much faint as cautious, as if he didn't want to be overheard.

'Damian!' Anna gave a false, rather embarrassed laugh. 'After all this time! Where are you? I hear you're married.'

He interrupted her quite brusquely. 'Anna, I can't speak for long but I've got something rather important to say and I want you to promise me that you won't get us into trouble.'

'What sort of trouble?' From joy to fear, that sudden transit that, after all, was so familiar to her.

'Anna, I know where Fiona is . . .'

'Oh my God, *Damian* . . .' She clutched her chest.

'You've got to give me your word first. Anna . . .'

'Tell me quickly where she is.'

'You must give me your word you won't shop us to the fuzz.'

'But, Damian . . .'

'You must protect us. We've done nothing wrong, but something serious has happened and I'm running out of coins. I'm calling from a call box and if you don't give me your word I'll have to go.'

'Reverse charges!' Anna cried, but afraid he might not ring back said quickly: 'I give you my word. Where is she?'

'Your oath you won't let us get into trouble . . .'

'Look, my oath . . .'

'I *have* to go, Anna. But Fiona is sick, very sick. Now listen and I'll tell you where she is and you'd better get here soonest.'

CHAPTER 17

Peter and Anna drove at speed through the night, crossing Dorset and Wiltshire into the Gloucestershire countryside, pausing every now and then for Anna to consult a map. They spoke very little, preferring to listen to music on the car stereo, Mozart and some Vivaldi, to try and calm their agitation.

There was really nothing to talk about until they knew what had happened, Damian having rung off as soon as he had given them directions. In many ways, Anna felt this journey must be both the worst and longest of her life, though it took under three hours before they arrived at the open gates of the large house standing well back from the road.

It was a place of some size and the imposing front door had opened even before they stopped the car and Damian, followed slowly by Arizona, came over to greet them.

Peter wore a polo top sweater, jacket and flannels, Anna a baggy sweater and Marks & Spencer jogging pants. They had only stopped to pick up some money and pack an overnight bag.

'You got here very quickly,' Damian said awkwardly.

'Where is she?' Peter demanded looking at him.

'This is my husband, Peter.' Anna tried to temper Peter's annoyance, the result of his anxiety. 'Damian, Arizona,' she indicated them briefly.

Everyone nodded. It seemed no time for social niceties. Also, to Anna, it seemed light years had elapsed since her brief fling with Damian.

'Hi, Arizona!' she acknowledged her.

'Hi, Anna!' Arizona's voice sounded lifeless, frightened; all the former confidence and heartiness was completely lacking. She wore a caftan festooned with beads, but was very far from her old self.

Anna was looking impatiently towards the house.

'She's not here.' Damian's voice was strained. 'There's a cottage on the grounds. When my grandfather owned the place it was quite something and the gamekeeper lived there. They . . .'

'How did she come to be here?' Peter's tone was still threatening and Anna remembered how frightened Damian had been and nudged him, saying to Damian: 'You'd better lead the way.'

'I'll wait in the house.' Arizona turned towards the door. 'I'll have something ready for you when you come back.' She held out a hand to Damian as though giving him strength. Anna's feeling of apprehension mounted to panic. Damian turned and led the way around the house, across the lawn towards the outbuildings and a cottage that stood some distance away, a mere shadow in the dark. It was nearly midnight and the welcome, familiar hoot of an owl came from somewhere way back in the woods. How Anna wished they were home and not here; that Damian's nocturnal call had never happened. There was a light on in the cottage but the door was locked, and as they stood in front of it rigid with tension Damian produced a key, looked at them and gave a deep sigh.

'I'm terribly sorry,' he said.

Peter pushed past him, closely followed by Anna. They went immediately into the room where the light came from. A very low light was on by the side of a divan in which, huddled amid bedclothes pulled right up to her chin, lay Fiona, the tip of her head just visible. There was a noxious smell in the room which Anna couldn't place: not drugs, not urine nor faeces.

Maybe a mixture of all three, plus decay, damp. She shivered with horror at the notion that Fiona should end up in a place like this.

Damian lurked in the doorway while Peter hurried over to his daughter's bed. Then he stopped and looked over at Anna.

'You do it,' he said.

'Do what?' She went up to the bed.

'Touch her . . . see if she's . . .'

Suddenly the truth struck Anna; the stillness of the figure on the bed, the stench which she now realised was vomit.

Remembering that the female of the species was stronger than the male, two members of which species now seemed heavily dependent on her, she went over to the bed and slowly drew back the covers, stared at the ashen face, eyes closed as if in a deep sleep. But there was no sign of breathing; instead from her half-open mouth a sickly dribble seemed to have congealed, perhaps for days. Anna touched Fiona's jugular, put another hand against her cheek. It was as cold as marble.

'I think she's dead.' She turned to Peter. 'Oh, my darling, I am so so sorry.' She flung her arms round him as he raised his head and gave a cry like an animal caught in a trap. Anna cradled him for a moment feeling the tears on his face. 'I think she just fell asleep . . . I'm sure she felt no pain. She seems so peaceful.'

And indeed Fiona did look peaceful, curled up in her familiar foetal position, her finger resting against her chest looking as though it had slipped from her mouth. For some reason Anna thought of the tale told in the Bible of the daughter of Jairus: 'she is not dead but sleepeth'. Would that same miracle could bring Fiona back to life.

Peter still seemed incapable of movement so Anna turned to Damian and said quietly: 'We simply must call the police.'

'Anna, you *promised*,' Damian looked pathetically over to her.

'I didn't know she was dead,' Anna said in as gentle, as reasonable a tone as she could. 'The police must know, Damian. If you had nothing to do with this you have nothing to fear.'

'Of course I had nothing to do with it.' Damian

kneaded his hands. 'But I wanted to tell you first, to explain . . . We knew nothing. We found her like this. Called you at once.'

'You didn't know she was *here?*' Peter said looking incredulous.

'Oh, yes, of course we knew, but . . .' Damian hung his head as if lost for words.

'Why don't we go over to the house?' Anna said in a practical tone of voice, 'and you can tell us what happened. The police will be able to find out when Fiona died, and the longer you leave it the worse it will be.'

'But it was *nothing* to do with us.'

'Still, not reporting a death is an offence, I'm afraid. Let's get it over with. As you say you know nothing; and I believe you. All that will be required is a statement.' She looked around: 'I suppose Errol has done another bunk?'

Damian nodded. 'I think Fiona's been like this a day or two.'

Anna went back to the divan and drew the duvet up to cover Fiona's head. She let her hand rest there for a moment, wishing with all her heart that she could bring the dead girl back to life like the daughter of Jairus. Then she put her arm through Peter's and drew him towards the door.

Damian, having already preceded them, waited for them outside.

'Leave the light on,' Peter said suddenly turning to Anna as her hand reached for the switch. 'I don't want her . . .' and then he began to weep

415

softly again. 'I don't want her to be alone in the dark.'

Anna left the light on and shut the door without looking at the bed again.

As they followed Damian back across the yard she thought it was like a mournful procession of hurt, bereaved, frightened people. When they got near the house the front door again swung open as if Arizona had been watching their progress through the grounds.

Inside it was cold. It also smelt of damp and neglect, as sinister as the doomladen cottage.

'I've made tea and sandwiches,' Arizona said as they trooped into the hall.

'Thanks.'

'I don't suppose you had time to eat,' Arizona went on.

'No, we didn't.'

'Maybe you'd like a whisky?' Damian led them into a room full of bulky, old-fashioned furniture.

'Whisky would be nice,' Anna said, rubbing her hands, and while Damian went out and Peter slumped into one of the chairs she looked around.

It was a large depressing room, almost a time warp of a past age. Obviously in its heyday the house had been one of the great places of Gloucestershire. The Bradleys were unknown to Anna but, doubtless, they had been a name in the county. The double entrance doors through which they'd entered gave way to a large baronial hall which, like the room they were now in, appeared to have seen better times.

The wooden floors were covered by rugs of undoubted antiquity, and probably value, but most of them were threadbare and beyond repair. The furniture was heavy, some of it good; but it must have been years since it had seen any polish. The sofas and armchairs were covered in a variety of materials: brocade, leather, even chintz, but they were all frayed and looked as though they were home to numerous small, unwelcome creatures. Heavy chandeliers hung from the smoke-darkened ceiling, their crystal lozenges yellowed by time, and on the floor and the rickety occasional tables were lamps, some with their shades askew, some with large burn marks; others lacked shades altogether and the naked bulbs winked unflinchingly in the gloom.

With an unsteady hand Arizona poured the tea into mugs which Damian passed round. His hands too were unsteady. Both had clearly had a profound shock.

Damian offered sandwiches which Peter declined. Anna took one out of politeness.

'Errol came to us about a year ago,' Damian said, sitting opposite Peter. 'He was looking for work and had heard through the grapevine that we lived here. Errol was in a bad way, depressed and heavily into drugs. He told us about Fiona and the baby which he guessed must have been born by then. He felt he couldn't cope with the baby, but I think he did love Fiona.'

'Love her!' Peter exploded. 'The way he treated her. You call *that* love? Leaving her in

417

the lurch when she was pregnant and stealing everything he could lay his hands on.'

'He had a very bad habit.' Damian sat uneasily on the edge of his chair. 'He kept on trying to give it up, but he couldn't.'

'I wish you'd told me,' Anna said bitterly.

Damian gave an expressive shrug. 'How could I know what would happen? I didn't know he'd go off with Fiona. By then, it was too late anyway. The thing with Errol was that he couldn't take responsibility. When he came to us we were sorry for him and let him stay in the cottage. He said he wanted to kick the habit and go back to Fiona. You might have heard I inherited this place when my father died. I would like to restore it to what it was, but it's a terribly expensive business. The little money my father left went to my mother who wouldn't let me have a penny because she disapproved of my lifestyle. My grandfather had entailed the house for me. My mother and I never got on. When I turned up to claim my inheritance with Arizona she tried to prevent me coming into the house.'

'Called the *fuzz*.' Momentarily Arizona came to life, showing something of the old sparkle. 'His *own* mother.'

'Mother had no legal right,' Damian said, 'and it was soon sorted out. She left and not long after that Errol turned up.'

'How did he know where you were?'

'He always kept in touch with some of the brethren who knew where we were.'

'What a pity,' Anna murmured.

'It was not a good day when Errol found us, but we didn't know that. There was something very likeable about Errol and I was happy when he went off with Fiona. I thought it would change him permanently. In many ways I do think he did want to settle down and come off drugs. But it's so hard once you've got a habit. He said he wanted to try, and would do up the cottage and give us a hand with the house.' Damian glanced towards the ceiling. 'It has almost as many leaks as the warehouse.

'For a while we all worked well. Errol seemed a lot better and to have ideas about making a nest for him, Fiona and the baby. He got in touch with her. Then she arrived one day in her car, some luggage, not much, but no baby.

'They seemed very happy together, but we never spoke to Fiona alone. We understood, however, that when the place was in order they would collect the baby, maybe get married.

'However this didn't last long. Errol was back on his habit and we think he got Fiona on to it. We saw less and less of them and there was obviously no work going on either at the cottage or here. They wanted to be left alone. We respected that. We had our own problems; what to do about the house, harassment by the social services who said we shouldn't be claiming benefits . . . you know, the usual sort of thing. Then Errol started to stay away and leave Fiona alone. I guess he was stealing to finance his habit. By then Fiona had probably started on it too . . .'

'If only you could have let me *know* . . .' Anna tried hard to stem her rising anger.

'Look, we aren't into the business of grassing on other people, Anna. You know that. We let everyone lead their own lives, as we like to lead ours. Don't we?' He looked over at Arizona who nodded her confirmation. It was bitterly cold in the house and Anna felt as though her body was petrifying. 'Well this time he stayed away, and the car was there and there was no sign of Fiona. Arizona went over this afternoon . . .'

Arizona suddenly put her hands over her face, bent so low that she nearly touched her knees, rocked from side to side. 'It was so terrible,' she murmured, 'something I'll never forget.'

'She was dead?' Anna whispered, and Arizona nodded.

'I simply didn't know what to do. I knew it was too late to call a doctor and we should tell the police, but we have had *so* much trouble with the authorities. You know what bastards they are. And you are so kind, Anna . . .' as if pleading with her Arizona held out her hand, 'we hoped you'd understand that we did our best.'

Ex-Labour Councillors daughter
in drug tragedy

An inquest was held on Fiona Livingstone, stepdaughter of Mrs Anna Livingstone, once a prominent Labour Councillor tipped at one time as a future Member of Parliament. Mrs Livingstone and her husband Peter testified as to their daughter's mental state at an inquest held in Gloucester on Friday. Nineteen year old Fiona Livingstone was found dead in a cottage on an estate in a remote part of Gloucestershire where she had been living with a man who has since disappeared.

A pathologist testified to the cause of death as being due to an overdose of an unusually pure form of heroin compounded with a large quantity of alcohol. The Coroner heard evidence from Mr Damian Bradley, on whose estate the cottage is situated, that Miss Livingstone had missed her parents and her baby whom she had left in their care.

Police said that all attempts to trace Mr Errol Murphy, who lived with Miss Livingstone, had failed.

Superintendent Francis Morris said that there were a number of deaths from overdoses relating to pure heroin in the area and attempts were being made to find the dealer with a view to charging him with manslaughter.

The Coroner expressed his condolences to Mr and Mrs Livingstone, who he said were in no way to blame for the tragedy. Mr Damian Bradley was also completely exonerated from blame.

Anna sat on an upturned packing case, the

pages spread out on her knees. At times the report had been blurred by tears, and when she finished she gave her nose a good blow.

It was three months since Fiona had been found dead, the inquest having twice been adjourned while the police tried to find Errol, who they believed was the main supplier of drugs in the area. It was thought now that he had escaped abroad.

The Coroner had released Fiona's body for burial in Dorset in a grave next to her mother, and almost at the same time a purchaser had been found for the London house. Completion was due tomorrow.

One more trip from the removal lorry and the house would be empty, ready for its new owners. Anna put the paper on one side and got up, pacing restlessly to the window, looking out, and back to the paper again. All the papers had carried reports, one even giving a brief history of her career: prominent Labour Councillor, well known solicitor, regular do-gooder, the implication being 'look where it got you?' The business of the squat was revived and raked over again, and a link with it, Fiona and Errol established.

It had been a dreadful time; so much going on and so much speculation, which was unjust, which had caused the Coroner to emphasise that she and Peter were in no way to blame for what had happened.

But the papers didn't let it go at that. Why should a nineteen year old girl run away and leave her baby, if she was properly treated at home? If people understood her? Perhaps there was an element of disapproval on the part of her establishment-minded parents? Did she get all the help and understanding she had a right to especially from someone who spent hours, perhaps too many, doing voluntary work? To compound it all Anna was a *stepmother:* and the stereotype of the dreaded stepmother who made no effort to understand her stepchildren was reviewed, with many case histories presented from fact as well as fiction.

Anna saw the removal van draw up outside the front door so went down to greet the men.

'Just one load,' she called, 'and that's it.'

'All to the Barbican, Mrs Livingstone?'

'All to the Barbican. The stuff for the country all went down yesterday.'

She stood watching them while they put the boxes containing books and various ornaments, a couple of chairs and a small chest from the hall, into the van.

'That all, madam?'

'That's all.' She stood on the steps watching them as they shut the back of the van, locked it and, with a wave, jumped into the cab.

She followed the progress of the van as it went slowly downhill and disappeared round the corner, out of sight. in the front garden the SOLD notice creaked eerily in the wind.

She walked back into the house, and went slowly through the rooms, checking that they were all empty, nothing was missed. First, hers and Peter's. How many times had they made love in the double bed which had now gone to the Barbican? How many rows, reconciliations, talks behind the closed door? Too many to remember.

She closed the door and then walked along the corridor to Fiona's. Once again she stood outside, aware of that bunched-up feeling, the knot in the pit of the stomach, as she gently turned the handle and stole inside. Nothing remained of Fiona except a few marks on the wall where her pictures and posters had been. There had stood her bed, there she'd curled up, finger invariably in her mouth, eyes staring balefully, reproachfully, at Anna.

Anna's eyes suddenly filled with tears and going over to the window she leaned heavily against the sill. No, memories of Fiona, especially in later years, were not good. There had been good times in the early days, but later as a teenager . . . she shivered recalling the unkind press reports. The inveterate do-gooder who could not manage her own stepdaughter.

True or false? Anna wiped the tears from her eyes, but still the garden was seen through a blur.

She knew that, although she had meant well, trying to change the lives of others by good works had brought about disaster. If she had not been involved in the squat the meeting between Errol and Fiona would never have taken place and that, surely, was the biggest mistake she had made in her life. She had not checked up on Errol; his background, his ability as an artist. Would she regard *that* as criminal if she read about it in the papers? How could a woman introduce her daughter to a thief, a drug addict, some even suggested a murderer?

But she had, and she would never forget it. Good intentions gone sour.

Guy's room had fewer bad memories, mainly because the change in Guy had blotted out the bad ones. He was an industrious student at an agricultural college who had done well in his first year exams. He'd worked all summer at the house and with a neighbouring farmer looking after stock, cutting hay, learning some of the mysteries of farming.

She left Guy's room, checked on the two guest rooms, the bathrooms, and then ran downstairs and did the same with the kitchen, breakfast room, dining room, study, living room. She went over to the French windows that led on to the balcony and, opening them, stepped outside for a moment gazing into the garden which had the neglected rather bedraggled look of late summer, especially when those who had once tended it so lovingly had neglected it. She looked for the blackbird she had fed every day with scraps from the breakfast table. Sometimes he would be sitting on the railing waiting for her when she got home at night.

But today he was not there.

There will be other blackbirds she thought as, sadly, she closed the window, bolted it and, gathering up a few things in the hall, left the house by the main door.

She ran down the steps and put everything in the boot of the car. That, and the back seat, already bulged with the bric-a-brac of moving house.

She went back to close the garden gate and then stood for a moment gazing up at the house. How sad and empty it looked with the curtains all gone, either to the Barbican or the jumble. The new owners, who she had never met, wanted to do the place over, so even carpets had gone. She didn't blame them. It was how she had felt about Hall Farm.

Anna turned abruptly, got into her car and drove to the end of the road, eyes straight in front of her looking to the future, leaving the past behind.

It had been a heavy day and now, with a pile of files high in front of her, she sat scribbling in the last of them. Opposite her her client sat on the edge of the chair, eyes anxiously on Anna's face.

She was a young mother whose partner had left without giving an address and the authorities were after him and her because they felt she knew where he was. She didn't. Anna was sure of that. She was honest, caring and frightened. She lived in one room with her baby and was entirely dependent on welfare. Now the CSA were threatening to take her to court because they thought she was shielding her partner.

Anna finished making her notes, closed her file and leaned towards her client. Summoning up yet another smile for the umpteenth time that evening she said as gently as she could: 'Valerie, I'm leaving the Centre tonight. This is the last time we'll meet.'

'Oh, Mrs *Livingstone*,' the woman's concern was palpable, 'you said you'd come to Court with me.'

'I was hoping to see you through; but I have so many problems of my own at the moment that I'm giving up all voluntary work.'

The young woman continued to look dejected.

'There's a very *nice* person taking over from me. A caring person. She will know all the details of your case and,' she indicated the stack of files beside her, 'others. Believe me, she won't leave a stone unturned to get you justice.'

It was nearly eight. Peter would be waiting in their new flat in the Barbican. Tonight would be their first night there, but also the last for some time. The following day Anna was off to Dorset and there was a lot to do. She opened the door and ushered her client out. The last time she would do what had become a familiar task for several years now. The corridor was deserted and all the helpers had gone home. She had already said goodbye to them and promised to drop in to see them from time to time. The usual thing. One very seldom did. She was pretty sure she would never see her neighbours again, or her fellow councillors, though for the time being she would keep in touch with the law firm if only by fax, telephone and letter because of her consultancy work.

She saw Valerie to the door and stood for a moment while they exchanged mutual good wishes. Then she watched her disappear in the mass of people thronging the pavement on that warm September evening.

She was deserting them: the people of the streets, of the squats, of single bedsitters; the loners, the rootless ones, dwellers in a great city.

A breeze suddenly blew in from the street ruffling her hair. It was a warm dusty breeze with a whiff of curry from the take-away round the corner, but as she raised her head and sniffed it she imagined that it smelt of newly mown grass, green banks full of wild thyme, white cow parsley and yellow, lemony tansy.

Anna shut the door, locked it firmly, chucked the key back through the letterbox, walked along the street, turned the corner, not looking back.

AFTERWORD

The car slowly edged forward, the lights kept on changing from red to yellow, then green, but before she could make any headway they changed back again to red. She was terribly late and burst out in a sweat; her hands gripping the wheel of the car were damp. Suddenly there was an enormous crash from the rear and her car was propelled with lightning speed through the traffic, which seemed to part for her almost miraculously, allowing her, like the fast forward process on a video, speedy access along Wigmore Street up Portland Place all the way to the Council Hall.

She left the car in front of the steps and dashed out of it, despite the phalanx of traffic wardens advancing towards her, wagging their fingers. 'I'm late, I'm late,' she cried like the White Rabbit, and dashed up the steps to the Council chamber hotly pursued by the traffic wardens. As she entered, the debate taking place suddenly stopped, all sound ceased and those present turned accusingly towards her.

'I'm so sorry I'm late,' she began but David Cole rose from the leader's bench and began berating her.

'You're *always* late, Anna. How do you suppose you can do your job properly? You're letting everyone down. Letting the Party down . . .'

'Letting the *Party* down!' the members chorused in unison and, rising in a body, advanced towards her at the same time as the doors burst open and the army of vengeful traffic wardens surged in waving their parking tickets which they began to shower on her.

Anna woke with a start; sat upright in bed, heart pounding, nightie drenched, her face also covered with sweat, a choking sensation in her throat. There was an aura of light around the drawn curtains. Dawn.

The dream had been such a jumble of events from the past, not the first time she'd had it in the years that had passed since she'd settled in Dorset, abandoned the life in the town to become a country dweller.

Her hand sidled across the bed for the warm, comforting, reassuring presence of Peter. Empty. Peter was in town, she remembered. It was midweek and he came down at weekends, sometimes for longer in the summer.

Anna got up, spent a penny, drank a glass of water and returned to bed. She lay there for a long time, quite still, until gradually sleep reclaimed her again.

The next time she woke someone was snuggling into bed beside her, a little warm body next to hers.

'Good morning, Mummy.' Loving, warm lips against her cheek.

'Good morning, darling.'

That precious time of day she and Harriet had exclusively for each other, though at the weekends it was shared with Peter. She, unquestioningly, was 'Mummy' and always had been, Harriet too young when Fiona died to remember her. Peter, however, was 'Grandpa'. The division seemed strange but logical; no one queried it.

Harriet was now four, bright, intelligent, beautiful. She attended nursery school part-time to which Anna took her every morning and picked her up again at lunch time. Or, sometimes, if Anna had something to do, Sal picked her up, or Guy might go over and get her, or she'd spend the afternoon with one or other of her friends.

Anna sometimes wondered how they would deal with the problem of explaining to Harriet her origins, how they would be able to judge when was the best time and how they would be able to tell.

Harriet was a reflective child, not a prattler, and she and Anna lay companionably together, not speaking, Anna almost beginning to doze off again because of her disturbed night. She felt a finger on her cheek and opened her eyes to see Harriet staring earnestly at her.

'Are you alright, Mummy?'

'Just tired, darling.' Anna turned to look at the clock. 'Goodness, look at the time! We'll be late!' and with a squeal Harriet tumbled out of bed, and Anna followed her as far as the door and watched her scamper along the corridor to her

431

room where she was quite capable of brushing her teeth, splashing some water on her face and dressing herself.

Anna went to her bathroom, ran a bath and jumped into it, lying there for a moment, eyes closed, as the horrors of the nightmare returned and then slowly receded again.

On the way downstairs she called into Harriet's room and found her dressed in her jeans and T-shirt, struggling with the laces of her little trainers. Swiftly Anna knelt and tied them for her, bows were still rather a problem.

'Done your hair?' she asked, gazing into the eager, upturned little face.

Harriet shook her head. She was still babyish enough to want Anna to do things for her, and Anna liked doing them. Grabbing a hairbrush, she began to brush the fair curls back from Harriet's head; making a semblance of a parting. Then there was the little ribbon to tie on for a top-knot.

Harriet sat on the bed watching her, and impulsively Anna leaned forward and kissed her.

'I do love you,' she said.

'I love you, Mummy.'

Anna held out her hand and together they went downstairs for the quick breakfast that preceded the trip to school.

It was possible to love somebody as though they were your own, providing you began early enough, Anna thought as she walked the two golden labradors, Dover and George, along the path by the river. She had no misgivings at all about abandoning work and London life entirely to care for Harriet. She occasionally 'consulted', but cases were few and far between. Financially they made do, thanks to Peter's job and the growing success of the farm.

It was not the life she ever expected to have to choose, but now she was glad that, although to some extent it had been forced on her, she had wanted it, had prepared for it. She owed it not only to Harriet and Peter, but Fiona. Now she was making up to Fiona for her unwitting neglect of her in the past or, at least, she was trying to.

It was a beautiful June day and, in the distance Guy was inside the cab of the combine harvester harvesting the first of the grass crop that would be used to feed the cattle in the winter. They came to the spot where the dogs liked to take their dip in the river, and where Anna threw sticks for them as they splashed in and out retrieving them and laying them at her feet so that the whole absurd but pleasurable process could be gone through again. When it was all over, Dover and George shook themselves vigorously and she darted away just in time to save herself from a soaking.

They'd got George and Dover as puppies, part of a thoroughbred litter, and the names were on the pedigree George St George and Dover St George. They were that beautiful honey-gold, with soft almond coloured eyes and sleek heads, and as they sped ahead of her Anna saw that the combine harvester was coming towards them and the dogs ran eagerly towards it though taking care not to get too near.

Guy stopped the machine and climbed from the cab.

'Hi!' he called.

'Hi!' Anna called back, walking towards him. 'Lovely day.'

'Lovely.' Guy looked up at the blue sky, the tiny wisps of clouds scudding towards the distant hills.

'Will you have this field done today?'

'I expect so.' Guy addressed himself to the dogs who made a fuss of him.

Guy lived in the cottage. He was now twenty, had passed all his exams and ran the farm with the aid of two experienced hands. Anna did a lot of the bookwork, the tiresome details required by the Common Economic Policy which had finished the Hansons. She, however, liked this aspect, and with her neat and tidy mind was good at it. They were dairy farmers, with fields full of wheat, maize and rape whose golden glow had just faded. It was difficult to imagine in the strapping young man she saw before her now that sullen, difficult teenager. She thought that not only was Guy content with his work but Fiona's death had a lot to do with his transformation.

'Why don't you come for dinner tonight?' Anna asked.

'Anyone else coming?'

'No, just us.'

'I'll bring Honey,' Guy said.

'Do.' The dogs were now far ahead along the bank and Anna whistled at them. 'About seven?' she said.

'After milking.'

'See you.' Anna stood back as Guy climbed into his cabin, started the noisy engine again and, with a wave, drove on.

Anna hurried along the track after the dogs, her senses sharpened by the beauty of the scenery round her. The variegated greens of the trees overhead and the cut grass under her feet, the fading cow parsley mingling with the bright yellow buttercups by the side of the bank. The swift-flowing river as it cascaded over the waterfall by the bridge.

Honey and Guy, naturally it seemed, had, despite a slight age difference, teamed up and lived at the cottage together. Honey went on with her job and drove every day into Blandford, but at night and weekends she helped at the farm. It was a situation that seemed to suit everyone. Guy had a mate, Honey had a purpose and Sal nursed her hopes for the future.

Anna reached the gate by the bridge where the dogs obediently waited for her. She slipped on their leads and they trotted by her side as she walked along the main street of the village, up towards the farm. Her walk by the river brought her full circle. It was about three miles and she did it every day — winter, summer, rain, sun. She found in the country that one lived continuously in comfortable clothes and wellies. She thought you could hardly have walked up Regent Street in wellies, but in Blandford or Sturminster Newton they were *de rigueur*. No one cared. No one looked.

She passed Guy's cottage, a place she hardly ever visited, even though Nancy's studio was now a garden shed and all vestiges of her and her daughter's lives as painters had gone. She knew inside the cottage it would be clean and tidy, beds made, floors shining. Guy, now that he was a farmer, was meticulous, and Honey seemed to be a willing home-maker.

Anna walked past Sal's cottage but knew she'd gone to see a friend in Bristol. She passed the pub and waved to a couple of people who were about to go in, declining the offer of a lunchtime drink.

As she was about to turn up the hill she stopped by the churchyard. It was almost the anniversary of Fiona's death. They would go there on the day with flowers but, on impulse today, she went through the gate, tied the dogs' leads to the post and walked slowly up the path, past the church, towards the graves that, surrounded by simple twin headstones, lay by the wall shaded by an elderberry tree, just bursting forth.

It was difficult to assuage guilt and find peace. It took a long time.

But at last the Livingstone family had found

it. And in burying Fiona, Anna thought, they had finally buried Nancy too. Mother and daughter secure in each other's company.

Anna stole away from the graves, unhooked the dogs from the gate and began to climb the hill towards home. She realised that gradually she had been liberated from guilt and grief, free to enjoy her life with Peter and with Harriet, Fiona's child who, in some way, had become theirs, tied to them by blood.